Mr. Ugly

WOL-VRIEY

Burning Bulb
PUBLISHING

Mr. Ugly

WOL-VRIEY

Burning Bulb
PUBLISHING

Mr. Ugly
By **Wol-vriey**

Burning Bulb Publishing
P.O. Box 4721
Bridgeport, WV 26330-4721
United States of America
www.BurningBulbPublishing.com

Cover artwork by Anton Rosovsky.
Author Photo: Lolade Akinsowon © 2014.

First Edition.

Paperback Edition ISBN: 978-1-948278-07-2

Printed in the United States of America

The gates of a cemetery must always be left open; so that the living can get in, and the dead can get out. (Necromantica 36:4:21)

PROLOGUE: THE RETURN

Evil is like yeast: a little goes a hellishly long way . . .

Malicia

That July was the summer when Malicia Howard got out of the Taunton State Hospital after her fifteen-year incarceration there.

Most folks who get released from lunatic asylums are believed to be cured. However, in this case there was some doubt that Malicia Howard actually was fine now. Several psychiatrists at the Taunton State Hospital were convinced she was faking normalcy. These doctors felt Malicia still held tight to her delusions. They believed she'd pretended to give them up solely because she wanted to be let out.

Fifteen years of considered madness is sufficient to drive anyone sane.

Whatever the diagnosis and prognosis of her sanity—whether actual or pretend remission—the fateful morning came however, when Malicia Howard was set free from the asylum and boarded a cab from the city of Taunton back home to Raynham. It was a very short trip, one which, seeing as the two towns abutted on each other, Raynham having begun life in 1639 as part of Taunton, was a drive of less than five kilometers northward.

Malicia's return home wouldn't have been such a big deal for the town (which had moved on in her absence), except that in sharp contrast to Malicia's doctors, many of the older folks in Raynham (those who remembered *why* she'd been locked away) had never believed she was crazy in the first place.

These good townsfolk all believed Malicia Howard was a witch.

The primary reason they'd been happy she'd been locked away back then, wasn't because they thought she was crazy, but because lunatic asylums didn't allow their inmates access to the kind of diabolical paraphernalia required to stir up a supernatural ruckus.

In other words, a locked-up Malicia was a *safe* Malicia.

But that was then. This was now. It was probably for the best that no one realized that Malicia had been released, or was heading home again.

Until the trouble started, that was.

***

Malicia Howard arrived in Raynham unexpected and unannounced on a warm Wednesday afternoon. She rode quietly into her hometown in a silver cab. As the cab rolled through the town, she stared from its windows at the buildings, the streets, and the people, taking in as much as she could of the changes a decade and a half had brought to Raynham. She'd heard about and expected some of it, but she still felt a shock of dislocation at seeing buildings in places she didn't remember them being. And other buildings missing from where they should be.

But, she asked herself honestly, *how much of my memory of anything is accurate after all these years?*

***

Malicia's real name was Alicia Mildred Howard (née Edwards). She'd gotten the nickname Malicia (from 'M' and 'Alicia') after a high school incident.

14-year-old Alicia Edwards had been having a 'bad period' day and Ronnie Gribble had been bullying her. Snotty Helen Baumgartner, who'd been in the girl's toilets when Alicia had been changing tampons, had told Ronnie about it. And Ronnie, a loudmouthed braggart, who at age fourteen already looked like the thug he was destined to grow into, had later loudly remarked about Alicia's blood stinking up the classroom.

Alicia hadn't said anything. She'd felt ashamed, as if she was the only girl in the class who bled on a monthly basis. She'd looked down into her lap and tried not to weep.

Ronnie though, seeing a victim, hadn't been able to leave well enough alone. He had to humiliate Alicia further. With his normal swagger, he'd left his desk and strode over to the blushing girl's. No one stopped or cautioned him. Half the class were enjoying the spectacle of Alicia's embarrassment, the other half were too scared of the class bully to say anything that might make themselves his target.

"Hey, Alicia," Ronnie said, with the eyes of the whole class on him, "didn't you hear me just now? You're smelling, you know. Like bad meat. You should just go on home."

Alicia, normally quiet and reserved and nerdy and obedient to authority, had snapped. That her womb was aching badly hadn't helped her temper any.

In the sudden rage that overcame her, she'd pulled a pair of scissors from her schoolbag and driven them all the way through Ronnie's right hand and into the top of her desk.

There was a moment of perplexed disbelief in the class, as though the air supply had been collectively sucked from all their ninth-grade lungs. Then Ronnie let out a loud yelp of pain.

Now that her reaction was over, Alicia gaped too. It was the first time she'd ever exerted an ounce of strength in defense of herself, and look at what she'd done. Ronnie's hand was pinned to the desk and there was blood squirting everywhere. Blood was squirting up around the base of the scissors. Blood was also seeping out from under the pinned palm. For a moment, Alicia hoped Ronnie's blood wouldn't stain her textbooks inside the desk.

She looked up at him to apologize for hurting him. He was staring back at her in horror. He looked like he'd have loved to cry, but he knew boys didn't cry and he'd be letting down the team if he let on just how much pain he was in.

Over on their left, Helen Baumgartner had just fainted, as had Sally Fields, who'd likely put Helen up to tattling in the first place.

Alicia looked back down again. By now, Todd Laine and Harry Howard, friends of Ronnie's, were hard at work trying to free his hand from the desk.

Bemused, Alicia had gotten up and let them open her desk.

Todd took one look at the two inches of scissors speared through the wood and turned to gape at Alicia in horror. "How the hell did you do this?" he'd asked.

"I-I-I don't know!" she'd gasped back apologetically, now certain she was really going to be in trouble. "Something seemed to come over me!"

"It's the power of malice," Harry Howard loudly proclaimed. Young Harry fancied himself a philosopher. "Never anger a teenage girl named Alice." He'd turned and grinned at Alicia. "And so, Mildred Alicia Howard, I hereby dub thee Malicia henceforth."

"Malicia, Malicia!" a chorus went up around the classroom, accompanied by some banging on desks.

"Just unpin my goddam hand," Ronnie growled at his friends, "and let me kill this stupid menstruating bitch!"

On that threat, something snapped inside Alicia Edwards again. She'd had enough of Ronnie Gribble. She'd pushed Todd and Harry out of the way, then grabbed hold of Ronnie's ears. "Listen," she'd whispered loudly so the whole class heard, "the next time you come near me, I'll stab you through your wiener."

She was clearly serious. The blood instantly drained from Ronnie's face. Nodding in fear, he backed off from her. At age fourteen he instinctively knew that you didn't want someone sticking sharp objects through your penis.

"I'm sorry, baby. I didn't mean to hurt you like that," Ronnie said from his safe distance. The boy said this automatically: it was what his father always told his mother after reducing her to tears in his latest drunk rage, usually by which time there'd be blood streaming down some part of her face, most times her nose. It was a town wonder how Louise Gribble still looked so pretty after sixteen years of being married to the brute.

Nurse Hollis had entered the classroom then with her first aid kit and everyone had quietened down. The fainted girls were carried off to the Nurse's Station and then they got down to freeing Ronnie's hand from Alicia's desktop.

Try as they might though, no one could get the scissors out of the desktop. By the third attempt, Ronnie fainted despite two shots of local anesthetic and they gave up trying to use force and instead fetched a circular saw and cut him free and took him off to hospital.

Needless to say, Ronnie Gribble kept well away from Alicia Edwards from that day onward.

Discipline? There was lip service paid to it. Everyone knew Ronnie was a bully. Besides, he *had* to have started it—what else was the boy doing over at Alicia's desk when it happened? And anyway, no one who wasn't there really believed Alicia had stabbed him. Where would that skinny girl find such strength? The general belief was that Ronnie had been fooling around with her scissors and had fallen on them.

And once the story got out about what Ronnie Gribble had been *saying* that had caused Alicia to snap? Well, that was it: in addition to having that hole and all those stitches in his right hand, Ronnie also found himself being threatened with expulsion from school for 'sexual harassment of a fellow minor.'

So Alicia walked free. No more bullying. No one dared.

But in many respects, the fallout was worse than if she'd been suspended from school. Harry Howard's nickname of 'Malicia' stuck to young Alicia Edwards like a nameplate affixed with Araldite. After a while even the townsfolk began calling her 'Malicia.' And her friends and family did too.

When, fifteen years later, she married Harry Howard, Malicia realized she was in the strange position of being a woman whose husband had given her not just her last name, but her first name as well.

***

Now, Malicia smiled at the memories. All that had happened fifty years ago. Her smile turned bitter. Harry had died after eighteen years of marriage, leaving her their bookstore and their son Peter.

It was a bittersweet memory. She'd had a blissful marriage, but the aftermath—what had happened when Harry was no longer around to protect she and her son—had been just awful.

Finally, Malicia's smile turned cruel.

Oh, she thought, *I've got a million scores to settle with this stupid little town and I sure as hell will settle them all. Before I'm done, everyone here in Raynham will be weeping. Just like I was shedding bucketloads of tears back then.*

The cab turned off Elizabeth Drive and rolled up the short driveway to Malicia's front door.

Home again after all these crazy years.

Malicia Howard stepped down from the cab onto Raynham soil. The cab driver unloaded her single suitcase from the trunk. She paid him and he left. She watched the car turn south, watched its taillights vanish. Then, finally left all alone, she looked around for a while. Just herself and her thoughts now.

No one observing the quaint old woman standing in the restored stone driveway would ever have suspected the rain of calamities she intended to unleash.

Malicia Howard was sixty-four years old. She was small and slight, with long gray hair and once-bright-blue eyes now faded almost sky-pale. She'd once been very pretty. On the few occasions that she smiled nowadays, one still saw traces of that ancient attractiveness, but for the most part, her good looks had faded away in the madhouse, absorbed into the walls of the series of padded cells she'd occupied.

All that remained now in her face was a memory of beauty, fleeting flashes as empty as the wistful reminiscences of a one-time world famous concert pianist now no longer able to play the instrument due to arthritis.

Crow's feet and liver-spotted hands, these were fashion accessories to her old-woman look.

At the moment Malicia wore a long black dress and sensible black shoes. *Sensible*. This was the precise word one would use to describe Malicia Howard: that she looked *sensible*. She looked like a favorite aunt. One's first impression was to like her very much.

It was almost noon, but the sky was overcast. The heavens seemed to be brooding. They seemed to suspect her bad intentions and disapprove of them.

She smirked at the sky. *Dislike all you like,* she thought. *I'm going through with it no matter what.*

True to her name, raw undiluted malice now coursed through her veins. After regarding the street for a while, bemused by all the latest models of cars, and how the few girls that crossed the foot of her drive seemed next-to-naked in the summer warmth, she turned and regarded her house instead.

The house was large and was painted white and brown. It had two stories, a cellar and a loft. The upper floor was living quarters; the lower was used commercially. Back in the day, the lower floor had housed she and Harry's business: the Mr. & Mrs. Book Emporium.

After she'd been locked away, the lower floor had been rented out. Her brother-in-law Raymond—Harry's older brother—had handled the business transactions for her. The most recent tenant had been a dentist, but six months ago she'd gotten married and moved up to Boston.

Malicia stood staring at the building. Once informed of her imminent release from the Taunton State Hospital, Ray had carried out extensive renovations on the house. The lower floor hadn't needed much work; it had been kept in good repair by its series of occupants. The upper floor, however, had needed refurbishing: for fifteen years its sole function had been one of storage.

Ray had spent the past month renovating the house, fixing the floors and the roof and windows, and finally, a week ago, also getting the water and electricity and other utilities turned back on. Ray had also stocked the place up with food for her.

Malicia was forced to smile. In a way, being crazy for so long at the state's expense had done wonders for her finances. In her absence, the small nest egg that had come from Harry's life insurance had now multiplied to quite a substantial amount, and the bank was waiting for her to come pick up her cards and checkbook and start spending the money.

Suddenly she felt tired. Age was telling on her.

Or maybe I'm just not used to being outside anymore? Have I been caged for so long that freedom's pleasure is diluted? Or is this just the excitement of being home again?

She picked up her single suitcase and strode up to her front door. She got out its key from her purse and let herself in.

"I'm back," she whispered to the house.

***

Ray had done a great job with the restoration. He'd done almost *too good* a job: her house smelt brand new—it lacked the memories Malicia sought, handholds and footholds for her anger to latch on to. This no longer seemed like the house she remembered.

But when she ascended to the upper floor, she felt more at home. Here, among the stacks of books and other scattered paraphernalia in the living room, she easily retrieved her past.

Staring at Harry's books, she felt tears fill her eyes. Then she saw her son Peter's picture on the wall and her tears became a flood. And when she stared over at the solitary metal funeral urn seated on the mantelpiece over the electric fireplace—undisturbed at its resting in fifteen years—her flood of liquid anguish became a relentless torrent of remembered sorrows.

She'd not cried in ages—in the asylum it did little good, was perceived as further evidence of mania or hysteria—but now she let herself go, let out fifteen years of rage and frustration and horror. She stood in the midst of her yesterdays and wept her heart out.

When she could weep no more, Malicia began searching through the piles of books scattered around the upper apartment. Ray had offered to unpack and arrange them all for her before she got home, but she'd refused the offer. Many of these books were priceless antiques. As part of its trade goods, the Mr. & Mrs. Book Emporium had purchased/owned lots of first editions, many of books long out of print. By themselves, these rarities were sufficient reason for Malicia not to want her brother-in-law's workmen to handle the stock.

14

Not for fear of theft—she didn't believe a blue-collar worker had sufficient mental acuity to appreciate the value of a 200-year-old book on the Industrial Revolution, or a genuinely autographed copy of Tom Sawyer; but because, for that same reason (that they couldn't appreciate the books' value) such workmen were certain to manhandle and unintentionally damage the books.

But there was another, more specific reason why Malicia had asked Raymond Howard not to open/tamper with the books now piled around her. This was because of the content of several of the books in question.

***

Towards the end of his life, Harry Howard had become very interested in the occult.

By the time of Harry's death, he'd amassed a huge collection of books and tomes on magical lore, volumes covering everything from innocent water-witching to the grossest sorceries and human sacrifice. He'd even somehow/somewhere come into possession of a copy of the dreaded Necromantica—a book containing the most obscene spells imaginable; a book made from bound pages of human skin, and with its text written in human blood and feces.

Not supernaturally inclined herself, Malicia had initially been very worried by her husband's interest in the arcane. But seeing as he never tried to cast the spells in the books, or sacrifice any cats or dogs or local teenagers to the disgusting and blasphemous deities etched within the Necromantica, she'd soon gotten over her fears.

With retrospective wisdom, Malicia was right to be worried. Harry's occult book collection did prove to be a huge danger, but only after his death, and in such weird circumstances as would have been impossible for anyone to predict beforehand.

***

Now, Malicia searched carefully through the book piles. Her second reason for not wanting Raymond's workmen to help her open and arrange them was that she didn't want them misplacing Harry's magic books.

15

She needed those magic books now. In particular, she needed her late husband's copy of the Necromantica.

That evil book—the Necromantica—had begun this mess she was in. Well, the damned book would finish it too.

It took her a long time to locate the Necromantica. While searching for it she found each successively unveiled book's smell of age both intoxicating and sad. Saddest of all were those books ruined by damp and mold infection. Each time she opened a package of such destroyed volumes, she felt a pang in her heart, as if irretrievable chunks of her past had gone to waste up here in her absence.

Several times Malicia broke off her search and laid down in bed to rest. Each time she did this, she wondered why she felt so old. Was it because she *was* old, or was it because she was surrounded by testimonies to her age? *Are my memories aging me?* At these times she wondered also if she'd have the strength to see her plan through.

Finally, she found the right package. She unwrapped it with trembling hands.

As the light fell on the Necromantica, revealing its covering of tanned human skin, a cold smile spread across Malicia Howard's old face.

Yes! she thought in evil delight, feeling thrills of pleasure course through her old veins. *Hell yes!*

But suddenly she felt very weary again. She staggered from the book-filled living room into her bedroom and fell into bed.

It was time to sleep. Tonight she had work to do. A lot of horrible work to do.

She fell asleep and had pleasant dreams in which she was stabbing everyone who'd hurt her.

***

On the stroke of the hour of midnight, awake and alone in the living room of her home, Malicia Howard began to cast a spell . . .

The old woman sat cross-legged before a pentagram etched in a pile of ashes she'd spilled on the green rug.

Earlier, after waking from her nap, Malicia had prepared and eaten a sparse dinner—she'd microwaved a plate of baked beans and some beef stew. After dinner, she'd then painstakingly cleared the middle of her living room of books. She'd carefully shifted her precious stacks of arcana to the edges of the parlor, lest they either hinder her motion or come in contact with fire. The job had taken her almost two hours to complete.

While clearing her space she'd again been reminded of how old she was—of how her youthful vigor had fled her like a scared bird—of how she'd spent most of her middle-age in a series of padded cells, doped out of her mind. Her memories of the ill treatment she'd endured at the hands of the skeptical doctors and nurses only firmed her resolve to get even with everyone now.

The room was dark except for the light from the single large red candle that Malicia had placed opposite her, on the other side of the ash pile. On her right lay a small kitchen knife.

Holding the Necromantica open with one hand, she recited the spell slowly, with deep feeling. The words she spoke had an unpleasant ring to them. Had anyone been listening on this horrible night, they'd have had no doubt that Malicia was up to no good.

"L'leh fos retsnom eye mote moc,
L'le weeh twonk iem rewsna,
L'lepss ihtfot seuqer ehtt narg,
L'lewu oyyap l'liw I seydna."

Though spoken softly, the potent words echoed in the living room. As sharply as if the floor was tiled, not carpeted. Her voice bounced off the walls and drapes as if they were made of stainless steel.

Malicia recited her spell. The darkness in her living room thickened. Soon, every part of the room, except for the small area around her and her pile of ashes and her now-sputtering red candle, was pitch black, absolutely impossible to see through.

And in that surrounding wall of darkness, Malicia heard voices. Unpleasant voices interested only in doing evil. The demigods of the chasm.

"What do you want?" the voices enquired of her. "What do you desire of us, old woman? Speak, and if your desire amuses us enough, then we will grant your wish."

"I want revenge," Malicia whispered back. "Revenge on this whole damn town. Terror and bloodshed beyond compare. I wish to seed pain in human hearts like one sowing corn in a field. I wish to reap its harvest of agony too."

"Pay the price then," the voices whispered. "Quench our eternal thirst and you'll have exactly what you desire."

Malicia nodded. Then she picked up the knife from the floor. Without hesitation, she sliced her left forearm open; a deep incision. Holding her arm out over the ashes, she let the blood spill on them. The voices in the darkness now babbled excitedly. She felt an invisible mouth attach itself to her arm and suck. She felt both shock and pain, unseen teeth digging deep into her flesh and tearing at it, hurting her further. She gaped. She stared. But there was nothing to see, nothing except blood leaving her body and vanishing in midair, while the voices that promised to grant her evil wish tittered insanely everywhere.

On the floor, the pile of ashes now began smoking as though a fire burnt under them.

The relentless bleeding began making Malicia feel faint. She feared that in their excitement, the creatures in the darkness would accidentally drain her dry.

About her, the darkness was thickening yet further. In addition it was pressing in on her. Finally, the darkness extinguished the red candle and left the room pitch black.

She saw nothing anymore. The black pressed on her eyes like it was sucking them out of her skull.

The strain of the ritual was really telling on her now. She felt her consciousness leaving her body.

"Don't kill me!" she gasped in fright, when it felt as if her heart was stopping from a shortage of blood to pump. "I've given you what you requested. Do for me what I ask in return. Bruzz, Bruzz, Bruzz! Kan'an'nan Bruzz!"

The voices tittered louder. The suction on her wound lessened.

"Do not fear, old woman," the unseen creatures said. "We have already kept our own part of the bargain. All that you have in mind you shall have."

Malicia's one fear as she collapsed back and fainted, was that the beings she'd summoned hadn't *already* drunk her to death.

Malicia Howard wasn't scared of dying. She just wanted to see the harm she'd caused first. Those expressions of agony on her tormentors' faces would make her both her miserable life and her death worthwhile.

PART 1: UNDEAD SUMMER

If the Devil didn't exist, men and women would create him to fulfil their heart's desires. (Necromantica 1.1.1)

CHAPTER 1

Chris

The time was close to midnight, just about ticking over from Thursday into Friday. Young Chris Burke was riding his bicycle down Judson Street. He was headed home.

Chris was returning from his best friend John Ames's house. The pair of them had been drinking and playing *Dark Souls 3* on John's Xbox One.

Chris smiled as he considered the road ahead. He hadn't too far to go now; just a couple more turnings and he'd be home.

He was all tired out, the movement of his feet mechanical on the bike's pedals. What he needed at the moment was to fall into bed and fall fast asleep, in anticipation of the early morning hangover. Not good, that, seeing as he had to be up at six in the morning to help his father at their grocery store.

Even right now, he thought he'd had too many beers to be riding a bike. He was delighted that you couldn't be arrested for drunk driving on a bicycle. You weren't endangering anyone except yourself.

18-year-old Chris Burke was tipsily rejoicing over how he couldn't kill anyone with his 21-speed Ozone 500, when the dark figure stepped out of the short patch of woods just after the Ninas Way junction.

Maybe it was because Chris was drunk, but the figure seemed to move incredibly fast. One moment it was *beside* the road, two moments later it was *in* the road, directly in Chris's path. It made no attempt to cross the road either; just stood there.

Chris tried to go around it, but his reaction wasn't quick enough to prevent a collision. He hit the figure and went flying off his bike.

He hit the sidewalk a short distance ahead. He rolled once, then lay still.

He reflected thankfully that he'd not been too tipsy to remember to wear his crash helmet. He wasn't hurt; just dazed. Bruised too from the impact, with, from the feel of things, a skinned knee.

He sat up to clear his head. The person who had caused his accident—it was a man in a blue suit; that much he could tell in the street-lit half darkness—had pulled his bike over to the sidewalk and was now walking towards him.

Chris prepared to give the man—had to be some drunken bum— a piece of his mind.

He began getting up; readying himself for a lecture and if necessary, a good quarrel.

But then, once again moving faster than was humanly normal, the man in the blue suit was suddenly right beside him.

Chris now got a good look at the man's face. What he saw was so unlikely that he couldn't even scream. Seeing that gruesome visage, Chris's legs turned to rubber and he landed hard on his behind again.

And there was the smell to contend with too. The man smelt rotten, as though he'd just unearthed himself from his grave. And his body . . . his body . . . the state of his body made no sense to Chris's mind.

Get up and run! his mind screamed at him. *Flee! He's going to kill you! He's going to—!*

Chris stopped thinking. His mind's warning was clearly right, but it had come too late: The man had just produced something from his blue jacket. A long blade that glittered silver in the streetlight.

Chris let out a single yelp of fear, but then the silver blade descended and silenced his protests. The blade neatly sliced his voice box in two. His intended screams instead exited his throat as a frenzied wheeze which no one could possibly hear.

Unable to protest and too stunned and tipsy to resist the assault, Chris was dragged off the sidewalk and across the grass bordering the road. He was dragged off beneath the trees, where he'd be invisible to passersby.

What followed next was a violent medley of different types of pain, a symphony of agonies that swept through Chris's body like a virtuoso violin performance by Paganini.

Till finally the pain ceased. And by the time it did, young Chris Burke was delighted to be able to die at last. By then, merely dying felt like a blessed release.

CHAPTER 2

Apache and Sully

Friday Morning:

"Damn, whoever did this to the kid really friggin' hated his ass."

The speaker was Detective Frank Sullivan, better known as just 'Sully.' A short, rough-looking young man with black hair and dark eyes, Sully was staring at Chris Burke's remains with a look of intense disbelief on his face. His disbelief was composed half of shock at the brutality of the boy's death and half of wonder that a murderer could be so clinical and thorough at dispensing death to his victim.

Sully's partner, Detective James 'Apache' Johnson said nothing. Apache, a tall, dark man in his mid-fifties, had investigated a lot of really bad killings over the years. To him, this was just one more.

***

'Apache' had gotten that nickname during a high school history class about The battle of the Little Bighorn (aka Custer's Last Stand), when one of his classmates had remarked that he looked like Sitting Bull.

This, of course was merely the dangerous working of the juvenile mind in evidence, seeing as neither Sitting Bull nor the young James Johnson were of Apache blood at all, the great Native American holy man being Lakota and the young student now being summarily renamed having a Wampanoag mother and an Irish-American father.

Still, as in Malicia's Howard's case, the nickname had stuck. There was no arguing either that 'Apache' (as everyone, including his parents, called him from then on) did look the part: he had a long stern face, thin lips and a nose like an eagle's beak.

His most distinguishing physical feature, however, was his black ponytail. It was rare to see a policeman with his hair pulled back and banded up like that, and it made Apache Johnson easy for the Raynham citizens to recognize and remember. And also, though stern-looking, he was an easygoing man and friendly with a large percentage of the townsfolk.

***

The detectives were standing just inside the woods on the west side of the Ninas Way–Judson Street corner.

The corpse had been found by an old woman, Mrs. Haverstock. Early that morning, she had been out walking her poodle, when suddenly the dog had yanked the chain from her grasp and dashed off into the woods. Mrs. Haverstock had followed after the poodle. Once in there amidst the trees, she'd caught sight of the dead boy, shrieked loudly and fainted.

It was Doug Harper, a 14-year-old out delivering newspapers a little later that morning, who'd noticed Mrs. Haverstock's feet poking from the bushes and gone to see what was wrong with her. On seeing the two bodies, Doug had dashed out into the road and alerted passersby. The passersby had dialed 911, then taken Mrs. Haverstock to hospital. Doug Harper, who'd discovered the bodies, had been promptly returned home, being no longer in any mental condition to resume his paper route.

And Apache and Sully had landed the case.

"There's no doubt that someone had it in for the kid," Sully insisted.

Apache grunted. He generally let Sully do their talking. Good cop, bad cop routine. Sully played 'bad cop' great; Apache had used to do it great too, but he'd mellowed with age. Instead of replying the younger man, he stared at the fresh corpse. Something about it had begun giving him a very queasy feeling. It wasn't just the violence of the death either.

This murder had been excessively brutal. Chris Burke had been cut to bits. His belly was open and his guts were strewn in red lines across the grass. In addition, skin and flesh hung off his arms in long strips. The blood splashed everywhere assured Apache that many of the cuts had been made while the boy was still alive and dying, not after he'd expired.

They couldn't see the expression on his face; it too was a shredded mess. Whatever blade the murderer had used had been ruthlessly sharp and efficient, cutting clean and deep. At some places on his head, the facial skin and muscle were completely peeled off the underlying skull, as smoothly as if the flesh was merely beard scraped off a redhead's chin.

Apache winced. The face was so slashed up that it couldn't be used as ID. They knew it was Chris Burke dead here mainly because the young man's bicycle was lying by the curb, and also because his father had called the station this morning saying he'd not come home last night and asking if the police were holding him for drunkenness or some other violation.

Apache didn't envy Chris's parents when they had to ID their son in the morgue.

Yes, this young man *had* died a horrible, brutal death. But beyond that, Apache sensed something more as he stared at the new corpse. It hadn't yet begun smelling, but the summer sun was rising and the sooner they put the kid's stiff in a meat locker, the better.

Apache frowned. *It's the summer again, ain't it?*

". . . So what do we do now?" Sully was asking. "Standard investigative procedure?"

"Huh? Yeah, nothing else for it." Apache was certain Sully had been saying more, but he'd been so caught up in this thoughts that he hadn't heard him. He nodded grimly. "We ask around, find out if anyone saw or heard anything last night that could add up to a lead. Then we await the forensics results."

Sully was pointing. "Forensics just got here." He waved them over. "Guys he's all yours . . ."

They crossed the road to sit in their car, an unmarked dust-colored Ford. Sully got behind the steering wheel. This was normal: Apache generally left all the driving to Sully.

"What's bugging you, old man?" Sully asked, not starting the motor.

"What d'you mean, what's bugging me?"

"You know . . . you're distracted. I don't think you even heard half of what I was saying back there." He paused, then added, "It can't be the state of the corpse. You've been a cop for over thirty years. You must've seen worse shit than that."

"Sully, it's that time of year again."

"Huh? What time of year?"

"It's the damn summer. The summer jinx is back to hassle us."

Sully laughed once he realized what his partner was talking about. "The summer jinx? C'mon, old man. Stop trying to spook me."

Apache grunted. He pointed across Sully, out of the car window. Doing so brought into sharp focus the older detective's singular deformity: a large portion of Apache's right palm was missing. Between the bases of the thumb and the little finger, a huge chunk of flesh looked to have been scooped out of the man's hand. It was an old wound, surgically fixed ages ago, so that Apache now had two long scars from the surgery that had repaired the wound. It didn't seem to hurt anymore; though Sully sometimes saw Apache unconsciously rubbing the scars.

The missing scoop of flesh had some noticeable effects on Apache: For one thing, he needed to tilt his service pistol to the right to keep it properly balanced in his palm. And also, Apache's pinkie finger didn't bend at all; it stuck out perpetually stiff and frozen.

Most times Apache wore gloves to cover his deformity, but sometimes he clearly forgot, like today for instance,.

Sully had once asked Apache about the palm wound. Apache had shrugged the question off. Sully had then assumed it was a war wound and hadn't pressed the matter.

Now, Apache grunted and nodded out of the car at the woods where the forensics investigators were setting up shop. "Kid, that— what we just saw over there—ain't any kind of a normal murder."

"You've got no proof of that yet." Sully didn't really appreciate being called 'Kid' and 'Son' (and occasionally even 'Boy') by his partner. But seeing as how Apache's daughter Rebecca was older than he was, he put up with it. He retaliated in his own way, by calling Apache 'Old Man' whenever the feeling took him.

"I can feel it in my goddamn bones," Apache said. "By the time this is over, both you and I are gonna be wishing that this here today *was* merely the work of a serial killer."

Sully hid a smile. There the old guy went off half-cocked again, jumping the investigative gun on some superstitious tangent. "You already know I disagree, old man," he said. "But let's wait and see."

Beside him, Apache pulled his hand back down to his side. "You know," he began quietly, "maybe I'm wrong this time. Maybe the kid just got into a fight with some bikers over a woman or some drugs and *they* slashed him up like that."

Sully nodded. "Maybe. Bikers don't take crap from no one. You piss them off and they've got no compunctions about punching you an early ticket to go settle accounts with your maker."

Apache nodded grimly again. "Yeah, maybe in this instance I am wrong. Well, I sure do hope I am." He scowled at Sully. "Start the damn car and drive. Let's go see that kid who Burke's dad says he went to visit last night."

***

Apache was a widower. He had a married daughter, a pharmacist who lived up in Boston and sometimes visited with his twin granddaughters.

Sully, on the other hand, wasn't even married yet. Sully had a girlfriend though, a young divorcee with two kids.

The pair of detectives got on well enough, with the usual conflicts across the generation gap: Apache thought the 'kid' was too quick on the draw, while Sully thought the 'old man' needed to lighten up a bit.

Sully was young and brash and not given to superstition. He'd only been with Raynham PD for a year now, and put no stock in the old wives tales the town seemed cursed with.

Everyone, his girlfriend Tilly Brandon inclusive, seemed to think their town was jinxed. Sully didn't get that. He didn't like it either. Believing that ghosts lurked around each corner could only hamper law enforcement. Even his partner had the supernatural heebie-jeebies.

Sully was seriously considering putting in a transfer request to another unit. His only stumbling block to leaving Raynham was his relationship with Tilly Brandon, whom he deeply cared about.

***

The visit to see John Ames proved a waste of time. The teenager's testimony, confirmed by both his parents (who'd been home at the time), was that he and the dead boy had played *Dark Souls 3* on the

Xbox till about a quarter to twelve, when Chris had left for home on his bicycle.

That was the last time they'd seen him. The shock on John Ames's bearded and pimply face when they'd broken the news of his friend's death to him couldn't be faked. He'd begun trembling. He'd staggered back to sit on a chair and almost been unable to reply their questions, his voice was shaking too much.

"Scratch him off as a suspect," Apache said when they left the house. "We're looking elsewhere for our killer."

Though his comments echoed Sully's own thoughts, Sully hated the displeased tone of Apache's voice. The older man's statement had echoed with the feeling that he'd have loved John Ames to be responsible for Chris Burke's death, as it would simplify matters.

Sully disagreed with that. *The old guy already sounds like he thinks ghosts committed the murder.*

All that Sully saw unravelling in the near future was a sordid case of some drugged-up bikers with a grudge against the dead kid. Maybe Chris Burke had run off with their drug money or raped one of their old ladies.

Once they got the forensics report, the bikers should be easy enough to track down.

CHAPTER 3

The Summer Jinx . . . or, What Apache Was Worried About.

Raynham, MA was a small town.

Though (to most of its resident's minds) cursed with much more than its fair share of unfortunate happenings, most of these incidents tended to occur in the summer months.

Apache Johnson had long pondered on that. He'd wondered why, for three-quarters of the year, life went on nice and easy here, and then between July and September, it seemed as though Hell had literally been let loose on the town.

The closest he'd come to an understanding was to assume that the summer madness followed the tourists and holiday makers into town.

Raynham, though not a particularly well-known tourist spot, nonetheless attracted a good number of visitors, ironically because of the very notoriety of its rumored horrors. Horrors that Apache and the rest of the Raynham, MA police force had made a career of hushing up, lest their town get a really bad reputation; the sort of bad reputation that would attract the attention of Capitol Hill.

Apache for one wasn't looking to have his hometown turned into a paranormal research laboratory.

The truth, which Apache and almost everyone else living in Raynham were blissfully unaware of, was that their peaceful little town was built on one of the 666 gateways linking Hell to Earth, and that those gateways were always more active (as in, easier to access) during the summer months, when the weather, being hot at that time of year, was closer in temperature to that of the infernal nether realms.

CHAPTER 4

Chelsea

Saturday Night.

Chelsea Byler slowly peeled off her work clothes. The time was 11:30 p.m. She'd just gotten home from work and was both tired and hungry.

Once undressed, she padded into the bathroom to pee.

Take it easy, girl, she told herself as she sat on the toilet. *You're home now. You can let your hair down.*

Chelsea did feel a bit stressed. She worked as a Department Manager at the Walmart Supercenter over on lower Broadway. She handled the Stationary Department. It was a good job, but sometimes, like tonight, it seemed like more work than salary.

While peeing, she checked her fingernails. These were each about an inch long and done up in diagonal red and black stripes. Party nails really, but she liked them; they added a touch of glamor to what was really a mundane job.

Her cousin Danny Foster said her flashy nails made her look like a high school senior. Danny would know: under the stage name of Deirdre Fabulous, Danny moonlighted as a drag queen on weekends at a number of gay clubs. He knew more about makeup and manicures than she did.

Chelsea peered down between her legs. She studied her toenails. Unlike her fingernails, these were trimmed short and painted a simple brown. They could do with a repainting; the brown was flaking off. But Chelsea couldn't be bothered to retouch her pedicure. Who looked at one's toenails anyway? Not when, in her case, she wore covered work shoes or sneakers 24/7.

She stopped examining her nails and got off the toilet. She cleaned up and flushed, then used a sanitary wipe between her legs for hygiene's sake.

She considered having a shower now. She decided against it. From past experience, right before going to bed was always best for her. Then she'd sleep soundly and wake up bright-eyed and raring to go.

Walmart waits for no woman, she thought in amusement. It was her favorite saying. She come up with it one afternoon while thinking of the crazy amounts of organization it took to run even one store in the Walmart retail chain. She'd gazed proudly at her portion of the magnificent whole, beamed at her sales associates as they assisted customers from aisle to aisle, and coined the expression.

She slipped into a bathrobe and then smiled at her reflection in the mirror over the washstand. She was a slim blonde. Twenty-eight years old and fresh-faced.

Satisfied with her appearance, she sashed up her bathrobe and returned to her bedroom. She paced quickly through the bedroom into the hallway and headed for the kitchen.

Alright, so what am I gonna eat? I'm so not in the mood to cook anything now. Aw, it'll have to be cookies and milk again tonight.

She stepped inside the kitchen, flicked on the lights and opened up the fridge.

Then she heard a noise. She froze and listened. The noise came again.

With a surge of alarm, Chelsea realized that the noise was coming from inside her house.

There's someone here in the house with me. An intruder.

Her eyes spread wide. She totally forgot about eating dinner. She straightened up. She shut the fridge. She listened some more.

Oh, there was no doubt about it. She wasn't alone in the house.

Chelsea considered screaming. She decided against it.

Maybe the intruder doesn't know I'm back home from work yet. No!—He knows that! My car is parked outside and all the house lights are on! So he knows. He's here now specifically because I'm home. He wants me. Oh, he wants to rape me!

With that terrifying thought in mind, Chelsea grabbed a knife off the kitchen counter. This of course, was the right time to call the police, but her cellphone was in her handbag in her bedroom. The cordless landline was out in the living room, but getting to it now . . .

Stepping outside of her kitchen didn't seem the smart thing to do, at least not until she'd determined the intruder's exact whereabouts in her house and calculated how much time she'd have to make the necessary phone call.

The sounds she was hearing confused her. She was certain they were footsteps. They had that solidity and repetitiveness of purpose which suggested a human intruder, along with a ponderousness that marked the intruder as male . . . but . . . but (and this was Chelsea's biggest problem) the footsteps also seemingly had no fixed location. At first they'd seemed to be coming from the front of the house, but then, a moment later, they'd sounded at the back—in her bedroom, she thought. The problem with this was, she'd heard no intervening sounds of the intruder running from front to rear of the house.

So maybe there was more than one prowler? That too didn't make any sense. If more than one person was invading her home, how come then that she kept hearing just one set of footfalls at a time?

She realized she needed to stop being scared and take some action. One thing was certain: she wasn't fighting. The knife she clutched in her whitening fingers was only for self-defense. Also, forget about dashing out into the living room and shrieking into the phone. She wasn't going out there and exposing herself. She didn't own a gun and this intruder might have one.

She needed to get away.

In theory, flight should have been simple enough. Even though making a break through its delicately latticed windows was out of the question, Chelsea's kitchen still had three exits. Two of these three potential points for departure were however inconvenient: In addition to being locked with a key, the side door that led outside the house also had a large padlock on it. And the handle to the dining room door (which route would have enabled her to easily dash through her living room to her front door and hopefully escape outside and reach her car) was bad; the door couldn't be opened from the kitchen.

Which meant that Chelsea's only route out of her kitchen was the door to the hallway.

Yes, she could attempt to leave by the side/outside door. But to do this, first she had to retrieve the key to its padlock from the top drawer of the kitchen counter (which was certain to make a loud noise), then she had to unlock the padlock (which would make another noise), before both unlatching and unlocking the door itself (two additional noises, both of which she knew from experience were louder than the previous two); and then lastly she had to actually open the side door and leave the house. This final action would add yet more unwanted sound to the equation of her escape; the issue with all these noises being, that if the intruder in her house didn't already know where she was, she'd be informing him of her location, and he'd be on her before she could make it safely outside.

Better to maintain this current stalemate, she decided. *I'll wait till he comes to me. All the better too if he has no idea which room I'm in. I'll surprise him then, not the other way around.*

She could hear him pacing at random through her house, the unnerving thread of his footsteps abruptly sounding at different parts of the cottage with no delays in-between, almost as if he was everywhere at once. Chelsea fought down the fear that swamped her as she considered this impossible fact.

Yet it would be easy to surprise him. The hallway door opened to her side. She was hidden behind it. Even if he looked into the kitchen, she'd be concealed until she decided to reveal herself.

Once he sets foot in the kitchen, I'll see through the crack between the door and the wall how tall he is and leap out and stab . . . !

She waited. Her heart seemed to have leapt up into her mouth; it felt to her like she was chewing on it with each heartbeat. She glanced out at the night, wishing she'd had the foresight to remove the metal latticework that prevented burglar access through the kitchen windows.

The footsteps sounded loudly now; apparently the intruder was right outside in the hallway. Right outside the kitchen door. Chelsea shivered. Her fingers tightened painfully on the handle of the knife.

One major problem she had was how the open door faced the hallway. She couldn't see who was out there without sticking her head through the doorway. A terrifying vision of her making that mistake—sticking her head out of the kitchen door and feeling it disconnect from her body and fall to the ground—almost made her pee herself in fright.

Chelsea waited with the knife raised. She formulated a desperate plan:

The moment he steps inside here, I'll stab him in the eye, then I'll dash past him for the bedroom, lock myself in there, grab my phone and call the police. Then I'll start yelling to attract the neighbors' attention. If I scream now, he may throw caution to the winds and just kill me anyway. But once he knows the police are coming, he won't dare.

She now became aware of the intruder's smell. It was utterly disgusting! The terrible smell made her gag. Whoever was out there smelt like rotten meat. Like a T-bone steak left out in the sun till grubs had begun crawling over it.

The smell perplexed her. *Is the guy carrying a dead cat with him, or what?*

They remained in stalemate like that: he outside, she inside; separated by an open door.

She began panicking, wondering what he was doing out there.

Is he masturbating to thoughts of killing me? Is that what he's up to? Why isn't he coming inside to kill me?

No, she didn't want him to come inside the kitchen, but at the same time, the knowledge that he was right outside there, and that only a plasterboard wall separated them both was threatening to make her faint.

She could almost hear him breathing on the other side of the wall. She was certain he could hear her breathing too.

And what if he comes inside the kitchen and I stab him and I don't hurt him enough? Oh, this is what the gun lobby are always on about guns being good for female health!

Then she relaxed slightly. She'd just realized that she could still get away: she'd been staring her escape directly in the face and not even realized it.

Chelsea's panic had made her overlook a simple fact: she could lock the hallway door. The key was right in front of her, sticking out of the keyhole less than a foot from her left hand. And once she'd locked the hallway door, she'd have sufficient time to unlock the side door and get outside.

She extended her hand to shut the door, then paused.

I need to think this out properly. She was sweating profusely now, desirous to let out her panic in a series of loud screams, but not daring to do so. The rotten smell coming through the open door was addling her brain. It was impossibly bad. It was making her feel faint.

She did a quick mental calculation:

Alright, once I lock the door, I'll first dash over to the counter, retrieve the key to the padlock, hurry and unlock that, then turn the key in the lock. . . . No, no, no! First I'll turn the key in the lock, then I'll retrieve the key to the padlock. That way, if I'm delayed in opening the padlock or drop the key, I'll still . . . Oh, fuck this!

Chelsea slumped against the wall. She'd confused herself. She was breathing heavily now. She didn't get it: how difficult could it be to simply slam one door shut, unlock another one, and run for her life? It ought to be the simplest thing in the world, right? But her current straits—knowing that the person after her was right outside and was toying with her emotions and playing on her fears—was preventing her fight-or-flight reflex from working properly. Even though she could get away, it seemed better to stay where she was and take the guy on.

Look, just lock the damn door already. I'll definitely be gone from here long before he breaks into the kitchen. The main thing I need to do is ensure I'm quiet, quieter than a butterfly, so he thinks I'm locking myself in here for safety and not because I'm trying to escape the house. Then I'll dash across the yard to Mr. Thomas's . . . No—once the door is locked, I'm gonna start yelling for help, while . . . Just lock the goddamned door first, dammit!

So that's what Chelsea Byler did. She slammed the kitchen door shut and locked it. Once she'd heard the key click in the lock, she spun around and hurried over to the side door. She smoothly (and quietly) unlocked it, then suddenly remembered to unlatch the chain as well. Afterwards, she felt a thrill of dread.

Imagine getting the padlock open and the door hooks 'cos I'd stupidly left the chain on! And the guy's breaking in the kitchen door then.

So far though, this last hadn't happened. She could hear no sounds coming from outside in the hallway. Surely he knew where she was now. He had to know. Or had she been lucky enough to make her move when he'd gone back to exploring the house?

Whichever it was, Chelsea wasn't hanging around to ask questions. The bad smell had lessened but not vanished completely. So he might still be out there, building up strength to charge the door and bust it off its hinges. Or—*Shit! I damn well forgot*—he may simply have walked around to the dining room entrance to the kitchen. It would open easily from the other side.

Chelsea had been about opening the counter drawer to fish for the padlock key. Now, realizing this fresh source of danger, she instead hurried across to the living room door and quickly locked it.

She leaned against the door for a few seconds to get her breath back.

Then she realized that the rotting smell in the kitchen had once more increased in intensity. She spun around and saw why.

She was no longer alone in the kitchen.

What the . . . ? On seeing the person now locked inside with her, Chelsea Byler felt crushed by Fate. Her situation reminded her of something her cousin Danny always said about trying to pick up straight guys for a quick fuck when he was done up in drag: "Well, sometimes I'm a hit and other times I get hit." In guise as Deirdre Fabulous, Danny was so beautiful that most men couldn't tell the difference. Most happily visited Deirdre's body via the back door once she coyly explained, "Oh, baby, I hope you don't mind traveling down Poo Avenue—I'm having my monthly little-girl troubles." But once or twice a guy hadn't been drunk enough and then Deirdre had gotten the full 'goddamn queer' homophobic treatment, complete with a black eye or two.

Chelsea suspected that tonight was her own 'get hit' night.

She didn't even realize she'd dropped the knife she'd been holding on to for protection. The sound of it clattering on the floor tiles announced its loss to her. She didn't bother bending to pick it up. To her stunned mind, it made little difference if she was armed or not.

The sight before her made little sense.

The man (she assumed it was a man) standing in front of her was a mockery—a total travesty—of human life.

He was tall; much taller than she was. He was dressed in a dirty blue suit. A bright blue suit. Just trousers and unbuttoned jacket; no shirt or tie beneath. He was wearing shiny black shoes, but his ankles bulged grotesquely over the top of each shoe, almost as if he'd had to shave off a part of his feet to fit them into the footwear.

He also had on a black hat from beneath which projected a matted mess of light brown hair.

Now Chelsea understood the reason for the horrible smell everywhere. This man facing her was *dead*. He had to be. To her horrified mind, a living person couldn't possibly look this shockingly ugly. Or stink like he did.

His face? At first Chelsea's intruder didn't appear to have a face. But then she realized that he did. It was just that his face seemed pulped, with its human features all completely effaced and destroyed. The man's face—indeed his entire head—was a swollen purple mess through which grubs and worms wriggled beneath the surface of the skin. An evil-looking, unnatural black ichor continually seeped from cracks in this mess of a face and dripped onto his shoulders and chest.

His chest and the rest of his body looked just as awful as his face did, all bruised up and black-and-purple and swollen and busted open.

Yes, his entire body was as fucked-up as his face. Everywhere also dripped the same disgusting black pus onto his blue suit; his pants were soaked through with black liquid patches.

His hands were huge gloves of puffy flesh, totally ruined, but somehow still fully functional. The fingernails were long and black and cracked. One or two were missing, their previous locations now festering sores.

Chelsea took all of this in in a moment's glance. He was there in front of her and she had no choice but to see him for the horror that he was.

The scariest detail of all, however, wasn't how frightening this intruder looked. No, the way Chelsea viewed it, the really terrifying thing about her current straits was that the kitchen door which she'd locked was *still* locked. The man hadn't broken in here: he'd either walked through the wall or teleported himself inside her kitchen.

"Stay away from me!" she gasped.

"Stay away," he repeated, in a voice that hissed like air escaping a punctured car tire.

She noted an additional impossibility now. It wasn't that this dead and rotting man didn't have a mouth or other facial features. She'd just missed them because they were all out of position. Chelsea's mind boggled at what she was seeing. Usually a mouth was at the bottom of the face and eyes were at the top, right? But this dead guy's mouth was on the right side of his face—at nine o'clock on a clock face—and . . . well, he had two side-by-side pits opposite it at 3 o'clock which she assumed contained his eyes. That settled, she figured his nose was the puddle of black mess in the center of his garbled features. She couldn't make out any nostrils, but still, the puddle had a familiar symmetry to it, despite the shards of bone projecting from it. Maybe the guy even had ears too, jumbled up somewhere in that twisted and pulped muddle that served as his head.

His teeth were all shattered: jagged out-of-line rocks in the black pit of his mouth.

What is this horrible thing doing in here? What does it want from me?

"If you come any closer, I'll scream!" She wondered why she wasn't screaming already. But something was keeping her jaws locked. A large part of this vocal paralysis came simply from how baffled she felt, but there was also her subconscious desire not to inhale any more of the dead man's nauseating dead-rat stink than she absolutely had to; and if she was going to yell, she'd first need to gulp in a huge mouthful of air to power her scream, which would mean filling her lungs with this repulsive creature's rotting air.

"I mean it, man. You dare come any closer to me and I'll goddam scream for help!"

"Scream," he repeated after her. "Scream."

It sounded to Chelsea as if he was encouraging her to scream. She tried to oblige him; she really did. But then this horrible stinking man pulled something from his suit and her terror froze her throat and lungs again.

It was a straight razor—the kind that barbers use to shave people. The kind that movie mobsters use to slit people's throats. Only, this razor had to be the largest one she'd ever seen.

Chelsea's eyes widened with a horrified understanding.

Then the dead and decaying and horrible and stinking man crossed the kitchen floor in a single step and grabbed Chelsea Byler by her throat.

While she gasped for breath, he began slashing her up. The first slash cut easily through her bathrobe and went deep into her chest, slicing down through her left breast and across towards her liver. Blood erupted from her pale flesh like roses blossoming in the snow.

Now Chelsea did scream, but it was a scream of silence; the man was choking off her voice.

She was in more pain than she'd ever felt before.

In self-defense, she dug her fingernails into his chest and clawed away at him. His flesh was pulpy and soft; it shredded easily beneath her assault and she felt the bones and organs beneath his skin.

But her clawing him didn't deter him in the least.

He cut her again. This time the razor slipped in between her right ribs and sliced open her lung. Chelsea's agony doubled. When he relaxed his grip on her throat and she found sufficient strength to vocally vent her terror, she was surprised that instead of a loud terrified noise, bright red frothy blood bubbled up out of her lips.

He slashed her again, this time across the forehead, peeling the skin and flesh down to the bone. Blood spurted onto his hands. Blood ran down her face, getting into her eyes. He moved his hand in a blur and now the pain was a fire burning down her right arm. She'd by now given up on trying to claw him off her. She was in too much agony. She was also choking up a lot of blood in her efforts to scream. It was becoming hard for her to breathe. When she inhaled, her lungs felt full of liquid.

She looked up at the intruder's face, seeking mercy. There was none to be seen. Though his mouth didn't move, she felt that he was laughing at her.

She looked out of the kitchen window. The moon was out, wind rustling the leaves of the trees.

She looked back inside at this man, this monster who was murdering her. She was still perplexed. She had no idea why this twisted and rotting parody of a human being was killing her.

Then he shoved her back against the door to the dining room, raised the straight razor high above his head, and began slashing mercilessly at her, now literally cutting her flesh into shreds.

Chelsea's blood splattered everywhere.

CHAPTER 5

Apache and Sully

"No point debating that it's the same killer, is there?" Sully asked. He figured that much was obvious. He doubted that his partner had any doubts on that score either.

Apache nodded. "It's the same fellow, alright. And a real sick and sadistic bastard he is too."

The detectives were standing in Chelsea Byler's kitchen.

It was just after 2 p.m. on Sunday afternoon. They'd been summoned here after Chelsea's cousin Danny Foster had called 911 and reported spotting blood splashes on her kitchen wall.

Danny had stopped by to pick Chelsea up for lunch. Her car was parked outside the house, so he'd known she was home. She'd not answered her front door, so he'd tried calling her phones instead. First her mobile, then her landline. When she'd not answered those either, even though he could hear both ringing inside the house, he'd become worried that something had happened to her. He'd then walked around the cottage, peeking in its windows. Danny hadn't seen any sign of Chelsea, but the blood splattered around her kitchen was enough reason for him to dial the cops.

Now, Danny was outside in the living room, crying into his hands. He'd followed Apache and Sully into the house when they'd broken down the front door, but once he'd seen Chelsea's corpse he'd burst into tears and fled the kitchen.

Sully found Danny Foster rather effeminate, with his slicked-back blonde hair, pale green pants, purple shirt and brown-and-white shoes. He thought the guy looked like Prince.

He noticed that the guy knew Apache though. But then, Apache seemed to know just about everyone in Raynham. That wasn't hard, he'd decided: Raynham was a little town, population of 15,000. Which broke down to about just four thousand families. Raynham was the sort of place where after a while, everyone was either directly involved in everyone else's business, or heard about it secondhand.

To be honest, Sully couldn't actually fault Danny for being upset at what had been done to his cousin. He too was very upset. He just wasn't the type to cry over spilt blood. Still, Sully was really angry that anyone could do this to another human being:

Just like with the Chris Burke murder two days ago, Chelsea Byler had been sliced to pieces.

Her face, for instance, was almost completely peeled off of her skull. Its meat and skin hung in jagged red strips, some of which had lost the battle with gravity and dropped into her lap. Her mouth hung open and the single blue eye that still remained in its socket—the left one—gaped open with horrifying intensity.

Chelsea was sitting open-legged on the kitchen tiles, with her back against the dining room door. Her entire torso was a shredded mess, an explosion of gore that had plastered the strips of her ripped-up bathrobe to her skin. At the moment it was impossible to tell which of the many red ribbons dangling from her were skin and which ones were cloth. The destruction of her body was that complete.

Her innards gaped a grisly red from five or six deep holes that had resulted from the depth of the numerous vertical and horizontal slashes that had turned her body into a morbid chessboard. The flesh missing from these holes hadn't been pulled out of Chelsea. No, just as had happened to the muscles of her face, these chunks of skin and flesh too had fallen out of her when the supports holding them in place were all severed.

In short, she'd been butchered. Her blood was splattered everywhere, over the floor, on the counter and on the fridge. Some of it was even up on the kitchen ceiling.

Sully felt sick to his stomach. In addition to the sight of the victim upsetting him, there was also a bad smell in the kitchen, a rotting odor that might be either a blocked drain or an overfull trashcan.

Sully looked at Apache. The older man didn't seem to have noticed the faint stink, or maybe he too assumed it was just rotten meat in the kitchen trashcan.

Apache turned from staring at something on the countertop to staring at Sully. Sully raised an eyebrow to let him know he had his attention.

Apache gestured around the kitchen. "Alright, son, now how do you read this? I mean, considering the circumstances, what would you say happened in here?"

Sully thought. There was a lot to think about. "Well, first of all, we need to assume that she—"

With a grim laugh, Apache preempted the younger man's reply. "You were gonna say she knew who killed her, weren't you?"

He nodded. "She must have. She let him into the house, didn't she? All the doors were locked from the inside when we got here, so she must have been the one who let him in."

"You're overlooking something, kid. And I think you're overlooking it intentionally, because you don't like the implications of noticing it."

Sully frowned. "What're you getting at, old man?"

"Kid, if dead Miss Byler here let her killer in, then who let him out again and locked the door after him? And slipped the chain on the front door too?"

Sully hazarded a guess: "There were *two* killers?"

"C'mon, you know better than to pretend that. Okay, forget that for a minute. Consider this additional mystery—how come she's this sliced up, with all this blood everywhere, and there's no bloody footprints in sight? Not a single one? And, Sullivan, don't'cha dare tell me the guy used a spear and did it from a dry distance."

Sully was about retorting, but Apache gestured to him to wait. "And, yeah, one more thing, kid: remember that we had to break in here 'cos the kitchen door was *also* locked from the inside?" He pointed to the dining room door against which the dead woman sat. "Luckily, we picked the right one to bust through, else we'd have dislodged all the evidence."

Sully didn't immediately reply. He honestly didn't like what this was adding up to; mainly because it wasn't adding up at all. "Okay," he said finally, "I agree that this *is* odd. We'd best let Forensics figure out how the guy got in. But"—a pleading note entered his voice—"can we just look through the house anyway, check out the windows for bloodstains and such like? Maybe, just maybe, the guy hasn't left yet." Sully laughed nervously, then gestured at the dead woman's half-faced stare of agony. "You never know, old man, a sicko like this just might hang around to mock us in person."

Apache shook his head like he thought Sully was nuts. But next he got out his gun. "Alright, get your rod out. We'll look around, if it makes you happy. We won't find anything though, rest assured about that."

Sully knew Apache was telling the truth, but he needed a pretext to leave the kitchen. The bad odor seemed to increase the closer he moved to the corpse, as if she was already rotting. But she clearly wasn't, so what was causing the smell?

***

Apache knew that Sully just wanted out of the kitchen. He sympathized entirely. Looking at dead Chelsea Byler, with all that vicious damage to her body and all the holes in it, was giving him the creeps too.

They searched through the house. They'd already alerted the station to the situation they'd found here. A forensics team was on its way over, but like Sully had suggested, it did no harm to look, and yes, it got them both out of the gruesome kitchen for a while.

"You satisfied now?" Apache asked Sully three minutes later, after they'd both confirmed that, no, whoever had murdered Chelsea Byler hadn't used any of the windows to get out either.

"Yeah," Sully grudgingly admitted.

"Alright then," Apache said gruffly, "let's get our asses back to the kitchen and see if we can notice anything else before Forensics arrive."

"I wonder what's keeping them anyway."

"Most likely the knowledge that the corpse won't be going anywhere till they get here."

A quick peek into the living room showed both detectives that Danny Foster was still seated how they'd left him, with his head in his hands and his shoulders shaking from his sobs.

"C'mon, Sully, let's do this quick," Apache said, stepping out of the hallway and back into the murder scene.

This time they ran their eyes carefully over everything, looking for something incongruous, something that made no sense. But then, this case already made no sense, so they were really looking for things that made additional no-sense.

It was Sully who noticed it. The rotting smell . . . He squatted down beside Chelsea and had a good look. What was making that smell?

Then his eyes narrowed. "Hey, Apache, I think we got something."

Apache turned from looking behind the fridge. "Yeah? What?"

Doing his best not to step in the blood everywhere, Sully reached over to the dead woman and, using a ballpoint pen, raised her left index finger. To do this he had to dislodge her entire left hand from beneath her thigh. She was already stiff, but he managed to work the hand free enough to show her fingers.

By then Apache was by his side. "What you got?"

Sully pointed with the pen. *"This."*

Trapped under Chelsea's long red-and-black fingernails were scoops of what had to be skin and flesh.

"I think we just got our first break," Apache said. "We seem to be staring the murderer's DNA right in the face. She put up a fight for her life and scraped his skin off."

"I don't think so," Sully replied, a look of disappointment stealing over his features. "There's way too much flesh under her nails. It can't be his . . . not unless he's made of corned beef. And as far as I can tell from the smell, this is rotten meat under her fingernails. I've been smelling it since we got in here." He looked enquiringly at his partner. "Man, can't you smell it?"

"Yeah, I've been smelling it too," Apache admitted. "But I thought it was just the trash. Some working girls don't have the time or the energy to clean up their own messes." Then, as though he'd just thought of something horrible, he looked *really* worried. "Aw shit, no . . ."

Sully hadn't noticed. Still crouched over the dead woman, he was too intent on his own thoughts. "Looks like we may have to involve the Feds in this." Before continuing, he once again scanned the dead woman; her one eye staring sightlessly into emptiness from a face devoid of half of its meat and skin; her straw-colored hair looking like it had been used to mop up blood; her torso so sliced up, she'd have to be cremated—no undertaker could repair this level of skin and tissue damage; chunks of her flesh on the floor between her legs like she'd been about eating herself for dinner . . . odd, this last thought, because she'd died in her own kitchen.

He looked up at Apache. "A serial killer this sick must've have struck before. He must have. Okay, maybe not here in Raynham, but elsewhere in the state or across the country. I can't think of any other explanation why he'd be carrying rotten meat on him." Then, at a thought, his face blanched up white like he'd puke. "Aw no—I sure hope this isn't some other victim's body he was carrying around or wearing like a skin."

"No, kid," Apache replied, "we definitely don't involve the Feds."

The words came out brusque and hard, with a cold cutting edge to them that Sully had never before associated with the older man. He felt like he'd been slapped hard in the face.

Apache seemed to sense this. His voice a little softer, he added, "At least not yet, we don't. Not till we're certain that this is a serial killer we're dealing with."

Here we go again, Sully thought glumly. *The old guy's gonna start harping on about paranormal causes again.*

But Apache didn't. He didn't say anything; just stared at the dead girl. And every once in a while, without realizing he was doing so, he'd rub that portion of his right hand where all the flesh was missing.

"You're right 'bout one thing though," he said finally. "Even if that ain't the killer's DNA under her nails, it'll provide us a clear lead as to where he's murdered in the past. If he is a serial killer, that is."

Now it was Sully's turn to brood and make no comment. *What else can it be but a serial killer, old man?*

***

They left the kitchen to go sit in the living room and wait for Forensics.

Danny Foster was still out there. He'd gotten his head out of his hands now and just looked miserable. He'd clearly loved his dead cousin a lot.

None of the three of them said anything.

Apache could tell that Sully was wary of Danny. It amused him. Sully clearly had a niggling feeling that the kid was gay, and it was bugging him. (Sully was right, Danny Foster *was* gay.) Apache understood that. The average straight man's problem with gay men wasn't that they couldn't stand them. No, it was that they were scared the gay guys were going to hit on them and try to fuck them in the ass; and they didn't know how to handle that.

Apache shrugged. Let Sully work that out for himself.

For his own part, Danny was a good kid. He worked in the children's section of the Raynham Public Library, which was about two hundred yards away from the police station. By all accounts he was a hard worker too.

That, to Apache's way of thinking, was what was important, not who you were busy kissing at midnight.

"Man, where the hell have Forensics gotten to?" Sully growled all of a sudden.

"Sully, I already told ya—those guys don't need to hurry; they know the corpse ain't leaving here without first talking to them."

"Yeah, yeah." Sully leapt up and went outside.

Apache stared after him. Then he looked at Danny. "You okay, son?"

Danny slowly nodded. "I-I-I just don't understand how anyone could do that to her. Chelsea was a nice, wonderful person. How could someone cut her up like that? Like they completely hated her guts. How could they?"

Apache frowned. "Son, there's some really sick people in this world. You know that just like I do. It's just unfortunate that they came knocking on your cousin's door last night."

Danny nodded. Once again, tears filled his eyes. Apache's words clearly made sense to him, but the horror of what he'd seen was still deep in his soul.

"You know what?" Apache said softly. "Why don't you go home now? There's nothing you can do here, and we don't need you for the investigation at this point. We'll call you if we need to confirm any details about Chelsea's movements last night. Alright?"

Danny nodded again. He slowly got to his feet. Apache stood up too. Arm around Danny's shoulders to steady him, he escorted the young man to the front door.

There, Danny turned and held Apache and wept like a baby on his shoulder. "Please, please, please, man, find out who did this to her. Find out who did it! She didn't deserve to die like this!"

Then, pursued by demons of grief, Danny turned and staggered off to his car, a red Toyota Corolla.

Danny drove off. Sully took his place at Apache's side.

"He definitely isn't a suspect," Sully said.

Apache nodded. "Nope, he ain't. I'm not sure I should've sent him home though. I just hope he doesn't go kill himself from grief. Or get drunk from grief and kill himself afterwards."

"If you know where he lives, we can check on him later. Ensure that he's okay."

Apache hid his surprise. Sully wasn't normally the sort to show concern for other people's feelings, particularly in this case where the age-old homo/hetero problem had raised its head.

"Yeah," he agreed, "we'll call him later. They'll have his cell number at the station."

"Well, the nerd squad finally got here," Sully noted, pointing to the two police vans just pulling into the front driveway. "Time to leave."

So they did. Apache though, first requested a thorough analysis of that rotten meat under the dead woman's fingernails.

He wanted to know exactly whose corpse it had come from.

He hoped it was an animal's. He was certain he was wrong.

CHAPTER 6

Apache, mostly

After questioning Chelsea Byler's next door neighbor Mr. Thomas, who'd neither seen nor heard anything suspicious the previous night, the two detectives drove over to the Walmart Supercenter on Broadway to make the usual enquires about the dead woman. Neither of them imagined they'd turn up anything of use at the department store, but until Forensics got back to them with some concrete data, there was little else to do.

As was normal, Sully drove their car. He had the radio on, was listening to the news.

Apache spent the trip to Walmart pondering Sully. Occasionally he glanced over at the young man sitting beside him. Brown suit, dark blue shirt, maroon tie and shoes. The kid was a sharp dresser. His face was ordinary enough: well-tanned complexion, gray eyes, short brown hair, largish nose and thin lips now curled into a grimace as he reflected on Washington's latest political upheaval. Sully looked every inch the stereotypical police officer who didn't take nonsense from criminals—neat and well-behaved, with a house in the suburbs and a doting wife and kids. Just a young man doing a necessary job of giving crooks hell, and committed to doing it well.

Apache liked Sully. But even so, he couldn't help pondering the difference between the old, experienced brand of detective, represented by himself, and the new sort, represented by his partner Frank Sullivan, who'd learned detective work from textbooks about cases solved by older generation guys like himself, and whom, armed with that book knowledge, now thought they knew more than those old guys.

To them, suspect fingerprints and blood samples and DNA analysis and cellphone records were the Holy Grail.

Take Sully here, for instance:

So okay, yes, the kid *was* smart. He had a good brain and a good intuition for what made criminals tick. He was a good cop.

Apache sighed as Sully turned a corner. The problem was, kids today watched too much television. By his own account, Sully here spent all his free time watching *CSI*, *Cold Case*, *Law & Order*, *The First 48*, and other cop and legal dramas with his girlfriend Tilly. Sully actually owned a copy of the complete box set of *CSI* DVDs. He owned the *Major Crimes* box set too and several others.

It was getting to where young police officers were having trouble separating fact from fiction, trying to apply law enforcement entertainment rules to their jobs.

Apache grimaced. Now, when he'd been young he'd never had time for TV watching. Most nights—before his daughter Rebecca came along and disrupted things with her toddling demands for breast milk and attention—Apache would have Beth on her hands and knees in their bed. She'd be sweating along with him, groaning and gasping for more, till finally she'd be begging him to stop, pleading with him not to kill her with his sweet manhood because it felt like he was pushing it through her cervix with each thrust.

Beth had had great breasts. He'd loved playing with those creamy globes; loved caressing and sucking on her chocolate-brown nipples, enjoyed squeezing her breasts while they made love. Feeling her chest pressed against his always resulted in getting him as hard as a rock and ready to rumble in bed.

Apache sighed at the sad memory of her death. Breasts aside, Beth Johnson had been a wonderful woman in every way and he missed her dearly. They'd had some great times together, both in and out of bed.

And that was how it was meant to be.

But these young boys and girls of nowadays? Nah, they'd rather watch cable TV than make love. Wow, how the times had changed.

Besides, back then we didn't have all these silly modern cop dramas anyway. Nothing to interfere with a young couple's passion.

They drove past a line of stores outside of which happy holidaymakers strolled. Apache glanced at them with approval. These people having fun weren't the sort who made trouble. Psychos, on the other hand, got their fun from making trouble for these people.

And then he and Sully had to clean up the madman's messes.

They were almost at their destination now. The massive Walmart building was visible five hundred feet farther down Broadway.

Apache returned his mind to his thoughts. This thing about police officers watching too much TV really bothered him.

The problem was, on those TV shows everything was solved by logic. In television Policeland, everything had an explainable cause. No matter how impossible or supernatural the clues at first appeared to be, the good detectives would finally unravel the 'paranormal mystery' into something plausibly mundane.

There, all else was science fiction. There was no place for the mystic.

He frowned. *Yeah, they do have some paranormal cop shows on TV too, but those are accepted as sci-fi by all and sundry.*

So, how was he to convince his partner Sully here that they weren't after a serial killer? The young man had the evidence right in front of him, but, as trained by TV dramas, he was doing everything in his power to rationalize it all away.

Still, I can't really blame the kid, Apache admitted to himself as they pulled into the Walmart parking lot. *In this instance, I'd LOVE for him to be right and myself wrong. I've just got a gut feeling that that ain't the case here. Not by a long shot.*

CHAPTER 7

Malicia

It was around noon on Monday.

Malicia Howard smiled as she watched the blue pickup truck depart her yard. That was her brother-in-law Raymond leaving. He'd been over to check on how she was settling in and also to have a look at her dripping kitchen taps.

The pickup's brake lights flared a bright red for a moment at the foot of the driveway, then dulled again to their stained-glass emptiness as the vehicle made a left turn. Raymond Howard waved back once, then sped off.

When the blue pickup truck was out of sight, Malicia turned back into the old house. She felt completely drained of energy. She'd put on a good show for Ray, had done her best to look and act strong, but she felt far from it. She was still weak from all the blood loss during her magic ritual. She was currently taking a herbal potion to revitalize herself and had also found a 'good health' spell in one of her magic books. But despite both of these treatments, she knew it would be at least another week before she really felt like herself again.

The pain and drain had been worth it though. She smiled at the bandage on her left forearm. Beneath it, the gash was still open. The wound had stopped bleeding and a herbal salve had prevented infection, but it needed stitches to close it properly, or else there'd be a horrible scar and she'd never be able to wear a short-sleeved blouse out again. It was a true quandary. She needed a doctor, but didn't dare visit one. Any physician seeing her wound would naturally assume she'd attempted suicide, and she couldn't have that.

After spending fifteen years of her life locked away, Malicia had no desire to ever visit an asylum again. She'd explained the bandage to Ray as covering an allergic reaction she'd developed to something under the kitchen sink while checking to see why her taps were leaking. He'd seemed to buy that. He'd been kindly solicitous, asking if she needed to visit the doctor, which she'd easily shrugged off.

It had helped that she'd not slashed her wrist during the ritual. A recently-crazy woman with a freshly-bandaged wrist would be a red alert to anyone, even her doting brother-in-law.

Standing inside her bookshop, Malicia felt pleased. Her smile broadened to a grin. Already, she knew, the panic had begun and was spreading. Spreading like an infection. She'd *felt* both deaths—they'd given her energy, further motivation to tread the dark path she'd embarked on.

Soon, this entire town would be terrified, squirming in the grip of the fright she'd created. It was a lovely feeling.

Malicia looked around her bookshop. Most of the newly installed bookshelves were bare, but she'd begun filling those on her far right. In her weakened state, it took her hours to do. She first had to carry the older books downstairs, then unpack them, then work out which went where.

She'd marked out the sections: Science, Arts, Fiction, Self-Help, and others. Over in the far right corner were ten cartons of newly purchased paperbacks that she'd not yet opened. The revolving book racks they were intended for stood black and glossy beside them. She'd have time for those later.

But she was getting her feet under her again, reconstructing her past in her present. In just a short while, she should have everything back to normal in here.

A sudden dizzy spell made her stumble forward and sit down, plumping herself on the short step ladder she used when stocking the higher shelves. She sat there for five or so minutes, bent over and breathing deeply, wondering why she felt so old.

Is it the weight of responsibility of seeing through what I've set in motion? I don't think so. I've no regrets over what I've begun. And I'm not worried either.

Bent over like she was, the bandage on her arm pressed against her forehead. She knew her payments weren't over. They never were when one dealt with devils. Would her infernal benefactors empty her veins next time?

She shuddered at the thought, then smiled. *In that case, it's a good thing I've not had the wound stitched up yet.*

She wiped the smile off her face. Being drunk to death wasn't a joking matter.

Occasionally she caught glimpses of the demon things, like darker shadows residing inside her house's own shadows. She'd turn to pick up a book, for instance, and see the shape of a tall man with too many arms stepping back into the gloom, or something like a spider, but with a tentacled head, rising back up into a corner of her bedroom ceiling. The 'darknesses' (as she'd named them) neither attempted to harm her nor approached her. They were simply there, best friends she didn't like at all. However, rather than reassuring Malicia by their presence, the darknesses made her shiver. They were like premonitions of evil she was keeping as pets.

Malicia also worried that the darknesses in her house were spying on her for the powers they represented. The only reason for this she could imagine, was so that she didn't change her mind and try to reverse her revenge.

The thought that they considered her so weak amused her. *That won't ever happen, you fools. I'm in this till my last drop of blood is spilt. You shadows can drain me dead if you like, but I too will drink my cup of revenge like it's a fine wine . . . drink it until it's empty and its juice of vengeance is replaced by the red blood of my victims.*

The thought enlivened Malicia. Feeling stronger now, she sat up straight again. She looked around her bookshop, taking pride in the great restoration work that had been done: in the clear wide windows and the glossy wood paneling and the new sales counter with its little blue cash register and black laptop. The floor was brown and purple carpeting; it would take a lot of dirt from the myriad of shoes she expected once she opened her doors again, hopefully by next Tuesday.

There were still a few things to set in order before the Mr. and Mrs. Book Emporium could resume business again though. In addition to all the books that needed arranging, the shop sign wasn't up yet. A friend of Ray's was designing it. Ray would be over to hang it up before the weekend.

Malicia stood up. She stared at the ten cartons of new paperbacks on her right. *Do I feel up to putting their contents on the shelves?*

No, I don't, she decided. *They'll keep till Wednesday. By then I should be strong enough to handle them.*

Then she smiled. *Oh, but there's really no need for me to wait that long. I'll just have Betsy arrange them for me when she comes over this evening.*

Betsy Driscoll was her niece, Ray's daughter. Betsy had earlier phoned to say she'd be visiting later in the day.

Malicia hadn't seen Betsy in almost two years, the last time being when Betsy had accompanied her father to the asylum. It would be nice to see the girl again; she'd not had any female company since she'd gotten home.

With that pleasant thought in mind, Malicia Howard climbed the stairs behind the bookstore to her apartment. She felt well enough now to have lunch and a short nap before her niece arrived.

CHAPTER 8

Betsy

Three months ago, Betsy Driscoll had arrived home from a weekend trip to Springfield to discover that her husband Sammy had left her.

Sammy Driscoll had eloped with a girl named Luisa. He was now down in Mexico. Not New Mexico, but actual south-of-the-border Mexico.

Sammy and Betsy had been married for six years. She'd been nineteen when they'd wed, and had been head-over-heels in love with him. Her husband was a handsome sandy-haired man who smiled a lot. Everyone who knew the couple had always assumed they were happy together.

And they had been happy; until Sammy met pretty young Luisa Gomez.

Betsy arrived home the night after Sammy left Raynham to find a note stating that he'd left her, that he wished her all the best, and that he'd be forwarding the divorce papers through his Reno lawyer.

Betsy was mad. She was understandably livid with rage.

Then she'd broken down and wept piteously. She was a woman, after all. She was completely heartbroken.

She'd wept a whole lot. For days and days she did nothing except wake up in the morning, get drunk, and then cry her heart out until it was nighttime and she could again seek the solace of slumber to escape the pain of her loss.

She'd tried calling Sammy, both using his cell number and also through WhatsApp and IMO, but he neither answered the phone nor replied the endless messages she left on his voicemail. He ignored all her text messages. Not once did she see an indication on her phone that he'd opened/read any of them. Her emails were similarly ignored.

All of this really hurt Betsy. She wondered why Sammy was being so cruel to her. It wasn't as though they'd had a major fight over anything. They'd always gotten along really well with each other, so why was he now refusing to even communicate with her?

It seemed to her as if Sammy was trying to erase their relationship. To rewrite their shared emotional history. He was behaving as if she'd never existed. As if she didn't actually exist now. As if he'd already completely forgotten her and overwritten her place in his heart with his mistress.

She got really mad again. Such cruelty as he was showing her deserved punishment. Sammy had broken her heart and she was going to break him in return. She'd . . . she'd . . .

Betsy wondered if law enforcement could help her find her runaway husband. Her father and Raynham Chief of Police Tina Kravitz were good friends. Or maybe, it would better if she hired a private investigator. All she needed to know was exactly where in Mexico Sammy and Luisa had eloped to. Once she knew that, she'd travel down there in disguise, with a handgun, and shoot him dead. And that little tramp Luisa wouldn't escape her either.

No, she wouldn't kill Sammy. She *loved* him. All she would do was force him to come back to her. She would most definitely kill Luisa though, quietly and somewhere out of the way, so Sammy wouldn't know who'd murdered his slut.

Once the pretty Latina obstruction was removed, Sammy would be hers and hers alone.

She harbored these thoughts for two weeks, then gave them up. She returned to being miserable again.

Betsy slowly came to accept that she'd lost Sammy for good.

And once past that point, her onetime passion for Sammy Driscoll quickly turned into intense hatred. He'd ruined her life and she was bent on getting even with him. Sammy Driscoll might be half a continent away, but he was going to pay dearly for the emotional pain he'd caused her.

***

Now . . .

Betsy Driscoll got down from the step ladder and stretched. Her arms ached from all the book arranging she'd been doing. Betsy was certain it was the blasted encyclopedias that were responsible for her aches.

Aunt Malicia was upstairs at the moment, fetching some more books, so Betsy had a moment to catch a breather. She sat on the ladder and relaxed, working each of her wrists in turn to ease the slight pains.

Betsy Driscoll was a tall brunette. Twenty-five years old, she was quite attractive, with nice blue eyes and cute lips. But she was also a little overweight. This was mainly because Sammy had loved eating unhealthy stuff (just about everything the health professionals advised against eating) and she, being his wife and having to cook the unhealthy stuff for him, always had to taste it to ensure it was properly prepared.

That was the joke she'd used to tell everyone anyway, only now it didn't sound funny at all. Now it was just another thing to be vengeful for.

Betsy shifted her legs beneath her long blue skirt and kicked out with her black shoes, distractedly scuffing her feet over the dark rug which was already flecked with scraps of cardboard and discarded twists of packing paper. She fluffed out her white blouse to let air through to her skin. The evening seemed too warm to her; but that was just the result of all this unaccustomed exercise: climbing up and down the ladder, and extending her arms back and forth like she was doing aerobics.

Her left thigh twinged and she rubbed it.

Ooh, I'd never once imagined that putting books in order could be so much work.

Even arranging the paperbacks took some effort, because one had to balance half a shelf's worth of them in the crook of one's arm, just so, and then pick out one or two at a time and stow them in the right places. Now she understood the importance of book carts, a purchase Aunt Malicia needed to make quickly.

Aunt Malicia.

As a teenager, Betsy had often wondered why her crazy aunt was called Malicia by everyone and not Mildred or Alicia which were her real names.

Her father had finally told her the story of Mildred Alicia Edwards, Ronnie Gribble, and the pair of scissors that went through Ronnie's hand and also through the desk. Raymond Howard had been in eleventh grade at the time it happened, and he clearly recalled how he'd paled with fear on hearing Harry's story of how much blood had squirted from Ronnie's hand and how they'd had to trash Malicia's desk with a circular saw before they could free it.

Betsy, who was having bullying hassles of her own with a couple of female classmates at that time, had been impressed. She'd thought her aunt was supremely badass to face up to the bully like that. Betsy hadn't been bold enough to try out the 'scissors and palm' defense for herself, but since then, her cloistered aunt had become a kind of heroine to her.

And then, there were all those other things that Betsy had heard about her aunt . . .

Most of this she'd gleaned from town gossip, usually when the older townsfolk—her aunts and uncles and their friends—were speaking. No matter how much she'd pestered her father with questions though, he'd refused to divulge any additional information about her aunt to her.

Her mother wouldn't tell her anything either. The most Betsy that was finally able to work out from the little she'd heard, was that her Aunt Malicia was a witch of some kind. Aunt Malicia had apparently caused some trouble during a courtroom trial, but it had all been hushed up by the town authorities. By all accounts, the story had never even made it into the papers.

Betsy wanted to ask Aunt Malicia about that. It was an awkward question to pose though:

I can't just ask her if she drinks blood and rides the Broomstick Express at night, can I?

She tilted her head and listened. She could hear the old woman moving about up there. It sounded like she was searching for something amidst the piles and piles of literature Betsy's father had stacked for her.

I really wonder why she insists on moving everything herself, when dad's workmen can bring all her books downstairs and fill the shelves too, in a tenth of the time it's gonna take both of us to do it.

For a moment her eyes misted. One of those workmen, Chuck Jennings, had been catching her eye a lot recently. Chuck was tall and muscular and cute and didn't currently seem to have a girlfriend. The only thing stopping her making a play for him was her father . . . he might not approve of her dating his employee.

Betsy began wondering exactly *what* her aunt was doing upstairs.

She decided to go see. She was bored with sitting around doing nothing, and she figured she'd fetch herself a drink too. She doubted that Aunt Malicia had any liquor in her kitchen, but there were certain to be sodas in the fridge.

She got up and climbed the stairs.

When she entered the living room, her aunt was just settling herself onto the single unoccupied couch, all the other available seats being covered with cartons, both large and small.

"Sorry, girl," Malicia apologized, "but I keep tiring out. I keep forgetting how old I am."

Betsy nodded. "You want that I should carry some stuff downstairs for you?"

Malicia waved a hand. "No, no. I'll be okay in five minutes, then we can resume." She gestured to one of the less-filled armchairs. "Clear the boxes off that one and have a seat."

Betsy got to work clearing the cartons off the armchair. Halfway through doing so, she happened upon two books, over which had lain a pile of ancient newspapers. The first book was titled *Black Magic for Beginners: Practical Spellcasting.* It was a small hardback volume and was clearly very old.

At first she mistook the second book for an encyclopedia—it was large and heavy—and winced at the strain to her poor arms if Aunt Malicia insisted on stashing it too on one of the top shelves alongside the others. The book's title had faded, apparently from its great age.

Then she realized there was something really odd about the book. It was a pinkish/off-white color, and though its cover seemed to be leather, there was something unpleasantly familiar about this leather:

The way it was crinkled reminded Betsy of a dead person's skin, as viewed in a casket at a funeral.

Is this human skin? she wondered. *Is this book actually bound in human skin?*

A series of deep shudders ran through her. Her trembling had two sources. The first of these was an instinctive revulsion, a natural disgust that anyone would consider using part of a human body as packing for their literature.

The second cause of Betsy's shuddering was a deep excitement.

So it's true! All those rumors about Aunt Malicia are true. She really is a . . .

She had no idea she'd begun smiling. A cold smile that left no doubts as to its desire to do nasty things.

Quickly, drawn on by her curiosity, she opened the skin-bound tome. Its pages were thin, each one made of the same human-leather, with words inscribed in either a bright red ink or a deep brown one. Accompanying the script were scary illustrations done in the same red and brown inks. The dual inks had an alarming, eerie brightness to them.

About half of the writing in the huge volume was in English; explanations of, for instance, how to cause blindness, or make someone hideously ugly, or give them a cancer.

The other half of the writing was the spells. Though all written using the English alphabet, the incantations were as meaningless to Betsy as though inscribed in Portuguese: words and phrases like 'Bruzz,' 'Toh si l'leh,' 'Noit abrut sam,' 'Boku Ninin,' 'Natas,' 'Goot koodanz,' and such gibberish.

However, despite her inability to grasp their meanings, these words and phrases still conveyed to Betsy impressions of their being immeasurably old. She felt them as magical voyagers from the time of the world's youth, and had fleeting glimpses of their ancient power.

The book itself seemed to her to be the expression of a hugely evil mind, one seeking release into the human world. The book both thrilled and upset her. Touching its pages gave her a sense of things she didn't need to know, of secrets better left unlearned. Holding it felt like holding eons of inscribed darkness.

Betsy had no idea that her aunt had been watching her closely. Her first hint of this came when Malicia said:

"What you're holding in your hands, girl, is the Necromantica."

Betsy shut the scary book and looked at her. "The Necromantica, auntie? What's that?"

Malicia Howard smiled a weak smile. "Actually, what you're holding is just a teeny-weeny part of the Necromantica. The actual Necromantica is the LOTUS—the Library Of The Unholy Sciences. It's a collection of magical books numbering in the thousands, some say six thousand, six hundred and sixty-six volumes in all, each one more horrible and more powerful than the last. For the most part, the LOTUS doesn't exist on Earth, but in the realm of Hell called SADE."

Betsy shuddered again; from fear this time. She could barely make sense of what she was hearing. "If this LOTUS library you mention doesn't exist on Earth, how'd you get this copy?"

Malicia shrugged. "Sometimes fault lines develop between the realms and things fall through; sometimes books get stolen; sometimes folks pay the price in obscenity and bloodletting to borrow the books from their demon keepers. My late husband—your late uncle Harry—may have been one of the latter category. I can't say for sure: I was never interested in the occult while Harry was alive. The book was his."

"Does it work?" Betsy asked. Her breathing was very shallow now. Anyone hearing it would think that she, and not the old woman, was the weaker one. Indeed, Betsy felt breathless, like one standing atop the Rockies and staring down at the world. She felt like she'd just made the world's greatest discovery. She felt like Columbus discovering the New World.

"Does the book do what it claims?" she meekly enquired.

Her old aunt nodded briskly back. "Oh yes, it certainly does. I was skeptical myself at first, but then I discovered the horrors that lie just beneath the surface of God's clean reality; all easily accessible and useable if one is willing to lose one's soul."

Betsy grinned, her teeth as bright as lamps. Outside, the sun lost a part of its luster. The evening took on foreboding tones of color.

The old woman raised herself to a sitting position. She smoothed down her pale sundress, then slipped on a woolen pullover because of the falling temperature.

"Now, Betsy dear," she said, "yes, I know you're glad to see me and all that, and I'm delighted to see you too, but I think there's something else to your coming, something you've been wanting to tell me about all evening since you got here; something you need my help with fixing."

This close to her heart's desire, Betsy almost faltered. Oh, but she couldn't ask for that! She wouldn't! "Oh, it's nothing, Aunt Malicia. Honest to God, it's not. Just some childish wishful thinking. Just a 'what if' thing."

"Now, now, Betsy, I can see that you do want something from me," Malicia said gently. "Please, stop trying to pull the wool over my aging eyes; my sight's bad enough as it is. So, what is it, girl? Don't be afraid; I don't bite."

So Betsy Driscoll bit the bullet: "Well, see, auntie, my husband . . ."

***

Malicia listened in silence to her niece's tale of her husband's betrayal and her impending divorce. Another sordid tale of a trifling man. It was a familiar story, one she'd heard times without number while in TSH: sane women running crazy after the husband began sleeping with either their sister or best friend or worst enemy or mother or daughter or maid or secretary; and in some cases even two or three of those at once.

Then the cheating man left, and the poor abandoned woman was left with a nightmare of neuroses and insecurities, confused about her own femininity and unsure if she was truly woman enough to satisfy a man. If she didn't have a good support system of caring friends and relatives, she could easily wind up in the madhouse. Some women who found themselves in this situation just gave up on men altogether and became lesbians.

Yes, Malicia had seen and heard it all before.

Some men were just pigs. Just horrible creatures.

Betsy finally broke down and wept. With tears streaming down her face, she finished: "And so, auntie, I really, really, really, really, really, *really* want to pay him back in some way."

"Do you want him to come back to you?" Malicia asked. "The books can grant you that."

Betsy wiped her eyes and stared. "You can actually make that happen?"

Her aunt nodded. "Yes, certainly. Cast the right marital fidelity spell and Sammy will come back to you, meek as a lamb, and he'll never, ever stray from your side again."

***

Betsy considered the request: *Hmm, do I want Sammy back? Do I really?*

Staring down at the skin-bound book in her hands, she thought the option over carefully.

If I get him back . . . but everyone knows he left me for another woman.

It was painful to consider. Right at the base of things, she didn't want to be alone. She was honest with herself.

Yes, pathetic as it is, I still love Sammy, and yes, I do want him back, but . . . not yet. No, not yet. Why should my philandering husband have an easy ride home to me after all the suffering he's put me through? Sammy needs to suffer too. Then he'll know to treat me better on his return.

So, instead of just swallowing her hurt pride and requesting a marital fidelity spell to return her errant husband to her side, Betsy lied to her aunt:

"Hmm . . . no, I don't love the son-of-a-bitch anymore. I just want to hurt him." She figured she could easily pretend to change her mind later on, and plead with her aunt that she'd been wrong and now that Sammy was certain to have seen the error of his ways, she wanted him back again.

"Yes," she repeated firmly. "I want Sammy to suffer like he's making me suffer."

Malicia nodded. "Alright then, we'll do that." She frowned. "What sort of suffering do you wish him to have? Do you want his manhood to stop working?"

Oh, Betsy was very tempted to leave Sammy with a permanently limp penis. But . . . she considered, there was the factor that she planned to forgive him after a while. What if the penis damage couldn't be reversed? All she'd have done then would be to stab herself in the sex organ, wouldn't it?

"No," she replied. "That's too ordinary, isn't it? Every time a man hurts a woman, she shoots him in the dick? I want something classical, something really evil."

She smiled at her aunt. "If a man had hurt you the way Sammy hurt me, what would you do?"

Malicia didn't immediately answer. Instead she got to her feet and hobbled across the crowded living room to a large chest of drawers.

She pulled open the top drawer, lifted a large wooden box out of it, then returned to the couch. This time she gestured to Betsy to come sit next to her.

Betsy did so. Malicia opened the box. Betsy gasped. The box contained four dolls, each one six inches long and two inches broad and carved from a light brown wood. Each more ugly than the last. All four dolls were dressed in identical little blue suits, black shoes, and had tiny black plastic hats on their wooden heads. Two of the dolls had bloodstains on them that looked recent. The dolls were recessed in slots in the box. The box had slots for six dolls, but two of them were empty.

"Auntie, what are these?"

Malicia smiled coldly back. "They're voodoo dolls, Betsy dear. I was thinking: how 'bout if we give your husband a set of afflictions that you can turn on or off as you wish?"

As the implications of her aunt's statement sank in, Betsy began giggling.

***

They got to work. Betsy was surprised by how easy it was to set up. All that was required was a little of her own blood and something that belonged to Sammy. Betsy winced when her aunt slit the base of her left thumb, but she figured the pain was worth the gain—she intended making Sammy feel a lot more pain than this before she forgave him.

Betsy also had something of Sammy's to hand: She'd been carrying his breakup note around in her handbag for the past three months.

Her aunt burnt up the note, then mixed its ashes with Betsy's spilled blood. Then, opening another book—not the Necromantica—to a brightly colored page depicting several demons violating a praying nun, she recited a spell.

Finally she smeared half of the blood-ash mixture on Betsy's forehead and the other half on the head of one of the voodoo dolls taken from the box.

Betsy blinked. The dark mix had seemed to vanish inside the doll. She felt her own forehead. The wetness there had also vanished. She did her best to hide her surprise.

"That was to link you both together," her aunt told her, "so the doll does what you tell it to."

"Wha-what *does* it do?"

Malicia picked a large pin out of the box. "Now, let's say you want Sammy to have a headache. Then you do *this* . . ." She pricked the doll's forehead with the pin. "The headache will last until you pull the pin out. If you want to give him a migraine . . ." She plucked the pin out of the doll's head and then stuck it back in again, this time pushing it in through one ear and out of the other one. "You do this and he'll think his head's exploding. No amount of any kind of medication will be able to relieve the symptoms."

She peered closely at her niece to make sure she understood.

Betsy was fascinated. "Can I try it?" she asked.

"Be my guest." Malicia handed her the doll. It seemed to be made of soft wood and felt oddly warm in Betsy's hand. Warm and damp, as if it was sweating out the bloody mix it had just absorbed. Its morbid heat easily penetrated its little blue suit.

Most of all, the doll seemed evil. This evil went beyond its mere facial ugliness (an ugliness unerringly reproduced in the others in its box); Betsy felt as though she could sense the doll's heart. And what she sensed was an utter blackness that for a moment terrified her.

"Don't be frightened of it," her aunt whispered. "It isn't ever going to hurt *you*." Then the old woman smirked coldly. "For Sammy though, it's a totally different ball game. I almost pity him."

"Well I don't, auntie," Betsy said, feeling a sudden eerie empowerment. She lifted up the doll and pulled the pin out of its head. Then laughing, she stuck the pin into the left side of its little blue suit. "Hey, darling, have an ulcer!"

She wasn't sure, but it almost felt as if the doll twitched in pain. Betsy liked to think it had anyway. Just to make certain that the ulcer was really happening to her husband, she shoved the pin in further.

"Now that that's settled," Malicia said, "put the doll away in your purse and let's get back to arranging these books downstairs. Say, dear, can you come over again tomorrow evening?"

Betsy nodded enthusiastically. "Yeah, sure, auntie." She stashed the little wooden figurine away in her purse, making sure that the pin she'd stuck into it was still firmly in place, then returned her attention to her aunt. "So, which books do you want to move first?" Then smiling, she pointed down at the skin-bound Necromantica. "I'm sure this isn't one of them, is it?"

They both burst out laughing at that.

Betsy went to the kitchen and got herself a Coke from the fridge and poured her aunt a glass of orange juice.

After refreshing themselves with the drinks, they resumed moving the books downstairs to the bookshop.

CHAPTER 9

Sully

Frank Sullivan enjoyed watching television. Mostly *CSI*. He found watching actors play cops and robbers a soothing release from spending the day playing cops and robbers.

Apache was wrong: Sully didn't own just *one* copy of the complete *CSI* DVDs box set; he owned *three* copies of the collection. He kept two copies at home, and one over at his girlfriend's place, so he could watch it there.

Tilly Brandon watched *CSI* along with Sully. She did it to humor him mostly. She preferred romantic dramas and comedies.

So, on most of the evenings that Sully was over at Tilly's house (which was most evenings of the week), they watched cop TV together after putting her kids to bed. Then they turned in themselves, made love and went to sleep.

Then, the next morning, Sully left Tilly's side to go play cops and robbers again.

PART 2: PIECES OF A MEAT PUZZLE

Sex and violence are the grease that lubricate human life.
(Necromantica 53:12:99)

CHAPTER 10

Ronald

Monday night. 11:47 p.m.

Ronald Snelson turned off Britton Street onto Broadway. He was walking home from his girlfriend's house. Teresa Badger lived just four hundred yards away from him, in a house she shared with two friends. Ronald, who lived down on Broadway almost opposite the Slap Shotz Gastropub, always chose to walk to her place, rather than driving.

This late at night, walking gave Ronald Snelson time to think about life. This close to midnight, the streets were mostly deserted. The only folks outside were the odd wino and others like himself, guys who lived so near those they'd visited that motoring there and back was a waste of gas.

The moon was up and the sky was clear. Air moved in gentle gusts. It was neither too warm nor too cold. Leaves rustled and insects chirped.

Occasionally, a solitary passing car ferried its yawning driver homeward to bed. Except for the streetlights like electric trees, it was a dead world. Even Ronald's footfalls sounded dead, his shoes hardly making a sound as he strode through the silence.

He thought back over the evening. He'd expected he and Teresa would be making love tonight, but she'd just started her period and was hurting and . . . well they'd sat holding hands with her head on his shoulder and watched one of the Syfy Sharknado movies. Crazy impossible stuff that nonetheless had had them both almost crapping their pants with laughter at the corniness of it all.

Afterwards, they'd kissed a bit and he'd left for home. Teresa worked for a law firm and had to be in court tomorrow. Before shooing Ronald out the door, she'd both taken a sedative and set the alarm on her phone for 6 a.m.

Ronald, an elementary school teacher, also had to be up early, but in his case the kids wouldn't really mind if he was a bit drowsy.

The children in his class were generally a well-behaved lot, except maybe for Tilly Brandon's son Marvin who was a bundle of mischief.

But all in all, life was fine.

Such were Ronald Snelson's pleasant thoughts as he approached the Stop N Go Express gas station opposite the start of Britton Street's lower half. (Divided by about fifty yards of Broadway, Britton Street was split in two.) Just a hundred and fifty yards further to go and he'd be home.

Of course, once through his front door, he'd call Teresa to see if she felt any better. Then he changed his mind about that. It wouldn't do to do so. Considering the sedative she'd taken, Teresa might already have fallen asleep by now and he'd only succeed in startling her and waking her up again.

No, I'll call her in the morning.

Ronald had now arrived at the Stop N Go Express. With pleasant images of Teresa's face in his mind, he looked left, at the gas station. The Stop N Go convenience store had closed for the night. He watched a small green sedan roll in and stop in front of one of the pumps. (The station had two pumps.) A woman got out of the green car and began punching figures into the pump. Ronald returned his attention to the road.

That was when he saw the man up ahead. Quite close to him, about twenty yards away. A tall bulky man in a blue suit and a black hat.

The man's abrupt appearance startled Ronald. *I only looked into the gas station for five seconds at most. So where'd he suddenly appear from?*

Ronald was still walking towards the mysterious figure. They were both actually standing in the road. At this part of Broadway the sidewalk was on the opposite side of the road. On Ronald's side, only a thin stretch of lawn and a curb separated the gas station premises from the highway. Late as it was and with no vehicles in sight, Ronald had seen no point in crossing over to the sidewalk. Any driver coming towards him would be on his side of the road. He'd simply step up onto the grass to avoid being run over. Of course, there were drunks behind wheels to contend with; but that couldn't be helped. Drunken drivers were the night pedestrian's eternal bogey.

The man in the blue suit hadn't moved since his appearance. He just stood there as if waiting for Ronald.

That didn't bother Ronald Snelson too much. Now that he was over his initial shock at the man's sudden appearance, he was prepared for trouble. Ronald was himself tall and muscular and he didn't scare easily. He'd boxed in high school and college and could handle himself well in a fight.

So long as this guy in front of him wasn't packing a gun, of course. Bullets beat the hell out of muscles any day.

Ronald tensed himself, warming up just in case the blue-suited figure wanted a fight. He flexed his fingers into fists and released them again. He repeated the maneuver, getting himself ready to throw a knockout punch. If this fellow in blue wanted trouble, the fight would be over before the bell for the first round had even rung. Hell, the ring-card girls wouldn't even have finished their circuit of the metaphoric ring before Ronald had laid the guy out. Ronald would hit the guy one punch upside his head and that would be that. Lights out, baby.

There was a streetlight opposite the gas station, and in addition, the station's own fluorescent lighting lit up the road at that point. Ronald could see the man ahead very clearly. And he disliked what he saw.

The man in the blue suit was a freak of some kind. Either that or he'd been mangled in a bad accident. But anyone who'd been this badly mangled had no business being out of a hospital bed.

Or maybe he should be in a grave somewhere. This additional consideration came as the wind changed direction and Ronald smelt the man for the first time. *Gosh, even gangrene doesn't smell this bad!*

But that smell was the fact of the matter. The man had a misshapen head; his face was a featureless warped ball of rotting meat. He had rotting skin that wept black liquid from long suppurating tears, and hands that were swollen to thrice normal size, with cracked black nails.

The rotting man reeked of death and the corruption of the grave. He seemed dead because he clearly *was* dead. Dead and yet walking. He was something that belonged in a campfire tale, not here on Broadway on a Massachusetts Monday midnight.

He was quite close to Ronald now, not because he'd moved, but because Ronald, in his confusion, hadn't stopped approaching him. Disbelieving what he saw, Ronald had walked nearer to the man to see better.

When Ronald finally stopped stepping up to this mess of human flesh in blue clothes, barely two yards separated them.

After taking a really good look at him, Ronald decided that fighting this man (thing? monster?) wouldn't be a wise idea. He decided he'd be a lot better off just ducking around him, crossing the road, and running hard and fast till he arrived home safe and sound. And once home, he'd lock himself inside, fastening all the doors and windows. Yes, he'd lock himself in his bedroom and then he'd make certain to leave all the lights on all night, so that not even a shadow could worm its way near him.

"Man, what the hell happened to you?" As scared as Ronald was, he couldn't resist asking the question. When someone looked this fucked-up, you had to know what they'd done or who they'd pissed off so you could avoid making the same mistake they had.

While awaiting a reply, he peered left, into the filling station. The lady at the gas pump was still there. She seemed to be having payment trouble with the machine. Maybe it was taking its time with returning her credit card.

The rotting man now shuffled a step closer to Ronald, his stink arriving first like an outrider.

"Ron," he said. He had a really queer voice, like Death's voice in the movies. Breathy and full of built-in echo.

"Ron," he repeated.

Ronald decided to take the man's advice. "Run," it sounded like he'd said, though he might just as well have been saying Ronald's name. Whichever it was didn't matter though. Either way, Ron didn't intend hanging around. While speaking, the man's mouth had opened in the *right side* of his face, rather than down near his chin, and it had revealed a tongue all black and swollen and crawling with worms. And, impossibly too, what looked like a little fish skeleton wedged between his tongue and his shattered front teeth.

And where the hell are his eyes?

The man spat out the fish skeleton.

For a moment everything hung in stasis around Ronald Snelson. His heart pounded in his chest; veins visibly twitched in his neck and forehead; he heard the woman at the gas pump loudly curse the machine; a lone owl hooted; the wind lifted the brim of the dead man's hat, revealing matted wormy hair; black goop plopped to the ground from the man's festering body.

71

The one thing that didn't happen was a car driving past. At the moment, Broadway felt like somewhere out in a parallel dimension.

It's like the world has ended and I'm here talking with Death.

Time unfroze. The man moved his disfigured and swollen hand down inside his suit and felt for something. "Ron," he repeated.

Ronald was just about to set off running for home, when the man whipped out his hand again.

Ronald caught the sudden flash of bloody silver in the streetlight's glare. His training as a boxer instantly kicked in: instead of fleeing, he was ready to fight again. He flung up his hands to guard himself.

Before the man could slash down at him with the blade, he hit him in the face with a hard punch.

The man's head rocked with the punch and snapped to the left, then righted itself. The man didn't falter, he just stood there. Ronald flung another hard punch, with the exact same results.

Ronald was shocked. Not so much because the rotting man was still standing after being hit so hard, but because of how the man's head had felt on each contact with his fist.

His head had felt smashed. With each blow, Ronald's hand had sunk into its pulp-like flesh to the knuckles, almost an inch deep. That was to be expected from how swollen and puffy the man's head looked, but . . .

But . . .

It had also felt like all the bones in the man's head were broken.

Ronald had no idea how that could be so. Crazier still, the second punch had opened the man's eyes, both of which were set, one beside the other, in the *left half* of his face.

Ronald had no time, however, to ponder on either of these discoveries, because at that moment the rotting man slashed him down his raised left forearm and he realized he was in a fight for his life.

Ronald howled. The blade had opened up his arm from wrist to elbow, shearing part of the muscle completely off the bone beneath and spilling blood onto the road. There was now a long gap in his shirtsleeve through which his wound was visible. Ronald tried to keep his guard up to throw another punch, but the blade flashed at him again. He grabbed at the man's wrist with his left hand. He thought he'd caught it, but a shearing pain in his hand a moment later made him realize that he'd caught the razor instead. Another moment, and the blade had cut through his hand and was slashing at his neck, with two of his fingers severed from his hand and falling to the ground. Behind the oncoming weapon, the man in the blue suit loomed like a bullying menace.

Ronald sidestepped the blade. It missed his throat, but then, instantly redirected, it caught him in the middle of his face instead. He yelled in pain. The attacker had sliced his nose off.

By now, all Ronald's intentions of defending himself had deserted him. He just wanted to escape his rotting attacker.

Blood jetting from his mutilated face, he turned to run back the way he'd been coming, but the blade instantly bit into the back of his head, stunning him with the pain of its path through the flesh of his scalp, pain like acid eating into his skin. The man's pulpy fingers also got a firm grip on his hair. Meanwhile, the air Ronald breathed was now mixed with blood. With his nose gone, each breath felt like someone was mashing toxic marshmallows into his brain.

"Help!" Ronald shouted to the woman in the gas station, who he could see watching him in shock and fright. "Call the police!"

The woman ducked behind her green car and stared at him from there.

The man spun Ronald around and slashed at his face again. The blade opened up Ronald's cheek. More blood spurted. The man still had a firm grip on Ronald's hair and was using it to hold him in place while he cut at him. Ronald realized that to get away, he needed to free his head. With his face and body screaming in pain from half a dozen wounds, he grabbed hold of the man's left hand, which was tangled in his hair, and slowly forced it away from his scalp.

Then the man slashed him in the neck. In a sudden surge of fear, Ronald kicked out at him and punched him in the face again.

The rotting attacker fell back, but not for long. In the interim before he closed in again, Ronald realized that he was clutching something in his right hand. He looked down at it.

He'd pulled one of the man's fingers off. The severed finger looked like a decaying sausage with a chunk of bone stuck in it. It was fat and sticky, covered with wormy slime.

Ronald quickly threw it away. The severed finger landed next to his own severed nose.

Seeing his nose there on the ground brought home to Ronald how mortal he was. How close to dying he was. An overwhelming panic filled him. He turned to flee again.

But the man in the blue suit grabbed his hair again. This time he didn't give Ronald the chance to turn back around and confront him. Instead, he tripped him up, then knelt on his back. Then, while Ronald howled in pain, the rotting man sawed at his head, cutting a jagged line around his hair.

Ronald only understood what the man was doing when he felt an agonizing jerk on his skull, and a moment later, saw something like a bloody brown cat drop in front of his face.

That was when he realized he'd been scalped.

While he lay there gaping in disbelief at his entire scalp lying on the road in front of him, the man in the blue suit really began slashing him up.

It didn't take Ronald Snelson long to die after that.

CHAPTER 11

Lynn

It was exactly as expected: when you had an emergency, the emergency number didn't work. Lynn Nilsson kept redialing, but no way; her damn phone simply wouldn't connect.

(Had she been less scared, she'd have realized she was dialing 9111 instead of 911.)

She kept glancing back at the Stop N Go convenience store, wishing it was still open and she could run into it for safety.

After her fourth abortive attempt at summoning help for the man being butchered out in the road, Lynn decided to get the hell out of there.

She'd been crouching on the passenger side of her car. Now she ran around to the driver's door and leapt in. She dropped her phone on the other front seat and started up the engine.

Lynn put the car in motion. In her panic, she almost rammed the green Audi into the second gas pump. She calmed down a little, reversed the car, then went forward again.

This time she drove slowly. The graphic murder was still occurring nearby, but she was far enough from it to escape by simply flooring the gas pedal and making either a left or a right turn.

I'll survive this, just so long as I don't panic again and this time stomp the brake instead of the gas pedal if the murderer runs at me. Somebody just died over there; the important thing is that it wasn't me . . . and I'd better take care not to become a victim too.

Twenty yards separated her from the violence. Unable to resist viewing the gory spectacle, she slowed her car further, almost to the pace of a snail's crawl, then took a good look at it. She could see clearly what was happening.

And it was shockingly savage. The man who'd killed the other one—he had a blue suit on—was now pulling out chunks of his victim's innards and flinging them around, sort of as if his hands were shovels and he was digging a hole in the other man so he could bury something inside him.

Lynn got a firm grip on her bladder. She managed not to wet herself. She was amazed at one detail: So far, in the ten or so minutes since she'd arrived then found herself trapped here at the filling station, not a single car had driven past. She made a mental note never to stop here again for gas this late at night.

Her phone suddenly beeped. Lynn glanced at it where it lay on the front passenger seat. It was giving her a 'battery low' warning.

Don't you dare die on me, you! I need to call the police once I'm safely away from here!

A sudden noise made her look up again and out of her windshield. She took one look outside and almost fainted.

The murderer was now walking right beside her car, out in front of the hood. He walked with a slow shuffling motion, like a drunk.

B-b-but . . . but I only looked away for a second. How'd he get over here so fast?

She instinctively hit the brake before she ran into him. Her car stopped about a yard away from him. She froze in her seat. For whatever reason, he seemed not to have noticed her and she didn't want him too.

Or maybe he's had his psycho fill of murder for tonight and can't be bothered about me. Or maybe he only kills men!

She glanced over at the victim. She had a wild fantasy that all she'd witnessed had been mere playacting, and that the supposedly dead man would also just get up and trudge off, maybe in the opposite direction.

But of course that didn't happen. The dead stayed dead and the blood splashed all over the blacktop stayed red.

The killer, his blue suit streaked with gore, had now stopped moving. He'd turned and was now staring into her car, looking directly at her. He raised his right hand and she saw the bloody razor with which he'd murdered his victim. Silver streaked with red that still dripped.

Her heart stuttered as though it would stop on each beat.

With her headlights on and the station lights on and the streetlight on, Lynn Nilsson got a really good look at the killer's face. A really good look of the kind that she'd never be able to unsee again if she lived a thousand years.

She knew exactly what she was staring at. His accompanying stink of putrefaction, blown by a malevolent breeze into her car, confirmed everything.

Finally, the man in the blue suit smiled at her, lips moving in the right side of his face. Then he turned away from Lynn, took two steps forward into the night and vanished.

Vanished. Without the slightest hint or premonition of his departure, he was suddenly gone.

How Lynn didn't faint from the shock she'd never know. Immediately the horrible man vanished, she floored the gas pedal of her Audi and raced out of the filling station.

She wanted to get as far away from there as was humanly possible. At the moment, even being safely home didn't seem safe enough.

CHAPTER 12

Betsy

Betsy Driscoll felt delirious with ecstasy. She moaned softly. She was at home and in bed, masturbating with a banana.

It wasn't her fault. Betsy was a normal, well-adjusted young woman currently suffering from Bad Husband Syndrome, some of the symptoms of which were: intense sexual frustration, shortness of temper and randomly occurring headaches.

Betsy definitely considered masturbation the second-best option, but when there was no husband at home, being one's own best friend got the job done nicely too.

Betsy had first slipped a condom over the yellow fruit before inserting it into herself. She didn't want to contact any weird diseases. She dreaded going to an STD clinic and being told she had 'ape-pussy.' Just imagine that!

Also, not wanting to overly stretch or stress her still-tight womanhood, she'd selected a banana of medium length and thickness. In fact, she'd done her best to match the tropical fruit to the size of Sammy's member. Sammy had a short and fat penis, and it also tapered noticeably from base to tip. Bananas didn't taper though, but she was making do.

When randy, use whatever you've got handy.

The batteries in her vibrator were flat. Betsy's usual remedy to this was to use a cucumber; but she was currently out of those too.

It was a weird situation to find herself in: *I was in Walmart shopping just this morning. They sell both batteries and cucumbers there. In fact, they sell everything there. All I needed to do was buy me some.*

But she hadn't, and so . . .

Betsy groaned in pleasure and rolled on the bed. She still had all her clothes on, including her shoes. All she'd done to get started after hurrying into the bedroom with banana in hand was pull up her skirt, slip her panties to one side and insert the fruit.

She slid the rubber-sheathed banana between her wet sexual lips and moaned softly. The banana wasn't as good as either Sammy or a vibrator. She wasn't even sure it matched the cucumber—it was too smooth, lacking the textured protrusions which the best sex-toy fruit should have.

But it was getting her off. *Abandoned pussy can't be choosy,* she thought as her body tingled deliciously.

At the height of Betsy's orgasm, her vagina contracted so tightly around the banana that it popped and squeezed out its white insides.

She managed to keep a firm grip on the improvised dildo, sliding it in and out a few more times until her pleasure had ebbed.

Then she lay there, her clothes rumpled up, pulped fruit between her legs, grinning deliriously. Her eyes roved from the Elvis portrait on the wall to the open window, with its fluttering drapes.

Afterwards, Betsy wiped herself clean. Then she got up and undressed.

Then she tied the banana's remains up in the rubber and dropped it at the foot of the bed. She would dispose of it in the kitchen trashcan.

Though Betsy had a trashcan at the foot of her bed, she resisted the temptation to discard the condomed banana in there. She'd tried that once before, with a cucumber. She'd been dashing off to work in a hurry and hadn't even taken the time to seal the condom first. She'd forgotten all about the discarded cucumber till four days later, when the vegetable had liquefied in the trashcan and, in addition to gluing itself to the can's bottom, had stunk up her bedroom.

Alright, she thought calmly. *Orgasmically, I'm good now.*

She now felt unstressed. It had been very late when she'd left her aunt's house. All that book arranging had exhausted her.

And I'm still going back there tomorrow.

But yet, for some reason, the moment she'd stepped through her front door, she'd felt totally overwhelmed by sexual passion. She'd noticed the bunch of bananas on the kitchen counter and thought 'Why not?' And matters had proceeded from there.

She lay back down on the bed to savor the moment. She tried to understand what had gotten her so aroused.

Is it 'cos I was flirting with that guy in the checkout queue at Walmart?

The man in question had looked incredibly hot in his white muscle shirt. He'd had pecs and abs like he ate barbells for breakfast and his black jeans had been skintight, with a nice fat bulge in the front . . . But then his girlfriend had joined them by the checkout counter.

Or maybe it's 'cos I'm thinking of asking Chuck out? Daddy won't like that tho'. But hey—screw what daddy likes! She felt happily defiant. *I haven't got Sammy and dad can't stop me having fun . . .* Then she glanced over at her handbag and laughed. *Oh, but I do have Sammy, don't I? I've got Sammy right where I want him—in the palm of my hand.* She recalled the pin she'd stuck in the voodoo doll's side. *Yes, my runaway baby misses me so much at the moment that it's giving him ulcers.*

Lying there on her back, Betsy had a good giggle over that.

And so, yes—I am going to date Chuck Jennings. Whether daddy likes it or not.

That settled, Betsy turned her thoughts to other things. Suddenly she felt hungry.

Oh, I haven't had any dinner yet. She and her aunt had worked till about 8:30 p.m., and then they'd sat talking and laughing. Aunt Malicia had told her some really crazy asylum stories—like the one about the man who'd fallen in love with his bed and had made a hole in his mattress so he could have sex with it and get it pregnant with twin pillows; and who then violently refused to change his room because that would be like having an affair with another bed. In the end, to keep him quiet, they'd moved his darling bed to his new room too.

And while Betsy and her aunt had chatted, the happy hours had slipped past and Betsy hadn't felt hungry in the least.

But now . . . now I really need to eat something.

The vigor of her afterglow had begun giving way to a pleasurable drowsy feeling. She sat up, grabbed the banana off the bed and headed for the kitchen.

As she stepped along the short hallway to the front of her house, she ran her dinner options through her mind. She'd originally intended to microwave a curry, but now . . . she felt too drowsy for spicy food, and the pepper in the curry was certain to rile up her stomach too.

She decided to just make herself a sandwich. She had some sliced chicken breast in the fridge and a loaf of brown bread. And she'd earlier bought a jar of pickles and some olives and cheese.

Once in the kitchen though, Betsy changed her mind. She was about discarding the banana in the trashcan when she decided to eat it instead. About half of it was still good. She'd slice that part up and use it in her sandwich—along with one more from the bunch.

She altered her former recipe. The brown bread could stay in the scheme of dinner, but the chicken and the pickles were out.

She opened up the fridge and had a look. As a result of her morning Walmart trip, her fridge was well-stocked with groceries. She was spoilt for choice of what to put in her sandwich.

She tapped her fingers against the fridge door and pondered: *Now what goes with banana and bread? Okay, I've got peanut butter . . . and I'll use some of those almonds and maybe apples . . . no, no—no one makes an apple sandwich . . . and . . . Hey, is that what I think it is?*

In a shadowy corner of the middle rack, stashed behind a tub of low-fat yoghurt, lay a solitary cucumber. Betsy was struck by the amusing thought that the vegetable had been intentionally hiding itself from her back there in that secluded nook of the fridge. Or else, why wasn't it down in the crisper where it belonged?

How'd it get up here anyway, except I used it for sex and really liked it and put it back in the fridge to use it again?

In fact, now that Betsy really thought about it, the cucumber looked rather familiar, like it would fit perfectly inside her body.

She looked over at her vaginally-demolished banana—some fruit just wasn't up to the task of really satisfying a lady in bed—then she picked up the cucumber and returned it to the crisper. The main advantage of this vegetable was that it didn't require batteries to work.

Yup, I'm an carnivore with a vegetarian sex life.

She grinned pityingly at the cucumber. *Sorry, veggie, but you're gonna get fucked again and soon too. You'd better start praying that I find myself a steady man soon, or else . . . you'll be on pussy-duty a whole damn lot.*

A frown now creased her brow. *Okay, where was I? So, what goes well with bananas and peanut butter in a sandwich?*

CHAPTER 13

Apache & Sully

That same night, around about a quarter to one.

Detectives 'Apache' Johnson and 'Sully' Sullivan were over on Broadway, standing amidst a young man's remains. 'Amidst,' because most of his innards were scattered around him. Several coils of the corpse's intestines were even out in the middle of the road. The two detectives had diverted the single car that had so far come this way over to the other side of the highway, so it didn't squash their stiff's displaced guts into the road surface.

Sully had been performing cunnilingus on his girlfriend Tilly when the phone call from the station shattered the mood. As a result, he wasn't in the best of moods.

Apache, on the other hand, single but nonetheless unable to sleep, had been watching a *CSI* DVD that he'd borrowed from Sully, trying to discover what young detectives found so awe-inspiring about the series.

"This sicko gets messier each time," Sully said. He looked over at his partner. "It's clearly the same guy, right?"

Apache nodded grimly. "Yeah, it's him alright. Same MO as the others: body sliced to ribbons, most of the face peeled off the scalp, and disemboweled, with his innards strewn everywhere."

Sully bent down and examined something white near his shoe. He flinched on realizing it was half of an eyeball. When he regained his composure, he said, "Yeah, only this time, he screwed up big time. He killed this guy in public, in front of a witness."

Apache scratched his chin. The harsh lighting gave his ponytailed hair a garish blue tint. "Yeah, the son-of-a-bitch did," he agreed. "Only problem is, where's the damn witness? The operator said her phone switched off suddenly just as she began giving directions."

After saying this he took a few moments to study the gas station, looking for the CCTV cameras. Maybe they'd have caught something of use. But no, no joy there: the two cameras he could see were both aimed inwards, towards the gas pumps. There was little chance that they'd have recorded the skirmish that had resulted in this man's bloody death.

Sully said: "You don't think *she's* the one who did this, do you?"

Apache didn't reply. He studied the human carnage around them. They didn't yet know who this dead guy was. They could tell from his clothes that he was young, but that was all. The dead man was certain to have some ID on him, but the way he was laid out, with his intestines draped over his jacket and ribbons of peeled skin all over his crotch, not to mention the blood on seemingly every inch of his clothes, had prevented the detectives from searching for it, in case they moved or dislodged some vital piece of evidence.

They weren't being overly cautious here. In contrast to the first two bodies they'd found, there were already a couple of weird things about this one. For one thing, near the corpse were several dark patches on the road. The patches were more or less dry now, but they appeared to have been mud.

Both Sully and Apache had knelt and sniffed them. They smelt rotten.

Even stranger than those was the fish skeleton Sully had noticed. Lying right at the border of the thin lawn separating the gas station from the road, this fish skeleton—merely three inches long—might have escaped their suspicion as a piece of evidence, except for the fact that it too was coated in places with the same dried black mud. They'd knelt and smelt it. It also smelt rotten.

Once again Forensics and the meat wagon were on their way over. In a sense, Apache and Sully were merely placeholders, ghoulish sentinels keeping graveyard shift watch over the latest set piece in the killer's sequence of destruction.

Sully repeated his question: "I'm wondering, old man: That supposed witness who called in about the murder. You don't suppose she's really the one who fucked this guy up like this?"

"Nah," Apache replied. "I don't think a woman did this. See the way the killer scalped him? That would take some real strength to accomplish."

"Yeah, I get what you mean, old man." Staring at the removed scalp, Sully had a sudden worrying thought that the killer might be one of Apache's Native American cousins who was getting angry with 'Paleface' about two centuries too late. He didn't dare make that joke though. Apache was certain not to find it funny in the least.

The night hung dark on them; both the darkness outside and the darkness inside the killer's head. This killing hung as damp on their shoulders as waterlogged clothes.

Apache went on: "Besides, this dead guy here's a big fellow—looks to weigh somewhere between two-forty to two-sixty pounds. A girl couldn't jump a guy this well-built. No, of course she could, but she'd have to surprise him to do it, and if you look around, except she hid behind the gas station sign over there, there's nowhere else for her to ambush him from."

Sully considered the Stop N Go's sign. While the metal pole holding it up *was* slightly thicker than the kind seminude women cavorted around in gentleman's clubs, the lower end of the sign itself hung three feet off the ground. Any attacker's legs were certain to be visible from the road to someone walking that way, and if that person was female, a good portion of their waist would likely be visible too. Sully grudgingly agreed that it would be stretching probability rather thin to assume the sign would make a good hiding place for an insane female with a literal axe to grind.

And, of course, once again, there were no footprints around the corpse. That was the second thing the detectives had noticed on their arrival here, once they'd gotten over their anger at being gifted another dead body.

"Also, look at the mess whoever did this made of him," Apache said. "Sliced his fingers off, then butchered him like a coyote's dinner. So, from the way things are now, I'd say the witness was being straight with us, and that like she said, a *guy* did it."

"So we rule out another potential suspect," Sully agreed. He turned from looking at the corpse to staring up the road towards the upper Britton Street junction. "Maybe the batteries in her phone just ran down," he said over his shoulder.

"Yeah, or maybe she's having a major nervous-breakdown-threatening freak-out and turned the phone off herself, so that she don't have to talk to anyone else tonight. We'll most likely get a follow-up call from her later today."

"Alright, so once Forensics arrive, we can both . . . I got some wet pussy to go finish eating."

"Hey, Sully, I got a question for ya."

"Yeah, old man, what is it?" Sully was still looking away from the body and gazing into the Broadway distance. He had a weird impression of this case now coming towards a solution, the way the houses and trees further down the highway gave one the illusion of their meeting together at a point.

"Kid, help me refresh my biology for a minute. Just how many fingers does a human being have on their left hand?"

"Five, old man. Why?"

" 'Cos this dead guy here? Well, he seems to have *six* fingers. And . . . hold on a second . . . Oh, you're gonna love this, kid: one of 'em seems to be rotten."

"What?" Sully spun back around. Apache was kneeling beside the scalp on the concrete. He'd moved the scalp a little, to see better. Sure, that wasn't standard procedure, but there couldn't be any other forensic conclusion other than that it had been sliced off the victim's head, so . . .

"At first I thought it was part of his left ear," Apache explained. "But that's his left ear over there, attached to that slice of his cheek; and it's all complete, so I had a look, see?"

Sully looked. Yes, there was a finger, a complete finger, on the ground beside the scalp. And no, its condition didn't seem in any way healthy. It looked old and was both swollen and decomposing.

Sully didn't know what to think about this. He didn't want to think about this. So instead he asked, "Old man, does it still have its fingerprint?"

Apache rolled the digit over. He bent and squinted at it, shone his flashlight on it, then gave up.

"You have a look, Sully. My eyes ain't too good this late at night and in this lunatic lighting."

Sully took his place beside the scalp. He was tempted to pick the finger up, but decided not to. Forensics might need its accurate location in their attempt to correctly reconstruct the details of the crime. He bent and peered at the rotted finger. It stank horribly. As badly as the flesh under the dead woman's fingernails at the last crime scene. The only reason they'd not located the severed finger by stink alone had to be that the wind was blowing its smell away.

He shone his flashlight on the finger, studied it for a while, then straightened up and nodded.

"Yes, it looks to still have its fingerprint. There's an eroded patch on the left, but I think there's enough there to determine the stiff's identity."

Apache nodded. "Good."

Then, while Sully got back up to his feet, Apache strode out into the road to divert an oncoming garbage truck around the two tubes of human intestine lying there.

The truck's noise was why Sully didn't hear Apache softly mutter: "Or enough to identify the *killer's* identity, son . . . yeah, the killer's."

CHAPTER 14

Betsy

Tuesday.

The new day was a wet one. It rained quite heavily, the water coming down in sheets.

Betsy Driscoll made it from her car to her front door without getting soaked too badly by the sideways gusts of water. It was about noon now. She left her dripping umbrella in the hallway, pulled off her wet shoes, and then hurried into the kitchen to brew herself a cup of coffee. While the percolator worked, she changed out of her black mourning clothes in the bedroom and toweled her hair dry.

Betsy felt miserable. She felt sad and depressed.

Worst of all, she felt pursued by something invisible.

Betsy was just returning from Chelsea Byler's funeral. Chelsea had been a good friend of hers since high school.

Chelsea Byler had been cremated. Her funeral service had taken place at the Sowiecki Funeral Home in the next-door city of Taunton. (There was no real distinction between both towns; Raynham had after all started out as a part of Taunton.) For some reason, there didn't seem to be any funeral homes here in Raynham. It wasn't like no one ever died here though.

Betsy had initially been confused as to why Chelsea had been buried so fast and with such a minimum of ceremony. It had seemed as though there'd been a rush to get her corpse out of the way. No obituary notice either in the local papers or on Facebook. Nothing.

Betsy had only learnt about both the death and the funeral at the last minute: this morning, when Danny Foster had phoned to invite her. Danny had explained that he'd been so distraught over his cousin's passing that he'd forgotten she and Betsy were good friends.

To hear that Chelsea was dead had been shocking enough. But then there was also the question of *how* she'd died.

The story Danny had at first told Betsy was that Chelsea had been horribly mangled in a machinery accident at work. But, seeing how Chelsea worked in the Stationary Department at Walmart and mostly dealt with pens and office supplies there, that explanation hadn't made much sense to Betsy. In that paper-intensive work environment, exactly where could she have found the machinery to mangle her? About the only machines she'd have to touch might be an office calculator or a laptop while performing inventory.

Betsy couldn't deny though, that something really messy and violent had happened to terminate Chelsea's life. At the funeral, there'd been no viewing of the corpse. The casket had remained shut all through the service until the committal—"ashes to ashes, dust to dust"—when the curtains had covered it for good.

The funeral had been a miserable affair. Everyone had cried, particularly the small representative contingent from Walmart.

Chelsea's widower father Jerry Byler had sat in front looking ashen, more stone-faced than a statue. Betsy had almost expected him to collapse and die there and then so he could be cremated along with her.

Chelsea's aged maternal grandparents had been there too; the white-haired old couple looking like they could see her ghost in the funeral hall.

Danny Foster had wept all the way through the service.

Amongst those in attendance, Betsy had spotted Detective Apache Johnson, who she knew from a distance. She'd figured the detective was a friend of Chelsea's father.

The funeral service had given Betsy mixed feelings. In one sense she was as miserable and horrified as everyone else in attendance. Beyond any shadow of a doubt, she'd been fully immersed in the communal atmosphere of sorrow that pervaded the little funeral chapel. The main room's décor was a mixture of bright and somber colors, the overall color scheme designed to both inspire reflection on one's loss and inspire hope for the future: deep wine for the rugs; mahogany framework of ceiling beams; subtly-patterned cream wallpaper; indirect lighting that maintained just the right frame of mind.

Sitting there amidst everyone else, Betsy had felt an intense pain. The weeping rain outside, Heaven's waterfall on the roof of the funeral home; tears—corresponding personal waterfalls—in the eyes of the mourners; and also her own emotions drawn from her personal well of sorrow. Yes, for those forty-five minutes she'd spent escorting Chelsea into the afterlife, Betsy had been fully immersed in the experience of loss. Indeed, departing the funeral home had felt to her like an escape, a harrowing rebirth from the jaws of death into the welcoming embrace of life.

So, yes, she'd felt intense grief.

But . . . mixed in with her sadness, had been a deep appreciation of the fact that she was still alive.

With all my problems, she'd thought, *I'm not dead. I'm still here.*

There was a temporariness to her rough experiences which, surrounded by sorrow, she'd learnt to appreciate. Death had a finality to it. Death was the period at the end of life's sentence. Marital troubles and other bothers were merely punctuation: commas, semi-colons at best. But—and here she'd winced as Chelsea's coffin was hidden from view by the curtains—death meant it was *over.* For good.

She'd felt grateful and blessed beneath her cloak of sorrow.

After the funeral, she'd chatted with Danny for a while. Danny was very handsome, but as queer as they came: limp wrist, mincing steps, feminine posture and gestures; at times he behaved more like a woman than she did. She'd not known too many of the other mourners, so remaining with Danny had freed her from an awkward situation—one where it was too early to leave, yet she'd have nothing to do and appear to be loitering, a ghoul feeding on negative emotions.

But she'd also had a secondary reason for singling out Danny Foster as her companion. She'd wanted more information on Chelsea's death. The air of mystery wasn't delicious enough: her curiosity needed something more meaty to eat.

If Betsy's curiosity was as bad as the proverbial dead cat's, its metaphorical feline cousins and the allegorical dogs were still dropping as liquid from the heavens. The rain had started during the service. It was coming down as if God Almighty himself was weeping for Chelsea's passing. Betsy had wondered how she was ever going to reach her car without getting soaked to the skin. She'd not checked the weather forecast before leaving home and as such had left her umbrella in her car.

After she'd gently prodded him long enough, Danny had pulled her aside. They'd walked around the corner of the building so they were alone, staring out at the drenching countryside.

"Betsy, I'm only telling you this 'cos you and my cousin were real close," Danny began, dabbing tears from his eyes with a purple hanky. "So you can't tell anyone else what I tell you, understand?"

She'd nodded, her curiosity at fever pitch now. "Yeah, sure. I'll keep quiet about it. But why all the secrecy anyway?"

"She was murdered," Danny told her. While Betsy gasped and flung a hand over her mouth to stifle a yelp lest someone heard, Danny went on: "Some psycho sliced Chelsea up like sandwich meat."

"For real?"

"I saw it myself. I was the one who called the cops. It was so bad that the cops and her family want to keep what happened a secret."

Murder? Detective Johnson's presence here at the funeral now made perfect sense to Betsy.

Danny had then gone on to tell her what he'd seen. Then, while Betsy struggled to come to terms with what she'd heard, he'd begun crying again.

She'd hugged the sniveling young man, which annoyingly, made her feel worse, not better, as though she was absorbing his misery into herself.

She was glad when they separated again.

After that, she couldn't leave the funeral home fast enough. She'd dared the rain without an umbrella (completely soaking her shoes in the process), leapt into her car and driven home.

And now here she was. Sitting in her living room with a warm mug in hand and feeling pursued. Pursued by all those others' pain; pursued by her memory of a grinning and vibrant Chelsea Byler . . .

Pursued too by something she didn't understand.

At the moment, it felt as though she was carrying her own personal disaster with her. The feeling was a vivid and a cancerous one. It spread to each corner of the living room that she looked at, like black slime dripping down the blue-and-white wallpaper.

Her hot coffee seemed to be turning to iced tea in her guts once she'd swallowed it. She shuddered and tried to find some pleasant thoughts to warm herself with.

After a few attempts she latched her mind on to something satisfactorily nice to dispel her inexplicable worry.

Yes! she thought triumphantly. *I did it.*

'Doing it' referred to her walking up to Chuck Jennings and shaking her breasts in his face until he'd gotten the point that she wanted to sleep with him and had asked her out.

She'd stopped by her father's workshop on her way home, found Chuck all alone in there, managed to temporarily cast aside her gloom over Chelsea's death, and taken her chance on Chuck rejecting her advances. To her delight, he'd seemed delighted that she liked him like that.

Yes!

It was a victory, particularly since she'd done it right under her father's nose. Old Raymond Howard had walked in on them less than a minute after they'd made their date. If he'd known what was going on, he'd not said anything.

Now that she thought back on it, Betsy suspected that her father was aware of her flirting with Chuck, but had been relieved that she was trying to put her life back together again after being dumped by Sammy. (At the moment Betsy was unemployed and reliant on handouts from her parents for everything, including help in covering the mortgage payments for the house that Sammy had callously burdened her with.)

Raymond Howard had never liked Sammy Driscoll to begin with.

I did it, Betsy thought again with glee. *Chuck and I are hanging out at Rudy's tomorrow night!*

The thought really lifted her mood. For one thing, it meant a welcome break from her vibrator-and-fruit-and-vegetable sex life. A long-needed break and hopefully for good. Damn that evil, no-good Sammy for leaving her sexually high and dry the way he had! Of course, sex wasn't the most important component of marital life, but once you'd gotten used to having it on a regular basis, dry spells such as Betsy was currently experiencing weren't appreciated in the least.

True, Rudy's Truck Stop wasn't haute cuisine, but it was a fine start, and besides, she knew Chuck Jennings didn't really have money to burn. He worked for her father, who was a stingy old fuck who never paid anyone well, one reason why he and Sammy hadn't ever gotten along.

"Sir, how the hell am I supposed to take good care of your daughter if you won't pay me a good wage?" had been Sammy's irate question to Raymond Howard on the day he'd quit family employment to go start his own business.

Betsy's mind now went to the voodoo doll her aunt had given her. At the moment it sat on her nightstand, on top of a picture of Sammy (to hopefully give it extra potency). The pin was still stuck in its belly. Betsy hoped Sammy's new ulcer was almost killing him.

Betsy had decided that in the interim before she forgave Sammy and asked Aunt Malicia to bring him back to her side, she was going to have some fun of her own. Date a few men and party a lot. Not for too long though. One could easily grow used to that kind of hedonistic lifestyle and then marriage would lose its sex appeal.

And I don't have any kids yet. And I sure as hell don't wanna have them for some drunken one-night-stand who'll name the boys Jack and Daniels just 'cos those are the names he likes best.

She sipped some of her coffee—which now tasted warm again. *Now, let's see: how long do I plan on staying single for?*

It was a hard question to answer. Fun or someone? Was being flirty and footloose better than marital fidelity?

But I didn't have any marital fidelity, did I? If I did, I'd not be doing this crap now, would I? It's Sammy's damn fault that I'm currently half-divorced. Yes, I'm half-divorced. Half-divorced. Not married, not divorced; hung somewhere in the middle like a mismatched sock on a washing line.

The thought that she'd been so used infuriated her.

All of a sudden she felt terrible again. She felt like shit. She felt horrible, rock-bottom down in the dumps. She felt like a lump of delicious, pungent Swiss cheese being relentlessly persecuted by evil unhygienic mice.

I've spent my entire adult life in this marriage, and now it's suddenly over.

Since Sammy left, Betsy had been riding a rollercoaster of bad emotions. She'd discovered that it was a total lie that heartbreak got easier with time. In reality, it got harder. In Betsy's case, the further she traveled in time from the night she'd returned home to find her husband gone, the worse she felt. She'd imagined that since her visit to her aunt, the worst was over for her. She'd been wrong; if anything, at the moment she felt poorer than ever.

Her misery squeezed her like a fist. It raked her bruised heart with iron claws.

She felt the full weight of her abandonment crushing her.

Yes, I HAVE been abandoned. I loved Sammy with every ounce of my being, and look how he treated me in the end. Screw him!

Anger filled her. She found it hard to understand how he'd left her so easily. One would naturally assume that after fucking a woman's body for eight years (they'd dated for two before getting married) a man would develop an addiction to it. A junkie craving for your wife's pussy. A dependency on the hole you were always inserting yourself into. At the very least, loyalty to the homestead vagina was to be expected, in appreciation of past pleasures granted to the man's penis and in anticipation of those years of equally sweet pleasures to come.

But no, Sammy had transferred his need for vagina elsewhere. As if hers wasn't good enough for him anymore.

Every emotion a betrayed woman had ever felt gnawed at Betsy as she sat on the couch watching the news. Most of the news was reviews of President Trump's governing style. CNN, in particular, really seemed to have it in for him. Betsy was still confused as to whether or not she liked the current Mr. President.

She leapt up from the couch and tramped into her bedroom.

She stared at her bed. She had a sudden nasty vision in her mind of Sammy and Luisa Gomez having sex on this very bed. Denting the mattress with their passion. She imagined Luisa on her back with her legs folded back onto her shoulders, while Sammy was thrusting hard into her and groaning how much he loved her sweet young body . . . and Luisa moaning back and telling him she loved his penis and dripping erotic juice from her vagina and . . . and . . .

In a fit of rage, Betsy stamped her way over to the left nightstand and grabbed up the voodoo doll. The ugly miniature asshole in its blue suit and black hat and shoes.

She yanked the pin from the doll's belly.

Then: *Hey, Sammy, have a migraine instead!* Like Aunt Malicia had shown her, Betsy shoved the pin all the way through the doll's head, from ear to ear.

As the tip of the pin exited the other side of the doll's head, she thought she heard it shriek in pain.

In fright, she dropped the doll on the bed. She gaped at it in alarm. Its ugly face stared back at her; its painted-on black eyes unnaturally spiteful.

Damn, I'm so glad its anger isn't directed at me!

Betsy waited, but it didn't say anything else. She decided she'd just imagined what she'd heard. She almost convinced herself that that was the case.

With trembling fingers, Betsy picked the doll off the bed. It felt nauseatingly warm in her hand, its wooden flesh now seeming almost as malleable to the touch as a human's.

She dropped it back on the nightstand. But she couldn't stand the gaze of its eyes, eyes that seemed to say: "You've hurt me, you bitch, and I'm gonna hurt you too; just you wait and see if I don't. I'll get you for this. I'll—"

Betsy didn't wait to imagine the rest. She quickly pulled out the nightstand drawer and dropped the doll inside it.

She slammed the drawer shut. She was grateful that she could no longer see the doll.

Then she dropped onto the bed. She lay there on her back, legs straight, arms outstretched by her sides, staring at the ceiling.

She began weeping, the tears trickling sideways to the edges of her face. All of a sudden Betsy felt terrified. And it wasn't just the voodoo doll she'd shut away in the drawer scaring her either.

She'd just had that horrible sense of a vindictive presence hovering around her again. Something unwilling to let her be. Something which would love to rip her to shreds if given a chance to do so. Something as brutal, relentless and unstoppable as the man who'd murdered poor Chelsea Byler.

She fell asleep and dreamt that a rotting monster was throttling her.

CHAPTER 15

Apache, Sully & Tina Kravitz

"This is just gettin' worse by the day," Tina Kravitz told the two detectives seated opposite her in her office.

It was just past noon and the Raynham Chief of Police was disgusted by her town's latest inexplicable mess.

"Three stiffs now," Sully agreed, shifting slightly in his chair. "Chief, I don't know how long we're gonna be able to stall the FBI from getting involved."

"Yeah," Apache morosely agreed beside him. "I hear the State Police are already running copious database checks for a serial killer match." Apache had just gotten in from attending Chelsea Byler's funeral. His mind was full of funeral gloom. The rain pouring outside wasn't helping matters either. This midday had something essential missing—sunlight.

Though he knew Jerry Byler, the dead girl's father, Apache had attended her funeral more out of a sense of social obligation than anything else. Apache had also been the one who'd explained to the distraught man why they needed to say Chelsea's death had been accidental.

Jerry Byler was old school Raynham folk; he implicitly understood the summer madness. Once he'd seen the slashed condition of his daughter's body, he'd known that's what it was. Jerry knew the town's curse claimed victims each year; the only real question when each July rolled around was what manifestation the curse would take this time, and who'd be adversely affected by it. He'd quickly agreed to go along with the tale of a machine mangling Chelsea at work.

John and Mary Burke, the parents of the first dead boy, had also agreed to say nothing, either to their extended family or to the press.

"At least till we get this thing wrapped up," Apache had told them. "We don't want the murderer either getting famous or getting away with it."

John Burke had nodded, his eyes grim. He too was of the old stock.

Apache had left it at that. He wasn't good at PR, and besides, he didn't really believe this particular killer was interested either in becoming a celebrity or escaping justice.

Sully, on the other hand, who looked and sounded like he was designed for PR, didn't see the point of covering up anything. As far as he was concerned, the air of secrecy which at the moment shrouded everything was merely aiding and abetting the killer to continue his spate of violent butchery.

Tina Kravitz sighed deeply. "This whole thing is a whole lot worse than you two possibly imagine," she said.

The Raynham Chief of Police was a corpulent but very pretty woman. Blonde and in her early fifties (she and Apache had attended the police academy together in the late 80's), she was an energetic and efficient mountain of female flesh, one totally dedicated to maintaining law and order in her little town.

Now, as she sat staring at Apache and Sully, her gray eyes reflected the weight of worry on her shoulders.

"The forensics reports for the first two bodies just came in," Tina went on. "At my request the tests were sped to the front of the queue."

She paused; maybe for effect; maybe because she really didn't know what to say; maybe because she knew what to say, but didn't wish to say it, as she knew how crazy it would sound.

Sully and Apache waited. Sully expected to hear about serial killers.

Apache expected to hear something different. Another reason he'd attended the funeral was to see if anyone there looked or acted suspicious. It was dumb, but had been known to happen: murderers attending their victims' funerals to gloat on the misery they'd caused. Usually these emotional ghouls stood out among the genuine mourners because no one knew them. But not this time; the gloom at Chelsea Byler's funeral had pervaded the air like a perfume prepared from dead rats.

"I'll cut straight to the chase," Tina Kravitz said finally. "You guys were right about that rotten meat under Chelsea Byler's fingernails being from a dead man." She sighed again. "The problem is, *who* that dead man is."

"Chief, a corpse is just a corpse is just a corpse," Sully pointed out unnecessarily.

Apache frowned at him. Tina shook her head at Apache. "Let the kid talk; he's got the right to be young. We both were once too."

Then, with a palpable air of misery to her words, she went on: "Alright, before I let you two in on the corpse's identity, let me just say this: it's been confirmed, so I don't want any arguing about it afterwards. It's hard enough for me to accept myself." She held up a fleshy hand to forestall their questions. "Yes, yes, yes—it's been *confirmed*. Twice. The first kid who died—Chris Burke? Well, the forensics guys found scraps of skin—abdominal skin they think it was, some hairs in it—on the handlebars of the kid's bicycle. They think he rode into the killer and the impact scraped the skin off."

"Alright, alright, Tina," Apache said impatiently, "just get on with it, please; the suspense isn't doing my heart any good."

She shrugged, which was like watching a mountain shake. "Alright, but like I said, I don't want any arguments afterwards as to identity. The DNA results all came back conclusive on this one."

"Tina, please . . ."

"The dead man is Peter Howard. Or *was* Peter Howard."

On hearing the name, all the blood drained from Apache's face. Memory gears strained in his mind, pulling up a face from the aging detective's youth and holding it before him again. A young, handsome, slightly sad face.

"Peter Howard?" he asked in surprise.

Tina nodded. "Yes, Peter Howard. *Our* Peter Howard. One and the same."

"But, Tina . . . but . . . yeah, I know he's dead, but . . ."

The rotund Chief of Police shrugged at Apache's confusion. "No 'buts,' Apache. It's him. Your reaction to the news exactly mirrors mine when they told me. So then I asked them to redo the DNA tests, to make absolutely certain of it. They did; the results came back positive again. It's Peter Howard beyond any shadow of a doubt."

"But that's impossible!"

"Yeah, it is," Tina glumly agreed. She leaned back in her chair, placed her hands on her desk and said nothing more. These two men were her best detectives, let *them* figure the puzzle out. The endless brainwork required to crack crazy cases like Raynham habitually threw up was a pain in the ass; it was one of the reasons why she'd long ago quit legwork for the administrative side of police life. As the boss you just told people what to do and let them work out how to do it.

Sully now thought it time to join the conversation. He didn't see what the fuss was all about. To him, it was more worrying that they'd so far been unable to contact the lady who'd witnessed last night's murder. What if the serial killer had followed her home and had butchered her too?

Sully said, "Hold on. I don't see what the fuss is all about here. Is this Peter Howard that you're both so worried about dead, or isn't he?"

"Oh, he's dead, Sully. He's stone cold dead."

"Yeah, he died fifteen years ago. Just before Malicia went to the loony bin."

Sully grew even more confused. Scratching his head, he asked, "Chief, who is Malicia?"

Tina said nothing; she just sat looking miserable. Apache answered for her: "Kid, Malicia Howard is Peter Howard's mother. Crazy old lady, been locked away in the TSH asylum for fifteen years now."

"Not anymore, Apache," Tina corrected him. "She got out last week. Moved back into the old house."

"What!?" Apache's face now took on the same perplexed look as Sully's. "Malicia's back in town? Why weren't we informed?"

Tina shrugged. "We were. Mandy filed it under 'Miscellaneous.' She had no idea who Malicia was and didn't think an old woman being let out of the asylum was something worth bothering me about. According to her, it wasn't like the old girl's a sex offender. I think I see her reasoning . . . at least until I got these damn forensics reports this morning."

Apache nodded grimly then lapsed into silence. Sully noticed that his partner had unconsciously begun rubbing the missing portion of his right palm again. He wondered what that was all about.

With neither the Chief nor Apache saying anything, Sully decided it lay with him to move the conversation and investigation forward.

"This seems relatively cut and dried then," he said.

Tina immediately looked 'interested.' "Say what's on your mind, kid."

Apache preempted Sully: "Don't, son. Just don't."

"But . . . !" Sully protested, feeling cheated. "You haven't even heard me out, old man."

Apache groaned. "Son, I'm trying to prevent you from embarrassing yourself in front of the Chief, okay? Alright, just settle down and let me run your thoughts by you, then correct if I'm wrong."

"Alright." Sully settled back down in his seat. It was actually a relief not to have to vocalize what he'd been thinking. Almost immediately he'd started talking he'd had a sinking feeling that his speculations would be shot down.

"Now," Apache began, "what you're thinking, Sully, is that we've got a grave-robbing serial killer here, right? And that, seeing as Malicia Howard just got out of the madhouse, it's certain to be her? Ha ha ha!" It was a cold laugh, unnerving because it held no mirth whatsoever. "You think Peter's ma is the one placing bits of his corpse at each murder scene. And that we can just arrest the old woman for grave-robbing and murder. Am I right, son?"

Sully nodded slowly. Those were his exact thoughts.

"Well," Apache continued, "let's go over the case facts once more. First of all, remember how all the doors and windows were locked from the inside at Ms. Byler's place." He looked at Tina for a moment. "Forensics come up with any explanation for that?"

She shook her head. "They're as baffled as you and I."

Apache went on: "Second, Sully, remember how we both agreed that it'd have to be *a man* who'd killed last night's victim and not a woman. Particularly not an *old* woman. Malicia must be in her mid-sixties by now and that young man from last night was a big fellow." He looked at Tina again. "We never got the kid's name."

She winced. "You're not gonna like knowing it then. It's Snelson. Ronald Snelson."

"*The* Snelson? Please, Tina, tell me it ain't the same Snelson."

"Yeah, the very same one. His grandson."

"Aw, shit, no."

Sully was now delighted that he'd let Apache take over doing the talking. Apache looked like he'd be physically sick right here and now in the office. And Sully still had no idea what the fuss was all about.

Okay, so the kid is dead. Okay, so his mama is crazy. So what? Case solved. It's even great that she's mad. Science has proven that insane folk are capable of astounding feats of strength. All she's doing is killing people, then leaving bits of her son's corpse around to confuse everyone that we've a zombie serial killer on our hands. She may even be wearing her son's skin. Just like . . .

At this point, Sully realized that the Chief was staring pointedly at him. She was shaking her head.

"What, Chief?" Sully asked.

"I can read your mind, young Frank Sullivan," Tina Kravitz said gravely. "And no, no, no, don't even go there."

"I wasn't . . ."

"Just listen, Sully. Malicia Howard *can't* be the one leaving parts of her son about."

"Why not?"

"For the simple reason that Peter Howard was *cremated*. There's no parts of him left to be left anywhere."

"Cremated? Aw, c'mon, Chief. You're shitting me, right?"

Apache rolled his eyes. The kid still didn't get it. "She ain't shitting you, Sully. Peter Howard *was* cremated fifteen years ago. I was at the funeral service; we both were."

"So how come then that we're finding fresh rotting pieces of him now? Or are you saying he's a twin? They do have similar DNA, and fingerprints too."

"No, he wasn't a twin."

"Then *how?*"

Chief Kravitz got to her feet, leaned her obese bulk over the desk, and glared at them both. The desk creaked as she settled her weight on it. "That's what you two need to find out. And fast at that, before anyone else gets murdered."

"It can't be the living dead," Sully said stubbornly.

"Maybe, maybe not," Apache said.

"It ain't zombies. There's no such thing as zombies."

"Maybe not in *CSI*, son, but they do exist in horror flicks."

Tina was still standing. She moved over to the north window of her office and stared disgustedly out at the afternoon.

"Oh, and one more thing," she said, turning back towards the two seated men. "On and under Chelsea's corpse, as well as beneath all that blood splattered everywhere, Forensics also found several puddles of putrescent black liquid, of the sort that might have come from a corpse retrieved from a pond or bog. There were similar smears on the grass around Chris Burke's body too. And . . . I suspect that both the fish skeleton and the mud recovered from beside Ronald Snelson's corpse came from exactly that same body of water."

On hearing this last detail, Apache looked sick again.

Chief of Police Tina Kravitz watched him with troubled gray eyes. "I don't like what you're thinking, man," she said. "I'm tryin' real hard not to think in the same direction too."

Apache said, "Well, there's still that severed finger we found near the Snelson kid's body. That'll either confirm the murderer as a somehow resurrected Peter Howard or someone else playing tricks on us."

"Yeah," Tina gloomily agreed. "I'm praying it's a prankster."

Apache scowled. "It's a shame that the gas station CCTV cameras were angled inward, not out. All they show is a scared woman ducking behind a green Audi. We can't even read the vehicle number."

Tina nodded. "Oh, we'll find her soon enough. She bought gas, didn't she? I've asked the gas station for their pump payment records. They gotta send a request through to the bank, that's why the delay."

"Yeah, I'd forgotten 'bout that." Apache reached behind his head and scratched an itchy part of his scalp under his ponytail. "I really, really hope the kid hasn't woken up from the dead though."

Resurrection? Woken up from the dead? Where the hell does all this nonsense end? Sully said nothing. There was nothing he could say. It was hard enough just listening to this crap. He wondered if maybe the police force shouldn't consider reducing their compulsory retirement age to fifty, or forty-five even. That way, old officers like Apache and Chief Kravitz here could be put out to pasture long before they permitted delusional and fantastical ideas to get in the way of their job of law enforcement and they became a danger to society.

All we've got here is a serial killer! There's no need to be so mysterious about this. It's just some crazy person digging up rotting bodies!

He felt like screaming it at Apache and the Chief.

But, of course, seeing as both his companions had seniority on him, Sully took care not to say anything to that effect, or even to let his feelings of pity, mental condescension and disgust reflect on his face.

So instead, he said, "Malicia's a really odd name, isn't it?"

Apache was about replying him when a loud knock sounded on the office door.

"Come in," Tina Kravitz called out, on which response the department secretary Mandy Emmel poked her head in through the door.

"Chief, we've located Lynn Nilsson, the woman who saw last night's murder," Mandy said.

Tina, Apache, and Sully looked at each other, then Tina asked: "Where is she? Here in the station?"

Mandy shook her head. "No, Chief. I asked her to come over to give a statement, but she refuses to leave her house. She sounds scared as hell on the phone."

"I don't blame her. She give you her address?"

"Yes. She lives at the Chestnut Farm Apartments, off North Main Street."

Tina nodded at Mandy. "Okay. Is she holding the line?"

"Yes. What should I tell her?"

"Tell her that two of our detectives, Apache and Sully . . . no . . . Detectives Johnson and Sullivan, will be over to talk to her in a little while. Tell her not to let anyone else into the house except for those two names. And they'll show her their badges too."

Mandy nodded and withdrew. Tina looked at the two men. "Well, boys, this is the break we've all been waiting for. Hopefully, this woman's statement will help us crack this case wide open. Once we've a positive visual ID on the perp, we can bring him in and ask him how he managed to get hold of Peter Howard's nonexistent remains."

Apache looked hard at Tina. "You know that this is about to get even more messed up, right?"

She stared back helplessly at him. "I know what you mean, man. I can sense it in my bones that you're right. But . . . but . . . but, let's just follow the letter of the law here, okay? At least until we're sure it's time to throw natural law out of the window?"

Apache nodded and got up from his chair. He turned and headed for the office door.

At the door he looked back. "You coming, Sully?" he growled. "I need a damn driver."

"Yeah. Right behind ya, old man."

Following along after him, Sully was relieved that his partner hadn't argued with the Chief. Now hopefully, they'd be able to get some real police work done on this case. He noticed that Apache was once again scratching the portion of his right palm where that massive scoop of flesh was missing.

Before they left the station, Apache slipped a black glove over the hand, like he was Michael Jackson.

CHAPTER 16

Malicia

"When will you pay the final price?" the voices in the darkness asked Malicia. "You still owe us . . . still owe us!" The voices were soothing and at the same time mocking. They teased and raged, pleaded and threatened.

"Soon," she whispered back weakly. "Very soon you'll have the rest of what I promised you."

"Good, good," came the eerie response from the wall of blackness. The blackness filled her living room. Yes, it was early afternoon, but no one entering Malicia's living room would think so. Here it was evil's midnight. Here, the darkness was all-encompassing, permitting not a single ray of hope or compassion entrance to its premises.

The only spaces that the inky blackness didn't fill were those occupied by the red pentagram Malicia had drawn on the green rug, and by her couch. She lay on that couch now, weak but blooming with the vitality of wickedness, as much a paradox herself as the unseen creatures she conversed with. The pentagram on the floor radiated a weak purple glow that was sufficient for her to see by.

Once again, the creatures were bleeding her, her blood leaking in a handwriting-thin stream from her left forearm to a point over the pentagram, where it vanished. This bleeding was nothing compared to the first and was merely being offered as praise to the darknesses.

The darknesses were pleased with her; they didn't wish her dead yet.

Malicia moaned gently. The pain of her draining felt almost orgasmic. She was in as much ecstasy as on her wedding night thirty-five years ago, when Harry's erection had teased her sensitive vaginal tissues into a frenzied bliss that had seemed never to end; when she'd soaked the bed sheets with both her sexual fluids and her ecstatic salivation.

Three dead so far, and more still to come. Wonderful!

She moaned softly as the bleeding stopped again, leaving her just enough liquid life to run her heart. The next bleeding would be in a week's time, long enough for her to have recovered her strength. The darknesses might be evil, but they weren't stupid: they understood that if they drank her to death, they'd have no more blood until someone else summoned them from the Outerness, their realm of intense night. And how many humans even knew that such a realm existed, less knew of the nightmarish spells required to open its salivating portals?

So she'd live for now.

But there was still the issue of the 'Final Payment' to consider. She shuddered at the thought of what they wanted from her.

Then she hardened her heart. *But I'll give it to them. Yes, I will!*

Three corpses so far. Each successive death and mutilation (or mutilation and death) more vicious and sickening than the last. She'd had vivid mental flashes of each corpse. She'd been very satisfied with how they'd looked. The darknesses hadn't lied to her that they'd quench her thirst for revenge.

And all the work of my own hands.

She lifted her hands. She studied them in the pentagram's purple light. True, they didn't look impressive in the least—just the slightly liver-spotted pre-arthritic hands of an old crone; but—she grinned at the thin dribble of blood now falling from her arm onto her dress— but she'd accomplished a lot with them.

No, not my hands. Peter's hands did it. Peter is taking revenge for me. For both of us!

"Hey, I want to see him," she requested of the darkness.

"See who, old woman?"

"Peter, of course!" Then her voice wavered and became uncertain, pleading. "You will let me see him, won't you?"

"Yes, you can see him, old woman. He is ours, as you too are ours now."

And Peter came to her. She didn't recognize him, but then she'd not recognized him back then either, after what they'd done to him. He walked out of the darkness into the room. He looked tall and magnificent, a beast machine of flesh, a monster designed now to kill and nothing else.

He stepped up close to her and she smelt his rotting flesh. It smelt wonderful.

Feeling energized by his very presence, she stood up from the couch and gripped him tightly, pushing aside the folds of his bloody blue suit and letting her face sink into his pulpy decaying chest, taking his wet charnel stink deep into her lungs, preserving it as a memory of him, something to think back on and savor between his killings.

She clung to him as if he was the mother and she the child. The wet goop dripped from the holes in his body. It stained her black. She reveled in it. She opened her mouth and drank the foul-smelling, nasty-tasting liquid. She sucked it from his body and filled her mouth with its foulness and swallowed it. The slimy taste of his corpse fluids gave her a deep thrill, an excitement unlike any she'd ever felt before.

All the while he held her close, his swollen fingers pressing her deeper into his body, as if . . . as if he too missed and loved her.

She pulled away and looked up at his ruined face. "Show me how you do it." She stepped back from him. "Yes, Peter, give me a demonstration of how you kill them. I want to feel a little bit of their pain in my own flesh. It will help me appreciate your hard work better."

He didn't wish to hurt her. She sensed this.

"Do it, Peter!" she snapped at him. "Do what your mother tells you to!"

He obeyed her. She hardly saw the hand move into and out of his suit again—its motion was that fast. But the next moment, she felt an intense burning pain tear through her chest. In a wonder of agony she looked down at herself. Clearly out of consideration for her, he'd struck her between her breasts, not across them. She watched the yellow dress fabric separate and a thin line of blood about eight inches long form along her pallid skin.

She looked back up at him.

"Again!" she screamed. "Again!"

This time there was no hesitation in his response. The huge hand flashed like an axe handle; the glittering blade descended and once again scorched her flesh with its agonizing fire. This time he'd slashed her down the side of her left breast. She'd felt the blade open her up and the pain rush into her body.

She raised her hand so he wouldn't cut her again.

"Go and do much evil, Peter!" she gasped. "Always remember, mother is proud of you. I'm *very* proud of you, darling!"

Like synchronized parts of a single living machine, they both moved at once, falling away from one another. She dropped back onto her couch; he fell back into the wall of black nothingness from which he'd come.

She lay there savoring her wounds. The pain made her feel stronger than ever before. It had been delicious to see the corpses, but now that she could feel their pain too, it was so much sweeter. So much sweeter.

"See, old woman?" the darknesses whispered to Malicia in amusement. "We keep our promises. We always do."

"And so will I," Malicia Howard assured them, relishing the burning pain in her body, feeling nourished by the filthy corpse-drainage of her dead son. "Yes, so will I. Thank you. Thank you so very much for helping me accomplish all of this."

CHAPTER 17

Betsy & Malicia

"Hello. Aunt Malicia, is that you?"

"Yes, Betsy darling. Is everything alright? You sound a little flustered."

"I'm a little worried, auntie."

"Worried, darling? Whatever about?"

"Well, it's this voodoo doll you gave me? Ever since I got it home yesterday, I've been having the weird sense that I'm not the only one in my house. I keep feeling like there's someone else at home with me, even though I've looked through the entire house and I'm all alone. It's scary as hell. I even looked under the beds. What's going on?"

"Oh, there's nothing to worry about, darling. It's just your voodoo doll going about its daily business."

"Yeah, I thought that might be the case . . . but . . . but . . ."

"But what?"

"But . . . why is it going about its business here in my place rather that down in Mexico where Sammy is?"

"Oh, rest assured that at the moment Sammy is in a huge amount of whatever nastiness you've inflicted on him. What *have* you done to him so far? Just the pin in the belly still?"

"I removed that one and used it to give him a migraine instead, then I used another pin—say, I can use any pins I want, right?"

"Yes, you can. Just don't use too many or you'll kill him."

"Hey, I can actually kill him doing this?"

"Not directly. You'd have to destroy the doll to do that. What I mean is, too much inexplicable pain may drive him crazy enough to kill himself."

"That may be a good thing."

"Not in your case, dear."

"What makes you say that?"

"Well, I saw the look in your eyes when I asked you what you wanted to do. You were really hesitating. You clearly wanted him back, but only after torturing him for a good long while."

"I'm that easy to read?"

"I'm just experienced at reading people, that's all. I had loads of practice in the asylum. . . . Now listen carefully. Don't worry about the odd feeling you're getting about not being alone at home. Remember what I told you: the voodoo doll is a strong and malignant force. What you're sensing is its evil power. It's operating from your house, so that's to be expected. But there's utterly no chance of it harming you, Betsy. So don't you worry none about that."

"You're certain about this? I mean, it not harming me?"

"Of course I am. The pins you're sticking in it don't harm it in any way, they just use it as a channel to reach your husband. And remember, I bonded it to you using your blood. So you're safe."

"Oh, I'm so, so relieved to hear that."

"So, fill me in, dear, exactly what did you do? Where else have you got pins stuck in little Sammy?"

"Well, there's one in his liver, one in each of his feet—the soles—and one in his chest, so that he'll have trouble breathing. Yeah, that's all I did. I think so, anyway—I was a little drunk? . . . It isn't with me right now, so I can't tell you for sure. I'm calling from the living room and the doll is in a drawer in the bedroom."

"You're an evil little niece, you know."

"I'm a woman scorned. And remember what they say about us?"

"Alright, alright. But remember, don't overdo it or you'll regret it. And whenever you think he's suffered enough, come and see me and I'll . . . hold on a minute. Before I forget, there's something I want to talk to you about. Your daddy just left here—"

"Dad was over there?"

"Yes. He came to hang up the new bookshop sign. It's really nicely done—white with blue letters; you'll like it. But where I'm going with this is . . . Betsy, your daddy says you're not working at the moment?"

"Yeah, auntie. Sammy's fault again. After he left, I got to drinking. I was working at a travel agency at the time. I turned up at the office drunk once or twice and got fired."

"That's really sad. How'd you like to work for me instead?"

"Work for you, at the bookstore? That'd be great! But surely, there isn't a whole lot to do at the moment?"

"There will be. I'm already getting orders from folks who want stuff. Mostly the sorts of books that I don't keep on the front shelves, if you get my meaning. And I need to order more of them in; some from places like eBay, others from dealers outside the USA."

"I understand."

"And besides, I'm an old woman now. Keeping up with all your modern computers and software and web searches and eBay auctions is a headache to my aging brain. You should be good at that stuff, darling. All of you young girls are."

"I'm okay at it, I guess. I used to handle bookings at the travel agency."

"So it's a deal then? You'll come work at the bookstore?"

"Yeah, sure, auntie. . . . How soon do I start?"

"Next week, once I open up."

"Cool. So I'll be over this evening then to finish arranging the books."

"Oh, I was going to call you about that, Betsy. Let's postpone it."

"But why? It's no trouble at all. I'm free for the rest of the day."

"I'm just feeling a little tired at the moment. I need to take things easy for a day or two. On Thursday or maybe Friday, or even over the weekend, we can finish setting up and still be ready to open our doors early next week."

"Yeah, you do sound tired. You want that I should come drive you to the doctor's?"

"No, no. It's nothing that a little rest won't cure. I'll be fine, don't you worry about me. Of late, I've been a little anemic, that's all. It started just before I left the hospital, but I've pills for it. I think I missed my morning dose today, that's why I'm feeling so under the weather."

"Do you need me to get you anything? Groceries or stuff like that?"

"No, no, darling. But I'll be certain to give you a call if I do. Thanks for offering to."

"Alright, auntie, take care of yourself."

And you too, dear. You sound a little tired yourself."

"Not tired . . . sad. I just got in from attending Chelsea Byler's funeral."

"Jerry Byler's daughter? She died?"

"Machine accident at Walmart. They were offloading something huge from a truck and the crane dropped it on her. Splattered her like a bug that's hit a windshield."

"Oh, that's just horrible. That's just horrible. I-I-I could hear it in your voice that you weren't happy, but I thought it was just this Sammy affair. Darling, are you *sure* you don't want us to just bring him back home now?"

"Nah."

"You sure, Betsy? A woman needs a man in her bed. A man keeps you really warm at nights. And sometimes in the day too."

"Oh, I know what you're hinting at, but I'm fine in that regard— I've got a plastic boyfriend, he just needs batteries. Maybe if this was the winter I'd have relented. But right now it's summer—there's already too much damn warmth as it is. I can definitely survive being lonely for a month or two longer. By mid-autumn though, I'll definitely want the philandering dick back, minus the philandering, of course."

"Sure? Really sure, girl?"

"Yeah, I'm sure, Aunt Malicia. Let Sammy enjoy his ulcers and liver cirrhosis and migraines and chest pain and excruciating arthritis of the feet for a month at least."

"Alright, darling. We'll do it like you want. Now, before I hang up, remember what I said: Don't worry yourself about the doll I gave you. The evil you're sensing isn't in any way directed at you. In one sense, it's almost like a protective shield watching over you. Just try and get used to it."

"Alright, auntie, I'll try to view it like you say. I'll do my best to adjust to the weird vibes."

"Okay, I'll hang up now. I need to go take my pills and have a little siesta. Oh, you young ones don't know what you're enjoying by not being old. . . . Bye, darling. I'll call you if I need you for anything."

"Thanks, Aunt Malicia, you're absolutely the best. Bye."

CHAPTER 18

Malicia

After getting off the phone, Malicia Howard lay in bed thinking.

She thought of the past. She thought of how she'd been robbed of fifteen good years of her life. She thought of the lunatic asylum she'd wasted away her prime in.

Of course Malicia Howard held no fond memories of the Taunton State Hospital, but, like it or not, it was now an inerasable part of her history. No one would ever talk about her again without mentioning those fifteen years of her perceived madness.

She'd lived there, hating the place. She'd altered as it had. It had changed and it had changed her too. Or maybe *she'd* restyled and rechristened it: transformed it from a hospital to a prison by her unnecessary presence there. A mental institution maintained its raison d'être so long as it housed the insane; but once the sane resided there too, surely its value to society and its very existence must be called into question?

It was an impossible query to answer.

She'd witnessed the Taunton State Hospital's lows. She'd been there in 2006 on the night of the great fire. She'd again shared in its pain in 2009, when large parts of it had been demolished.

She'd endured as it had. She'd suffered as it had.

Today the TSH was a sedate 48-bed institution, with a women addict's recovery program and a substance abuse treatment center. Of course, it still had its padded cells for the crazies too.

It's a lot like me, she realized. *A relic of the past slightly out of place in these modern times, but determined not to vanish into historical obscurity.*

This fresh insight almost depressed her. But then she redirected her thoughts from the past to the future and smiled evilly.

CHAPTER 19

Apache, Sully and Lynn

At the Chestnut Farm Apartments, Lynn Nilsson was so scared that it took the detectives five minutes to convince her to take the chain off her front door and let them in. All that while Apache kept up a chain of soothing chatter and he and Sully kept their badges in view.

"Well, I don't see what we're gonna do 'bout this now, Mrs. Nilsson," Apache said finally. "You're the one who invited us over. And I don't think that what you wanna discuss can be said through this crack in the door. Except maybe you want us to go back to the station and return later?"

That got through to the frightened woman. She removed the chain and let the door swing open. She backed inside slowly, like she was preparing to flee if the detectives turned out to be other than they professed themselves to be.

The detectives stepped inside the apartment.

Even now, Lynn Nilsson was still shaking, trembling violently like she was freezing. She was a brunette of average height. Mid-thirties. Long disheveled hair, small nose, and light-brown eyes with a transom of blue eyeshadow. Tiny pinhead earrings.

She was dressed like she'd been about to go out when they arrived. No, like she'd just gotten in: her cream-colored pantsuit was violently crinkled up, as if she'd slept in it.

Sully made a mental note that whatever this woman had seen had been really bad. Just seeing how spooked she was was spooking him in turn.

Once inside Mrs. Nilsson's living room, they discovered she'd covered everywhere with silver crosses made of duct tape. She'd taped crosses all over the walls and all over the three doors that left the living room. She'd also made huge crosses on both sides of her hallway entrance.

Apache was still pondering this when she began sobbing.

"Now, take it easy, Mrs. Nilsson," he said. "Everything's under control now."

She dabbed at her eyes and pointed to chairs. "Please sit down, officers."

With the two men in the room, she seemed to recover herself. They politely declined her offer of coffee, turned on a voice recorder, and asked her what she'd seen.

They listened in silence. What she described in her trembling voice fit all the evidence recovered at the crime scene. A tall man in a blue suit and a hat had attacked Ronald Snelson with a glittering knife. (Forensics said it had been a straight razor.) He'd fought back, and even tried to run away, but the man had overpowered him and viciously sliced him up.

At this point in her tale Lynn Nilsson was herself overpowered by another sobbing fit.

"Why didn't you call us from the filling station?" Sully asked. Not unkindly, to Apache's relief.

"I tried to . . . I really did. . . . But . . . but . . ." She wept a little more. "I was so scared that I . . . I . . . So I decided to drive off, to just get the hell out of there, but then . . ."

"What happened then, ma'am?" Apache asked softly. All the silver crosses on the walls were affecting him too, particularly the way they reflected light as though they were themselves razors.

"Well then, I looked down for a minute and he was suddenly right there in front of my car and I stopped."

"Hold on a sec, ma'am," Sully interjected before she could go on. "When you say, he was 'suddenly there,' do you mean that he sprinted over from beside Ronald's corpse?"

She shook her head. "No, no, he didn't. My phone beeped that the battery was running down. I took a little look at it and next thing he was walking . . . walking in front of my car. All covered in blood. A second ago he was twenty yards away and now he was right there. And then . . . and then he looked at me and then vanished."

"Vanished, Mrs. Nilsson? What do you mean, he vanished?"

She stared adamantly at them both. Both men had the impression that despite her horrors, she'd thought long and hard on how to explain what she'd seen to them in a way that wouldn't invite mockery, and had finally decided to just come out straight with it.

"I mean exactly what I said," she said quietly. "He took two steps and vanished. Like—Poof!" She gestured an explosion with her hands. "Suddenly he wasn't there anymore."

"He turned a corner?"

"No, the ugly bastard disappeared into thin air. He *vanished!*" She began sobbing again. "You've got to believe me, officers. I saw him. I saw it happen."

"We want to believe you, ma'am," Sully said coldly, "but it's real hard."

She glared at him. "I know what I saw and that's what I'm telling you." Her eyes, already well-reddened from weeping, now acquired the additional crimson tint of anger.

Apache quickly recognized the danger signs. Trust Sully to antagonize their only witness. The last thing they needed now was for this lady to clam up and refuse to tell them any more.

"Now, now, Mrs. Nilsson, please don't misunderstand us. What my young partner here"—he darted a quick 'keep your damn mouth shut' glance at Sully—"meant to say was, that he believes you, but well, we're cops, so we'll need more details so we can work out where the killer vanished to." He flashed the upset woman what he considered to be a reassuring smile, then went on: "But, hey, let's forget about that little detail for a moment. You said you saw the killer's face. What did he look like?"

It was a simple question. But Lynn began trembling again, wringing her hands in her lap and looking like she was sitting on the toilet and straining to eject a stubborn turd.

With Apache flashing warning glances at Sully, they both waited till she'd composed herself again.

"He was dead," she said, in a voice so horrified that it sounded like she was back there again and seeing the killer face-to-face. "He was a *zombie.*"

"But that's impossible!" Sully blurted out.

This time, wrapped in the spell of her gothic recollection, Lynn Nilsson paid no attention to the young man. Or rather, she wove his disbelieving thoughts into her own. "Yes, that's what I thought myself at first. But I was wrong. He was dead. He was rotting all over—his blood-splattered suit was open and his chest was bare—and a horrible blackish liquid was running down his chest. And . . ."

"His face," Apache gently prompted. "Ma'am, what did his face look like?"

"I was coming to that," she replied dreamily. "He didn't really have a face. It was just a large bruise that he had for a head. Just a swollen mass of pulp like the inside of a rotten fruit. Or like a patient with really horrible head cancer that's eaten up all his facial features. He had no eyes or ears or nose, just that swollen and bruised purple mass of head. I think he had a mouth though: there was a wide slit on the side of his head"—she traced an imaginary line from her nose to her right ear—"that looked like a mouth. I mean, there were teeth in it, detectives. At least, I think those were teeth in it. And—"

"Mr. Ugly," Sully said without thinking.

"Huh?" Apache said.

"Yes," the woman agreed. "Mr. Ugly. A real Mr. Ugly he was. That same blackish goo was pouring from under the brim of his hat onto his blue suit and down to the ground. And he stank like bad meat—rotting meat. The wind brought the smell of him into my car and it was all I could do not to throw up all over the steering wheel."

She came out of her trance of recollection then and looked at both men. "I'm finding it really hard to put this into words; but trust me on this: he was dead and rotting. I can't explain it, but there was no doubt in my mind whatsoever that I was staring at a walking corpse."

Yeah, right, Sully thought. *Lady, you watch too much TV.*

The name 'Mr. Ugly' had come to him in a flash, and he supposed that now it was going to stick, because it just had that *ring* to it. But he didn't believe any of it—the witness's description had just been incredibly vivid, that was all. Almost like she'd really seen what she'd described. But of course she hadn't. She couldn't have.

He'd noticed Apache's face though. Apache was looking at Lynn Nilsson like everything she was saying was the gospel truth and he was having trouble disbelieving it, rather than having trouble believing it.

Only it's all unfiltered BS, isn't it? If it happened like she says it did, then I'm President Trump!

But he only said: "The way you're describing this, ma'am, it sounds like you were there watching him for quite a while."

Apache nodded at the question. It was a good one.

But Lynn Nilsson's answer was equally as good: "No, I don't think I stared at him for more than fifteen seconds, tops. Then he walked off and vanished like I told you men. But a face like that isn't something one ever forgets. I'll be seeing that face in my nightmares forever, detectives."

"And after the man vanished," Apache said, "then you drove back home here, called the police and went to bed . . . no, you couldn't go to sleep, could you? That was when you taped the place up like this?"

She nodded. "Yes, yes, yes. My phone died while I was talking to the operator and I plugged it in to recharge, and that's when I decided to take some precautions in case the monster came here looking for me."

Apache looked around at Lynn Nilsson's emergency redecoration. Yes, the duct-tape crosses looked like knives themselves: supernatural knives with razor-sharp edges.

"You sure did use a lot of duct tape," he remarked. "How come that you've so much of it at home?"

She shrugged. "My husband's company makes it. We always have several boxes of duct tape in our store."

"And where is your husband at the moment?"

"Joe's down in West Virginia speaking to prospective clients. He won't be back till Sunday morning."

"Mrs. Nilsson," Sully asked, "are you sure that what you saw was actually the killer's face? Couldn't he have been wearing a mask?"

She instantly shook her head. "No," she firmly replied. "It *was* his face. I told you his suit was open. He didn't have a shirt on, his body was all the same as his head; everything continued in the same rotting way from his head to his body."

Sully nodded. He glanced down at the voice recorder. He was glad he wouldn't have to explain this wacky statement to anyone. Clearly, the lady *had* seen something, but what? A guy in a super-realistic Halloween costume three months early? Whatever she'd seen though, it clearly couldn't be what she'd described. That would be crazy.

His thoughts were disrupted by the ring of Apache's phone.

"Hello . . . Tina? . . . Yeah, we're with Mrs. Nilsson right now. . . . What? . . . Yeah, sure, we'll fill you in once we get back. . . . No, not over the phone: you wouldn't believe this."

He hung up and scowled at Sully. "Yeah, that was the Chief. It gets worse, kid. The fingerprint from that severed finger we found at the gas station came back positive for Peter Howard."

Sully could only gape at him.

Apache said, "Yeah, I feel about the same way as you look, kid. But . . . I think everything's beginning to fall into place now. I think I see where all this is coming from and leading to."

Sully, however, didn't see a damn thing. As far as he was concerned, nothing was falling into place. If anything, everything had just gotten more complicated. Like a jigsaw puzzle that was already missing pieces being chopped into yet smaller pieces

"Well, thanks, Mrs. Nilsson," Apache said, getting to his feet. He gestured around the apartment. "I don't think you need to keep redecorating though—the killer's unlikely to be around your way anytime soon."

"Why? Have you caught him already?" Her voice was very hopeful.

He shook his head. "Nah, it's just a hunch I've got." He saw the return of fright to her face, and added, "It's like this: Well, he didn't come after you last night, did he?"

"No, but that's only because of all these crosses I put up everywhere."

Apache doubted that was the reason, but he nodded anyway. "See, that's great then. All you need to do while going about your daily business, is wear a crucifix. So as not to be obvious, you can wear it under your blouse. Carry one or two along with you in your purse and car when you go out too. That should dissuade the zombie."

She nodded slowly, like she saw his point. Sully, meanwhile, was rolling his eyes and trying not to show his exasperation. He leaned forward and picked up their voice recorder, checked that it had actually captured the woman's statement, then switched it off and stowed it away inside his suit jacket.

"Alright, we're leaving," Apache said finally. "Feel free to call us if you remember anything else that you saw or that maybe you'd forgotten. Also, we may invite you over to the station to confirm a few details. Or to ID the perp when we apprehend him. Just try not to worry about it."

She saw them to her front door, but wouldn't step outside. After she shut the door behind them, both men heard her replace the chain.

Hearing the tinkle of the chain, Sully said, "She's definitely still worrying about it, old man."

Apache shrugged. "I don't blame her. Watching a guy get butchered like that and seeing *what* did it would be enough to give anyone the heebie-jeebies. She'll hopefully get over it with time."

They took the elevator back down, walked to their squad car and got in.

Apache told Sully: "Kid, shoot us like a bullet over to Elizabeth Drive. You and I need to pay Malicia Howard a visit."

"Aw, man," Sully growled, "don't you think we're taking all this a little too seriously?"

Apache smiled humorlessly. "Son, we ain't taking it seriously enough. We're about to start doing that. Shut up and drive."

CHAPTER 20

Apache & Sully

Neither detective said much on the short drive over to the Mr. & Mrs. Book Emporium. This lack of speech was helped in part by Sully accidentally tuning the radio to a college radio alternative rock program. This forced them both to listen to a very noisy band called Slain Jane. Apache couldn't believe anyone would actually title a song 'Shit Lipstick.' The lyrics went:

"Come here and tongue my ass, boy,
You're gonna tongue my ass, boy,
You'd better tongue my ass, boy,
Or I won't play with your love toy.
Hey, get over here and tongue my backside pristine clean,
Just like a pretty-boy love machine . . .
That's an order, boy!

I'm giving out shit lipstick!
I'm a givin' you some shit lipstick!"

Both men were in similarly mentally fugued states. Sully let the song play. After what he'd just heard where they'd just left, he lacked the energy to be sufficiently outraged by this song to change the channel. For his part, Apache couldn't be bothered to protest and demand that Sully find something sane for them to listen to. He figured the next song in the DJ's playlist couldn't be this bad.

In this state of mind they pulled up in Malicia Howard's driveway. Sully parked the squad car. They sat in the car, looking around the yard.

Sully scowled. "Gone fifteen years you say, old man? The place still looks in good shape. Lawns all neat and everything, with no weeds on the driveway; fresh coat of paint, clean windows, and not a single bit of trash lying about anywhere."

"It was rented out. But I know what you mean. Last time I drove by here—maybe four months ago—it was all overgrown with weeds. Ray must have fixed it up when he heard she was getting out."

"Who's Ray?"

"Raymond Howard. Her dead husband's brother. He runs a house renovation business."

They got out of the car and approached the front door.

Now, with each step nearer to it they took, the handsome old house developed a more menacing aspect. It was still a neat and attractive building (painted a bright brown and white), but something, particularly around the upper floor, didn't seem right about it. The air about that upper floor appeared to quiver as though it hung over a fire. Seen through it, the high roof seemed to be wavering, its black and gray shingles switching places as though they were dancing.

Sully found that he was shivering. He wondered where the chill had come from unannounced on this warm afternoon.

On lowering his eyes from regarding the eerie rooftop, Apache saw a white face peering from an upstairs window on their right. Then the white face was quickly blotted out by white drapes.

Sully stepped under the blue-on-white bookshop sign and up to the front door. He was relieved to be under the eaves, out of sight of that strange air overhead. He knew there had to be a logical explanation for the weird visuals, but knowing that didn't stop him being instinctively spooked by the view.

Sully rang the doorbell.

No reply came from within. He rang again. When again no reply came, he gave Apache a perplexed look.

"Old man, I could've sworn I heard someone moving around in there right before I pressed the buzzer."

Apache grimaced at him. "Oh, she's in there alright. Keep ringing. She always was as stubborn as a mule." Apache didn't look spooked. He just looked grim. As far as he was concerned, this house's weird ambience was merely confirmation that Malicia was up to her old tricks again.

Sully kept ringing. When that brought no response either, Apache took to banging on the door. "Hey, Malicia, open up! It's Apache Johnson! I wanna talk to ya!"

This too brought no response. Sully kept his finger down on the buzzer. He could hear its strident bee sound echoing through the space behind the wall. He began worrying that they weren't in the process of driving the recently cured woman in the house crazy again.

Apache thumped louder on the door. "C'mon, Malicia, open the damn door! It's Apache! I just wanna say hi!"

This got a response: "I don't wanna see you, Apache! Leave my damn home or I'm gonna call the police!"

"Malicia, in case you've forgotten—I am the damn police! Goddammit, old woman, don't tell me you haven't changed a bit in all this time."

"Just go away, Apache. If I ever wanna see you I'll send for you. And for heaven's sake, tell that young idiot with you to stop shredding my eardrums!"

This last was shrieked out with such vehemence that Sully instantly took his finger off the buzzer. He looked at Apache. "So what do we do now?"

Apache shrugged. "She don't wanna see us? I guess we'd better leave then; best thing for our good health. Old woman like her? She could get mad enough to shoot us both through the door. She'd claim she didn't know it was the police."

"But that's crazy. No sane person would shoot at cops."

Apache lowered his voice to a whisper. "She just got out of the loony bin, remember? The jury's likely still out on how sane she is." He gestured to their car with his head. "Kid, let's just go."

He turned away from the door, then turned back and yelled, "Alright, Malicia, have it your way—we're leaving! Welcome back home to Raynham!"

"Just go away!" she screeched back. "I don't need your damn welcomes! I hope you and this entire God-damned town all rot in Hell. And you all will if I have anything to say about it!"

And then, to Sully's immense surprise, there came the clear sound of loud sobbing from behind the door.

Apache caught his eye. "Let's just leave," he mouthed at him.

They walked back to their car. Before getting in, both men stood and regarded the house again.

"The building looks weird in some way, don't it?" Apache asked Sully, to gauge his response. "I mean the upper floor. It ain't anything you can clearly see, but it's almost like it's flickering in patches."

"I see it too, old man," Sully replied. He'd begun shivering again, and just wanted to be away from here. Yes there *was* something decidedly strange about Malicia Howard's house, but he didn't doubt that it had a logical explanation. He said, "It's most likely an optical illusion caused by the sun overheating the air over the roof. That's why the shingles appear to be moving sideways. You know, just like how the air over a campfire always looks somewhat distorted, as if you're peering through water. I think all these really tall trees around the building are preventing proper air circulation."

Apache began shaking his head at his young companion's analysis, then caught himself and nodded instead. "Yeah, I guess you're right, son. Too bad we can't get a warrant and search the damn building, see if she's building fires on the upper floor or in the attic."

"You're joking, right?"

"About which of 'em? The crazy house or the crazy woman who's returned home to it?" He tapped the roof of their police cruiser. "C'mon, let's head back to the station and discuss this with Tina. Maybe she *can* get us a warrant on a technicality—something like a fire-hazard—to enable us inspect the premises for evidence of any illegal stupidity." Then he checked his wristwatch. "Nah, not so fast. It's way past our lunch time and I'm starving. So, first we swing down by the Dunkin' Donuts on the New State Highway for takeouts. *Then* we can go fill the Chief in what we've discovered so far."

Apache stared once more at the brown and white two-story house. "I wonder what she's really up to up there? She surely ain't baking bread in that oven, that's for sure."

Sully didn't say a word. They got in their car and drove off.

Yes, even though he couldn't admit it openly, Detective Frank Sullivan knew Apache was right about something being off here.

Sully wanted to get away from Malicia Howard's home before he started sharing Apache's point of view: that that strange shimmering clearly visible around the upper floor of the Mr. & Mrs. Book Emporium had supernatural causes.

This is supposed to be a murder investigation, he groaned inwardly. *Well, it was one, but now it seems almost completely derailed. First, that crazy Mrs.*

Nilsson telling us that Ronald Snelson was killed by a dead man, and now this! And Apache is eating it all up like a late breakfast!

Or maybe, he thought, swinging their Ford onto Pleasant Street, which led down to the New State Highway aka Route 44, *maybe this still is a murder investigation. But if so, it's the oddest one I've ever been involved in.*

Sully was relieved when he stopped shivering and began feeling warm again. That took a while to happen, but by the time he'd pulled up outside the Dunkin' Donuts to buy their lunches, he felt as right as rain again.

CHAPTER 21

Betsy

Wednesday.

At around 9 p.m. on Wednesday night, Chuck Jennings's pickup truck pulled up in front of Betsy's house.

Chuck and Betsy had been out at Rudy's Truck Stop, which was situated by the overpass where Broadway crossed the Blue Star Memorial Highway.

They'd had a greasy dinner in Rudy's and then danced a little, but they'd not drunk too much. Both of them were looking to get laid and, as Betsy had sweetly pointed out when her date wanted to order them both a third round of beers, Chuck had to remain sober enough to drive them back to her place.

Chuck reached across Betsy and opened the passenger-side door. "Ladies first."

They both got out and met in front of the truck. Then, arm-in-arm, they walked towards the front door.

While Betsy got her house keys out, Chuck looked around the yard. He stood there in his denim clothes feeling pleased with himself. This was logical enough: Betsy Driscoll was a very pretty woman. Chuck had often stared at her wistfully and wondered what his life would be like if she were his lady instead of Sammy's. And seeing as he worked for her father, he'd run into her on a regular basis.

Now, he stared appreciatively at the woman as she went through her purse, audibly humming to herself. She had a good figure, that was for sure. Well-padded without actually being fat. Shapely, full breasts that bulged out her white halter top; a plump but cute behind that her blue shorts were showing off to great advantage; nice legs; and well-shaped ankles and feet in her blue high heels.

She turned and saw him appraising her. She giggled. "Like what you see? You'd better like it, boy, 'cos you're gettin' it whether you like it or not."

They both laughed. He moved forward and grabbed her plush behind. "Oh, I love it, babe."

She playfully shoved him off. "Hold your horse, stud, I gotta get the door open first."

He held on to her, hands cradling her soft hips, while she slid the key into the door and clicked it open. She put on the lights and they both stepped inside.

Almost at once, Betsy felt the voodoo doll's presence. An angry, malevolent ambience lurked in the shadows where the lights weren't yet turned on. She could practically feel that she and Chuck weren't the only ones there. Something unholy had just welcomed them home.

"Do you sense it?" she asked Chuck.

He looked curiously at her. "Sense what, babe?"

She realized she wouldn't be able to explain what she sensed without appearing kooky and possibly dousing his ardor and ruining their fun, so she shrugged it off: "Forget it, baby. It's nothing. I'm a little stressed, that's all." She leaned forward and kissed him. "But, hey, that's what you're here for—to help me unwind—ain't it, sweetheart?"

"You can bet your sweet ass it is, honey."

They made an untidy beeline from the hallway to the master bedroom. They were both in a hurry. Along the way, Betsy kicked off both of her shoes, then slipped off her halter too. She dropped the top on the hallway rug. Chuck unhooked her bra and discarded it.

He cupped her breasts from behind. She gasped at the feeling of his strong male hands on her soft female skin. He squeezed gently and her nipples instantly stiffened.

She moaned and slipped from his grasp. She crooked her finger at him and stepped into the bedroom, pausing in the doorway to shake her behind seductively at him before reaching along the wall to flick the lights on.

Once she'd illuminated the bedroom, she looked lustfully at him. He was right behind her. The front of his denim pants were bulging, his erection obvious even while he was still unbuckling his belt. He was panting like a thirsty dog and gulping, his Adam's apple rising and falling like a piston.

Then the voodoo doll's bad vibes hit her again. This time the feeling was even stronger. Considering the problem with a corner of her lust-inflamed mind, Betsy thought she knew why this was: the doll was in the top drawer of the right nightstand, and the drawer was open. Her fault. She'd been looking for a misplaced set of earrings and in her excitement when her date had pulled up outside her house and honked his arrival, she hadn't remembered to shut the drawer again.

It occurred to her that she'd be lying right next to the doll while they made love. She shook her head: *Friend of mine or not, I'm not having sex with that creepy thing nearby. I don't care what Aunt Malicia says about it not harming me. How do I know what it's actually gonna do once I'm not paying attention to it?*

One thing Betsy definitely didn't want was for the voodoo doll to mistake Chuck Jennings for her runaway husband, and for it to then inflict all of her curses on him just as they began getting busy. She could almost *see* the doll's foul essence in her bedroom. It was like invisible plumes of steam wafting out of the open drawer.

She decided against having sex in here. She grinned at Chuck, who'd now gotten his pants and underpants and shoes off and was stroking his hard penis.

"Hey, I got a great idea," she said. "Let's do it out on the living room couch."

But it was too late. Even while speaking, Betsy had known it was too late. Chuck had that horny 'Too late, woman!' look in his eyes. And the way his manhood was throbbing threateningly at her . . .

His hands on her shoulders, Chuck gently but firmly backed her towards the bed. She went with him willingly. She wanted him too. It was just the doll . . . the doll . . .

Alright, I'll just shut the drawer.

But even that wasn't happening. Before Betsy could do a single thing—reach towards the nightstand or anything—Chuck had upended her onto the soft mattress. Next, he'd pulled off her panties (all she was still wearing at that point), spread her legs, and was going down on her.

"You've got a lovely vertical smile," he said, and kissed it, sticking his tongue deep into her interior as if her vagina had a tongue of its own that he wanted to French kiss.

Ah, whatever, Betsy decided. *The doll can watch if it likes.*

The feeling of evil was still thick in the room, but Betsy discovered she could ignore it. All she had to do was close her eyes and concentrate on the man busy licking her clitoris and vagina, and the doll's malice faded like storm clouds melting before the sun.

So she did just that. She relaxed into the delicious feeling of Chuck's mouth on her sex and her anus, and of his strong fingers gently massaging her thighs. She enjoyed the exquisite sensations of cunnilingus after three months of enforced abstinence and cucumbers and a banana.

Yes, masturbation was fun and was highly recommended for lonely people by sex therapists and medical professionals worldwide, but it wasn't anything like having actual sexual contact with another human being.

The pleasure went on for a long time. Her hands went from caressing Chuck's shoulders to running her fingers through his dark hair, to squeezing her own breasts. She had major nipple hard-ons—both nubs of flesh felt electrified. She came twice from the cunnilingus, then felt Chuck remove his mouth from her dripping sexual opening.

She opened her eyes now. Chuck was rolling on a condom. He had a desperate fire in his eyes.

"Quick! Come inside me!" she gasped in equal desperation. By now, the evil voodoo doll was all but forgotten.

He obliged, sliding in deep and filling her to the brim. She gasped and resumed having orgasms. She shut her eyes again and travelled in darkness on the waves of sensation his penis gave her flesh. Then she felt him stiffen on her and she opened her eyes and stared into his, sharing the sweet despair of his climax, wrapping her arms and legs tightly around him as he ejaculated.

He shuddered on her as if he was dying, then went on limp on her. She drank in the sensation of his orgasm. It felt like he'd transferred a part of himself to her.

He rolled off her. He lay on her left panting. She stroked his hair. It had been very good. She remembered she was half-divorced. A part of her felt guilty. But guilty about what? That she was cheating on Sammy, who was cheating on her? She realized she was merely being silly thinking like that. Screw Sammy. Sure she still loved him, but this man beside her in bed was all she needed right now.

She felt nice and satisfied and at peace with herself and her vagina for the first time in ages. Prior to this it had occasionally felt like her vagina was angry with her for cheating it of erotic sensations, for depriving it of a man's swollen organ.

She turned and kissed Chuck. As she raised herself on her elbow, she saw the opened drawer. Her concern must have shown on her face, because Chuck asked, "What's the matter, babe?"

"It's nothing, sweetie, just me being silly." She felt so close to him, so open and vulnerable, that she added, "Just some silly doll that I need to get rid off. The damn thing is creeping me out."

"A doll?" Intrigued, he sat up with his back on the headboard. "Lemme see it."

Betsy now felt that maybe she shouldn't have mentioned the doll. Better to keep her mouth shut and have Chuck think her a little weird, than to show him the doll and remove all his doubts on that score.

Still, against her better judgment, she showed him the voodoo doll.

Chuck took it from her and examined it. "Well, I can definitely see why you're creeped out. Damn, it sure is ugly. Yeah, Mr. Ugly." He ran a finger around the brim of its tiny black hat, then up and down its blue suit. Then he flicked several of the pins stuck in it. "Who stuck the needles in?"

She sighed, certain now that she was about making a fool of herself. And the sex had been so great too. She wanted him again and again; he'd make a very nice stopgap indeed till she forgave Sammy.

"I bought it like that," she lied. "I found it at a garage sale while visiting a friend in Dover."

Now he looked at her queerly for the first time. "Why'd you buy it if it spooks you?"

She shrugged. He'd bought the lie; her guilty secret was safe. "It was noon then; it looked less menacing. Once I got it home, though . . ."

"Yeah, I can dig that. I wonder what'll happen if I pull the needles out?"

"Don't!" She'd yelped the caution before realizing it was a foolish thing to do. What harm could removing the pins she'd stuck in the doll do, except to temporarily free Sammy from some excruciating hurt? And the relief *would* be temporary, because once Chuck left in the morning she'd be certain to stick all the pins back in again.

He gave her that odd look again, but then it transformed into a look of understanding. "Yeah, okay, babe, I get that it spooks you. I won't pull the needles out. I'm just fooling with it." He tapped the doll's head. "Ugly sucker though, you gotta admit. And it feels strangely warm, like maybe you've got a heater on in the drawer there."

"Put it down, Chuck. I don't like looking at it, that's all."

He shrugged and dropped the doll back on the nightstand. On top of it, beside the reading lamp, not inside the drawer. Betsy was at least relieved that the thing's face was turned away from her now. Earlier she'd imagined it was watching her.

"So what you wanna do now?" Chuck enquired. "Start on the wine we bought at Rudy's or . . ."

"Later," she said. "First, I need to pee." She kissed him and scooted off the bed, then added, "Then we'll bump and grind some more. You've no idea how long it's been since I last got laid."

"I can imagine," he said seriously. "You heard anything from Sammy yet?"

She shook her head at him from the bathroom door. "Nope, and I don't wanna hear from the bastard. So long as I've got you here, what do I need Sammy for?"

She left him grinning at her and hurried inside to the toilet.

She took her time in there. It wasn't as if she had a lot of water to set free, but, well, she was pleased with herself. She'd stepped out of her misery zone. She taken control of her life, gotten herself a new man . . . well, there *was* the small matter of what her father might say about her dating one of his staff to consider, but she'd always been able to wrap him around her finger in the past.

Betsy had been smiling to herself while thinking of the progress she'd made, but then, just like that, her thoughts darkened. She quickly identified the source of her unease: it was the voodoo doll again. Something was wrong, but what could that be?

She unrolled some tissue and wiped. She discarded that and unrolled some more. It was then that Chuck called out from the bedroom:

"Hey, Betsy, I really love this doll of yours!"

She sighed. *Oh, he's picked it up again, that's why I'm feeling so edgy.*

She was about relaxing, when Chuck said, "You know, its head's a separate chunk of wood. I wonder if it spins all the way around. You know, like toy heads do—"

His voice cut off there and was replaced by a sudden loud cracking sound, as if someone had broken a large flower vase on the rug. Then there was an ominous silence from the bedroom. Betsy's dread soared. Her delightful feeling of afterglow drained from her. In its place, huge hailstones of worry pounded on her mind.

"Chuck?" she enquired tentatively. "You okay out there, sweetie?"
No reply.
"Hey, man, say something! Don't scare me like this!"
Still no reply came from the bedroom.
Slowly, very slowly, Betsy finished wiping herself.
No, it's impossible, she told herself. *The doll can't have . . . it can't have . . .*

She didn't dare form the thought that her so-far perfect night had abruptly taken a turn for the bad. A feeling of terror hovered around her, but she resisted it with all her might.

Finally, she found the courage to exit the bathroom.

At first everything looked normal in her bedroom.

Chuck was sitting just like she'd left him, propped up on pillows against the headboard, long legs stretched out in front of him. He seemed to be grinning at the hallway entrance. The voodoo doll lay discarded on his right beside his open hand.

"Chuck, are you alright?"

But he didn't reply. He just kept staring at the door opposite, with its flooring of discarded clothes.

It was the way both of Chuck's hands lay motionless by his side that alerted Betsy to the fact that yes, something was fucked up in her bedroom. She'd been about relaxing a little, but . . .

She stepped closer, then noticed the thin trail of blood dribbling from the left side of Chuck's mouth. Then she saw that something was wrong with his neck too. His neck now looked much thinner than before she'd left him to go use the bathroom.

It took a while for Betsy to work out what the matter with her date was. And once she did, her shock was so great that she couldn't even scream. For that first moment of realization, she couldn't even breathe. The air froze in her windpipe and lungs, seemingly scared to exit into a world where logic no longer prevailed.

Her eyes widening in fear, Betsy looked down at the voodoo doll, then back up at Chuck's face.

Yes, he *was* dead, she got that. But it was *how* he'd apparently died that was the freaky factor here. She was seeing it, but . . .

How is that even possible? she asked herself in mounting disbelief.

To her credit, Betsy didn't panic.

With a deadly calm that bordered on insanity, she walked around the bed to where she'd discarded her purse by the door. There, she got out her cellphone and dialed her aunt.

While waiting for the call to connect, she stared in horror at the blue-suited figurine on her bed.

CHAPTER 22

Malicia

Malicia Howard was catching up on her bookkeeping when her living room phone rang. She checked the time on the wall clock: 9:41 p.m. She got up from the couch, picked up the phone, and accepted the call.

"Oh, Betsy darling, it's you. I hope everything's fine with you calling me so late at—"

"Aunt Malicia, the doll just killed Chuck!"

Malicia felt like she'd been punched in the gut. She already felt weak, but the shock of what she was hearing was close to giving her a heart attack. She retreated with phone in hand and sat down. She took off her reading glasses and put them down on the opened ledger.

"Aunt Malicia, are you there? Answer me!"

"Yes," Malicia replied tiredly. "I'm still here. Who's Chuck, dear?"

"Chuck Jennings. He's one of daddy's favorite workers. I was dating him to fill in the space left by Sammy's departure."

"Fill in the space? Oh, what a lovely way to describe lovemaking. So the two of you had sex, and then what . . . ?"

"Then I went to pee and while inside there . . . when I came outside, the doll had . . . well, Chuck had been playing with it and . . . Shit! I still can't believe it!"

"Believe what, Betsy?"

"Well, Chuck was just saying to me that he wanted to see if the doll's head would twist all the way around, and then I heard this horrible cracking sound and now . . ."

Malicia lost her patience. "And now what's happened? Stop this irritating suspense act you're putting on and tell me plain and simple what the hell has happened to your new boyfriend!"

"You could be nicer about it. This is your fault too."

"Only by association; I'm just guilty of being related to you. Betsy, what is it that the doll did to your boyfriend? What are you finding so difficult to describe?"

"Oh, it looks as though . . . okay, Chuck's head has been twisted all the way around so that now there's a knot in it. I mean, it's twisted in a circle so he's looking forward again. Actually, I think his head's been twisted around *twice*—one knot on top of the other." There was a short pause, but before Malicia could say anything, Betsy interjected into the silence: "H-h-how is that p-possible?"

Malicia sighed. "It's called *voodoo*, dear. The real question here isn't how it's possible that the doll killed your friend, it's—how could you be so dumb as to let him see it in the first place?"

"You're blaming *me* for this?"

"Who else?" Malicia's lips twisted up in anger, an anger which she tried not to convey in her voice as she replied her niece. This was a total disaster. Trust young people to make a mess of even little things. It was now very important that she calm Betsy down, so that the silly girl would follow the instructions she was about to give her.

"Now, don't worry, dear. This can be fixed."

"How? You're gonna bring Chuck back to life for me?"

"I really don't think you'd like a zombie lover. They tend to stink awfully."

"What then, Aunt Malicia? What the hell do I do now?"

"First of all, you need to remain calm. Don't panic, dear."

"I'm not panicking. But I am extremely upset."

"I can well imagine that you are. Was he good in bed?"

"Yes. Very."

"Don't worry about it. Sure it's a loss, but there'll be others. If you want, I can make you a queen bee, with hundreds of hunky men knocking on your doors and windows at all hours of the day and night." She giggled. "Of course, you'll get sore . . . *very* sore after a while, but too much sex doesn't ever seem to harm the ladies in the adult entertainment industry."

"Aunt Malicia, be friggin' serious, for goodness sake. I'm close to freaking out here."

"Just trying to help you see the lighter side of things, Betsy."

"There is no lighter side. I've got a corpse in my bed. I have to call the police and report Chuck's death, and I've absolutely no idea what to tell them."

Malicia winced, then she shrugged. Sure, she hadn't intended for this to happen, but the silly girl really should be more careful about letting men play with her toys. Now that fool had gone and killed himself.

"Just tell them what happened, darling: how you went to the bathroom to have a little girly piss-piss and by the time you got out, your lover was dead. And that you've no idea who or what killed him."

The thought and mention of the police angered her. Just when she was getting properly started, this threatened to throw a spanner into the works. First, that meddler Apache Johnson had come by yesterday afternoon, and now *this*. Argh!

For an enraged moment, Malicia had violent thoughts of inviting Betsy over here tonight and sacrificing her to the darknesses; the demons were certain to appreciate the girl's fresh young blood. But on further reflection, she questioned what being so petty would achieve.

Besides, even if the girl's stupidity disgusted her, Betsy was still Raymond Howard's daughter, and Ray was a good friend. No matter what she'd gone through since her Harry had died, Ray Howard had always stood by her. Whenever she'd needed a shoulder to cry on or a helping hand, he'd been there for her. For the past seventeen years, he'd been a rock of solace for her to rest on during her excessively stormy life.

No, Malicia would never do anything to hurt Ray.

"Hide the doll," she calmly advised Betsy over the line. "Do it before you call the police. Whatever else you do, hide the doll. And don't mention it either. Like I just said, just say you went to pee and came back and found him dead like that. Alright?"

"Yes, auntie. But . . ."

"But what, girl?"

"It ain't gonna make any sense to them."

"That's exactly what you want: for his death not to make sense. I've been hearing two or three rumors of late of some crazy happenings. People being cut up in atrocious but inexplicable ways."

"I-I heard s-s-some of those too."

"So just say the right thing and look as confused as you can, and the police can't blame you for anything. Mr. Jennings's death will fit right into the current mystery. Just something else which happened this summer that the cops can't explain."

"Alright, Aunt Malicia. Thanks. I'll do exactly like you said."

"Well, hurry up now and call 911. How long ago did he die?"

"Five or ten minutes. Why?"

"Just so that the cops and paramedics don't start wondering why you delayed in calling them. But it's alright—you haven't waited too long. If anyone asks, say you were in shock. Don't mention calling me tonight."

"Alright, auntie. I'd better hang up now. I'll call you tomorrow morning to let you know how it went."

"Okay, you go ahead now and do that."

But Betsy *didn't* hang up. Instead she said, "Aunt Malicia, I'm worried about something else too."

"What is it? And please, don't take too long this time to tell me. Remember you need to call the police."

"Okay. What's bothering me is this: with the doll killing Chuck like this, has it also killed Sammy where he is?"

Malicia sighed. *Even in the midst of her sorrow, the silly young filly is still worried about her no-good husband.* She rolled her eyes at her ceiling. *I must do my utmost best to reassure her.*

"No, it hasn't killed him," she replied truthfully. "Sammy's still okay where he is, enjoying all the misery you've so far inflicted on him."

"Are you sure?" This was a very nervous question. Malicia, peering out of a window at the night sky, wondered why Betsy didn't just forgive the man and let her work the spell to bring him home and tether him by her side. Of course, like most women below the age of menopause and thus still in the hot and fecund reproductive phase of their lives, Betsy's primary problems concerned men: first the one who'd run away and now the one she'd killed. Had Sammy not left her, she'd be worried about him leaving her, or his not loving her enough, or him dying on her and leaving her a miserable widow. In the realm of romance, women seemingly couldn't win.

But madness is an integral part of romance, Malicia understood. *Betsy wants to harm and punish her husband, but only because she considers him her personal property, which gives her the right to do to him whatever she likes. Hmmm.*

"Yes, I'm sure," she replied firmly. "At the moment, Sammy may be many things, but I assure you that 'dead' isn't one of them. He's only as badly injured as you lovingly left him the last time you played with your occult doll."

"Oh, am I so relieved to hear that. You're really sure of this, though? You're not saying it just to make me feel better?"

Malicia felt like screaming at her niece. *Doesn't Betsy have any brains at all? Or has one bout of sex liquefied them and drained them out of her sex hole?*

She managed to stay calm. "Yes, darling, your husband is perfectly fine. You have my witchy word on that. Now please get off the phone to me and call 911. If you delay much longer you'll need to lie to the paramedics that you fainted from shock."

"Okay, sorry for taking so long on the phone. Bye."

Betsy hung up. Malicia heaved a sigh of relief. She leaned back on the new couch and pondered deeply on the conversation she'd just had. Just the earlier part about the dead man.

Yes, grown men shouldn't play with dolls; the results can be fatal.

All things considered, it wasn't entirely bad; not the disaster she'd originally imagined. And besides, Betsy's boyfriend's death had its positive points: one way or another, the body count was rising. This young man's death would merely increase the townspeople's panic.

She got up. Ouch! Her movements had reopened the wonderful wound Peter had made in her left breast. Pain ran down her left side. She touched the wound; her fingers came away red.

This stuff will kill me, if I don't kill myself first, she thought angrily, the pain triggering a deep and violent surge of malevolence within her.

More than once since seeing Peter, she'd considered using a spell to heal herself, but the darknesses liked her weak and bleeding like this. Sometimes they strayed from their hiding places in the shadows and licked her. When they did this, her body flickered with pain; but with the pain came the pleasure of feeling their delight. Then, of course, came the fear of the 'Final Sacrifice' that they demanded from her.

Will I be able to give them what they want? Am I strong enough to take that final, irreversible step? I think I am; but maybe I'm not.

She looked around her living room. It was well-lighted now, its pockets of shadows vanquished by electricity since all the books had been moved downstairs. As for the darknesses themselves—her supernatural tenants—they hid in whatever dusky nooks they could still find in her living room—under the couch she currently sat on (she'd just felt one lick her leg), behind the television (where the shadows bent away from the light and were oddly curved rather than the expected straight lines), and even inside her shoes (when she'd slipped her feet into her slippers to go answer the phone just now, she'd felt something black and liquid and disappointed at its eviction squirt out as her toes went in).

The darknesses were everywhere around her, she knew. They were as much a part of the house now as its walls were.

Sometimes they even got outside, seeping through the walls and condensing on the windowpanes like dew on flowers. Then they danced in the air around the upper floor and roof, causing the air there to waver oddly and making onlookers ponder what was going on in the newly renovated building. She'd pleaded with them to stop going outside. It made the house look creepy.

Maybe they're even inside me now. They may have invaded my body as I lost blood. God knows I've bled enough for seven women and yet I'm still alive.

She frowned. *And . . . the Final Sacrifice still looms over me like the open mouth of a dragon.*

Her future looked grim indeed.

But then Malicia smiled. It was a feeble smile, one in which her lips were molded by the pain she felt in her weakened body. Nonetheless it was a satisfied smile. It had suddenly occurred to Malicia Howard that things had sped up, that events were now racing to a conclusion that might even already be out of her hands. Sure, she'd wanted things to move quickly, but now, with this voodoo doll mishap of Betsy's, things might just have accelerated a whole lot faster that she'd intended.

I need to take some drastic steps, she told herself. *This horror I've unleashed is more than worth the price demanded.*

As if they'd read her mind, when she settled back down on the couch after determining this, the darknesses under the furniture emerged like tongues and loving lapped at her legs.

CHAPTER 23

Betsy

After calling 911, Betsy nervously approached the bed. She found it weird, the way Chuck seemed to be staring right through her. She wondered if she should close his eyes, but then she decided the detectives wouldn't like it, it might be considered messing up the crime scene. And besides, what if he fell over when she touched him? If that happened, her story of non-involvement in his death might seem shaky.

So she left him just like he was, sitting up like that with that horrible knot twisted in his neck—it looked like a hangman's noose that had gotten under his skin and grown to become a part of his body, just like happened with trees sometimes, where the trunk and bark grew over and covered up a foreign object that had penetrated them.

She stood beside the bed trembling. Yes, Chuck was remaining exactly where he was, but, like Aunt Malicia had pointed out, the voodoo doll had to go.

The doll still lay by Chuck's right hand. Its ugly little head was positioned normally (face forward) on its body. This made Betsy wonder if Chuck had actually even begun swiveling the evil thing's head around before it had killed him, or if he'd completed a few turns first.

But where do I hide it? Where won't the police find it?

She ran her mind over the possibilities: the closets, under the bed, beneath that loose corner of the living room rug, behind one of the televisions, in one of her handbags, inside her long white boots, in the trashcan in the kitchen, in a suitcase . . . For something so small the list of potential hiding places seemed endless, but so too did the chances of prying law enforcement eyes locating the doll while carrying out the most cursory of checks.

In the end she decided on one of her hatboxes. She had six or seven of these; they were in the closet in the guest bedroom down the hallway.

That settled, Betsy leaned over the dead man and picked up the voodoo doll.

She instantly dropped it again. It felt . . . queasy. It was as warm as earlier, but now once again had that throbbing sensation to it that it had had back at her aunt's house. It felt like a living thing.

She stood there, terrified of it. She was aware, however, that she had no choice: *I have to move this disgusting thing before the paramedics arrive, or else . . .*

She was more worried about her aunt's reaction if she didn't hide the doll than what the police might think on finding such a curious object beside a dead body.

Particularly with all these pins stuck in it—they're gonna look at me real odd.

Still, after all the 'she's crazy' looks, the police would at worst just file the doll as evidence.

Aunt Malicia on the other hand . . . While on the phone to her aunt, Betsy had clearly heard in her voice just how upset she'd been by this blunder of hers. She'd sensed the old woman biting back her anger, not wanting to yell at her so as not to further aggravate this already bad situation.

But if I screw this up too, there's no telling what she'll do to me! She might get another doll, link it to me instead and start sticking pins into it!

That horrible thought galvanized Betsy into action. Firming her resolve, doing her best not to look sideways at Chuck's staring face, she bent again and retrieved the doll from where it had fallen in his crotch.

This time she held on to it. And holding on to it now, she felt not just its warmth and queasy throbbing, but also its malevolence. The voodoo doll seemed to be angry, but without any particular focus. It just bore its burden of evil, ready to hurt whoever ran foul of it.

This sudden understanding forced Betsy to take another look at Chuck.

Damn, you pissed it off, sweetie, didn't you? Or,—this time she looked down at the doll—*did you kill him just for the fun of it? You're made of wood. His twisting your head didn't hurt you at all, did it?*

She got no reply from the doll. But then, she'd not actually expected any. Violent and deadly or not, it was after all just a carved piece of wood.

She disliked holding on to it though. And now she thought she heard a siren.

She left the bedroom and hurried down the hallway.

Once she'd stashed the doll away, she felt calmer. She badly needed a drink though, something to stabilize her rattled nerves. She was starting to transition from the shock that had numbed her into an intense feeling of sorrow over Chuck's death.

It's so damn unfair, Betsy thought, with the first tears coming to her eyes. *He really didn't need to die like this!*

The doorbell rang. Betsy quickly walked to the front of the house to let the paramedics in. Passing the clothes strewn about the hallway, clothes she'd discarded in her recent passion, just made her sadder.

Now the tears came freely to her eyes. By the time she'd gotten the front door open, they were running down her cheeks in torrents.

CHAPTER 24

Apache & Sully

At about the same time as Betsy was letting the paramedics into her house, Apache and Sully were drinking together at the Liquid Solace bar over on Lincoln Avenue.

The bar was a quiet place, one conducive for conversation. The detectives were discussing the murders. They'd been arguing about cause and effect for almost two hours now, with Sully maintaining the skeptic's line, while Apache tried to get him to be 'more flexible' in his thinking.

"I don't care what you say, old man, ghosts don't return from the grave a-decade-and-a-half later and kill people."

"I know it's hard to accept, kid, but trust me, in this case there doesn't seem to be any other way to explain the evidence. Sully, think for a moment . . . remember everything Forensics said."

"Yeah, yeah," Sully countered. "I'll tell you what: Forensics need to recalibrate their equipment. Despite all we've seen, there's no such thing as magic . . ."

And so it had gone on all night.

But . . .

To an increasing degree over the past few days, Sully was just putting up a front. He no longer doubted that something weird was going on here in Raynham with this 'slasher serial killer' case. All the crazy evidence—the murderer's impossible exit from Chelsea Byler's place, the 'vanishing' reported by Lynn Nilsson, the fragments of corpse flesh from a man who everyone agreed had been cremated back when he, Detective Francis Jacob Sullivan, was still in middle school—all this had to mean something.

But Sully disliked its apparent meaning.

He was doing his best to hold on to his belief in a logical cause-and-effect universe for as long as he could. The only magic he was prepared to accept was the sort illusionists did on TV, which, once the secrets were revealed, always showed itself to be a hoax on the thrill-seeking mind.

But . . . well, there was just something about the way Apache had been speaking all this while that bothered Sully. Apache had been calm, presenting his argument logically, even though the house of his reasoning was clearly built on an illogical foundation. They'd had three whiskeys apiece, but not a hint of drunkenness had infiltrated Apache's statements.

Apache's calmness worried Sully more than all the crazy evidence did. This was because Apache was talking as if he knew something which Sully didn't. And all the while, he kept rubbing that ruined and mutilated right palm of his as if their discussion was triggering bad memories in his mind.

In fact, now that Sully thought about it, Apache had only begun rubbing his palm this much after the killings started. Prior to that he seemed to have even forgotten that a third of the flesh on his right hand was missing.

"Look, look, look," Apache said finally, his voice taking on an exasperation he'd not shown all night. I might as well just tell you the whole damn story."

"What damn story?"

"The whole Malicia Howard fiasco from fifteen years ago."

"If it's yet more of this paranormal craziness, I don't wanna hear it, man. You ain't gonna convince me anyway."

Apache rubbed his bad hand and laughed. "Oh, you wanna hear this tale, son. I can assure you that you do, 'cos in a way it's also the story of how my right hand got mangled like it is now."

He waved the hand in front of Sully's face. "So, you wanna hear about that or not?"

Sully nodded. He lifted his glass and sipped his whiskey. "Alright, old man, you've caught me with that one. I'm all ears. If there's one mystery I'm interested in unraveling, it's learning exactly what happened to your hand. You've been rubbing it a lot lately too."

Apache looked surprised. "I have?"

"Every chance you get. Usually when we're discussing the murders."

"I never even noticed." Apache laughed. "Well, I guess then that my subconscious is trying to remind me of some stuff I'd long ago forgotten . . . or ought to have forgotten. Anyway, I'll tell you what happened back then, and let you judge if there is a supernatural or not. Now, here's the thing: some of this I know from being there when it occurred; other things were related to me by reliable witnesses like Chief Kravitz . . . some other stuff we discovered as evidence . . . while the rest is just supposition, witness testimony and such like. But I'll try to make as much of a logical story of it as I can. You're gonna have to excuse me if I get my facts or dates or timeline muddled up on occasion."

Sully nodded. "Yeah, sure." *This had better be good,* he thought. But the chilly vibe already settling over their secluded booth assured him that this tale was going to be better than good.

"Alright," Apache said. "I'd best start right at the beginning. What happened was . . . Well, to start with, Malicia Howard never actually was crazy."

Sully looked surprised. "Hey, wait a minute now. The general vibe you and the Chief have been giving me all this while is that she's more batshit that a bat out of Hell."

Apache laughed and sipped his whiskey. "Crazy? Nah, Malicia never was crazy. She was just safer locked away. And so long as she kept asserting that she was telling the truth, the shrinks at the Taunton State Hospital assumed she was ranting and figured they were justified in keeping her there."

Sully looked shocked. "You're saying you locked away an innocent woman for fifteen years?"

Apache shrugged. "Not my fault—I wasn't running things back then. Besides, she ain't exactly innocent either. You must've noticed the amount of trouble she's already caused after being let loose for just a week. So, no, she wasn't guiltless. She just wasn't *mad* like everyone claimed she was. Well, alright, she was *mad*, but not in that kinda way."

"It's still wrong."

"And for some people it works. Sure, she's only been in there for . . . Well she ain't been incarcerated as long as Nelson Mandela was, so we can't elect her president, but governor of Massachusetts may be alright as compensation."

Sully gaped at him.

Apache waved his drink at Sully. "And don't you dare quote me anywhere on that—I ain't racist; I'm half Native American myself . . . that was the alcohol talking just now, not me."

"Just get on with the story, old man," Sully said, motioning to a waitress for another drink. "You're wearing my patience thin."

So Apache did. "Okay. Now, it all started with Tammy Byler. She was working—"

"Byler? Is she related to Chelsea Byler?"

"She was Chelsea's aunt, her dad's kid sister. Now, just listen and don't interrupt me again."

Sully nodded. He shut up, drank his fresh whiskey and listened.

Sully didn't want to believe any of what he was hearing, but sometimes things convict one by their very implausibleness.

PART 3: THE DEATH OF PETER HOWARD & WHAT CAME AFTER.

Enjoy whatever you employ; but take heed, for it may destroy. (Necromantica 420:4:32)

CHAPTER 25

I

Tammy Byler was working a summer job at the Mr. & Mrs. Book Emporium when she had the 'Great Idea.'

Tammy was eighteen years old and was just about to enter the Bridgewater State University to study Art History. She was tall, slim, smart, and should have been quite pretty.

But she had the most horrible acne imaginable. Her skin problem had begun when she was thirteen years old. Since then an army of zits had invaded her face in such profusion that it looked like she had a violent allergy. She had cysts and scars (from scratching) and horrible facial secretions and whatnot.

Her acne had been a source of continual embarrassment. It had caused her to withdraw into herself and made her suspect the motives of anyone who attempted to befriend her.

To Tammy's mind, 19-year-old Peter Howard was her only real friend.

At one time she'd also been close to Cleo Beauchamp, her brother Max's girlfriend. Cleo was nineteen too and had at first seemed to be a true friend. But Cleo Beauchamp was a fashion snob. She'd dropped Tammy like a hot potato once her prettier friends had begun questioning their relationship in a "What the hell is a hot chick like you doing hanging out with that ugly bitch?" sort of way.

Cleo's rejection had forced Tammy, who was already shy and retiring, completely into her shell. It was only when Peter Howard had begun flirting with her that she'd slowly and shyly reemerged from behind her emotional defenses, a twilight moth shrugging its way forth from a bruised chrysalis.

She and Peter had both graduated high school that June; he'd been her date to the senior prom.

And later that prom night, she'd also lost her virginity to him, in the back of his mother's blue station wagon. Getting deflowered had been a major relief to Tammy: that a boy had been able to see beyond the array of horrible acne scars on her face. During high school, she'd had endless naïve fears that she was doomed to spend the rest of her life as a virgin. But after all the dread and anticipation, she'd finally had sex.

Okay, it hadn't been exactly mind-blowing—she'd been too worried over whether she was doing it right to actually feel anything more than the ripping of her hymen—but she considered it a landmark experience. She'd been 'blooded.' Whether her tormentors liked it or not, she was one of the girls now. A part of that exclusive secret society of femaleness.

The sex had gotten much better since then. Largely because she'd realized Peter wasn't concerned about how messy her face was. He sweetly referred to her facial landscape of zits as her 'freckles'; which she really liked. And he always kissed her and looked directly at her while they made love, so she was certain he wasn't just using her to relieve his male urges.

It wasn't enough though. Tammy had been afflicted by her insecurities for way too long. Like a damsel in distress who'd died and resurrected as a zombie before her knight in shining armor overcame the dragon and rescued her, and who now tried to eat his brain instead of kissing him, Tammy had long ago reached the point where, even though she'd found a man who loved her for herself, she needed herself to actually be 'perfect' to feel lovable. Yes Peter loved her, but she wanted everyone else to love her too. Love her, not despite her imperfections, but because she *was* perfect.

At first this had seemed impossible to accomplish. She'd seen doctor after doctor and had faithfully taken all the medications they'd prescribed and used all the special cleansing soaps and skin lotions, but apparently nothing could be done to cure her acne. (She'd once even endured an alternative medicine therapy during which leeches were placed on her face.)

"You've merely a weird hormonal imbalance," the dermatologists all told her. "Try not to worry yourself to death over it. It'll clear up by itself by your mid-twenties, by age thirty at the latest."

Thirty? To a 18-year-old girl about to enter university and be stared at afresh by everyone, thirty was much too far off. Tammy had gotten ready to be embarrassed and the butt of 'Miss Ugly' jokes all over again.

She'd go home after each medical consultation and stare into the mirror. Her reflection would cry right along with her, its chin, forehead and cheeks so messed up by her skin condition that it seemed as if an enemy had smeared mud and pus over them or painted a lizard's facial features over hers.

Nothing Peter said could console her. It was going to be high school all over again. And worse still, Peter wouldn't even be there with her. He was remaining at home for a year to help his mother out with the bookshop. His mother still felt lonely after his father's death the previous year. Peter had explained that he couldn't leave her all by herself at this time.

Tammy had replied that she understood. And she honestly did, but it would just be so lonely without him in school with her.

But then, to pass the time until she resumed at BSU, Peter had gotten her this job at his family's bookstore. Most of what she did was bag and mail orders going out of town, stock the shelves and help clean the place. Mrs. Howard was a pleasant woman, who didn't seem to mind that Tammy was dating her son.

Tammy had no idea how she'd gotten the nickname 'Malicia.'

Tammy got on with her work. After work, she occupied her time with making love with and fighting with Peter. And in between the pleasant former and the annoying latter (which invariably led back to more of the pleasant former) she prayed fervently that her acne would miraculously vanish overnight and prove the doctors all wrong, so that come late August, she'd be able to begin her higher education as smooth-faced as the rest of the other college freshmen.

It was while trying to locate an order for mailing that Tammy came upon the late Harry Howard's store of magic books.

Of course, at first Tammy Byler had no real idea of the true worth of what she'd discovered. All that initially caught her attention in the books were the strange drawings; these arcane illustrations being of deep interest to her because she was shortly to begin an undergraduate course in World Art.

Then too, when she finally understood that she'd stumbled on Peter's father's occult library, she was skeptical that it could be of any real use to her—everyone and their old wives knew there wasn't really any such thing as actual magic.

But such was the level of Tammy's desperation to look 'normal' . . . and with the end of summer fast approaching, she had very little time left before she'd have to head up the road to BSU and begin the dreaded freshmen registrations and initiations.

What sorority in its right mind will accept me as I am now? she often asked her mirror, while agitatedly squeezing and scratching her forest of blackheads and weeping pustules. *Freak Freak Zeta? Even I wouldn't let myself in the house door the way I look now!* Then she'd rub on her latest medicated complexion cream and cry softly into her hands.

She decided to give magic a try. Maybe, just maybe, a spell could cure her of her acne.

She didn't tell Peter her plans. He loved her, but he was certain to discourage her. He'd be scared of her being disappointed by her failure to fix her errant complexion.

And she couldn't tell Mrs. Howard her intentions either.

According to Peter, there'd been a certain morbid mystery surrounding his father's death that smacked of paranormal causes: on a clear Saturday morning last February, and with no prior warning whatsoever, Harry Howard had suddenly dropped dead of a heart attack, a day after a full medical checkup had given him a clean bill of health. He'd been shut up in his study when discovered. The only possible clue as to what might have killed him was the book of spells open on his desk. The spell book was open to a summoning ritual invoking a demon called Boku Zenax from somewhere called SADE.

On finding her darling husband dead, Malicia had instantly passed out. It had been up to Peter to call for an ambulance.

So no, Tammy didn't dare mention anything to Mrs. Howard either.

But she'd decided to try it anyway. It couldn't be *that* hard to cast a spell. She doubted magic was as dangerous as superstitious folks always made it out to be.

Besides, Tammy reasoned, one had to remember that Mr. Howard had been *old*. He'd been almost fifty years old. She felt his age was a very important factor to consider. Had a young person of say, her brothers Max's and Homer's age died in the circumstances Mr. Howard had, she'd have been bothered. But old people died all the time. That was what being old meant, wasn't it? Being near one's grave?

Old people regularly had heart seizures too. Almost like rehearsals for their Big Exit. And apparently, almost anything could set one off. (Tammy's own father had spent a month in hospital last year after suffering a heart attack.) So it was most likely that Peter's father actually *had* died of heart failure, but the doctor had pretended to be perplexed just to hide his own incompetence.

Once Tammy had made up her mind to try a magic spell, she bided her time. In particular, she needed to wait for a day when she was all alone in the bookstore at closing time. Then she'd have the run of the place to herself, and not need to worry about disturbance from customers.

That day came soon enough.

II

That fateful Thursday evening, Peter reversed the blue Volkswagen Golf station wagon out of the driveway.

Tammy waved goodbye to her boyfriend and his mother. They were off to the coastal town of Plymouth (about 25 miles away) to visit a friend of Mrs. Howard's who was having her baby shower.

The vehicle turned south and soon vanished from view.

Tammy waited five minutes longer to ensure that the Volkswagen wouldn't return because Mrs. Howard had maybe forgotten her present or something. Then, brimming with an anticipation she found almost impossible to control, she locked up the shop and retreated into the study/library.

By now her heart was beating wildly and she was almost beside herself with excitement.

I'm gonna do it now, she enthused to herself. *In less than an hour from now I'll be free of my acne!*

She stood in the study doorway, running her mind over the preparations she'd made, in case she'd forgotten anything. She didn't think she had. It was just 'make the pentagrams, spill the blood and read the spell.' It was weird, she'd had no idea that magic was so uncomplicated. She'd thought it all involved the sacrifice of virgins and a whole lot of orgiastic sex and debauchery. Apparently it didn't. You just followed a few simple rules and got what you wanted.

At least, that's what the books she'd studied all said. Particularly the one she intended using—the Necromantica.

She imagined how her darling Peter would feel, when, on his return from Plymouth, she greeted him with her new face—one completely free of zits, blackheads and crusty scars. Oh, she was certain he'd be utterly delighted for her.

"Oh, however did you manage it?" he was certain to ask. And she'd whisper the amazing answer into his ear. And then, when his tired mother was in bed and fast asleep, they'd sneak into his bedroom and make celebratory love.

If he'd been turned on by her before, she couldn't even conceive of how turned on he'd be now. He'd likely come in his pants each time she smiled.

Oh, he'll just love me to pieces, she thought and tingled with delicious anticipation.

Tammy stepped inside the study. She shut the oak door behind her; very gently, in case some late customer had just pulled up outside and could hear her. She wasn't about reopening the bookshop for anyone.

Once the door was shut, she had no further need for caution. The single wall of the study not framed by books was covered by heavy drapes. Its windows had been closed for as long as she could recall. The late Mr. Howard had preferred to let the air-conditioning unit provide the airflow for his volumes of literature, and his widow had kept things the same way.

Working quickly, Tammy got out the items she'd cached in the study earlier in the day, once Peter had told her of he and his mother's evening excursion. Most prominent of these was a large white tarp with a red pentagram etched on it. She'd made this at home; she didn't wish to mess up Mrs. Howard's green rug with magic marker. The two other things were: a bundle of five black candles meant to be placed at the points of the pentagram, and a small jar containing some of her blood.

Tammy had at first been very bothered by the ritual's requirement for some of her blood. Her worry was that she might cut herself too deeply and bleed to death. But she'd solved that problem. Her period had begun just this morning and it was a heavy one. Each time she'd felt the cramps, she'd hurried to the toilet, sat on the seat, and held the jar under herself to collect her menses.

She regarded the contents of the jar now. About half an inch, slightly diluted with water so it didn't clot. It seemed a little lumpy, but it should do. Anyway, the Necromantica hadn't stated what part of the body the required blood should come from.

Tammy put down the jar of menstrual blood, then got to work arranging everything. This was easy enough. She spread the tarp with the red pentagram topside, then arranged the black candles at the tips of the star. Then she shucked off her clothes. According to the magic text, everything had to go, her panties inclusive. She didn't know why this was, but rules were rules.

When she was naked except for her tampon, Tammy got the copy of the Necromantica from the bookshelf.

Immediately she touched it she felt odd. Odd, as if she'd just charged the air with death. She disliked the feeling; it made her hurry up. The sooner she got this over with, the better.

The Necromantica was a strange book, for sure, with its pages of dry human skin and those suspiciously red letters that looked as if the pages were bleeding. It felt queasy to the touch too.

Following the instructions in the Necromantica, Tammy stood in the middle of the pentagram. She'd already opened the spell book to the right page; it lay on her right. She retrieved the jar of blood from where she'd placed it on the floor. Then, dipping her finger into it, she drew six bloody upside-down crosses on her belly.

Next came the really icky part of the ritual, the part of it which made her wish she'd bled her wrist instead: seeing as this was a beautification spell she intended casting, she had to smear the rest of the blood over the part of her that she wanted transformed.

Reluctantly, appalled by how gross it was, Tammy smeared her menstrual blood all over her face. Once past its awful smell, she really got into the spirit of things, dosing her acne with as much blood medicine as she could.

Finally, looking as red-faced as if her skin had been peeled off, Tammy set the little jar down. She'd emptied it. She wiped her hands on some tissue, picked up the Necromantica and began reading:

"Noos, noos, sey noos,
Lufi tua eb eblli
Yt'ter'pyrev.
Noos, os noos . . .
Oot gni kool doog eblli!
Enca live u oh teca fym ffo teg . . . !"

It was a long spell, and she'd already practiced it a few times in her mind. She ran it all the way through once and waited.

The first thing Tammy noticed was that the room got hotter. In just a short while it felt to her as though she were standing in a sauna. Now she understood the reason why the book said to take one's clothes off: in this kind of heat they'd be too uncomfortable to wear.

Next, the room grew darker. She maintained her courage as all the furniture faded from view. She was suddenly frightened by what she'd started. Yes, she wanted a clear and unblemished face, but maybe she'd overdone things by trying to get it this way.

The room was still darkening, with the fluorescent ceiling lamps completely doused by the evil force she'd invoked. Of that, Tammy was certain: she'd succeeded in her ritual. The heat in the room and the increasing darkness were heralds of the creature she'd summoned to grant her wish.

Finally, the borders of the study were in pitch blackness, the sort of impenetrable night that miners find themselves stranded in after a landslide. All around Tammy was darkness such as she'd never before seen or imagined.

All the light in the room now came from the pentagram she stood on. It was a sickly light, grayish rather than white, and was projecting from the evil red lines she'd drawn on the tarp, not from the white sheet itself. At the tips of the five-pointed star lay five black puddles of wax—the unseen arrival's heat had melted the candles.

Tammy took all this in as peripheral. Her attention was focused directly ahead.

Ahead of her, where the window drapes had hung, an aperture was opening in the darkness. It was an archway, a framing of black stone around a corpse-gray void from which came a slithering sound.

Inscribed over the archway were the red words: ENLIGHTENMENT.

I've done it! Tammy enthused. *I've done it!* She was sweating freely but that didn't matter in the least now. Nor did her nakedness matter either.

Here now was the fulfilment of her quest.

The demon she'd summoned had arrived in the archway. It was a hulking shape, large but obscured by the gray void it stood in, which swirled around it like mist. Its eyes were visible however, large yellow orbs that glowed and blinked and seemed reptilian. Its body seemed to swell and contract at random, as if it was either a fluid or had tentacles.

A wind of evil blew outward from the morbid creature, enveloping and terrifying Tammy.

"Yesssss?" it hissed at her. "You called, we came. What is your desire?"

"I-I-I wa-wa-want my a-a-a-a-acne gone! I-I-I wanna b-b-be beautiful! I wanna . . . !"

She was so scared that she'd have cut and run. Only, a glance behind her after the archway appeared had shown her that there was nowhere to flee to. The wall of surrounding blackness was complete. She'd entombed herself in a well of frozen ink. She couldn't leave it until she either got or didn't get what she'd come here for.

Even then, Tammy might still have turned and fled into the darkness, trusting that the door still existed on its other side. But the Necromantica plainly stated that she—the 'spellcaster' the book called her—was not to step outside of the pentagram she'd drawn until after the ritual was concluded. Doing so could prove fatal.

"We can grant your desire," the voice from the archway said. "Yes, we can. But we want something in return. We want blood. *Your* blood."

"I-I-I d-don't . . . !" Tammy stuttered. "I-I-I d-d-don't ha-ha-have any more of it. I used it a-a-all up summoning you."

She cast a glance down at the empty jar. *Aw shucks,* she thought, *I shoulda just cut my arm after all. How the hell am I going to find more blood for this thing?* She felt desperate. It hurt to be so close to achieving her heart's desire and then failing at the last hurdle. *Oh no, I don't wanna have to do this again!*

Worst of all, she had had a knife with her—the one she'd earlier used to cut the twine with which she'd bound the tarpaulin sheet. Unfortunately, this now lay out of sight (and possibly no longer in Earth's universe) on a reading desk that the darkness had swallowed up.

"You have blood!" the sibilant demonic voice whispered back. "You are female and you are bleeding now. We will take *that* blood from you."

Tammy heaved a sigh of relief. It was alright then. "Okay," she said, "you've got a deal. Fix me and then—"

She'd been about to say: "And then I'll throw you my tampon," but a sudden fizzy feeling around her face made her shut up. Her face kept fizzing, as if it was a wound and someone had just spilled hydrogen peroxide on it.

"What are you doing?" she gasped at the archway. The fizzing had begun stinging now.

The horrible yellow eyes blinked and the demon laughed. "We are granting your request," it replied.

Tammy felt a moment of searing pain when it seemed as though all the skin on her face had been ripped off. Then, just as suddenly, the pain was gone.

She lifted a hand and touched her left cheek. She was amazed. Her cheek felt baby-butt smooth. No more pus-filled bumps or scars. She raised her other hand to her face and felt her skin from forehead to chin. As she touched herself, her eyes widened in delight.

"This is amazing," she gasped at the creature in the archway. "My skin is okay again. It hasn't felt this smooth since I was twelve." She kept feeling her face, stroking what she was certain was a lovely milky complexion. Oh, how she wished she had a mirror here so she could admire herself. She was already falling in love with her new look.

"And now," her healer said, "it is time for our payment."

Tammy nodded. "Yeah, sure. Just hold on a sec while I get the tampon out and throw it to you."

"Halt!" the demon ordered, just as she gripped the tampon's string and prepared to pull it out. "Stop. That is not what we want."

Tammy stared confused at the creature. Behind its glowing eyes she thought she could make out horns, only there were very many of these horns and they were all wavering.

"B-but you said . . ."

"You will come over to us here at the border of the realms. We will suck the blood out of you."

"What? Hell no! I ain't doing that!" Tammy remembered very well the Necromantica's admonition to not step out of the pentagram.

She could almost sense the creature's cold amusement as it replied, "We have granted your desire; and so you must grant ours too. If you do not do so, we will take back the gift we have just given you. You will become ugly again, and now it will never leave you. This will be our punishment to you for wasting our time with this summoning."

The thought of going back to being 'Miss Ugly' again terrified Tammy even more than the thought of leaving the pentagram's protection. She'd just escaped for good the misery that had dogged her all her teen years and had threatened to carry on through college. Returning to that was inconceivable; she'd rather die instead. She didn't doubt that the creature could undo what it had done for her. As such, she didn't dare bluff it. If it called her bluff and went away angry now, would it return when she had a bowl of non-menstrual blood for it to slake its thirst on? She didn't think it would.

She imagined she could sense the demon's displeasure as the additional waves of heat that now poured from the archway. She was drenched in sweat now and had begun feeling faint.

"I'm scared," she pleaded. "I can't leave the pentagram."

"Oh, but you can," the demon encouraged her, its body rising and falling between the mist of the void. "The pentagram is to hold back the darkness, touching which would prove fatal to you. But between you and us there is no darkness, only the floor, which is safe."

"Why can't you come here to me instead?" Tammy asked. The creature's explanation made sense, but it sounded too glib, like a seducer. And besides, she really didn't want its horrible mouth on her vagina.

"Come, beautiful girl," it hissed nicely. "Soon the portal will close and we will depart. If by then you've not paid our price, we must take our gift back home with us. And next time you call us, the price will have doubled."

The creature's threat of departure terrified Tammy. "Okay," she said. "I'll come to you. Just give me a moment to compose myself."

"We await you."

"You'll be gentle, right? I mean, while sucking?" She was clutching the Necromantica pressed tightly to her breasts, sweating all over it. Paradoxically, the book was cool in the room's heat, a heat now so fierce that Tammy easily imagined that all the bookshelves hidden behind the darkness had long since burnt up. She was worried about her hair going the same route.

"Of course, of course we will," the demon reassured her, its eyes blinking and seeming to grow larger. "It will be a delicious feeling—the height of ecstasy. We just want the blood of life that you are wasting at the moment."

Alright then. One can't make a cake without breaking eggs. I'll just need to douche properly afterwards; like five or six times. It'll be horrible to lose the acne and instead contract an incurable strain of demon herpes.

Her heart beating like a drum, Tammy stepped out of the pentagram.

"Yes, come to us," the thing in the void whispered to her as she stepped onto a floor now made of hot bluish flagstones. "Come to us, beautiful girl!"

There was something in the demon's voice that worried Tammy: an anticipation she couldn't decipher. *Am I just hearing the thing's desire for my waste blood, or is it trying to sucker me? What does it actually want from me?*

"Leave the book behind," the demon advised. "You don't need it in here."

She realized she'd carried the Necromantica out of the pentagram. At the same time she thought she heard a hint of fear in the creature's voice. It was another warning she chose to ignore. She turned, put the horrible spell book down inside the pentagram, then resumed her slow progress to the archway.

Once she'd reached it, she discovered that there really was a separation between the realms. It seemed like a sheet of cellophane hung between her and the demon dimension— ENLIGHTENMENT, the etching over the archway proclaimed it to be.

"Come! Come! Bring us your blood," the demon whimpered in a frenzy of excitement almost pathetic in its intensity. The thing sounded like a junkie desperate for a fix. Its eyes yawned as wide as mouths and she saw that each yellow oculus had three pupils, each pupil a different color—red, blue, and green. And now too, she made out the creature's body much more clearly. It seemed to lack arms and legs. Its form writhed because it was covered with tentacles. The tentacles were all colored the deepest black imaginable; it was only by their ceaseless motion and when the shrouding mist curled through the spaces between them that she could determine their separate existence from the bulk of the demon's body.

She saw the creature in there waiting for her.

She had a final crisis of worry: *I really shouldn't do this! I really shouldn't do this!*

But, oh no, she wasn't about reverting to her previous ugly self. *They've fulfilled the greatest wish I've ever had and I'm not losing that!*

So, against Tammy's better judgment, she stepped into the void beyond the archway.

She'd not known what to expect, but in *here* was as hot as out *there*. The gray mist had a smell like rotten eggs and it took an effort not to barf.

She stood facing the demon. "Alright, I'm here," she told the horrible creature. "You can lick me all you want, but I have to get back out soon."

"You are going nowhere!" the demon told her. "You are ours now! All ours!"

Tammy began shivering. "But you promised!"

The demon laughed. "You should have remained inside the pentagram! You were safe there; we required no further payment from you. The blood on your face was sufficient in exchange for what we did for you."

"But . . . !" *Shit—this nasty horrible thing tricked me!*

Then Tammy realized all hope wasn't lost yet. She could still get away.

She spun around and leapt towards the archway.

She almost made it through, but the demon flailed out a tentacle and snagged her left ankle. The demon dragged her back towards it. She could hear it chortling in delight now. It pulled her off her feet. She fell forward and smacked her head on the hot stone.

Dazed, she felt another tentacle wrapping itself around her right ankle.

"Please, don't!" she pleaded. "Please, let me go!"

In response, Tammy felt her legs being pulled apart. Then she felt a tongue lapping at her private parts. A mouth began sucking on her sex.

She almost relaxed then. The sensation wasn't really bad: it was like cunnilingus but lacked any finesse.

She felt the tampon being slurped out of her body. She felt the blood stream from her womb and out into the sucking mouth. Though definitely scary and also incredibly gross, this wasn't too bad either: it was what the demon had said they wanted. So maybe it was merely scaring her. Maybe it would let her go once it had drunk its fill.

But then she felt the sharp pain of something biting her right buttock.

What . . . !? She raised herself on her elbows and twisted herself and looked back. Yes, a tentacle *was* pressed against her sex, lapping and sucking at it. But another tentacle—this one having four red eyes—was tearing a chunk out of her ass.

Agony flooded her body. The tentacle raised its head from the wound it had made. Horrified, she watched it wolf the torn flesh down. Its mouth was a bloody circle of teeth.

The tentacle's eyes seemed to wink at Tammy. Then it dipped down again and dug its teeth into the pit it had made in her flesh. It began sucking fat and blood from the wound.

Tammy screamed in horror and pain. She stared pleadingly up at the huge yellow eyes in the demon's tentacle mass.

The demon laughed mockingly at her disbelief. "Yes, we only want your blood," it replied her questioning gaze. "But we want *all* of the blood in your body."

After that, everything became pain. More tentacles detached from the mass of the creature and dug themselves into Tammy's legs. They anchored themselves like leeches and began emptying her.

Oh, the horrible pain! She could feel herself going, being drained out of her body. But she wasn't going down without a fight.

Hell no! Tammy thought desperately. *I've worked much too hard to become pretty to die in here and like this!*

She was close to the archway opening. She reached back out through it, once more puncturing the nylon-like barrier between Earth and this horrible place. She got a firm grip on the stone that formed the infernal entrance. The stone was impossibly hot, but she held on to it.

With a strength and a desperation born from the agony that now raged through her lower body, coupled with her fear of a fate worse than death if she died in this hellish place, Tammy began dragging herself out of the void.

The demon had a good hold on her, but the mass of its tentacles were slack. It was more concerned with draining her of blood than with stopping her escape.

Tammy was shortly to discover why this was.

Her body in a crises of combined agonies, her hands as hot as if they were on fire, she pulled her head and shoulders out of the archway. Then, bracing her elbows on the edge of the sizzling stone, she got her breasts through as well. Now she had sufficient leverage to place her palms on the side of the entrance and push instead of pull. This worked well and soon she was out up to her waist.

It was here that she hit the first snag. The demon had a viselike grip on her buttocks and legs. In fact, it was holding her lower limbs so tightly that they felt paralyzed.

The damn thing won't let go of me, Tammy realized in horror. *And since it can't pass through the archway, I'm stuck here like this.*

She twisted around onto her back and looked at her captor. It was hulked over her legs, a tentacled lion feeding. Its tentacles were attached all over her lower body. It was exsanguinating her so hard that her womb felt like it was collapsing inside her. The demon's eyes glowed, but it wasn't looking at her anymore. It was concentrating on its murderous task.

Shit, this damn thing ain't letting go of me no matter what I do. I don't wanna die like this! No! I'm pretty now!

"FRIGGING LET ME GO!" she screamed at it. She'd have beaten at it with her hands, but she didn't dare remove them from the burning stone. Doing so would mean her being dragged back through the portal again. And she knew that once that happened, she'd never have the strength to pull herself out again. At the moment she was functioning purely on raw courage and adrenalin.

"LET ME GO, YOU BASTARD, GODDAMMIT!" she shrieked again.

The demon neither responded nor complied with her demand. Its body merely throbbed with its feeding glee. She even thought she could see it swelling, bloating with the life it was stealing from her.

Then, young Tammy Byler discovered she had another, more immediate problem:

The archway was closing.

Like a set of elevator doors coming together in the middle, the sides of the stone entrance were moving inwards towards her. At the same time, the upper, arched portion of the hellish portal was descending towards her like a guillotine blade, coming down at rapid speed.

Forgetting her pain for the moment, Tammy began praying that, just like an elevator's doors, the portal's sides would stop and retract once they touched her body.

She was wrong. She had the shortest of interludes of a sensation of being compressed inside a hot ring, as if she'd fallen into a flaming rabbit hole and couldn't dig herself out again, and then . . .

The closing portal walls cut through her body like a hot knife going through butter.

III

"And that's how they found Tammy Byler," Apache said, speaking so quietly that Sully had to strain to hear him. He sipped his drink, then went on: "Tammy's upper body was lying beside the window drapes in the study. She'd been sliced cleanly in two. According to the medical examiners, the edges of the wound were surgically precise, as neat as if she'd been butchered using one of those sci-fi lasers."

"And the rest of her?" Sully asked.

"Was missing . . . and still is." Apache laughed. "Nah, they never found the girl's ass and legs. That was the first oddity of the case. But I do need to backtrack here, so you understand how everything went down, because of what happened afterwards.

"Okay, so what happened that night was that, Peter and Malicia Howard got home at about eleven o'clock, but then couldn't unlock the front door because the key was still in the lock. Remember, Tammy hadn't planned on dying. She'd intended to be out of the house before they returned from their trip. So, unable to open the front door, mother and son then made their way around to the back and let themselves in that way. The back door opened into a corridor that ran straight to the bookshop. On seeing Tammy's handbag lying on the bookshop counter, they began searching the house for her. That's how they found her in Harry Howard's study, with the white tarp on the floor with the pentagram and melted wax on it and that copy of the spell book."

"The Necromantica?"

"Yeah. Well, on seeing that there's only half of Tammy in the room, Malicia starts freaking out. It's Peter who called us, and we went over there—it was myself and Chief Kravitz who responded to the call. Remember this was fifteen years ago: back then Tina was still a detective like me. So, yeah, we went over there and we found everything exactly how I've just described it to you."

"You searched the house for the rest of Tammy Byler?"

Apache nodded. "Yeah, yeah, we did. We looked everywhere, though after taking one good look at that book of spells, Tina had already whispered to me that she doubted we'd find the rest of the kid. I was skeptical, of course. Back then I was a lot like you. I insisted that we look anyway. But even I could tell there was something wrong about that crime scene. For one thing, there was no blood on the dead girl whatsoever. I mean, she'd been chopped in half and there wasn't any blood anywhere? And second—and this was the weirdest thing I'd *ever* seen up to that point—her face was completely free of zits and scars." He raised a hand to still Sully's protests. "No, don't you say that that ain't a big deal. You didn't know this kid; I did. She had literally the worst case of acne you've ever seen in your damn life. Think for a moment of that geeky boy in your high school with the terrible skin condition, and then make his state twice as bad—yeah, that was Tammy Byler for you: skin so bad it looked barbequed. And so, to now see her with a *perfect* face—and I mean a Hollywood-actress-*perfect* face . . . So yeah, right off the bat it was clear that something weird had taken place in that house that night."

"Alright, old man," Sully agreed, "I can see how this is creepy and all, but how does Peter Howard fit into this? I mean, it's his girlfriend who got killed, not himself."

Apache laughed. "Calm down, son; don't jump the gun. I ain't even halfway through my story yet." He stared into his whiskey like it was a crystal ball and he could see the past reflected clearly in it. "See, the real problem started because . . . well, Tammy Byler's family all blamed Malicia, and in particular Peter, for her death."

"That's stupid," Sully said. "Not with all the evidence you've just mentioned."

Apache smiled. "If humans were a sensible lot, you and I'd both be out of a job, wouldn't we? Sure, it was dumb, but it's what happened. But then, the Bylers were always a silly bunch anyway. Okay, now I need to tell you a little bit about the Bylers:

"First was the dad, Bart Byler. He'd been in high school with Malicia. He knew all about the scissors incident—"

"Back up a bit. What scissors incident?"

"Ah, I forgot you aren't from around here. Once, while being picked on in high school, Malicia rammed a pair of scissors through Ronnie Gribble's hand and her own school desk. By all accounts it wasn't pretty."

Sully's eyes widened at the gross imagery. "She did that?"

"Yeah. But it happened like thirty years before this story that I'm telling you now, so don't ask me for the details. Apparently that's how she got the name 'Malicia' in the first place, 'cos her later husband Harry, who was good friends with Ronnie at the time, imagined she'd stabbed him out of sheer malice. . . . Why I'm mentioning it now is because, knowing about that incident, Bart Byler was always wary of Malicia Howard and apparently warned his kids to stay well away from her. Of course, he'd not counted on his favorite daughter falling in love with the woman's son. And then, of course, there was the additional twist to the tale that by the time Tammy and Peter were dating, old Bart was still recovering from his recent heart attack. And besides, the young girl had been so miserable for years because of her bad skin that Bart was delighted that she'd finally found happiness somewhere; anywhere, even if it was with Malicia's kid."

"I can understand that."

"Okay, so that was Bart Byler for you. He was a decent and hardworking fellow, though quite ornery, a trait that only worsened the older he got. Not completely a jerk, but still he could be mulish when he got some idea into his head, even if it didn't hold up to the light of reason. He said whatever he felt like saying and whenever he felt like saying it, and he didn't care if you took it the wrong way, or if he hurt you. Put simply, he was a rather unpleasant fellow to know.

"His wife Cissy was very different. You know how opposites attract? Well, now here you had a textbook example of it. Cissy Byler was sweetness and light itself. A delicate and pretty woman who loved everyone and wouldn't hurt a fly. No one I've ever met could tell me what she'd seen in her ogre of a husband, to make her marry him and then remain with him for four decades. Cissy was one of those people who really did give you hope for the human race and made this world a better place just by living in it. She was sweet and easygoing and courted neither trouble nor controversy. Apparently the most shocking thing Cissy Byler ever did in her forty years of marriage to Bart before the cancer killed her, was to get up one morning and announce that she wanted a divorce." Apache laughed. "It was that announcement of hers which sparked Bart's heart attack. And Cissy meant it too. She only relented when it seemed very likely that Bart would die if she went ahead with the threatened divorce. Apparently, he couldn't live without having her around to argue with. Nor she without him either."

He drank a little more whiskey.

"Yeah, and then there were the kids. The Bylers had six children—two girls and four boys. The boys were Max, Homer, Eddie, and Chelsea's dad Jerry, who was overseas with the army in Iraq at the time. All four sons were in their mid to late twenties when this happened. I think Jerry, being the eldest, was even in his thirties. Max was married too. No, no, he'd just gotten divorced. His wife had run off because he kept beating her and she'd taken his children with her, so now—"

"Why're you telling me all this extended family tree stuff?" Sully asked bluntly.

"Just hold on; you'll understand its relevance later. Alright, where was I? Yeah, I was saying Max Byler's wife Terri had run off, taking his two kids with her. So now Max had a new girlfriend, a young hellcat named Cleo Beauchamp. Cleo was bad to the bone, but she was the town administrator's niece, so she got away with a lot of misbehavior." Apache looked closely at Sully. "You following this so far?"

Sully nodded. "So that's the sons covered. "How 'bout the daughters?"

"I'm coming to those. But one more thing about the Byler boys: They were a rowdy lot. Max and Homer were the worst, apt to use their fists to settle an argument as much as talk. Both brothers were about six-foot-five in height and rippled with muscle, so I guess using their fists came easier to them than using their brains. We were always throwing those two in the tank to dry out after a night of carousing, usually with Cleo along too. Homer couldn't keep a girlfriend. There was a lot of debate on whether it was 'cos his dick was too big or 'cos it was too small.

"Jerry, the eldest son, was a bundle of energy. He could think a bit too. He didn't want to hang around this small town of ours; he wanted to see the world. So he left and joined the army. He fought in Iraq as a Major, got wounded and was honorably discharged. Today, he's back here running the family grocery business. Which leaves Eddie Byler, the youngest and smartest of the four brothers and also the only one of them we never arrested for any misdemeanors. Eddie Byler never even had time for girls, always had his head stuck in a book. The summer Tammy died, Eddie was in Europe, travelling with a group of friends on a science project. So, like Jerry, he had nothing to do with any of this. Eddie's a physics professor in UCLA now. There's rumors he's in contention for the Nobel Prize, for some shit that involves smashing neutrinos against each other.

"And so, now on to the Byler girls: Mary was third in the line of birth. I think she came after Max and before Homer. She was tall and pretty and took after her mother. I mean, she minded her own business, read her books and attended med school while her brothers were busy rabblerousing. Today, Mary is both a pediatrician and a preacher's wife, and is highly regarded by everyone. She lives over in Springfield with her brood.

"Which leaves Tammy, who'd apparently just killed herself. That anyway was the official coroner's verdict: Death by Misadventure. There were simply too many inexplicable factors in Tammy's death for any other conclusion to be reached. But not for her family. The problem was, that Tammy was Bart Byler's favorite child. She was maybe seven or eight years younger than her other siblings and was *really* close to her dad. So her death really hurt him. It hurt him a whole lot more than if another of his kids had died, even his older daughter Mary. And remember too, that Bart already had this thing in his mind about Malicia Howard. He didn't trust Malicia at all and now that suspicion had extended itself to her son."

Apache looked at Sully for confirmation that the other was following the story. Sully nodded back. Apache went on:

"Well, anyhow, long story short, Bart and his sons got the idea in their heads that Peter Howard had murdered Tammy during some Satanist ritual he'd conned her into participating in. I guess, in a sense you couldn't blame 'em, right? The police had found all the evidence for them. Pentagrams, black candles, book of spells, missing body parts? What else did you need to prove witchcraft? The only question unanswered was *who'd* been in the house when Bart's favorite daughter had died. We knew for sure that Malicia and Peter hadn't been at home—we'd crosschecked their story. The time they said they'd left Plymouth checked out, and also, on their way home they'd stopped at a filling station along Route 44 to buy gas, and the attendant remembered them, identifying them from the snaps we showed him. And even old Mrs. Fitch, who lived opposite the Howards and disliked Malicia, confirmed their statement of the time they'd arrived back home—Janie Fitch had been outside looking for her cat and had seen the Howards' blue station wagon turn into their driveway with both mother and son in it. So, no—*they'd* not killed Tammy. Whatever she'd done, she'd done to herself.

"But her family didn't see it like that at all. They all blamed Peter."

Apache paused now and sighed. To Sully, the sigh sounded more like a groan of pain.

"And so it happened," the older detective continued, "that one fateful night in late July, Max, Cleo, Homer and one of their friends kidnapped Peter Howard."

IV

Most violent crimes occur at night, when the sun has winked out of sight and the moon collaborates with the perpetrators.

So it was that night. The black pickup truck turned off Darrington Drive, and after motoring down a short dirt road, pulled up in a grove of moonlit trees beside Gushee Pond. Everyone got out.

Peter Howard was half-pulled, half-shoved out of the truck by Max and Homer Byler. Neither man had said a word since they'd grabbed him. They'd sat like stone statues in the rear of the truck, one giant on either side of the captive, while Homer's best friend John Burke drove the pickup and beside him, Cleo Beauchamp made conversation with herself.

***

Getting Peter away from home had been easy enough. Cleo had called him. She'd said she needed to talk to him, that she wanted to tell him what Tammy had told her the night before she died.

In other circumstances, Peter might have been suspicious. He knew Tammy and Cleo hadn't gotten along. Though their ages were close, he knew Cleo had blown Tammy off because she said 'Lil Miss Ugly' wasn't cool enough to hang out with. It was unlikely then that the two young women would have shared any confidences.

But Peter was deeply mourning his dead girlfriend, and anything that might help explain her fatal actions was welcome to him.

Which was exactly what his abductors had been counting on: that he'd be so grief-stricken that he'd not pause to question Cleo's true motives for calling him until it was too late.

Peter had told his mother where he was going. Malicia, herself still overcome with shock at what had happened in her house, had just nodded.

Peter had climbed into the blue Volkswagen and headed over to Rudy's Truck Stop to meet with Cleo.

Max Byler at the wheel, they'd run Peter off the road on the upper portion of Center Street, right after the Cedarmill Drive junction, that hundred-yard stretch of highway where there were no houses, and where this late at night there would hardly be any traffic and definitely no nosy pedestrians.

They'd planned the abduction to perfection, with Homer hiding down the road with a cellphone and alerting the others once Peter had driven past him.

They'd hidden Peter's car behind some trees and driven off with their captive.

***

Now, as he was roughly shoved out from the car, Peter realized his mistake. He also realized that it was too late for him to do anything about it. He had no chance of winning a fight with either of Tammy's brothers, both of whom towered over him by at least five inches and weighed twice as much as he did, all of it muscle. Even John Burke, the 'smallest' of the trio, was six-foot-two in height and built like a football player. (John Burke actually had played football in college, but he'd broken his hip during a championship game, and even after the surgery still had problems with pain.)

He wouldn't be able to outrun them either. Like they expected him to make a run for it, he'd been stood against the rear bed of the truck with the three men arranging themselves in a rough semicircle around him.

Peter knew he was going to have to either plead his way out of this or take the beating of his life. He had no self-defense skills. He was lanky and had never thrown an angry punch in his life. A reader, not a fighter.

I'm gonna get killed here!

They were parked/standing almost at the end of the dirt road, with thick forest on both sides of them and a sparse awning of overlapping tree branches. The road itself extended away to his right.

Looking left, he could see down the pond shore to the moonlit water surface which rippled with frogs in motion. The moon wasn't full, but there was sufficient light for him to make out the faces of his captors.

Both Byler brothers were dressed alike, wearing denim pants and dark, sweaty work shirts with rolled-up sleeves. Both men had long brown hair, thick noses, thin lips and large jaws. Max had a wild mustache and beard, Homer was clean-shaven. There wasn't sufficient light to see their eyes by, but Peter was well acquainted with the icy blue stares he was certain they were now projecting at him. They'd never approved of his relationship with their kid sister, but their father had told them to let him be since he was making Tammy happy.

Clearly not anymore though.

John Burke stood on his left, looking amused. John had short blonde hair and was dressed all in black leather. Personally, he had nothing against Peter, but he was Homer's best friend and would go along with whatever the brothers decided.

That left Cleo. Peter looked desperately at her. She too was on his left, outside of the three men, leaning back against the hood of the black truck. Tallish, slim yet busty, pretty, and with short ginger hair; dressed in a gray tank top and red shorts and boots. She was staring at him and smoking a cigarette. He saw that she was licking her lips. The desire for blood was on her. She wanted to watch him get hurt.

He'd been thinking of appealing to Cleo to plead with the brothers on his behalf. But, seeing the lackadaisical way she'd posed herself against the hood of the pickup truck, and remembering that she'd been the one who'd suckered him out here in the first place, he decided to address Tammy's brothers directly.

Since their arrival at this solitary place, the night had been silent with anticipation. Even the woodland creatures in the nearby foliage were silent. The world seemed to be waiting for what was going to happen. The tension had become a knife that would split the darkness in unequal halves and leave the night lying bleeding.

"So, what have you got to say for yourself?" Max finally asked Peter.

"It wasn't my fault," Peter pleaded. "Honest, Max, you guys have gotta believe me. I didn't—"

A hard slap to the side of his head shut Peter up. His left ear filled with a dull buzzing sound through which he heard: "Oh yeah? So whose fault was it then? Tammy's?"

Peter was still attempting to phrase an inoffensive reply to this when a blow to the gut doubled him over. Just like that, his dinner spewed out of his mouth. The puke went all over Max's shoes, riling him up even further.

Peter was aware of being hauled upright by Homer. "Now listen, kid," Homer said, "you ain't got no excuses you can make that're gonna satisfy us, alright?"

Peter nodded weakly, the taste of vomit thick in his mouth. His ear was still ringing and he could only manage short breaths.

Homer went on: "And that's 'cos it's because you had all of those evil books in your house in the first place that our baby sister found 'em."

"But it's a bookshop!"

"It doesn't matter what it is," Max said, taking over the conversation again. "What's important is what *resulted* from your having those bad books at home."

Peter resigned himself to getting the beatdown of his life. He figured he'd be lucky to get out of this without suffering any broken bones.

Then he thought of running for it. He just might have some good luck and get away. It was almost midnight now. If he went into the trees, out of the moonlight, he'd be almost impossible to see, even with flashlights. The brothers might not catch him before he reached the main road. And once on the road, he stood a good chance of a passing car framing the chase in its headlights. Once that happened, his pursuers would have to leave him alone.

Of course, if they *did* catch him before he made it to the road there was no telling what they'd do to him. But then also, he had no idea what they intended doing to him now either. It was better to try to get away.

Peter began plotting his escape.

Max was still speaking: "Our dad wants us to send a clear message to everyone in Raynham that you don't mess with the Bylers and get away scot free. He wants your witch of a mother to feel just as bad as he does now."

This statement got through to Peter. *They're gonna kill me?* He stared in horror at the semicircle of men cordoning him beside the pickup truck. "You're gonna kill me?"

"How smart you are, kid," John Burke said, speaking for the first time. He reached out and patronizingly patted Peter's head. "You got some brains in your noggin after all. Yeah, we're gonna kill you. Your witch-mother butchered Tammy and we're gonna do a similarly nasty number on you in return."

Peter swatted his hand away. Then he broke for it. He wasn't hanging around to be killed.

With their murderous intent now out in the open, Max had thrown another punch at Peter's belly. This time though, Peter ducked, so Max hit the side of the truck instead.

"Fuck!" the big man growled.

Peter headed left. John had just stepped nearer to Homer, leaving a gap between himself and the vehicle. Peter had intended to dart right, through the space between the brothers (that way was a direct route into the woods behind them, and he'd be able to run almost parallel to the dirt track and not lose his way while fleeing), but at the last moment he'd remembered John's old football wound. John had broken his right hip. Peter gambled on the injury meaning John wouldn't be able to turn fast enough to grab and hold him. Once he made it around the front of the pickup truck, he'd have the vehicle between him and his pursuers for a few seconds at least, hopefully enough of a head start for him to reach the forest without being caught.

He'd guessed right about John's old injury. As he slipped past John, the man twisted to stop him, then doubled up in pain, grabbing his right thigh.

"Shit!" John yelped.

Peter was past him by then and only heard the agonized sounds he made. Peter's adrenalin was pumping. His thoughts were focused completely on making it around the hood of the truck.

"Stop that God-damned son-of-a-bitch!" Max growled.

Then Cleo Beauchamp, whom Peter had completely forgotten about, stuck out her foot and tripped him up.

That was the end of Peter's escape. He went sprawling on his face and streaking towards the lake. He'd been moving so fast that once he lost his balance, he completely lost it. Worse still for him, the ground was both muddy and sloped down slightly. Peter ended up rolling over and over on his side. By the time he stopped rolling, he was so dazed that he was uncertain which side was up.

When he finally focused his eyes, he saw Cleo Beauchamp staring down at him, her face illuminated by the red glow of her cigarette. She was sitting on his belly so he couldn't get away again.

"Please help me, Cleo!" he gasped out hoarsely. "C'mon, Cleo, you and Tammy were friends. Plead with Homer and Max for me."

She grinned back and blew cigarette smoke in his face. "Now, dude, don't you dare tell my boyfriend Maxwell that I said this," she whispered, her pretty face glistening evilly in her cigarette's glow, "but personally, I'm so glad Tammy killed herself. She was too ugly to live—a face like that is a crime against beauty. Boy, you must really be into freaks, 'cos I wonder what the hell else you ever saw in that warty toad that made you want to fuck her. Or maybe you two always did it with a paper bag over her head?"

At that insult, Peter forgot his own straits. He attempted raising himself to choke Cleo. "How dare you talk about Tammy like that, you damn bitch! I'll . . . I'll—YEEEOOWWW!"

Cleo had jabbed her lit cigarette into Peter's right eye. He'd not been expecting anything of the sort. Before he could either blink or jerk his face away, the burning cigarette tip had made contact with his eyeball and Cleo was rubbing it in hard, as hard as if she was stubbing it out in an ashtray.

At the contact between grey iris and bright red cigarette tip, white-hot agony filled Peter's pink brain. An explosion of sparks flared inside his head. His eye felt like it was melting.

Shrieking, he fell back to the ground.

While he writhed in the mud holding his face and moaning, Cleo laughed down at him.

"So alright, man," she said, her voice heavily amused, "here come the guys now with the hammers. Don't worry 'bout a thing; you'll shortly be seeing that ugly cunt Tammy again, for sure."

She stood up off him then.

Hammers? Cleo's words slowly made their way through Peter's haze of pain. He only understood their significance when the first sledgehammer blow hit him in the side, smashing his ribs to bits.

After that, all Peter Howard felt was agony stacked on agony as the Byler brothers methodically worked him over with their sledgehammers, pulping his head and body as efficiently as if it were all mere eggshell.

***

"Well, I don't think anyone'll ever be able to put this Humpty Dumpty back together again either," Max said in a satisfied voice afterwards.

Homer and John both laughed loudly at the joke. Cleo, who was now dragging on a fresh cigarette, smirked down at the mess of gooey flesh that had once been a man.

To Cleo's mind, what remained of Peter Howard looked more like roadkill than a human being. It was just a horrible mashed mess, like looking at a pile of mince that had tried putting on human clothes, or a limp balloon of skin from which blood and meat and bone had squirted at random from a hundred tears. Peter's head was merely a flattened circle. She honestly thought the head looked like a jumbo pizza, with skull chunks as anchovies and brain pulp as cheese.

She lit two more cigarettes and handed one each to Max and John. Homer didn't smoke; he was already fishing around in the pickup truck's backseat for their beers.

"Yeah, that really was some thirsty work, wasn't it?" he said, passing cans of Bud Light around.

"Yup, it sure was," Max agreed. Personally he felt winded. It had taken them almost twenty minutes of relentless pounding with the sledgehammers before he was satisfied that their father would be satisfied with the results. Despite their immense size and strength, both he and Homer were sweating bullets. The beers went well down their thirsty throats.

John Burke hadn't done anything except keep watch. Also the sledgehammers were his. As was the truck too, Homer having explained to him that seeing as Max and himself would be the primary suspects during any investigation, it was important for their alibis that they appeared not to have left home tonight.

John was squeamish about getting involved in violence anyway. He was also thinking that if at any point push came to shove, he'd be able to argue his way out of a prison sentence if he could prove he'd not had any hand in the actual killing.

They stood around like that, smoking and getting a buzz from the beers. Occasionally one of them would make a joke about Peter's remains.

The jokes reminded Max of something he needed to do. He got out a Polaroid 600 camera and reeled off a few flash-snaps of the dead kid. Then, using a penlight, he examined the photographs carefully, to ensure they had the right angles and perspectives. He handed them over to Homer, who also examined them.

Homer nodded. "Yeah, dad'll be sure now that we didn't fuck up. He wanted revenge for Tammy and we delivered."

"Yeah, you guys *really* delivered," Cleo agreed, puffing smoke out towards the pond.

"So . . . how do we dispose of him?" John asked. "Plan A or Plan B?"

Plan A was to burn the corpse. Plan B was to drown it, hence their current waterside location.

"Plan B," Max decided. "We can't burn it here—we'll attract too much attention—so we might as well just throw it in the water."

So that's what they did. They tied some old barbells (also John's property) to Peter Howard's arms and legs. Then they carried the mess they'd made of him to the side of Gushee Pond and, after selecting a nice secluded spot, flung it as far out into the water as they could—about twenty feet.

Then they waited awhile to ensure the body wouldn't resurface. When after thirty minutes it still hadn't come up, they decided they were in the clear and left for home.

All four of them were satisfied with the night's work.

V

Apache smiled coldly. "For two weeks no one could find Peter Howard. Of course, we easily located his ride: we found the station wagon the next day, in the parking lot behind Rudy's Truck Stop. But no one had seen who'd parked it there. Remember though, that he'd told his mom where he was going. Once we'd spoken to Malicia, our suspicion naturally fell on Cleo, who'd been the last person to talk to Peter. Cleo's story was that she'd arranged to meet with Peter over at Rudy's Truck Stop, just to comfort him, but that he'd never shown up; so after waiting for half an hour, she'd gone back home to Max's house, where she'd taken some aspirin and gone to sleep 'cos she'd had a bad headache. The truck stop waitresses confirmed that, yeah, Cleo had come in, drank a Coke and left. Seeing as we'd already found Peter's car behind the building, this should have confirmed her story; except that, well, she seemed real nervous each time we spoke to her. Tracking the signals from Cleo's phone proved a dud too. She'd left her cellphone at Max's house. And unfortunately for us, a friend had called her there while they were out killing Peter, and Max's mother Cissy had answered. She'd said Tammy had a headache and was in bed."

"Hold on. You just said Tammy went back to Max's place. So what's his mom doing there? That's suspicious, ain't it?"

"Not really. Thing is, Max and Homer both lived right next door to their parents. The Bylers owned three or four adjacent lots along Courtney Way, up near where the Blue Star Highway crosses the Taunton River; I think most of the land on the south side of the road was theirs. So Cleo saying she went to Max's place meant the same thing as her going to his parents' house."

He sighed. "The Byler family alibi was more waterproof than a frog's back. Both father and mother swore that neither of their sons had left the house all night. Cissy Byler clearly didn't approve of what they'd done, but no way was she going to let her husband and two of her sons go to jail for murder, not after just losing one daughter . . . and besides—she asked us—if Peter *was* actually dead, where was his body? Yeah, that baffled us too."

"So how'd you find him?" Sully asked. This *was* one hell of a story, he thought.

Apache smiled again. "How we found Peter? The Devil's luck, something you couldn't predict in a hundred years that just somehow happened. Two weeks later, a family of four were holding a picnic around where they threw the body in the pond. According to what we gathered, they were from Halifax, just passing through town on their way south, and they'd heard about Gushee Pond and decided it would be a lovely place to stop and have a picnic lunch. Well, after having lunch, the mother and father both dozed off, leaving the two kids playing. One child was two, the other eight; they said they'd told the elder one to watch his little sister and wake them if there was any trouble. Long story short, ten minutes later, the mother wakes up and can't find her eight-year-old son. She panics and wakes her husband. Meanwhile, the two-year-old keeps pointing at the pond. Both parents assume that since she's doing so, maybe the missing boy's drowned in there. So the father strips off and dives in. He doesn't find the boy, but he finds Peter down there, all rotting and tangled up with the water weeds. When the father comes up for air, scared out of his wits, who does he see, but his missing son returning from a jaunt in the woods with a garter snake in his hands. The kid had apparently forgotten he was supposed to keep an eye on his baby sister and had followed the snake into the trees."

Apache nodded grimly. "Odd though, how it never occurred to any of us that he might be submerged in there. I mean, everyone was always dumping stuff in Gushee Pond anyway. Whenever folks wanted to throw something away but didn't want to pay the disposal costs for it, they'd just drive out there and fling it in the water. Or, if it was too large to throw far, they'd leave it lying somewhere around the pond shore. Once, some conscientious townsfolk organized a cleanup drive for Gushee Pond and collected a whole dumpster's worth of trash, including furniture, a house's worth of carpeting, tires, and TVs. So why not dispose of a human body in there too?"

He nodded again. "Yeah, so anyway, that's *how* we found Peter Howard. And let me tell you right off the bat, the first time Tina and I set our eyes on his remains, we wished we'd *not* found him. . . . What he looked like? You just picture it: try to imagine the results if two guys—each about six-foot-five in height and ripped like Mr. Universe—began hitting another guy with sledgehammers." He paused and peered at Sully, waiting for a reply.

"They'd pulp him," Sully said, gulping at the image his mind showed him, "break all his bones."

"Uh huh," Apache agreed with him. "I recall asking the M.E. why the kid's head looked so odd—it was just a shapeless, featureless sack of flesh with muddy brown hair showing at some points. Know what she told me? She said every single bone in his skull had been shattered at least thrice." He squeezed up his face, trying to remember something. "Yeah, she also explained that at some point during that sledgehammer demolition of his features, Peter's entire mouth, both upper and lower jaws had moved sideways to the right side of his face, and both his eyes—I mean their exploded, empty remains—now lay on the left. I didn't believe that was even possible until she demonstrated by using a pair of tweezers to pull open two holes on the left of his face, near where his ear should have been, and I saw some white inside."

He paused speaking because Sully looked sick. Sully used the oral respite to empty his whiskey and order an orange juice. No more alcohol for him tonight. He'd be driving them home and cops didn't DUI.

"Make that two," Apache told the waiter. When the man had left, he told Sully, "I've had enough alcohol myself for one night. I'm beginning to slur my words and I want to tell this story straight, so you'll understand where I'm coming from. Now, yeah, where was I?"

"Peter Howard's eyes and mouth had shifted to the sides of his face?"

"Yes, they had. They were actually in a straight line. You could go across his face in a straight sequence from his right ear—I mean, ear, mouth, what remained of his nose, right eye, left eye, missing other ear—like that."

"That's disgusting."

"Yes it was. And that wasn't even the worst of it. Remember Peter had been in the water for a fortnight by then. . . . When we found him, he was all bloated up, swollen and rotten. Some little fishes had even gotten inside of him; they'd just swum in through the rips in his skin and made themselves at home. Most had died, but at least one that I saw came out asphyxiating, angrily flapping its little body like it had been beached. Peter was dripping with some blackish liquid. I remember Martha—that was the M.E.'s name—making an incision in the dead boy's chest and this thick rope of black goop spurting out. On seeing it, Tina Kravitz actually leapt back in fright—she thought it was a snake. But it was just some mess of mud and whatever he'd had for dinner the night he was killed. And the rest of his body was just as bad. His hands were so swollen and shapeless, it looked like he had giant baseball mitts on. Son, you following this?"

"Yeah, but get off it already, you're making me wanna puke."

"Sully, I mean, do you get *the point* of this? I ain't describing this 'cos I wanna make you sick. Are you noticing the similarities between the description we've got of our current murderer and . . . Nah, you still don't yet, do you?"

"I'm still here, old man. And I'm still listening. I want to hear everything first before making up my mind as to what I think about it."

"Fair enough. So I'll go on then. So that's what Peter looked like. A total mess."

"Hey, if he was that fucked-up looking, how'd you know it was him?"

"A good question. We suspected it was—I mean, we'd been looking for him. And you gotta remember that he still had the same clothes on. His wallet was in his pants, which first helped us ID him, but we also did some DNA tests to make sure—got the DNA from his toothbrush and some hair cuttings and toenail clippings in the trashcan in his bedroom. And we got a few good fingerprints off his hands which, once shrunk to normal size again, matched those on the cover of his laptop and on its keyboard. So finally, we were sure it was him that we'd pulled out of the pond. As an aside, that's where Forensics got the DNA profiles and prints they used to determine that it's Peter killing everyone now."

Apache raised a hand to forestall whatever Sully might have been about to say. "And next came the difficult part: we had to tell his mama. Tina and I went over to the bookstore to see her. It went much better than we'd expected, which should have warned us that something was up. But Tina and me? We were both like you are now—skeptics—so we didn't cotton on that the old lady was . . . ha ha! Cotton on, huh? Now there's a good joke for you."

"I don't see what's funny."

"Oh, but you will, son. You most certainly will." He leaned back and sipped his just-arrived orange juice.

VI

They sat in Malicia's living room over the bookshop to commiserate with her.

". . . We're sorry, Mrs. Howard. We really are. We've confirmed that it is Peter. We can't even ask you to come down to the morgue to identify him. There's just no way you could possibly recognize him in the shape he's in . . ."

Malicia Howard nodded at Tina Kravitz's words. She'd known Peter was dead; she'd sensed it in her heart. She'd known too that he'd died horribly, brutally; murdered by blind, merciless fools. It had taken her a while to overcome her initial surge of grief, but now she was calm, wrapped around by a sense of purpose.

She even managed to smile.

She suspected that her two visitors found her composure ghoulish and unsettling.

"A cot'n did it," she finally interrupted the female detective.

"What's that?" Apache Johnson asked. "What's a cotton?"

"Not 'cotton,' as in fabric," Malicia corrected, "but *cot'n*. C . . . O . . . T . . . apostrophe . . . N. It's an acronym meaning 'Child of the Night.' " She laughed softly, morbidly amused at the detective's perplexed gazes.

"Can you explain better?" Apache asked. To Malicia's mature eyes, the young half-Indian man was handsome but rather brash. He seemed to fancy himself a movie star, particularly with that silly ponytail he'd made of his black hair. The other detective, Tina Kravitz, she'd known since Tina was a child. The fat blonde was farmer Ed McKinney's recently wed daughter. Tina was okay, she was very smart and was quite pretty for an overweight woman. She too was staring at Malicia with deep interest in her gray eyes.

Malicia had also noticed that so far, Apache was letting Tina do most of their talking.

"*Cot'n?* Children of the Night?" Tina prompted. "That sounds like the name of a motorcycle gang. You're saying some bikers killed Peter?"

She shook her head. "No, not Peter. The cot'ns were what killed Tammy."

They stared at her in confusion. She'd expected them to. She explained, not really expecting them to understand: "A child of the night is an infernal pan-dimensional entity. Or what you'd call a demon. Tammy summoned one of them and it killed her."

Their eyes reflected her image back at her. Their faces projected their disbelief. She noted, however, that both detectives were polite enough not to say anything. Both clearly thought that her grief at losing her son so soon after her husband's death had begun to unhinge her mind. She knew it was dangerous to go on—if she said too much her sanity would soon be called into question—but she also felt compelled to explain what she knew to the pair.

"I didn't at first believe in the supernatural either," she stated calmly. "But now I do. I went through the book of spells Tammy used—it had been in the house for years but I'd never once read it—and everything is listed in there: blood rituals, human sacrifices, how to raise the dead, even."

"There's no such thing as magic," Apache seemed impelled to say. She could see he looked nervous though, like he didn't believe his own words.

She smiled coldly at him, which rattled him further. "No, detective? So how then did Tammy miraculously lose her acne? And the rest of her body?"

Neither Tina nor Apache had a reply to that, so Malicia went on: "I've been searching through my late husband's books on magic and I've discovered the truth. I know now how—"

"Ma'am, we're just here to talk about Peter," Tina interrupted softly, clearly desperate to return the conversation to a safe and logical thread. She was obviously scared of this discussion degenerating into a debate on spooks and Satan worship. "We're really sorry he died like he did. He was a nice kid."

"We're going to do everything in our power to bring his murderers to justice," Apache added solemnly.

His eyes were still disturbed though. Malicia knew her words about the cot'ns had bothered him. For her part, Tina Kravitz just looked sympathetic. Malicia appreciated the young woman's concern.

"Tammy's family are responsible," Malicia said firmly. "My son had no enemies. Peter got along with everyone. So Tammy's folks have to have killed him. They killed him. They killed my son."

"We've no evidence of that yet," Apache said brusquely. "But rest assured we're gonna leave no stone unturned to catch Peter's killers. You've got my word on that, Mrs. Howard."

Malicia smiled coldly. Oh, this Apache was smug, alright; he thought he knew it all. Here she was, her whole family dead now and the detective was doing his best to overlook the obvious. But that was the job of the police, wasn't it? To ignore what was staring them right in the face and waste everyone's time rooting in the mud for evidence.

A sudden violent pang went through her. An intense taste for blood filled her mouth. She was going to have to give everyone a demonstration. She wouldn't stand for people thinking her dead son *had* actually killed Tammy Byler, and as such had gotten what was coming to him. Losing Peter was bad enough. She wouldn't let the people of Raynham remember him like that. Oh, no!

The detectives rose to leave. "So please call us if you remember anything else that might be of use to us in solving this case," Tina said nicely as Malicia saw them to the door.

She nodded.

"Remember what I said, detectives," she said, right before they walked across to their car.

"What's that?" Tina asked.

"That Tammy was killed by the cot'ns—the children of the night. She made a deal with one of them to fix her face and it went awry with disastrous results."

Tina nodded, but didn't say anything.

At that statement, however, Apache's face had crinkled up in—was it irritation, or anger, or fear, or just plain pity at what her grief was doing to her? She couldn't tell. He didn't look happy in the least now though.

She watched from the porch as they drove off.

She shivered. Even though it was early August, it was a cold evening.

Or maybe she was just shivering with repressed rage at the horrible loss she'd suffered.

VII

"Like I said, she was too calm when we spoke to her," Apache said. "Tina too commented on it while I was driving us back to the station."

"You? Drive?" Sully laughed. "You actually sat behind the wheel of a squad car with your foot on the gas pedal?"

Both men had by this time finished their glasses of orange juice, but neither of them had requested a refill: Sully, because the tale had begun enthralling him; Apache, because he'd become spellbound by his memories.

"I wasn't always this old," Apache grinned back at him. "But anyways, we should have noticed the signs that she was going off the deep end."

"Hey, I thought you said she wasn't crazy."

"She wasn't. That ain't the deep end I'm referring to. Just hold on, wait patiently till I arrive us there. So . . . so we got back to investigating. Just like Malicia had pointed out, everyone in Raynham and their three-legged dog knew that the Byler family had killed Peter Howard. There clearly wasn't anyone else who was angry enough with Peter to bludgeon him to death with sledgehammers. But the Bylers all held together and didn't say a thing. We tried all kinds of investigative tricks—veiled threats, hinting at non-existent evidence, hinting at having witnesses, stakeouts, what have you—to get them to slip up, but they didn't. That was, not until Homer had his fight with Crystal."

"Crystal?"

"Crystal Parr. The hooker."

"Oh, her. She's involved in this too?"

"Yeah. She got us the breakthrough we needed."

"How? What happened?"

"What happened was that, Homer, who didn't have a girlfriend—remember I said he couldn't keep one—hired Crystal's services for the night. She was in her mid-twenties back then and even more popular than she is now. Sexy as hell. So, according to her, she and Homer fuck, but then he refuses to pay her what they'd agreed on. She gets mad and they have a fight—a screaming match really, remember Homer's a giant, if he'd hit Crystal even once, there'd be almost nothing of her left. . . . Well, they're both drunk, and while they're growling at each other, Homer threatens Crystal. What he says is: 'If you don't watch it, bitch, we'll do you up worse that we did Peter Howard.' Now Crystal isn't so drunk that she's lost all reason, and in the spirit of the argument she questions him: 'So it was you that killed that poor boy?', to which Homer beats his chest and replies, 'Yeah, me and Max and Johnny and Cleo too. And if you become a nuisance, we'll get rid of your skanky ass the same way. Only, this time we'll stow your corpse in a drum so you'll never be found!'

"That instantly sobers Crystal up. She pleads with Homer that it's cool, she'll forget what he owes her, and that she'll be good and not make any fuss; and then she leaves his house. I think she even gave him another blowjob first before leaving, just to calm him down. The next day, though, she walks into the police station and reports everything to Tina. So now, we've both got a witness and know who was involved in the murder."

"Great," Sully said.

Apache shook his head. "Nah, not so great. The DA still says we can't arrest anyone. Not enough evidence. Crystal is more than willing to testify in court, but Homer denies ever saying that to her. It's a classic he said/she said situation. And besides, remember they were both drunk at the time. To further muddy the waters, Homer openly admits that he refused to pay Crystal after screwing her, and claims she's trying to frame him for Peter's murder out of sheer malice."

"Lots of malice in this case, old man."

"Yeah, a bucketful of malice. Now listen: So, we're stuck. We haul all four of them in for questioning, but don't get anywhere. They all insist they want a lawyer before talking to us, and when they do get one, all claim they didn't do it. We get a search warrant. We go through both of the Byler boy's houses, and John Burke's and Cleo's places too. We find nada. But we're still hoping one of them will crack. If that's possible, it'll most likely be John Burke. He wasn't as hard as the others and each time we'd have him in the interrogation room, the possibility that he'd go to jail for a long time seemed to scare him shitless.

"Then we get another break. Forensics find a discarded beer can near where Peter was dropped in the pond. It was tucked away under some tree roots; the initial investigation had missed it completely."

"Fingerprints?"

Apache nodded. "Yeah. And guess whose they were?"

"John Burke, of course."

"Yeah. The only problem is, as this is two months after the murder, there's no way to pinpoint the actual day when the beer can was left there. When questioned, John says he went to the pond to see where Peter was killed and drank some beer there in his memory. But we know we've got him rattled for sure now.

"So anyhow, to pile the pressure on, we arrested all four of them on suspicion of murder and the DA sets up a preliminary hearing. The evidence is wafer-thin, but we think we can swing it. Cleo and Max had also just broken up over the fact that he'd given her yet another black eye, and we think we can get her to testify against him—she clearly *wasn't* the one who beat Peter to death, she's much too little to even lift the sledgehammer . . . so if we get the two brothers and John we'll drop the charges against her. We've felt her out, but she's still adamant, still in love with Max and hoping to get back together with him. But we're certain that if we put enough pressure on her egg, the cracks'll start showing. Being charged with murder and facing a life sentence does wonders for a woman's sense of romantic loyalty.

"And so, that's how we all arrived at the Taunton District Court on Friday the 13th of October."

Apache grimaced. "I was there in court on that fateful day, and now I really, really wish that I hadn't been. I remember that day like it was yesterday. Judge Snelson was presiding—"

"Snelson? Is this Judge Snelson any relation to our dead Ronald Snelson?"

"Yeah. He was the dead kid's grandfather. The judge was a good, decent man; honest and upright. The old guy definitely didn't deserve what happened to him."

VIII

The courtroom session had only a few attendees that afternoon, less even than the number of pimples on Tammy Byler's face before she died.

From the middle of the right-hand aisle (as one entered) Detective James 'Apache' Johnson looked around the courtroom. He nodded. They'd not held any press conferences about the case, nor given any dates to the media, but nonetheless, some media vultures had managed to smell the reek of the corpse. Apache knew two of the five press folk in attendance. He waved and nodded to Sheryl Gump of the Taunton Daily Gazette and Matthew Collard of the Boston Globe. The other three he assumed were journalists because they were seated in the same rear row of the gallery as Gump and Collard and were engaged in conversation with them.

He returned his attention forward. They were still waiting for the judge.

Apache ran his eyes across the counsel's tables. First he studied the prosecution's table. Shannon Riley, the prosecuting attorney, looked calm and confident in her white pantsuit as she discussed a point of law with her team. Apache was certain her smile was a front: there was no way she could be confident with the scant evidence they'd found.

Beside Shannon sat Crystal Parr, wearing a long-sleeved blue dress with white collar and cuffs. Crystal had dyed her brunette hair red for the trial. This however, was her only attempt at looking hot and sexy.

The usually flamboyant young hooker looked a little flustered, as if certain that the moment she finished giving her testimony, she'd in turn be arrested and arraigned for serial prostitution. Or maybe it was the sensible clothing she'd been forced to wear to court making her uncomfortable, and she was dying to get back to her routine garb of braless tube tops, denim hot pants and eight-inch heels. Once a hooker, always a hooker. Damn, Crystal even had glasses on. She looked like a responsible young schoolteacher, not one of the Raynham menfolk's most prized sexual possessions.

Apache shifted his gaze to the defense's table. Seated beside defense attorney Jules Jordon, the four suspects looked calm enough: Max and Homer in matching black suits like they were attending a wedding or a wake; John Burke in a blue pinstriped one; and Cleo Beauchamp looking even more sensible than Crystal did in a simple white dress, a black jacket, and a necklace of fake pearls. Apache shook his head; it was amazing what a dose of 'we might go to jail' did for people's dress sense. Here, no matter how guilty they were, everyone looked sane and exhibited their best behavior. The cracks never showed until the cross examinations began.

Cissy and Bart Byler and the other parents of the accused were seated behind their children, in the first row behind the rail. Which made Apache look around for Malicia Howard. Surely she'd be attending this hearing? He didn't think she'd want to miss this.

He looked around, but at first didn't see Malicia.

He made his way forward through the aisle. He wanted to get a good look at the suspects' faces before Judge Snelson emerged from his chambers.

Once he could see the four clearly, Apache frowned. Max and Homer had barely-concealed smirks of amusement on their faces.

Cleo looked tense. She was also gripping Max's hand.

Not a good sign there, Apache thought. *It looks like they're already back together again. Fashion conscious as she is, maybe she needs a second black eye to balance out the first.*

John Burke was visibly trembling and not doing a great job of hiding it.

Let the spineless bastard sweat, Apache thought. *He knows we've pegged him at the crime scene with those fingerprints on that beer can. He's likely praying that the judge accepts his lie that he only went there afterwards. I really hope he cracks under the pressure. Damn murdering son-of-a-bitch.*

"You're hoping they're gonna hang themselves with their own tongues, right?" The voice was a soft whisper coming his way.

He turned to nod at his partner. Tina Kravitz was her usual pretty blonde self; bright and cheerful even though the proceedings were dull.

"More or less," he agreed. They walked back towards the center row of gallery benches. There, he got out of the way so she could walk in ahead of him. This took a little while: Tina Kravitz was a very fat woman, not one designed by nature to squeeze into tight spaces. And since getting married, she'd gotten even fatter.

"It's our only chance of convicting them now," he continued, speaking to her back. "We need to get them to turn on themselves."

"I hope they do too," she said as they both sat down. "Working this case just gives me the creeps. It ain't so much that they killed the young man that upsets me this much, but *how* they did it—pounding him to mush like that. Apache, you were at Peter's funeral, you saw how his momma burst into tears like she was dying inside."

Apache remembered Peter's funeral service, held at the Riendeau-Mulvey Funeral Home. In a marked contrast to when they'd visited her at home, that day at the funeral Malicia Howard had seemed like a broken woman. She'd looked ethereal, made of fluff, a rag doll with all the stuffing pulled out of it. Flanked by her brother-in-law and her cousins, Malicia had seemed lost, afloat and adrift on waves of sorrow no one else could possibly comprehend. The woman had remained in her emotional limbo until the coffin was wheeled out of the hall on its one-way, no-stop trip to the crematory. And then she'd broken down completely. She'd gotten so hysterical that her brother-in-law Ray Howard had led her out of the funeral hall and driven her home.

Tina pointed forward and little to the left. "Hey, Apache, there's Malicia now."

Apache followed her chubby finger. Peter's mother was seated all by herself in the third row of the middle section of benches. From their vantage point they had a good view of her profile.

"She seems recovered," he said.

"No," Tina said flatly, "that woman ain't recovered in the least." She nudged him with her elbow. "Apache, take a *good look* at her face. I mean a really *good* look."

Apache leaned forward and did so. He saw what Tina meant. Despite his logical brain telling him there was nothing to worry about, he felt chilled.

Chilled because Malicia Howard was laughing softly to herself. There was a look on her face that said, 'I know something you don't.'

He mentioned this to Tina.

"No," Tina promptly retorted, "She don't know anything that we don't. She's just going crazy. Look at her clothes, for chrissakes!"

Apache had already noticed them. Malicia Howard was dressed all in red. Red long-sleeved dress, red hat, red scarf wrapped around her neck because of the autumn chill outside, red handbag. Red the exact color of freshly spilled blood.

Then Tina's voice turned a little unsure. "You don't think . . . you think she's maybe smuggled a gun into the courtroom?"

Apache could easily visualize the bereft and enraged mother pulling out a pistol and putting bullets into the heads of the four suspects in front of her. Still, he shook his head. "She wouldn't be able to sneak it past the metal detectors."

"Don't be too certain, Apache. Us girls have hiding places that you men don't even suspect." Tina clearly meant this as a joke, but it didn't come off. Apache felt too tense to laugh. His unease was infecting her too.

It was at this exact moment that Malicia Howard turned to look at them, and with a psychotic grin on her face, winked. She waved to them. Her lips and fingernails were painted that same blood-red. She had on red eyeshadow too.

Apache froze, as did Tina. Why the hell would a bereaved mother wink at them? And why the hell was she all colored up like that?

Malicia looked forward again. She resumed laughing softly to herself.

"You're right, Tina," Apache said, "she *is* going crazy."

They had no further time to discuss it. Up on the bench, Judge Snelson had just taken his seat.

The judge was an old man, due for retirement any day now. Small, stout and gray-haired. Positioned there at the head of everyone, he looked like an idol they'd gathered to worship.

The judge banged the gavel and court was in session.

***

It didn't take long for the trouble to start. Not long at all.

It began when Homer Byler was in the witness box. He'd just taken the oath and prosecutor Shannon Riley had begun questioning him, when . . .

The courtroom lights abruptly dimmed. They didn't go off entirely. They just dimmed enough so it was impossible to see what anyone was doing. Everyone became shadows. What had been bright artificial noon a moment ago was suddenly late evening.

And so no one at first observed what Malicia Howard was up to.

***

Malicia had initially figured that with her red dress on, no one would notice when she cut her arm in the courtroom, just like with her other self-inflicted wounds. But then she'd seen those two nosy detectives behind her. They were certain to be watching her, so she'd decided a simple spell to dim the lights for a few moments would suffice till she got her show under way. Then the lights could come back up again. She didn't want anyone present to miss a thing.

While the court officials tried to work out the problem with the lights, or failing that, get the technicians to switch over to an auxiliary power supply, Malicia took advantage of the confusion to get busy. All around her, people were talking in hushed voices of varying loudnesses.

A woman yelled from the back of the hall: "Hey, someone's locked the doors! We're all shut in here!" A similar loud complaint came from the front of the hall on her left.

This too was Malicia's doing. Another spell had sealed off all the courtroom entrances. She didn't want anyone leaving till she was done.

She peeked quickly back at the detectives. Both were on their feet and exiting their seating row, apparently off to check the locked doors. Yes, they were: once out in the aisle they turned forward, exiting the rail gate and moving toward the right side exits. As with the other doors, several court officers were already over there trying to figure out the problem with its lock.

Good. No, perfect. Smiling, she reached into her red handbag.

In the three months since her son's death, Malicia had become very proficient in magic. She'd put herself through an intense crash course on the subject, learning everything she could. She'd figured it had to be easy to get the hang of: if Tammy Byler could do so with such regrettable success, then so could she. And besides, like Tammy, she only wanted to know a few things, just the stuff she needed to make today one of the most memorable days ever in the history of the Taunton District Court.

Now, unnoticed, she pulled back her sleeve and slit her left forearm with a sharpened nail file. Not her wrist: if she cut herself there the blood would be certain to spill into her palm, and she needed to be able to hold things. She cut her arm deeply so the blood would flow freely. Then she reached into her handbag again and brought out three things: two ugly dolls and a small jar containing a ground paste of dead worms, newt and toad guts, cockroach heads, and other horrible stuff like that.

The confusion around her was music to her ears. The judge was banging his gavel and asking everyone to calm down. But the hubbub just increased.

And it hasn't even really begun yet.

While whispering a spell, she held the little dolls under her bleeding arm until they were both soaked red. She let more blood drip into the nauseating mix in the jar.

Then grinning like a witch, Malicia spoke the spell to undim the courtroom lights.

She however kept all the doors locked shut. Now the fun would begin.

***

"And here we've got two bad-to-the-bone redheads," Tina had been joking about Crystal Parr and Cleo Beauchamp before the lights dimmed. "When it's their turns to be questioned, Shelby shouldn't bothering with calling their names. He should just say: 'We now summon the redhead for the prosecution to the witness box,' or 'The redhead for the defense.' Everyone in court will know who he's referring to."

Apache had thought it a great joke; one to take his mind off his worries. He'd been laughing.

But then everything just turned crazy on them, and he and Tina had found themselves running through shadows while all across the hall everyone made noises indicating different shades of confusion.

He and Tina were down at the right side door when the lights brightened up again. The doors still weren't opening, but with proper lighting now restored to the courtroom, that wasn't so much of a problem anymore. Worst case scenario? The doors would be cut through or blown open from the outside.

With the lights back to full power, Judge Snelson's voice now came over the speakers again. "Please take your seats, everyone, and let's resume the hearing. The appropriate department will have the doors open shortly."

People seemed to agree with him. Quickly, the small groups that had been forming at the exits dissolved and the benches filled again.

"We'd better get back to our seats too," Tina told Apache. Without waiting for his reply, she turned and headed back towards the gallery.

Apache followed a few paces behind her. When they reached their row, Tina once more entered in first. And again, Tina's massive body meant it took her awhile to reach her seat.

While waiting for his partner to make her way inward, Apache passed the time watching Homer Byler in the witness box.

And that was how he didn't miss a single thing that happened.

The prosecutor was about to resume questioning Homer. She'd just tapped her microphone to make sure it was working, when . . .

All of a sudden Homer began twitching. Next, the huge young man leapt to his feet.

Homer stood bolt-upright like that, fixed in place and trembling, while everyone in the courtroom gaped at him. To the detectives, he seemed to be having some kind of a fit. But then—and everyone present both heard and saw this—to the loud noise of bones shattering, Homer's body crumpled inwards. Homer began screaming in agony and didn't stop. He imploded slowly, his torso and hips moving inwards from both sides as if he was being squeezed between the giant jaws of a divine vise, his shattered ribs tearing bloody holes in his black suit.

Relentlessly then, while he howled in pain and spat and dribbled blood from his mouth and nose, he grew steadily thinner, while whatever force was crushing his torso continued doing so with implacable power. Thinner and thinner and thinner. Impossibly so; comically so even, though no one watching was laughing.

Every eye stared; all were horrified at what they were witnessing.

Then the invisible compressing force gave Homer a final merciless squeeze and his eyes gaped wider than ever and his guts exploded out of his mouth. The force dropped him then. He fell over the front of the witness box, with half of his intestines hanging from between his lips.

All this took thirty seconds to complete.

Homer's death would have produced enough confusion, but the same force had now also seized Max Byler. This time the force yanked him up into the air, holding him in space in the front of the courtroom. There in midair, it twisted him like a pretzel. Max shrieked for help as the upper and lower halves of his body were rotated in different directions—once, twice, thrice . . . six times in all. All the while, along with the horrifying visual of Max both vomiting blood and squirting more of it from his destroyed flesh, the noise of his shattering bones filled the air.

A large gush of Max's blood spattered Cleo Beauchamp in the face. She instantly fainted.

Beside her, John Burke shook with fear. John clearly thought he'd be the next one to die.

Unlike Homer's corpse, Max's body didn't topple over. The twisted corpse hung there in the air for everyone to see. The dead man's eyes were open; his stomach dangled from his mouth like a purple balloon he'd been blowing up.

So far, except for a few other women who'd fainted, no-one had moved. After Homer's inexplicable death, the court security guards had started towards him, but once the same unseen force had levitated Max, they'd frozen in place and just gaped up at him. Shock had frozen everyone. It was like morbidly watching that impossible-to-ignore Asian Tsunami disaster on TV: being revolted by what you saw, but nonetheless receiving the thrill of appreciation of one's own personal well-being from it.

Apache and Tina had been as confused as everyone else. They were still confused. Thoughts had been machine-gunning through Apache's head that Malicia Howard was somehow involved in what was going on, but when he looked forward at her, she didn't seem to be doing anything. She was however grinning at the deaths.

Then Apache looked up towards the judge's bench and gasped.

"Look!" he pointed out to Tina. "Behind Judge Snelson!"

It was a needless observation to make. Tina Kravitz could see it as well as he did. She'd noticed it before he had.

In fact, Judge Snelson was the only one in the courtroom *not* to notice the thing forming on the wall behind him. After just managing to sit through Homer and Max's deaths, the court clerk had abandoned her post on the right of the witness box and taken to her heels. Now she huddled over by the locked door on the right. Likewise the bailiff, who'd been standing almost directly under Max and had been 'rained on' by his squirting blood.

The judge, however, was still gaping at Max's suspended corpse. The old man looked stupefied. He appeared to be wondering if a horror of this magnitude deserved him having a heart attack or not. Even when the bailiff and two guards gestured furiously at him, trying to get his attention, trying to get him to either turn around or get out of his enclosure, he kept staring at Max. His problem was obvious: to his befuddled mind, it would seem utterly impossible for anything else happening to top what he was currently looking at.

No one present was about going up to the bench to forcefully remove Judge Snelson. No one dared.

The wood paneling behind the old judge bulged with tentacles. Large greenish and black tentacles that flailed. Amidst the mass of tentacles shone two large eyes. Huge yellow serpentine eyes that glowed with malevolent intent.

The thing coming through the wall exited it fully. It was about the size of a horse or a cow. It seemed to have three legs. Other than that, it looked like a mass of black worms that someone had twisted up into a ball.

For a moment, it hung over Judge Snelson like a melted Sword of Damocles, casting a strange shadow over the old man.

There was a hush in the courtroom. Even the guards, who'd been desperately trying to call outside on their radios, shut up and stared. (Their radios weren't working: one couldn't call through a magic shield. Every telecommunication device in the courtroom was similarly dead, including apparently the CCTV, which should otherwise have alerted those outside to the crazy courtroom happenings and brought swift help.)

Apache and Sully had gotten their guns out, as had most of the other law enforcement officers present, but no one had fired yet.

The shadow of the creature hanging over the judge finally alerted him to its presence overhead. He stopped staring at the corpse floating in midair in front of him. Following the distracted gaze of everyone else, he slowly lifted his own eyes to see what they were all gaping at.

He never finished the motion. He never saw the creature above him.

Suddenly the ball of tentacles dipped a few feet then rose again.

Once it had lifted again, everyone saw that it had ripped Judge Snelson's head off. In fact, the creature had done more than just rip the poor judge's head off: it had bitten off his entire head and shoulders. His arms fell to the floor. His torso remained upright, as though still overseeing proceedings. Blood jetted out from his exposed heart.

The monster meanwhile, floated forward and began eating Max Byler's suspended corpse.

Hardly anyone was paying much attention to this, however. Everyone was now screaming and making bee lines for the still-locked exits.

Because now, ten or fifteen more of the things that had killed the judge were coming in through the courtroom walls. The guards were shooting at them, but the bullets fired didn't look to be having any effect.

And this was when Apache and Tina really paid attention to Malicia Howard again.

***

Malicia Howard was delighted with the results she was getting.

After she'd had gotten through squeezing the life from both Max and Homer with the pair of voodoo dolls she'd brought to court, she'd decided it was time to summon the cot'ns. She'd thrown the dolls away, picked up her jar of bloodied witch-stuff and begun chanting the necessary spell. It was a simple spell, but one that needed constant repetition to keep the infernal gateways open.

Eid l'lal liw seimene ym noos, noos!
Meht l'lik, meht l'lik!

Once the first cot'n had eaten Judge Snelson's head and the other cot'ns had penetrated the courtroom walls and pandemonium was in full swing, Malicia decided to let everyone know who was responsible for what was happening, and why she was doing it.

So she leapt up on top of her bench—a fury in red clothes—and began screaming:

"Hey, Bart and Cissy Byler! Listen to me, you two old idiots! You didn't believe me that Peter didn't kill Tammy, yeah!? Well, I'm sure you believe me now, right!?"

The old couple she was addressing didn't hear her at first. They, along with John Burke's parents, were desperately trying to force open the left front side exit. Cleo Beauchamp was still out cold and her father was trying both to move her and not to become a victim of the creature that had killed her boyfriend. The tentacled thing hung above them, writhing and dripping blood while still eating Max's corpse.

Down at the front of the courtroom, the court clerk was long since dead, that hapless lady now merely a series of garish red streaks across the wood paneling behind where she'd once sat.

The cot'ns had begun killing people freely now, swooping down low and plucking them up into the air and pulling their heads and limbs off. Everyone was in a state of panic, trampling on themselves in their desperation to flee the courtroom.

It was only when Malicia mockingly yelled, "You can't get out! Not one of you will leave here alive! The children of the night will eat you all! I've sacrificed you to them!" that everyone stopped what they were doing and turned and stared at her.

And once the full import of her words hit them, they all resumed screaming again.

***

Amidst the frenzied panic consuming everyone, Apache did his best to think clearly.

He wanted to get close to Malicia Howard without being killed and eaten.

This seemed impossible to do. There were at least eight corpses in the courtroom now, each one covered by a squirming mass of black tentacles that was bloodily eating it. The cot'ns were messy feeders; every now and then a severed arm or leg would go flying through the air. The most recent of these airborne limbs had almost hit Tina Kravitz in the face.

Apache had pulled Tina down just in time.

"Just frigging stay down," he'd insisted. Now they both lay on the right aisle rug, while the monsters floated overhead.

One additional thing that surprised Apache was how the temperature in the hall had risen steeply since the monsters' appearance. Almost as if all the air conditioners had failed at once. It felt like a sauna in here now.

I guess I do believe in the damn supernatural now, he thought grimly.

Looking either up or down the aisle revealed bloody carnage. Like a punted football, a man's severed head was rolling toward them from the main entrance. In the opposite direction, at the front of the courtroom, they could see a hapless group of guards firing up at a tentacled mass that was falling towards them.

And amidst the screams and gunshot noises, Apache could hear Malicia chanting, her voice like the eerie tolling of a feminine doomsday bell. Occasionally, she'd break off her chanting. She'd yell, "Feed, cot'ns, feed! Children of the night, eat your fill of sweet human flesh! Feed until they believe me!" Then she'd resume chanting again.

Apache suddenly had an idea of how to stop her.

"Don't move," he warned Tina as he got to his feet.

"Where the hell are you going?" she queried.

"I'm off to shut the witch up."

"Just shoot her, man."

"Bullets don't work against magic." He pointed. "Look!"

She looked. Down at the front of the hall, one of the cot'ns had snared a court officer by wrapping its tongue around his neck. The other guards where firing at it, but the gunshots weren't making the slightest difference. The tentacled demon kept doing what it was doing: it yanked the snared man off his feet and flung him towards the rear of the hall. The screaming man cartwheeled over the benches, soaring over Apache and Tina, to finally crash down in a moaning tangle of broken limbs two rows behind them. The demon that had flung him had meanwhile latched on to another court officer and was eating him alive where he stood, while his terrified companions continued firing at it without any effect.

"I don't wanna shoot Malicia and find out that bullets don't work on her either, and wind up like that guy," Apache explained to Tina. "I need to get up close and personal with her."

She nodded. Apache didn't say any more. He didn't wait to consider his options either. He knew that if he did so, he'd stay here pressed down on the floor beside Tina.

I've got to stop her chanting! I've got to stop her chanting!

He crawled forward two rows, then leapt up onto the bench and hurried towards Malicia, who was standing up on its farther end, her red dress like crimson liquid flowing down her body. She was turned away from him and didn't see him coming. Despite which, he was forced to duck as one of the airborne balls of tentacles with glowing yellow eyes swooped low, coming in from the front of the courtroom. He got out of its way just in time. It went over him and landed on the broken-but-still-alive man its fellow demon had earlier hurled across the hall.

The man's screams as the monster bit into him caused Apache to look that way. He didn't want to, but the sound of the victim's anguish compelled him to. Malicia was still looking the other way, intent on her mockery of the Bylers, who, though white-faced, quivering with fear and sweating profusely from the impossible heat, were both miraculously still alive and cowering by the left front-of-courtroom door. John Burke and Cleo Beauchamp seemed to have so far survived too. As had the prostitute Crystal Parr, who was huddled down with them and who looked like she wished she was currently safely locked away in prison for her many sexual offences against public decency.

"You're gonna die believing, Bart, you malicious son-of-a-bitch! How dare you kill my only son because of that ditzy, pimply girl of yours!?"

"Please, Malicia, stop it!" came Cissy Byler's anguished plea, her voice filled with the pain of having watched her two grown sons die before her very eyes. "We're sorry, we really are! We do believe you now! Yes, we shouldn't have killed Peter! Just, please, stop killing everyone!"

Malicia seemed to relent for a moment. Her shoulders slumped and her head tilted sideways like she was considering relenting in her massacre, but then her body tensed again and she yelled: "Screw you,

Cecelia! You should have stopped that knucklehead you married from killing my young Peter!"

And then she resumed chanting again, while screams of distress resounded around the hall of justice.

Because of this interlude/discussion, Apache Johnson had enough time to get a good look at the man the demon was eating. He got a *really* good look at how it fed. Hanging above the man like an airborne jellyfish, the quivering pile of worms worked its green tentacles into the officer's body as if they were giant corkscrews, each one twisting in circles as it penetrated the victim's flesh. Blood squirted everywhere. Indeed, sucked up by the centrifugal force of the appendages' whirling motions, a lot of the blood actually flowed *up* the tentacles towards the demon's body, like cherry soda ascending straws. The man was dead in five seconds flat, and then the cot'n carved him up like he was a rare-cooked roast, using other tentacles tipped with deviously sharp blades. The resulting red chunks of law enforcement officer were pulled up into its underside, the dead man's guts unreeling as they were raised so that they looked like tentacles themselves, composite parts of the feeding monster.

Apache had seen enough. Indeed, he realized he'd been foolish to look at all. Not because he might have attracted the feeding demon's attention to himself, but because at any second while his attention had been diverted, Malicia Howard could have noticed him and summoned another cot'n to eat him too.

Now though, his mind full of the horror he'd just witnessed, he briskly stepped up behind Malicia and grabbed her with both hands. His left arm went around her belly to hold her tight to him, while he clamped his right hand equally tightly over her mouth.

He had a moment's wonder at how strangely 'wet' she felt, and then she was fighting against him with every ounce of strength in her body. She kicked and fussed and hit at him with her fists.

Then she began biting his hand.

Apache felt her teeth go through the skin of his hand. In an instant reaction to the pain, he let go of her mouth and staggered back. His palm already dripped with blood.

Malicia immediately resumed her chanting again. But in those fifteen seconds when he'd stopped her mouth, Apache had noticed a clear difference in the courtroom: the infernal temperature had dropped several degrees and two of the cot'ns had vanished, one fading into nothingness just when it had seemed as if nothing could stop it from ripping the head off the lady reporter from the Taunton Daily Gazette.

And now, as Malicia resumed her dire spellcasting, three more tentacle-demons appeared in midair.

Taking a break in her incantation, Malicia turned and spat at him. "To hell with you too, Apache! I wasn't going to kill you before, but now—"

Apache didn't wait to hear what she had planned for him. He leapt forward, grabbed her again, and clamped his bleeding hand back over her mouth.

Confident that her previous tactics would work again, she resumed biting him, while at the same time kicking and stomping on his feet and elbowing him and wriggling left and right and flinging her head back, trying to head-butt him.

He held on. Even when he felt her teeth go through the skin of his palm for the second time and this time sink into the muscle beneath, he held on. The cot'ns were fading fast now and Apache wasn't taking any chances on letting Malicia bring them back. If he made the mistake of letting her go he knew he'd be the first one she'd have them kill.

Yes, the cot'ns were dispersing, like wisps of black smoke dissolving into the air, or like balls of dyed cotton thread unraveled and borne out of sight on a spectral wind.

So he held on, held on while the blood spilled out from under his torn-up hand; held on through the excruciating pain that raced up and down his right arm and made it feel like his arm was being baked in a furnace; held on even when—horror of horrors—he felt the enraged woman in his clutches completely bite away the mouthful of flesh she'd had between her teeth and swallow it, then resume biting out a fresh chunk of his hand. He howled as her teeth sank into the raw wound but didn't let go of her mouth. He was losing blood from his hand at an alarming rate.

Still, Apache held on, because by now the courtroom was normal again. There were no cot'ns left in it anymore—no more whirling masses of flying black worm-things eating everyone.

The temperature had also dropped back to normal.

The only things out of place were all the corpses everywhere. And they were literally *everywhere*. All over the aisles, all over the gallery, and all over the well of space at the front of the courtroom. Bits and pieces of humans were strewn about like wet refuse spilled from a trashcan. Intestines hung over the backs of benches, quartered limbs littered the aisles, chunks of half-eaten viscera lay spilled all over the courtroom like leftovers from a lunatic's lunch. Scraps of human skin were draped over the bar like laundry; the far-left portion of the bar railing had even fractured and impaled someone's left arm—the rest of the victim was missing.

Chillingly, so far as Apache could make out, there didn't seem to be even one single corpse anywhere that was still whole. All those visible had more parts missing than remaining.

She-it! The goddamned demons had a real lunch party here today.

Apache held on to Malicia, who kept fighting him, seeking to free herself and bring back the cot'ns to resume wreaking her enraged vengeance on everyone. She bit off and swallowed more of his palm, drank the blood that poured from the wound, and did everything womanly possible to make him let go of her, including reaching back with both hands and feeling between Apache's legs for his testicles, which he barely managed to keep safely out of her way.

Then, just when he thought he'd have to let go of her, he felt someone tugging on his trouser leg. He looked down from the bench. Tina Kravitz was behind him, down in the space between the rows.

Tina was holding a taser.

"Let her go," Tina whispered up to him. "I got her anti-stress medication right here."

Malicia hadn't yet seen Tina. Apache nodded. He let go of Malicia and quickly stepped back. Tina immediately rammed the taser against Malicia's right thigh.

The jolt of electricity put the angry woman straight to sleep.

The incapacitated Malicia Howard settled down on the court bench. Apache turned to stare at Tina. Tina's suit was plastered to her body, soaked through with sweat, just like his was.

"I guess it worked then," was all he could say to her.

White-faced, Tina nodded back at him. She took one look at his ruined hand, managed not to throw up, then hurried past him to duct-tape Malicia Howard's mouth shut, before the woman revived again.

Then she got out a set of handcuffs and secured Malicia's hands behind her back, so that she'd not be able to get the duct tape off her face.

Apache's hand . . . his hand was a separate universe of pain, something eerily detached from him. While tightly gripping his right wrist to staunch the bleeding, he examined the wound's jagged edges. He wondered at how sharp Malicia's teeth were; it was almost as if she'd filed them to points. It was hard to believe the damage she'd done: in the shape of a roughly right-angled triangle, all the flesh from the base of his right thumb to the opposite end of the wrist and up to the base of his little finger was missing. The entire meaty portion of his hand. Vanished down Malicia's throat. He could see the bones inside his hand; covered with blood, but clearly visible now that the muscle covering them had been ripped away. Worse yet, he'd just discovered he could no longer flex his right pinky finger. Malicia had eaten the muscles and ligaments that worked it. Even his thumb didn't seem to work right anymore.

Apache gaped down at Malicia Howard in horror. Tina had just gotten through securing Malicia's ankles with duct tape.

"She ain't either about saying anything or going anywhere now," Tina said, a grim but satisfied look on her face.

Malicia's red dress had ridden up her legs when she'd sprawled on the bench. Apache thought the tops of her knee-length red boots looked bloodstained, but before he got a proper look at them, Tina was dragging him away from there.

"Come on, we need to get your hand looked at," she said as she led him out between the benches and up the right aisle, both of them stepping over pieces of dead people as they went. "We still can't get the doors open or call out, but there's a first aid kit at the back there." She scowled at him. "You may not be bleeding to death, Apache, but I sure as hell don't wanna be your partner if you've got witch rabies."

IX

"Fuck," Sully gasped in disbelief. "I'd never have suspected that's what happened in a million years. So . . . how'd you guys finally get out?"

"Fire department broke down the doors with axes. Once they got a good look inside, though . . ." Apache stared into the bottom of his glass. "Now you're not gonna believe this either, but what they told us later was, that no one outside—not one single person in the entire building—had even the slightest idea that anything weird was going on inside that courtroom." He nodded at Sully's surprise. "Yeah, that's right, son: all that time while we were fighting for our lives, everyone outside could still hear Judge Snelson conducting proceedings." He shook his head. "Don't ask me *how* Malicia did it. All I know is that she did. The CCTV didn't work either. The guys monitoring the cameras were having fun: eating donuts, drinking coffee and admiring prosecutor Shannon Riley's ass."

"Her ass?"

"She had a nice one. Almost everyone admired it. I did once or twice myself."

"Just go on."

"Okay, now on to the body count: Nineteen people died in there. But there were only two complete bodies. Eight of the dead—guys like Max Byler—only had maybe a hand or a leg left of 'em; they were identified by DNA matching. We did, of course, have most of Judge Snelson, but his head and shoulders were gone. Both the prosecution and defense teams were all dead. I think all that remained of Shannon Riley were her head, right arm and belly button, which had slipped out between one of the demon's teeth. Her great ass was gone, swallowed down a demon's throat.

"There was no logical explanation for what had happened, so the authorities made one up. It helped that aside from the journalists and court officers, the only others who'd seen what really happened—and survived to talk about it—were folks from Raynham. And most of the dead were cops—okay, two of the five journalists got eaten too—so in retrospect, it was easier than it might have been to sweep it under the carpet. The Raynham Board of Selectmen and Taunton City Council got together with the State Police authorities and concocted a story and fed that to the press."

Sully was intrigued. "What could they possibly say that anyone would swallow? I mean, once the story got out and the TV crews arrived?"

Apache laughed dryly at the question. "Oh, I'll get to that in a bit. But first things first: Now, the immediate aftermath of the massacre was that Malicia Howard was taken away, straight to the loony bin. The Taunton State Hospital ambulance collected her from the court premises and we never saw her again until last week. And never wanted to either. As far as everyone was concerned, she could rot

200

away in there. As Tina blithely put it: 'A witch out of sight is a law enforcement delight.' "

"But . . . if you guys knew she wasn't nuts, it wouldn't be hard for the shrinks to work that out too."

Apache laughed, a cold, cold noise that sounded like he had tuberculosis. "Oh, I worried about that too at first: that she'd be given a clean bill of mental health and we'd have to deal with her again. But that turned out to be a baseless fear."

"What d'you mean, baseless?"

"Oh, she helped us incarcerate her."

"She *helped* you lock her away? How?"

"Remember how I said she felt wet? Well, her dress *was* wet. And there was a very good reason—no, a very *bad* reason—for that."

"She'd been sweating? You said everyone was soaking because of the heat."

"No, no, Malicia wasn't sweating. I was holding on to her and she wasn't sweating. She was as cool as deodorant spray."

"So what then?"

"She was *bleeding*. She was wearing that red dress because she was bleeding."

"You mean she was having her period?"

"No, not that, Sully. Malicia was already well past menopause by then. The damn woman had cut herself all over her body."

"What?" Sully looked confounded.

"Yeah, I saw the photos myself. She'd sliced sixty-six little symbols into her skin. Most of the symbols were routine black magic shapes— upside-down crosses and pentagrams. But there were a number of other designs she'd cut into her skin, crazy squiggles that I'd never seen before but which nonetheless scared me shitless. Just viewing those things, you knew they were evil. All the markings were dripping with blood. In some places, she'd sliced herself open all the way down to the muscle below. And amazingly, the shapes weren't just on the front of her body: she'd also somehow marked up her back too, sliced *perfectly-shaped* pentagrams on her back. Never seen anything like that either before or since. It must have taken her literally hours to do . . . and . . . and just imagine the amount of pain she'd have been in while opening herself up like that. She'd have needed to be fueled by intense hatred to mutilate herself so severely.

"And . . . hey, you recall what I said, how before Tina pulled me away to get my hand looked at, that I'd noticed how the tops of the woman's boots looked bloodstained? Well, they actually *were* bloodstained: those red boots were literally filled to the brim with blood that had dribbled down Malicia's legs. How she'd ever walked into court in them without leaving bloody footprints is best left to the imagination."

"Wow," was all Sully could contribute. His face, though, told a story of equal parts disgust and fascination.

"Yeah, wow," Apache agreed. "Needless to say, with all that self-mutilation in evidence, combined with the cannibalism she'd performed on me, it was easier to get Malicia committed than declared sane." He laughed. "Now, here's the funny thing: we who'd seen what had happened couldn't talk about it either, else we'd obviously wind up locked away along with Malicia. But we now had another worry—that she'd somehow be able to cast spells on us from inside her cell."

"Did she? . . . I mean, could she?"

"You're starting to sound mighty convinced, son."

Sully frowned. "I'd prefer not to be. But, old man, I can tell that you aren't bullshitting me. I can feel in my bones that you're telling the truth. And the problem with that is . . . well, so far, your story's crazier than what we're currently investigating." Sully waved a waitress over and ordered another orange juice.

"Hell yeah," Apache agreed. "Oh, it was crazy as hell back then. And . . . if the past is anything to go by, I think we need to start hoping Malicia Howard has lost some of her witchery skills. Else, this 'Mr. Ugly' case we're tangled up in now may end up getting *really* ugly. So far, we've only three dead youths. Trust me—no way is that old girl satisfied with such a small number of stiffs."

"Go on, old man. So what happened at the asylum?"

"Yeah, I'd better finish the story; we can rap afterwards. Well, at first the shrinks at the Taunton State Hospital were loath to gag Malicia—said she wasn't doing anyone any harm and it'd be taking away her rights. They knew she'd eaten a cop's hand, but she'd shown no signs of violence since being committed. But . . . ha ha ha . . . their indifference didn't last long. Once two or three of the night staff reported hearing her chanting spells at midnight and seeing weird shadows on the walls of her room, shadows that looked like giant insects? . . . well, they gag-balled Malicia so tightly she most likely thought she was making BDSM porn." He laughed loudly. "Speaking of porn, that's where Cleo Beauchamp finally ended up. She left town the next weekend—hopped aboard a Greyhound bus bound south for Florida. She's been shooting adult flicks ever since. You may have heard of her. I can't recall her stage name now—Cleo Foxx or Cleo Cummings . . . something kinky like that."

Sully made a face. "Never heard of her. What happened to John Burke?"

"Nothing. He instantly renounced his rowdy ways and became an upstanding citizen. He hasn't gotten so much as a parking ticket in fifteen years."

"C'mon, old man, *nothing* was done to them? You said the Byler parents openly admitted to killing Peter in the courtroom."

"Yeah, but it was swept under the carpet too, all part of the cover-up. With Malicia safely locked away, no one wanted to reopen her can of worms. No one dared. So Peter Howard's death was filed away as 'Unsolved.' It's still a cold case, just one no one is ever gonna revisit."

"But what about the courtroom cameras? Surely they caught something on film."

"All that the courtroom cameras caught were swirls of writhing gas with people falling to pieces inside them. Could just have easily have been a bomb blowing them up. About the Bylers' confessions? Microphones didn't catch a thing over all the screaming going on. I heard the whole exchange only 'cos I was right behind Malicia at the time. Most important of all though, was that Malicia wasn't ever caught on tape. That wasn't because she wouldn't film, just that no one was pointing a camera at her; remember that most court cameras face forward, towards the judge and the jury and the witness box, not back towards the gallery. And remember too, that this was before video phones became routine. One journalist—Roy Bailey—*had* sneaked in a video camera, but he lost it while trying not to become a human sacrifice."

Sully mused on that a bit. His fresh orange juice had been placed in front of him. He took a sip. "Alright, so the case died that day too. But I'm still curious as to how you covered that much bloodshed up."

"We . . . they . . . got away with it mainly because everyone originally thought a bomb had gone off inside the courtroom. You know what *you'd* think if you were called over to a crime scene and saw bits of people lying everywhere and blood all over the walls. You'd instantly think 'bomb' too, right? Yeah, so that's what the SWAT guys initially assumed also. All we survivors tried to tell them different, but our talk of monsters was considered a mass hallucination, shared delusions resulting from some kind of gas the terrorists must have released into the courtroom before detonating the explosives. So that originally kept the press hounds at bay. Well, not exactly at bay; they didn't stop sniffing for the real story, but it kept them in the dark at least."

"Hey, but what about those reporters who were there? They're still going to write accounts of what they saw, and if their accounts agree, they'd—"

Apache laughed loudly. "Yeah, yeah, I know: even if they wouldn't be believed, they could still raise quite a stink with tales of government conspiracies and illegal weapons tests and cover-ups. And once they'd convinced the relatives of the dead that there'd been foul play, the authorities would have had to deal with all sorts of federal inquiries and lawsuits, yeah?"

Sully nodded. "Yes, exactly. So how'd you silence *them*?"

"Oldest trick in the book: both towns *paid* them to keep their mouths shut."

"Huh? Aw, c'mon, how possible is that?"

"Son, don't be naïve. People do all sorts of weird shit when enough money's involved. You ever heard the tale of the Great Wall of China?"

"I just know it's there, man, and that you can see it from space."

"Okay, the Great Wall was built to keep out the nomad invaders, right? Twenty thousand miles long, taller than a house, wide enough to drive a car on it, yeah?"

"Yeah, yeah, old man. And your point is?"

"Well, the invaders never fired a cannon at it; they never tried to breach the wall at all. They simply bribed the guards to let them through. Now that's the power of money for you. All that time spent doing all that legendary work and all for nothing in the end."

Sully laughed at that. Then he frowned. "But that was before the mass media. I don't see that kind of stuff happening now."

Apache sighed and tapped the tabletop. "Okay, I'll give you another example. You ever read the scriptures?"

"C'mon, old man, you know I ain't religious." He smirked. "And I know you aren't either. You're superstitious for sure, but not religious. But why're you asking anyway?"

" 'Cos of what we're discussing, about the journalists. See, I've got a cousin Tony, who's a priest. He's high ranking now—a monsignor or cardinal, I never could keep Catholic titles straight in my head. Once you ain't either the Pope or running a parish, it's all a mystery to me."

"I didn't know you were Catholic."

"I'm not. We're Episcopalian, but my aunt Paula married Mario Mancini, who was Italian, see?"

Sully wagged his head like a dog, trying to see where this was leading.

"Now," Apache explained, "a long time ago, so long ago in fact that I no longer recall if it was before or after Tony went into the seminary, he told me something. He said the thing he read in the Bible that scared him the most was the account of the resurrection of Christ in the Gospel of St. Mathew, where the Roman guards who'd witnessed the angel roll away the stone were paid to say that Christ's disciples had stolen away his body instead. Tony said that that account scared him even more than Christ being betrayed for thirty pieces of silver. He couldn't conceive that anyone would see a corpse come back to life and would lie about it 'cos he was paid to."

"Is that actually in the Bible?"

"I dunno. You just said it—I ain't religious either; I never checked whether it was in the Bible or not. I just took it on good authority, seeing as Tony was in the ministry or was gonna be, that he knew what he was talking about. But here's the thing, Sully: I've been catching crooks for thirty-odd years now, and whenever I've investigated a case with financial leanings—fraud, arson or murder for insurance money, white slavery"—he frowned—"you name it, man . . . whenever I've doubted the depths of human depravity that folks can sink to just to earn an illegal dollar, I always remember Tony's words and I shiver." He nodded to himself. "The only difference in our case was that Jesus wasn't resurrecting again, but that some demons had come out of the afterlife and murdered everyone."

Apache laughed coldly. "Long story short again? The reporters all took the money and shut up about it. Sheryl Gump from the Taunton Gazette was an ex-girlfriend of mine. She told me she was offered a quarter of a million bucks for her silence. Sheryl took the money and moved across the Pond to Europe, where there was less chance of her being eaten by the Creature from the Black Lagoon. One of the other two—David Yuzna, I think it was—even did an hour-long TV special debunking 'crazy rumors' that a UFO had crashed into the courtroom, and then also carried out an in-depth analysis of how Malicia Howard had systematically murdered everyone with grenades and whatnot. He even had experts on the show saying—"

"Hey, hold on, Apache! Just *wait*. Man, you just told me that Malicia was in TSH; how is she mixed up in all this again?"

"They made her the scapegoat, spread the rumor far and wide that she'd blown up everyone."

"Without evidence? Old man, it's clear that there wasn't any evidence, 'cos if there had been, she'd still be locked away now; and in the penitentiary for that matter."

"Yeah, yeah, kid, there wasn't any evidence. But the rumors were enough. And so long as the lady *was* shut away, and that somewhere far from any chance of public interaction with her, no one cared. I guess 'scapegoat' ain't exactly the right word for this case, but it's the nearest one I can come up with right now. I mean, whether she'd done it using bombs or demons, Malicia *was* responsible for all those deaths."

"But . . . but . . . it's just *wrong* . . . no trial . . . no—"

"Sully, for fuck's sake, stop being such a boy scout. It was the smart thing to do."

"Don't tell me you approved of it."

Apache grinned. "Yeah, I approved entirely. She was safer in her padded cell. Safer for everyone else, that is. Don't you look at me like that, kid. If she'd just eaten half of *your* hand, you'd have approved too."

X

After some discussion, the Raynham and Taunton town authorities realized that the public would believe whatever explanation they were given, so long as it wasn't what had actually happened.

In short, they could tell them *anything*, just so long as it wasn't the truth.

No one was ever going to accept that demons had appeared in court and eaten everyone, and had done so without anyone outside the courtroom hearing the commotion.

They would, however, buy a story of a crazed woman's terror attack on those she'd believed had wronged her. So that's what they got: Malicia Howard's rumored rampage . . .

Certainly, none of the evidence would ever add up . . . but law enforcement departments dislike doing paranormal arithmetic anyway. The Raynham and Taunton police departments, and the Massachusetts State Police were happy to pass the courtroom camera recordings on to Area 51 and forget all about them.

Once it had been agreed that Malicia would be the 'scapegoat,' the rumor mill went into overdrive. The hue and cry died down in a month, but by then the public were well aware that Malicia Howard had somehow sneaked a sawn-off shotgun and some Iraq-surplus experimental grenades through court security and the metal detectors.

Terrence Pratt, Raynham's town administrator at the time, had even had the genius idea of sleazing up the tale of exactly *how* Malicia had snuck the shotgun into court:

"Just say she hid it in her pussy," Mr. Pratt told his aides. "It's sawn off, ain't it? It should fit."

The rumor that Malicia had hidden her main weapon in her lady parts spread through Raynham and its neighbor towns like a forest fire in the autumn. Soon the tenor of discussions about the deaths changed. No one cared any longer why she'd killed everyone, they were more concerned with trying to figure out the length of Malicia's supremely capacious vagina, with estimating the dimensions of her exceptional womanhood, and with working out too how much stuff she could actually fit inside her body without it alerting metal detectors to the presence of foreign objects in the vicinity.

It was a hotly debated philosophical puzzle; one similar (and as equally unresolvable) to the age-old questions: 'How many angels can fit/dance on the head of a pin?' and 'Which came first—the egg or the chicken?'

Drunken college boys (already an irresponsible and disreputable species) also tried to figure out the composition of Malicia Howard's ass gas. These alcoholic scientists believed that it was the uncommon and supremely nasty pungency of Malicia's farts which had given the survivors hallucinations of monsters.

The Boston band Midnight Monday even recorded a pop song about it, titled *Gas Monsters From Malicious Mothers*. The Raynham and Taunton town authorities were amused. Mission accomplished.

PART 4: THE UNGRATEFUL DEAD

You'll find everything evil somewhere and something evil everywhere. (Necromantica 6:13:66)

CHAPTER 26

Sylvia & Larry

That same Wednesday night, while Betsy was trying to cope with the shock of Chuck Jennings' improbable death, and while Apache was busy filling Sully in about the past, a woman named Sylvia Cooper was being strangled by her husband in their single-wide trailer at the Oak Hill Mobile Home Park over in Taunton.

For poor Sylvia, this wasn't really anything new; Larry tended to beat her up at least three times a week. Usually this happened whenever she scolded him for drinking too much.

And tonight, she'd really scolded him; he'd given her additional anger fuel. Larry had stolen and spent the money she'd been saving to buy new clothes for their daughter Sandy. She'd hidden the money in one of her shoes. She'd thought it was safe there. But somehow, Larry had found the cash and bought four bottles of Jack Daniels whiskey with it.

It wasn't possible to get used to being an abused woman, but over the years, Sylvia had come to terms with her fate. She'd thrice run away from Larry, but she seemed to always pick the same sort of smelly and good-for-nothing man to shack up with.

Larry Cooper, a short, grizzly man with dirty blonde hair and untrimmed beard and mustache, was simply a despicable human being. Now, his mind overcome by the contents of the empty bottle of whiskey on the floor, Larry had both hands wrapped about Sylvia's neck and was squeezing hard. They were down on the dirty floor of their living room and he was sitting on her belly with his knees pinning her arms to her sides. She'd kicked and tried hard to throw him off her, but he was big and she was small and she'd discovered ages ago that once he was like this she couldn't budge him.

"I'm gonna kill ya, bitch," Larry growled, squeezing her throat harder still.

"Larry, stop!" Sylvia gasped, her eyes bulging. She beat at his thighs with her small fists, desperate to get him off her before she lost consciousness.

Yes, this *had* happened before, on countless occasions, and Sylvia had always survived the violent assaults, but Larry's rage tonight seemed different to her. Tonight, her husband's bloodshot eyes had a crazy glint in them that seemed to yell at her, "Ha, you silly bitch, tonight's the night I'm gonna kill ya for real! I'm gonna send ya packing straight down to Hell!"

Sylvia had on just a bra and panties, her normal wear for this hour of the night. Larry was wearing soiled blue underpants and a red T-shirt with white lettering that read: 'I'M TOO BROKE TO PAY FOR MY SINS.'

Sylvia was really having trouble breathing now. Her face was swollen up purple and the veins in her temples were bulging out from all the backed-up blood that wanted out of her head but couldn't find the exit door. Her thoughts were as foggy as a morning when mist had covered everything and reduced visibility to a mere five or ten feet ahead.

This is just crazy, Sylvia thought. She couldn't count how many times her younger brother had pleaded with her to leave Larry before he killed her. And she had left. But each time, she'd either gotten lonely, or tired of her mother's nagging (whenever she left Larry, she first stopped at her mother's home to drop off their daughter Sandy till she got her feet under her again), or her husband himself came to her all contrite and begged her to come back to him (because he was such a jerk that no other woman in her right senses would fuck him and cook for him). And she always went back (which maybe proved that she wasn't in her right senses either).

And now it looked like her brother's dire warnings were about coming to pass.

"I'm gonna teach ya not to defy me," Larry growled down at her, a drunken scowl etched on his flushed face.

"Larry, you're killing me," she gasped. It smelt as if Larry had just shit himself too. Now she'd have to clean up his damn mess. But she needed to be alive to clean up anything at all, and if she didn't get this drunken asshole off of her very soon, she wasn't going to be alive. If he kept throttling her for much longer, she was going to be stone cold dead. Deader than the damn plaice they'd had for dinner. She could already see dark spots swimming between her eyes.

My daughter's asleep in her bedroom and I'm being murdered out here.

But Sylvia knew Sandy wasn't going to wake up. The eight-year-old was used to the nighttime ruckus her parents made. To her the noise of domestic violence was as ordinary as the sound of the TV that she heard from the living room after going to bed. Most days now she slept through it.

And even if their fight was keeping Sandy awake, the young girl wouldn't be coming to her mother's rescue.

To her credit, Sandy *had* tried rescuing her mother in the past— hurrying out in alarm and beating on her father's back with her little fists, while yelling, "Daddy, daddy, leave mommy alone!" But it had always ended the same way: with her father using his belt on her too.

(The neighbors wouldn't interfere either. They were all tired of the Coopers' endless marital disturbances. A classic case of The Girl Who Cried Wolf one too many times.)

"You're killing me!" Sylvia gasped again. She wondered how much longer she'd be able to remain conscious. The black spots were now dancing before her eyes. The spots were bouncing like those balls that accompanied the words on sing-along songs on TV.

"Not as much as I'm gonna kill ya, you uppity skank! How dare you question my drinkin' habits! I'm a man, woman! I got all the right in the world to drink as much as I like. It's a damn human right!"

"Okay, okay!" she gasped at him. Getting the words through her throat felt as painful as pushing a baby out the other way. "You can keep the damn money! I won't say a thing about it anymore, I promise! Just stop throttling me!"

At that, a look of dubious sanity entered Larry's eyes.

"Alright, Sylvia, now I'm gonna stop killing ya," he slobbered, spitting all over her. He pulled his hands off her neck and sat up, swaying over her as the alcohol sloshed through his brain.

She gasped in several deep breaths of air. *Okay, it's over for tonight. I've survived again. But I have got to get away from this madman before he does me in for good. Once he's off to work tomorrow, I'm packing me and Sandy off to mom's. And this time, I'm not ever coming back. Not ever; no matter how much he pleads with me. I really almost just got murdered.*

Larry wagged a condescending finger down at her. "I'm gonna

212

resume my damn drinking now and I don't wanna hear nothing from ya, okay!"

"Whatever," she replied coldly, her voice and heart both filled with hatred for him. She had to speak slowly, because her throat really hurt, but she took care to enunciate each word clearly. "Just get off of me, you smelly bastard. And, shit, go wash your ass. You've fouled yourself. You smell worse than rotten eggs."

For a moment, he looked at her as if he'd hit her for sassing him, but then, he just scowled. "I ain't shit myself, ya idiot. You're the one that farted. I told you to stop feeding us all them damn beans and eggs, but you don't ever listen to me, do ya?"

Sylvia hadn't farted. She was certain she hadn't. No, she wasn't actually sure. She might have farted. She might even have pooped on herself during her struggles to escape him, but she didn't think so.

"Yeah, alright. Just get off of me! I gotta go check that you haven't woken up Sandy."

"Okay, but don't ya dare disturb me. Next time you do, I'll . . . urgghh!"

At first, because all her attention was riveted on his drunken face, Sylvia thought her evil and smelly husband had stopped talking because he was about vomiting on her. Used to him doing this too, she twisted herself sideways to escape the anticipated rain of regurgitated chips, fish and whiskey. But it didn't come, so she looked back at him again.

He was gaping at her in confusion. Someone half-concealed in shadows had a hold of Larry's blonde hair and was pulling his head back and was slitting his throat with a huge glittering razor. Sylvia watched speechless as the blood emptied out from the widening hole in Larry's neck as though someone had punctured one of those blood bank bags.

Almost before Larry could react, the blood had obliterated the top three white words on his red T-shirt, so that all that was left was: 'TO PAY FOR MY SINS.'

Sylvia remained speechless. She'd have liked to have screamed, but then the person who was killing Larry leaned forward out of the shadows and she saw his face. Or rather, his lack of one. The man's entire head was just a mess from which black slime dripped like diabolic molasses. Beneath the brim of his atrocious black hat, worms wriggled left and right as though they'd mistaken themselves for hair.

Sylvia now understood where the foul smell in the trailer had come from. The man's body seemed to be rotting. He wore a muddy blue suit and the flesh it covered was black and purple and punctured by chunks of wet and dripping bone.

Larry's eyes bulged as he died. He tried reaching up to fight his killer, but the killer swatted his hands away. Once, Larry got a good grip on the rotting man's right hand, but then, to Sylvia's additional horror, his fingers sank into the man's flesh. They sank in deep. His fingers easily penetrated the decaying skin, releasing squirts of black liquid that spattered Sylvia's breasts.

The man killing Larry carried on doing so. The damage to his hand clearly had no effect on him.

The rain of blood continued unabated. Its initial vigor now weakened, the emerging blood trickled from Larry's neck in red rivulets that first became crimson streams, and then rivers which cascaded down his front and sides to pool as red lakes on Sylvia's belly, and then finally drain like waterfalls to the floor.

By now, Larry Cooper was dead in all but name. With his neck slit wide open from ear to ear, his eyes nonetheless still stared wildly left and right about him, his brain fighting desperately to comprehend why, with his nose still working right, it was about shutting down from oxygen deprivation. But slowly his eyes turned dull and froze in place, his brain's neurons losing their battle to keep him functional against the stacked odds of a violent death.

Sylvia didn't dare stare up into the face of the blue-suited killer. She also didn't dare stare at her husband's face either, with its horrible view of his dying agony.

Instead, she riveted her gaze on Larry's T-shirt: 'TO PAY FOR MY SINS. TO PAY FOR MY SINS. TO PAY FOR MY SINS.' Like a crazy mantra, the words sizzled hot in her head like bacon in a nonstick frypan.

While black slop dripped off those parts of his rotting body exposed between the flaps of his blue jacket, the killer severed Larry's head completely.

He let go of the body. The headless form fell forward on Sylvia.

She lay there, paralyzed by fear. Her hands were still pinned to her sides. The blood on her felt like glue fixing her to the floor. She was rendered additionally immobile by Larry's weight on her. Now it was all dead weight, two hundred pounds of dead man.

She was also torn between her concern for her own safety and for Sandy's wellbeing. Should she get up and run to her daughter's bedroom to protect her? Or should she remain here and play possum?

She realized that the rotting man was bending over her. He was looking at her, though both of his eyes were on the left side of his face and contained grubs instead of eyeballs.

"Please, don't hurt us," she pleaded. Looking up into that awful pulped nothing of a face, staring up through the space where Larry's head had recently been, over the awful red mess that remained of his neck, she had no courage. There was no fight anywhere in her. None at all. At the moment Sylvia Cooper was confronted by something so far beyond her understanding that she might as well have been dreaming for all the sense it made.

"Please, don't hurt us!" she repeated in utter terror, feeling the spousal-abused strands of her mind close to unraveling completely.

In reply, the corpse-man (oh, she had no doubts that he was dead!) bent down closer and stroked her cheek with fingers like large putrid sausages.

"Not yet!" he whispered in a diseased voice. "Wait! Kill later."

His speech brought with it thick visible clouds of corpse gas that spilled from his horrible displaced mouth. The gas was of such noxious odor and consistency that it sped Sylvia towards unconsciousness.

She stayed conscious long enough to see the monster in the blue suit straighten up again. He was still holding Larry's severed head. He was holding it up, staring it in the face.

"Asshole," he said in that sepulchral voice of his. Then he vanished. Just like that. On his disappearance, Larry's head dropped to the floor and bounced a few times.

If Sylvia had been halfway to a blackout before, seeing Larry's head bounce like a ball was the last straw for her.

"At least I'm safe," she thought in relief. "And my daughter is safe too. And Larry's never, never, never, never ever going to beat me up again!"

If nothing else, being set free from her abusive husband was something to be grateful for.

And if the murderer thought she'd actually wait around for him to come back and kill she and Sandy, he was worse than crazy.

Unable to muster even the slightest iota of strength to free herself from his weight, Sylvia Cooper passed out with Larry's corpse still lying on her.

CHAPTER 27

Apache & Sully

After Apache was done with his tale, Sully was speechless for a while. Sure, he had questions to ask, but for those first few moments, the questions appeared redundant to him.

There was really just *one* question to answer now: *Do I believe this or not?* It had been easy enough while Apache was speaking, but now, in the minutes approaching last Call, Sully debated with himself.

***

Apache, meanwhile, wasn't saying anything. He'd left the younger man to his ruminations. He'd also decided that, seeing as he wasn't going to be driving himself back home, he could have another whiskey. Remembering Malicia Howard tended to have that effect on him. It was why he remembered her as little as possible.

He waited for Sully to make up his mind. Sully was staring hard at his glass of orange juice. His eyes were as riveted on the half-full glass as if it was filled with blood and he was trying to work out whose blood it was and who had spilled it.

Apache understood the young man's crisis. He'd given the kid irrefutable evidence, but would Sully still find an escape from believing what he'd heard?

Unconsciously, he began scratching his right palm again. Then he realized he was doing so and stopped. He called a waitress over. "Whisky sour, please, Denise."

She left to fetch the drink. Without realizing he was doing so, Apache once more slipped back into scratching his right palm.

***

At a flash of blue walking past their booth, Sully looked up. A tall blonde in a short blue dress, pretty, but wearing too much makeup, was striding towards the ladies' room. She had large breasts, high and firm breasts that bounced with each step she took. Her mammary endowment caught and held Sully's attention. He watched her pass through the door to the restrooms (her behind was nice and firm too), then returned his mind to his thoughts.

Apache's drink had just been delivered, and the old guy was taking a sip of it. Sully absentmindedly watched the waitress saunter off. She was shapely too.

"Your deepest convictions ain't hid in her butt, kid," Apache said.

"What?"

Laughing, Apache lowered his voice. "The way you're staring at girls' asses now. Like you think pussy is the route to truth." He smirked. "Well, it sure is the route to pleasure and to babies too, but . . . hey, make up your mind if you believe me or not, so we can get on with this. I'm an old man. I ain't got all my life to wait for your reply."

"It's hard, old man."

"What is? Your dick? Then stop studying for your masters degree at the university of T & A. Keep your eyes to yourself till you get home to Tilly."

Sully laughed. Then, picking his words carefully, he said, "I'll put it like this: I don't know if I believe what I've heard, old man, but I trust you not to lie to me. You've always been straight as my dad with me, even when I disagree with you." He frowned. "So let's say I believe *you*, even if the story I just heard doesn't deserve to be believed. How's that?"

Apache nodded. "Fair enough. That's good enough to work on." He lifted his drink . "So now that we're finally on the same bloodstained page here, let's consider what we've got. Alright, first of all, we now know *for certain* that it is a diabolically resurrected Peter Howard killing everyone."

Sully nodded. "The first thing we need to do is connect each victim to the killer. If we can establish a direct relationship between cause and effect, we may be able to predict where he's going to strike next. And if we know who the next victim is, we may be able to arrange an ambush."

Frowning, Apache shook his glass of whiskey. "I must admit though, that something else has also occurred to me—that it may be someone who's *possessed* by Peter's spirit doing the killings."

"Can't be. If it is, where'd he get the rotting flesh that's been turning up?"

"Yeah, good point there. Go on with what you were saying. I like this idea of ambushing the undead son-of-a-bitch before he can strike again."

Sully nodded. "Okay, let's examine those murdered so far for their connections to Peter Howard. Your call, old man."

It was Apache's turn to nod now. "Fair enough. Let's do it."

"First victim—Chris Burke."

"John Burke's son. That's a direct connection."

"Second victim—Chelsea Byler."

"Jerry Byler's daughter. He had nothing to do with the murder, but the poor girl was Max and Homer's niece, as well as Bart and Cissy's granddaughter, so . . ."

"Okay, that's a direct enough connection for me. And Ronald Snelson?"

"Judge Snelson's grandson." Apache frowned. "Now here's the difficult one for me to reason out: The judge had nothing whatsoever to do with the deaths back then. I mean, Malicia had him eaten before he could even rule on the case, and, knowing the sort of decent fellow the old guy was, he was more likely than not going to rule in favor of us taking it to trial. But she killed him. Okay, I understand that maybe, just maybe, she had some conspiracy thing going on in her mind about how the law was merely holding a show trial and were really planning to screw her over—remember I told you that both the prosecution and defense attorneys were killed too?"

"Yeah, I remember that. Go on."

"Okay, but that was back then. Why would she kill the judge's grandson now?"

"Shush! Not so loud, there's folks looking at us."

Apache glanced around the bar. "No one's lookin' at *us*—they're all searching for their missing souls in their alcoholic beverages. Kid, we're all drunks in here. An hour from now, no one's gonna remember anything we said."

"Yeah, okay. Alright, I agree with you that Malicia had no reason to kill Snelson's grandson. But remember also that Peter walked right by that witness at the gas station, what's her name again?"

"Who? Oh, Lynn Nilsson?"

"Yeah, Mrs. Nilsson. He walked right by her and didn't do squat to her."

They paused speaking. "That must've been one hell of a long shit," Apache said out of the blue.

"Huh?" Sully asked. "What are you talking about?"

His partner pointed. The tall blonde whose breasts Sully had earlier been admiring had just emerged from the restroom and was stepping back towards her seat, smoothing her blue dress as her hips swayed drunkenly. Sully once again found himself unable to stop staring at the girl's impressive cleavage. Wow, the lady was really stacked.

Apache explained what he'd meant by his comment: "She spent so long back there in the restrooms that she was either badly constipated, had the runs, or was sucking dick."

Sully frowned. "She's a hooker?" He wasn't looking forward to doing vice squad work tonight. He was off-duty (well supposedly off-duty, one never truly was off-duty during a murder investigation) and wanted to dedicate his entire mind to the puzzle at hand.

Apache laughed. "Nah, she ain't a hooker."

Sully didn't get the joke. "What's so funny?"

"That's Danny Foster—Chelsea Byler's cousin."

"He's . . . she's . . . he's"—the right pronoun eluded him—"a drag queen?" Sully gaped at the svelte blonde, who was now seated cross-legged with two male friends. "*That's* Danny Foster?"

"Yeah, the kid does a nightclub routine down in Rhode Island on the weekends. A few other places around here too. Performs under the name of Deidre Fabulous." He regarded Sully's stunned gaze. "He looks just like a babe, yeah?"

Sully nodded slowly, then looked away from Danny before the other might have noticed him staring. "Yeah, for real. I wouldn't even need to be drunk to ask him out on a date." Across the room, Deidre Fabulous was tapping her fingernails on a young man's arm and grinning a red lipstick grin.

"Wow, you mean those great tits are plastic?"

"Lotsa great tits are plastic nowadays, kid. Even world-famous ones. Artificial is the new real."

Sully gulped. "Yeah, I guess."

Apache similarly tapped fingers on the tabletop. "Okay, now back to business. So, Sully, we've two possible scenarios to consider here: It's either that Mr. Ugly is knocking off anyone who was even remotely connected with his death, distant relatives inclusive; or . . . that he's conducting a random rampage and Ronald Snelson just happened to be on the wrong street at the wrong time of night."

"With no way to prove either theory, which do you prefer?"

"I'd stick with logical cause. Shorter odds that way. We need to go with the assumption that the boy is doing his mother's bidding and not offing folks on his own initiative . . . or else, why would he leave John Burke alive and kill his son instead?"

"Maybe he's like Freddy Kruger? *Nightmare on Elm Street?* Sins of the father and mothers? We've got a similar scenario here: Dead murderer comes back and—"

"Son, it ain't the same thing. Peter Howard wasn't ever a child molester and he didn't kill anyone. And he ain't haunting anyone's dreams either. As far as we can determine, Mr. Ugly has been visiting in the flesh to kill his victims. It's making my brain hurt just thinking about it. I think I need another drink."

Sully shook his head at him. "Nah, how 'bout if I run you home instead? You have any more whiskey, you'll be too hungover in the morning to get any work done."

Apache nodded. "I guess you're right. I already feel like the Titanic going down."

They got up and walked to the bar to settle their tab.

"Hi, Deidre," Apache greeted the pretty drag queen and her friends as they passed the trio on their way out.

"Hi, Apache," Deidre whispered back in a very tipsy voice. "We were just discussing the benefits of double penetration. You're welcome to join us." On her comment, the two young men with her grinned sheepishly.

"Yeah, penetration's great," Apache agreed. "But I'm an old widower and I got a lot of crooks to catch tomorrow. You guys have fun working it out though. Just try not to tear whoever's ass up."

Sully did his best to keep a straight face.

The detectives stepped outside. The night air was a relief to them after the bar's smoky atmosphere.

They got into their squad car. Sully put the car in motion, turned off Broadway onto Center Street and headed south.

Apache lived five minutes away, off Route 44, on the lower part of Hill Street in southern Raynham. Sully's place was up on Carver Street, walking distance from the Liquid Solace bar, but his girlfriend Tilly Brandon lived on Leonard Street, on the other side of Route 44 from Apache and just three minutes drive away from Apache's house. Sleeping over at Tilly's like Sully intended doing tonight had the added advantage of making it easy to pick Apache up in the morning.

Neither man said much at first.

"We gotta keep a close eye on that kid Danny back there," Apache said after they'd been driving awhile, just as Sully swung the squad car onto Route 44 and the cool wind was clearing some of the whiskey from his eyes.

"Why?" Sully asked. "He's clearly not connected with any of this." Then he thought a bit deeper on it. "Oh, he is, isn't he? If he's Chelsea Byler's cousin, that means he's related to . . . shit, he's in danger too."

Apache waited till Sully had turned onto Hill Street before continuing: "Oh, Danny mightn't know it, but he's in more danger than just about anyone else in town. Remember how I told you that Max Byler's wife Terri left him 'cos he kept beating her?"

Sully nodded. "Yeah, I do."

"Well, she'd had two kids by then, a boy and a girl. Danny's the boy." Apache smiled sadly at Sully's surprise. "Yeah. Danny *is* Maxwell Byler's son. Four or five years after Max's death, Terri came back to Raynham. But she'd remarried in the interim and her new husband had formally adopted her kids, hence the name change."

"Oh, the drag queen is Max Byler's son." Sully was speaking to himself. The portion of his mind not occupied with steering the car was focused on making sense of the convoluted tangle this case was fast becoming.

"That young man is certain to be next in line to be killed," Apache said. "And he doesn't even know it."

"Maybe he isn't," Sully countered. "You know, I just had a bad feeling about this."

"Yeah?"

They were just pulling into Apache's driveway. Sully parked the car, then turned to Apache. "Remember what you said about 'logical cause?' Well, I think it just leapt out the window."

Apache scowled. "What are you talking 'bout, son?"

Sully explained: "Simple enough. At first we had three deaths, all of which we could somehow account for; so we agreed that Mr. Ugly has been killing the descendants of the folks involved, right?"

"Yeah. So? Hurry up, I need to go to bed. All those drinks we had are finally catching up with me."

"Old man, why hasn't Mr. Ugly killed Danny Foster yet? He's the most obvious target, and yet he's still alive."

Apache nodded. "Hmmm. Good thing I'm going to bed right now. I'm gonna need a whole night's rest to ponder that question."

"You said Max Byler had *two* kids. Where's Danny's sister now?"

"Sylvia? Oh, she's here in town too. Sylvia Cooper's her married name. She's Danny's older sister. She's married to some trailer trash piece of shit called Larry who beats her up on any pretext he gets. Sylvia Cooper is one of those people who are simply impossible to help. She won't leave the pig she's wed to and won't even press charges when he assaults her, so what the hell are we supposed to do?"

Sully realized they were in danger of getting sidetracked. He said, "And just to buttress my point: we haven't yet received any reports of Sylvia being attacked either, have we? So, I don't think—"

"Save it till morning, son," Apache said, pushing the car door open and stepping out. There was only so much his brain could hold and at the moment, the alcohol seemed to be edging reason out of the way. He shut the door and leaned back in through the window. "I'm serious about needing to go to bed, kid—suddenly I feel more beat than a piñata. But . . . tell you what: Tomorrow we'll both go see Sylvia Cooper and set up our plans to keep an eye on both of Max's kids and to ambush Mr. Ugly as well. How's that?"

"Fine with me," Sully replied. He watched Apache until the older man had let himself in his front door. Apache didn't even look back or wave. He just vanished inside his house and slammed the door behind him.

"Wow, he really *is* beat," Sully said softly to himself.

Then he turned the car around and drove off for Tilly's house.

Apache was right; it *was* time to go to bed. They'd both done enough work for the day. And besides, even if fake, those large bouncy breasts Sully had noticed tonight in the bar had kindled in him an intense and desperate need for Tilly's breasts. Hopefully the beautiful lady would be in the mood for some lovemaking tonight.

CHAPTER 28

Sully & Tilly

Tilly *was* in the mood for love.

"Let's do it outside in my car," she said.

Sully stared at her. "What?"

She nodded. "Yes, let's do it outside. *Please.*"

"I'm tired, baby. How 'bout if we do it like that tomorrow night?"

"No. Right now, and outside in my car." She licked his ear, making him shiver deliciously.

Sully was slightly perplexed. From the moment he'd arrived here, Tilly had been all over him, squeezing his crotch as if she couldn't wait to get him into bed. He'd restrained his own desire, but the feeling was definitely mutual.

And now this. She seemed to have changed her mind on the fly. Not about the sex, but about the fucking location.

"Baby," he protested, "please have pity on my poor dick. I don't think it can wait that long. It's hard and impatient. Erections can't wait, they need to be satisfied—ask any rapist."

"Outside," she insisted. "And you're a cop, not a rapist."

"A dick doesn't know its owner's occupation."

"*Outside*, Frank."

"Come to bed, baby," he whispered in her ear. "I wanna stir up your tongue with my cock."

Sully really just wanted some relaxed missionary-style lovemaking. But then Tilly pouted at him and he gave in. These moods took her sometimes and he'd discovered it was best to play along with what she wanted. The sex was usually good and sometimes it was even better than good.

"Okay, then," he agreed. "Let's go."

He'd made it over to the bedroom door before realizing that Tilly wasn't following him. He looked back. She was bent over and rummaging through her nightstand, with her large buttocks wobbling delightfully in her skimpy negligee. He loved her rear view, but his penis was hard and even this short delay in getting down to business was angering it.

"Come on now, baby," he urged. "You're the one who wants to do it downstairs. What are you looking for anyway?"

"Rubbers."

"Rubbers? I thought you were on the pill?"

"I am, silly. The rubbers are so you don't spill sperm on my car seats."

"Forget the rubbers, we'll do it outside on the hood. Inside or out, the car is still the car."

She nodded and walked over to him. She was tall, with pretty dark eyes and jet-black hair that she'd tonight clipped back in a ponytail.

She had large breasts. She claimed motherhood was to blame for this; but Sully wasn't sure that was really the case. For some reason he couldn't imagine Tilly with a moderately sized chest. Something about her—maybe the wide spread of her hips, maybe the length and slight convexity of her legs—made him think she was the kind of woman designed to carry a large bosom.

They left the bedroom. Tilly winced when Sully shut the door.

"Shush!" she cautioned with a finger to her lips. "We don't wanna wake up the kids!"

He nodded. The kids. 6-year-old Marvin and 8-year-old Lisa were asleep in the next room. It would be rather embarrassing if the two of them stepped outside and found their mother and her boyfriend both half-naked.

Sully was dressed in just briefs and slippers and had a visible erection making a tent of the front of his briefs. He wondered how married couples ever got it on with their children in the next room. But they did, didn't they? That was how additional little humans were made.

I'm not so sure I really wanna get married, he thought. *But . . .*

The 'but' was Tilly, who'd now impatiently begun dragging him down the stairs. He thought he was falling in love with this woman. Not with her hometown though—he still wanted out of this crazy place called Raynham, where creepy undead monsters could manifest at will and butcher innocent youths.

Tilly dragged him through the living room, through the kitchen, and then pushed him out into the garage. Then she flicked on the garage lights. The garage roller shutter was down, sealing them in and the night-world out. There was no chance of their being seen by unwanted eyes.

By the time they were standing beside her gray Ford Fiesta, Sully felt as if his testicles would pop from internal pressure. The sexual urge was as strong on him as stink on a turd.

Tilly seemed to sense his desperation. In five seconds flat she had Sully's underpants down to his ankles and was sucking hard on his hard penis. He stood there with one hand braced on the car and the other on his hip and let her have him.

His erection was firm and fat in Tilly's mouth. When he thrust forward, she felt it blocking her throat. To stop herself gagging, she backed off, licking along the rigid length of flesh. She concentrated on the swollen head, tasting it like it was a sweet. One of her hands squeezed Sully's balls, the other one toyed with his six-pack. Oh, Tilly just loved Sully's body. He was so fit, so tanned and sexy, and had such a HARD penis!

Tilly's sex was dripping. Her stiffened nipples felt hot, as if flames burnt in each one.

Once she had her boyfriend's penis good and wet, Tilly bent over the hood. She pulled off her nightie and stuck her buttocks out, offering herself up for penetration. She wanted it *deep*.

She whispered back at Sully, "Alright, give me that nightstick, Mr. Policeman."

With a gasp of relief, Sully spread her buttocks and slid himself inside her.

Tilly relaxed as she felt him entering her body. His penis was a loving hot plug filling her up.

He began thrusting slowly, reaching a hand forward to caress her clitoris at the same time.

She had both hands on the Fiesta's hood. She was doing her utmost best not to rock the car. Whenever she balanced against it, the vehicle tended to make a noise like something under the hood was displaced. This was an old problem, one that she should have had looked at long ago. It was impossible not to rock the car though—each time Sully's crotch smacked against her buttocks, her arms transmitted that force to the car and its front end dipped and creaked. She moaned and grunted with pleasure. It would be incredibly embarrassing if the kids woke up, came downstairs, and caught them like this. The vehicle was making a noise which seemed louder than normal in the garage. Even though she'd shut the side-access door to the kitchen, she couldn't be certain that the sound wouldn't still somehow penetrate the house walls and wake and alarm Marvin and Lisa.

She considered taking her hands off the hood and gripping her ankles instead. But the way she was positioned right now was just right for deep penetration. At the moment it felt like Sully's penis wasn't merely hitting her G-spot, but that it was reaching all the way in to her liver and kidneys. She could feel the man's erection everywhere inside her body; rising on each thrust to the uppermost ridges of her brain and also tunneling down to the soles of her feet. Her breasts felt like hot bowls of milk being stirred by the marauding penis.

So she kept rocking the car, gambling on not rousing her children.

But along with her concerns, she felt that slight thrill of the forbidden, the anticipation of her kids actually catching she and Sully at it, with the accompanying awkward explanation of what they were up to.

An especially sweet thrust made her gasp, "Oh, Mr. Policeman! I just love you!"

"I love you too, baby!" he grunted back.

Sully began thrusting faster. A hand on her shoulder steadied her against him. His other hand stroked her clitoris.

Tilly tensed up and then she was coming. She stumbled forward. She gasped and went limp. She felt as if she'd just turned to Jell-O. Her legs trembled and bent. She collapsed forward on the gray car, squashing her large breasts against its cold metal. Dripping sweat on it.

Sully was still going though. Holding her firmly about the hips now with both hands and pushing his hard manhood into her.

Tilly relaxed and let Sully enjoy her body. "Yeah, arrest my ass, officer! I'm placing my pussy in your protective custody!"

Sully gripped her waist like it was a horse's reins. "Yeah, I'm locking this pussy up right now," he grunted. "I'm arresting you for excessive sweetness, girl!"

"Give me that hard policeman's baton!" she gasped. "Come inside me, officer. I wanna feel your service revolver squirt its love-bullets all wet and gooey inside me."

What man could ever resist that sort of erotic encouragement? Sully groaned and ejaculated.

"Oh, Mr. Policeman," Tilly gasped, "it's so warm!"

Sully let go of Tilly's hips and his penis slipped out of her.

The penis's removal from her body was followed by a slow influx of warm air. She turned and gripped him and pressed her soft body against him and kissed him.

***

They returned upstairs to bed.

"My parents are coming to visit," she told him as they climbed the stairs.

"Oh, yeah?"

"Yes. They've heard so much about you from me that they're curious to see what you're like in person." She giggled. "Mom says she wants to see for herself if I'm telling the truth about how great you are."

"So you don't make another mistake, huh?" He laughed. He felt really good now. He always liked it when she called him 'Mr. Policeman' while they did it.

She grinned and stroked his cheek. "Maybe. You know how moms always think they know best. But I'll try and convince her that you're worth it."

They got into bed and lay quietly, their bodies relaxed.

Now that the lust had all drained out of him, Sully's mind returned to the night's earlier discussion with Apache.

Tilly was lying cradled in his left arm. Her eyes were shut, but she wasn't yet asleep. He watched the peaceful rise and fall of her large breasts for a while before speaking:

"Hey, babe, there's something important I need to know."

"Aw, Mr. Policeman, can't it wait till morning?" she replied drowsily without opening her eyes. "Your dick must've injected me with tranquilizers. All I wanna do now is dream."

He shook her a little. "No, tonight. It's important. It won't take long."

She opened her eyes. "Really? What is it? Is this about that spooky case you're working on?"

He nodded. "Yeah. Just a question really. Okay, now I know you're not originally from Raynham—that you only moved up here with your ex when you got married—but, Tilly, are you absolutely certain that you're not related to the Bylers in any way?"

She regarded him with surprise. "The Bylers? Who're they? Oh, oh, you mean that Walmart manager who was murdered? What's up with the Bylers?"

He sighed. "They're currently the Raynham family with the lowest life expectancy."

Tilly found this amusing. She burst into laughter. "You can't be serious."

"Darling, I am. Our serial killer seems dedicated to bumping them off one by one."

She stopped laughing, thought a moment, then shook her head. "No, there's no Bylers in our family."

"No marriage linkages? No cousins who married any, or aunts or uncle Bylers? Think carefully, baby. This nutcase we're dealing with isn't very choosy."

She shook her head again. "None. I'm certain of it. My cousin Jack married a Miss Brody and I've two nutty Barbanell aunts, but those are all. My sisters are Mrs. Smith and Mrs. Brown, and Jane—that's my brother Joe's wife—used to be Jane Levy."

Sully exhaled a long gust of relieved breath. "That's great then. Now that I'm sure you won't suddenly die on me, you can go to sleep."

She looked at him queerly. "You really love me, don't you, Mr. Policeman?"

He smiled. "It sure seems like it. I know I'd never forgive myself if anything bad happened to you." He leaned over and kissed her softly on the lips. "Alright, honey, goodnight."

"Goodnight, Mr. Policeman."

They fell asleep like that.

CHAPTER 29

Betsy

Thursday.

Betsy woke up at about ten o'clock the following morning.

Actually, her phone woke her up. It was her father, calling her about Chuck Jennings' death. The old man was irate. She listened to him loudly state that he'd told her more than once to stay away from his staff.

She heard him out in silence. She was too hungover and too upset to defend herself.

". . . Now see what you've gone and done. And to one of my best workers too."

"Dad, I'm sorry," she said once he'd simmered down. "I didn't know something like this was gonna happen."

"Well I did," the old man growled then hung up.

Betsy put down the phone and got out of bed.

Too bad I'm currently unemployed. This is the perfect sort of day when one needs a job to go to. Then she quit deceiving herself—today, a job wouldn't have done her any good: *I'm in no mental condition to go anywhere. If I was employed, I'd have had to call in sick today.*

She sat down and tried to get her head in order. It was hard going: she had a bad hangover.

After the paramedics had left last night; she'd gotten hammered on the bottles of wine Chuck had earlier bought. It was the only way she could think of to calm herself. Sammy had left some sleeping pills behind in the medicine cabinet, but she'd known that if she'd taken one of those she'd wake up depressed, and being already depressed, that more or less meant that she'd wake up feeling suicidal.

The ambulance men had been perplexed. They'd never seen anything like Chuck Jennings' death before—a man with his head twisted around twice on his neck. Betsy had stuck to the story she'd agreed on with her aunt, telling the confused men that she'd returned from the bathroom to find him that way. There was no visible sign of either a struggle or of foul play, so they'd strapped the dead man to a gurney and carried him off.

Weeping, she'd followed them out to their vehicle. After loading Chuck into its rear, they'd told her the police would likely be over to question her further. She'd nodded and watched them drive off. She'd stood there with tears streaming down her cheeks. She'd at first wondered why the cops hadn't accompanied them over, then remembered she'd told the 911 woman that her boyfriend had had an 'accident of some kind,' and not that 'something had killed him.' Which meant it was only when the body hit the morgue that the shit would hit the fan, if it ever did. She'd had no idea if she was relieved to not have to recount her miserable story for a third time in the space of an hour.

Once the ambulance was out of sight, Betsy had locked up again. She'd dried her eyes, then called her aunt. She'd told her how everything had gone, hung up, and begun drinking. She'd finished both bottles of wine and passed out in the bed. Sometime during the night, she'd gotten up and staggered into the bathroom to pee. That done, she'd staggered out again and passed out on the bed again.

And woken up just now. She hadn't dreamt, which was a huge relief to her. She was certain any dreams she'd have had would have been of Chuck.

She walked into the kitchen and made herself a cup of coffee. The drink did little to help her hangover, but its caffeine content bulldozed a sufficiently clear path through her mental haze for her to think straight.

She was trembling, her body shaking now in a delayed reaction to last night's events. The morning was warm but she felt frozen. The cold poured from her soul, neutralizing the coffee's heat, till she felt as though she could drink the entire scalding brew and not notice its fiery temperature.

Sitting on a living room couch in her blue dressing gown, legs crossed at the ankles, her brown hair in her eyes, she sipped her coffee and pondered.

That voodoo doll has to go, she thought. *It's leaving my house today, before it makes another corpse. Yes, just like Aunt Malicia says, it may be my fault that Chuck is dead . . . but, what if she's wrong?*

She decided the debate was neither here nor there. Already, since waking up barely thirty minutes ago, she could sense the voodoo doll's evil presence in her house. It was a very unpleasant sensation. Had Betsy been perceiving it with her physical senses, she'd have likened the feeling to the reek from an unflushed defecation when the toilet door is left open. Something really nasty that you knew you were responsible for.

She couldn't tell if she was sensing the doll so strongly because it was linked to her, or because it was angry with her.

Both scenarios held sufficient cause for worry: The first, because it was truly horrifying sensing the devilish thing's ill will towards others (towards everyone except herself, it appeared); the second, because if the doll got angry enough with her (because she'd dumped it in that hatbox last night; or because—and this was a definite possibility— she'd not been either nasty or demanding enough in her use of its powers), it might chose to ignore the magical restraints placed on it against harming her.

That's it, the damn thing is scaring me shitless. She was admitting this to herself for maybe the fifth or sixth time since bringing the voodoo doll home. It was utterly crazy to be frightened of the instrument of one's own revenge. *But I am. I feel like I'm unhappily married to the damn thing!*

Betsy made up her mind: *Once I'm clearheaded enough to drive, I'll return it to Aunt Malicia.*

That resolved, she relaxed a little. Her trembling subsided and she felt a little safer in her own house. All she had to do now was survive the doll for three or four hours. By afternoon, she'd be recovered enough to trust herself behind the steering wheel of her car, and then . . .

Bye-bye, doll!

She however still had the issue of her husband to consider. But her thoughts towards the marital deserter were gentler now. After witnessing Chuck's death, she wasn't about taking any risky chances with Sammy getting killed too. The voodoo doll was way too powerful!

Look, I'll just forgive Sammy and ask auntie to bring him back home to me, and chain him to my side so that we'll live together happily ever after. Yes, that's what I'll do. She's already said she'll do it for me once I'm ready. So when I take the doll back this afternoon—

The doorbell rang. After fingerstyling her hair until it no longer looked like a bird's nest, she got up and went to answer the door.

She opened her front door. A bespectacled middle-aged man stood there holding a large envelope. Parked in the background was a white USPS van.

"Are you Mrs. Betsy Driscoll?" the man asked.

She first checked that her bathrobe was shut and her cleavage hidden. "Yep, that's me," she agreed finally. "Mail for me?"

"Certified USPS mail for you, ma'am," the man agreed.

She coldly regarded the envelope. At first she wondered who could be sending her such a letter. Then she realized it could only be one thing. What she'd been scared of was happening: Sammy was serving her divorce papers.

Divorce papers. Yesterday, Betsy would have either broken out screaming or broken into a cold sweat. Now, however, she just smiled and accepted the white envelope from the man.

"You seem upset," the USPS man observed. "I hope nothing's the matter."

She shrugged. "There's always something the matter, isn't there? Life is just a damn crisis to be survived."

He shrugged back like he understood. He pointed to a slip attached to the envelope. "You'll need to sign this return receipt, ma'am."

She signed. He departed with it. She watched him leave.

As his white van bore him away, she stood in her doorway and took the morning into herself, swallowing its tastes, inhaling its aromas, absorbing its bright colors through her eyes and letting her skin savor its heat and the random caress of its breezes. She was very aware that outside here—in actual fact once she'd taken even that first step out through the door—the voodoo doll's influence was more than halved. She felt like she'd stepped from jail into freedom.

But, all good things must come to an end. Wincing, she stepped back inside, shut the door, put the chain back on, and then made her way back into her living room to see what the mailman had brought her.

As she'd expected, it was the divorce papers. From some lawyer's office in Reno, Nevada. She pulled them out, scanned a page or two, then decided 'Fuck it!' and packed them away again.

She smirked to herself. *I know I'm not signing these—there's no need to, since I'm having Sammy couriered cross-country to me.*

She really liked the idea of her husband wrapped up like a birthday gift and delivered to her front door by the USPS, all meek and apologetic.

First, he'll eat a lot of humble pie, and then—she giggled to herself—*he's gonna eat a whole lot of hair pie!*

Yes, that was what was going to happen. The image was a delicious one. Betsy visualized herself spread-eagled in their bed, her thighs split wide while Sammy worshiped her vagina with his tongue, singing its praise and making her squirm with pleasure and orgasm over and over again. She saw herself on her hands and knees while he tongued her from behind, imagined him licking her anus, which he hardly ever did (he said it was unhygienic) . . . she imagined him sucking her clitoris gently, then harder, sucking bliss into her body.

She came out of her erotic daze tingly slightly. This was a much better feeling than the previous shivering: where earlier fear had clutched her in its negative grasp, this simmering eroticism she now felt was entirely positive in its effects on her psyche, filling her with hope for the future.

Best of all, it was helping her push back her memories of last night's horrors with the voodoo doll.

I need some more coffee though.

She got to her feet and, cup in hand, headed for the kitchen. Halfway there, she turned back and returned to fetch the envelope with the divorce papers.

Seeing as they're useless anyway, I might as well dispose of them.

She had complete faith in her Aunt Malicia's ability to deliver on what she'd promised.

That decided, before pouring herself more coffee, she lit the two largest burners on the gas range and dropped the white envelope on them.

There was a lot of smoke and she didn't want her neighbors to think she was burning down her house, so she didn't finish destroying the envelope's contents. She just made sure it was charred enough that signing or mailing anything back to Reno was completely out of the question. Then she turned off the gas, doused the flames with water, and dumped the soggy resulting mess into the trashcan.

Bye-bye, divorce!

Then she picked up her fresh cup of coffee and left the kitchen.

Once more, she found herself making a departure from her initial plans. Instead of returning to the living room to watch some television, she turned down the hallway. Taking brisk purposeful steps, she headed for the guest bedroom.

There, she reached into the top of the closet and took down the hatbox in which she'd hidden the voodoo doll. She opened the box and smirked down at its blue-suited inhabitant. The doll regarded her back with unseeing eyes. She didn't touch it. She wasn't ready to feel its clammy unnatural warmth just yet.

The doll had seven or eight pins stuck in it, including the 'migraine' one passing from ear to ear.

Oh, Sammy can't be feeling any kind of great at the moment. But it serves him right!

"Before you return home to Aunt Malicia," Betsy told the voodoo doll, "you and I are going to teach my husband Sammy one final painful lesson in respecting a woman's feelings. Okay, doll?"

Was it her imagination, or was the thing actually smiling at her? No, that was impossible. The carved sadistic curl of its lips hadn't altered, but she was sure she felt approval radiating from it; a degenerate delight at being once more put to use doing the bad things it had been designed for.

She carried the hatbox into her bedroom and began rooting around in her dresser for her pack of razor blades.

By the time she got through with slashing up Sammy's buttocks he'd think he was sitting on burning coals!

235

CHAPTER 30

Apache & Sully

Though warm, this Thursday morning was overcast and looked like it might rain.

Apache and Sully were over at the Oak Hill Mobile Home Park, at Sylvia and Larry Cooper's trailer home, investigating Mr. Ugly's latest killing.

In contrast to the other deaths, this was a more sedate murder, with just the husband's head cut off.

Sylvia Cooper had remained unconscious through the night. She was okay now though.

Also unharmed was the couple's eight-year-old daughter Sandy. When questioned, the child had said she'd heard a commotion last night, but she hadn't thought anything of it because her parents were always fighting.

This time, Forensics had arrived at the crime scene before the two detectives. There were two reasons for this: Firstly, Apache had had a bad hangover and Sully admitted to oversleeping after some wild sex with Tilly. But the second and more important reason, was that the Oak Hill Park was situated in Taunton, not Raynham, so the 911 distress call had first gone to the Taunton police station. Only after the first respondents had determined the exact nature of the emergency, had the case been rerouted across to the Raynham PD, since it clearly had to do with their current 'serial killer' investigation. The Taunton police chief was as much 'in the know' as Tina Kravitz, and was as interested in keeping a lid on this as she was.

By the time Apache and Sully arrived at the Cooper's trailer, Forensics already had the two pieces of Larry Cooper up on a gurney, ready to be borne away to the morgue.

Two chalk outlines on the floor of the mobile home's living room now indicated where his body and head had separately lain. The trailer was filled with women and men taking measurements. One woman was swabbing up a puddle of the familiar black-mud mess.

After hearing both the mother's and the daughter's statements, Sully dragged Apache out of earshot into the trailer kitchen.

"This is confirmation of what I was saying last night," he whispered.

"I daresay it is," Apache readily agreed. "There really is no rhyme or reason to the deaths. But . . . Sylvia says he threatened to come back and kill her too."

"Yeah, yeah, but why the delay? What the hell is he waiting for?"

"I don't know. You don't know either. We're just gonna roll with it; the answers will come if we're patient."

"Old man, if we're *too* patient, there may be no one left in town to save."

Apache scowled at that. *There Sully goes again, being all melodramatic. Shows what use TV is to detectives: four deaths and he's already envisaging the zombie apocalypse.*

Then he glanced over at Sylvia Cooper, who was sitting on a living room couch and clutching her daughter tightly to her.

Appearance-wise, the new widow was simply an older, female version of her brother. Almost as if nature had known Max Byler wouldn't be around as a future reference point for the physical resemblance of his children, both Danny and Sylvia had inherited their mother's slight physique and delicate face.

Apache ran his mind over Sylvia's tale of last night's happening. It was the expected sordid story: Larry had been beating her up yet again when a man in a blue suit with no face and rotting skin had killed him.

Apache didn't doubt she was telling the truth. As glaring proof of the family altercation, Sylvia had two black eyes, a split lip, and her throat was bruised a deep purple.

Sandy, the little kid, was staring wide-eyed at everything, as if she wasn't yet certain exactly what was happening, or like she thought a cop TV drama was being filmed in her home. She looked like she thought her father had simply been called up to Heaven on vacation by God and would shortly be back home again.

Her mother looked similarly shell-shocked, but . . . Sylvia was also doing her utmost best not to show how pleased she was that Larry was dead. Yes, she *was* scared stiff over what had happened to her, but if one looked behind that, her relief at being unchained from her husband was obvious.

Apache didn't blame her; he'd always expected to hear someday that she'd stabbed or shot the dead man. With brutes like that, it was only a matter of time before the wife had enough and hit back, usually fatally.

(As a matter of fact, Larry Cooper's death was already being explained to the other trailer park residents as Sylvia stabbing him in self-defense while he was trying to kill her. No one was going to question the truth of that lie.)

Apache found it hard to feel sorry for the dead man. No, not just *hard*, he found it well-nigh impossible.

Larry Cooper had been all the things Apache couldn't tolerate: a lazy bastard, a bully and a braggart, and a drunk and a fool. He'd been one of those nasty people who made the world a worse place to live in. True, no one deserved to die the way he had, but everyone was going to say he had it coming to him. No one was ever going to shed any tears for Larry Cooper.

Apache had had to control himself to not laugh aloud on seeing the partly bloodied writing on Larry's T-shirt as the man was wheeled out of the trailer: 'TO PAY FOR MY SINS'? Everyone in Raynham was certain to be joking about that for years to come.

But that had been a mere flyspeck of comic relief on an elephant's turd of craziness.

Apache watched a female police officer escort Sylvia and Sandy Cooper into the little girl's bedroom so they could pack a few of her things. Sylvia had said she was off to stay at her mother's place.

Sully left Apache's side and slipped on a pair of latex gloves so he could join in the search for clues.

Left by himself, Apache leaned against the trailer fridge and pondered this latest twist in the case. He did his best to make sense of what really made no sense. He wondered where to begin plugging the leakage of logic before the dam of coherence burst and flooded the valley of reason all over again.

His phone rang then, an irritated buzzing like the noise of a thousand blowflies arriving late to feast on the dead man.

He pulled it out and checked the screen. He whistled. "Well, speak of the Devil and she appears."

He had no idea he'd spoken aloud until Sully asked: "What's up, old man? Why d'you look so shocked all of a sudden?"

Apache gestured him over. "It's Malicia Howard calling me," he whispered.

Sully's eyes widened. "For real?"

The phone was still ringing. One or two of the Taunton cops were looking at the Raynham detectives, wondering why Apache didn't answer the call.

Sully gestured at the phone. "You'd best see what she wants."

Apache accepted the call. There was a weird crackle of static in his inner ear and then Malicia's witchy voice: "Come and see me, Apache."

He raised an eyebrow. "Okay, but later. I'll—"

"No. *Right now*. Leave whatever you're up to and come over to my house *right now*. This is important."

"Alright, I'll be—"

"And come *alone*," she interrupted him again. "Don't bring your young assistant with you. What we're going to discuss won't make any sense to him and I don't want to have to explain or repeat myself."

"Yeah, alright. I'll—" But she'd already hung up.

"She wants me to come and see her right now," he told Sully.

"So, let's go."

"Uh uh, kid. She's says I'm to come alone."

"You can't do that," Sully immediately protested, his voice a harsh whisper. "Not after everything you told me about her. The woman's nuts. She's . . . she's . . ."

Apache shook his head. "We do it like she says," he said, adjusting his ponytail. "Exactly like she says. She's the only one who can stop this mess, and for the moment, until we find a crack in her armor, we'd best stay on her good side."

"But she's dangerous," Sully whispered.

Apache shook his mangled right hand at Sully; this morning he was wearing a black glove on it. "Don't you think I already know that?" He shrugged. "Don't worry 'bout me. I'll be fine. She likely just wants to gloat and mock our failure."

Sully grimaced at the blood splattered everywhere, then grudgingly escorted Apache out of the trailer.

"Keep on her good side, huh, old man?" he said as they stepped outside. "If this is the woman's *good* side, I'd utterly hate to see her *bad* one."

Somehow, Apache found that very funny.

CHAPTER 31

Apache & Malicia

"Well, here I am."

Apache pulled up outside the Mr. & Mrs. Book Emporium, parking the unmarked squad car a few feet from the front door. He had a bitter taste in his mouth and it looked about to get even bitterer.

He avoided looking at the brown and white house. The single glance he'd unwisely taken while steering the car up the driveway had shown him that the building still had that weird effect on the air around it, making it waver and dance like the haze over a bonfire, making the house's upper floor appear to shift and move from side to side like tree branches in a storm.

Apache had no desire to view that again, so once he'd parked and left the squad car, he kept his gaze fixed down on the stone walkway and headed straight for Malicia's front door.

The door opened even before the sound of the buzzer had ceased echoing. She'd clearly been waiting for him. She stood out of the way in the shadows to permit him to enter, then shut and bolted the door behind them both.

"Follow me," she said. "We'll talk upstairs."

She set off immediately after speaking. Apache took the briefest of glances around the renovated bookstore, noting how sedate and sane it looked, then hurried after the old woman who'd already turned a corner in the hallway and was ascending the stairs.

Why the hell am I having a sense of deja vu? he asked himself as he followed her up the stairs.

Then, in an unnerving flash, the answer occurred to him: *She's wearing the same red dress. Exactly the same red dress. No, that would be impossible—this one she has on now isn't old. It's new, but it's the exact same blood color as the one she had on the last time she fucked things up.*

241

He stared down at her bare feet on the stairs. He grimaced. Was she leaving wet footprints? The stairwell lights were off. He was unable to tell if her footprints were a liquid red or not.

Please let them not be, he thought.

They climbed the stairs slowly, with Malicia not turning round to make sure he was following. Each step up seemed to be taking her all of her strength and concentration. Once she was firmly placed on the next step, she would stop to catch her breath. She seemed so frail, yet an almost palpable menace radiated from her. It prevented him from trying to either steady her or help her up the stairs.

As he watched her hobble upwards, he formulated a plan in his mind: *If she's mutilated herself again like I think she has, that'll provide us with sufficient evidence that she's still 'crazy' and deserving to be locked back in her padded cell. And this time, I'll personally gag-ball her myself.*

Such were Apache's thoughts as he and Malicia Howard arrived in her living room.

Now she turned around. For the first time he saw her clearly.

Oh Fuck! Her lips were painted a bright red. She'd shaded her eyelids red also; they were garish crimson circlets around her eyes.

Scared that history was about repeating itself before his very eyes, Apache looked down at her feet. Though she'd not painted either her fingernails or toenails crimson this time, Malicia Howard was standing in a widening pool of blood.

Feeling his courage draining away, Apache looked back up at her face. She was smirking at him. She could tell that he was scared of her. It amused her.

"Malicia, you said you just wanted to talk."

She grinned. "Oh yes I do, Apache. Have a seat. I'll be right back."

She hobbled off into the back of the apartment, leaving bloody footprints in her wake. He sat. He felt trapped. He'd been wrong to answer her summons alone. He should have ignored the old woman's restrictions and brought Sully along. Sully could have waited outside in the squad car.

Despite which, he couldn't leave either. It would be the easiest thing in the world to simply hightail it down the steps now before she returned, and let himself out of this crazy house and drive off. But he couldn't do that. He had a responsibility to protect the public, and he had to live up to that expectation. If he left, what then? He and Sully already knew that Malicia was responsible for the killings. She alone held the key to undoing the havoc she'd set in motion. Despite his previous plan to simply shut her away again, Apache suspected that if they did so, the deaths would continue unabated anyway, and this time without even a ghost of a chance of stopping Mr. Ugly.

He looked around, noticing for the first time the red pentagram drawn in the middle of the light green rug and also the five glittering obsidian puddles spaced evenly around it that might or might not be melted candle wax. Also on the floor, and in the middle of the pentagram, lay an open weird-looking book with strangely colored, leathery pages. Apache had the worrying impression that he'd seen this book before, somewhere, a long time ago.

By imperceptible stages, the room was darkening. It took Apache a while to notice this. Once he did so, he tried to figure out why it was happening.

Across the room, the curtains were drawn. The darkness in the room however seemed to have little to do with light not entering it. And in any case, the living room lights were on. As far as he could tell, the darkness was emerging from the walls. As it thickened around him, the walls themselves grew murkier, till it seemed he was viewing them through a sheet of black smoke.

This is a witches lair! I need to get the hell out of here!

But then Malicia Howard walked out of the hallway, stark naked and carrying a knife in her hand. She walked through the darkness like she owned it. It split before her and reformed behind her. The fading light glittered off the long blade she bore towards him.

Seeing the knife, Apache instantly went for his gun.

"Put the damn gun away," she commanded. "This is well beyond your middle-aged machismo."

He holstered his gun again. His scalp felt prickly and he'd begun sweating. This wasn't from fear: the living room had begun heating up.

Just like last time. Exactly like last time. But . . . no, this is different: it isn't like she wants to eat the parts of me she overlooked the last time we were in the same room together. She just wants to talk.

Malicia was sweating too, large iridescent beads of water forming on her aged and wrinkled skin and trickling down her body like dissolved pearls.

Apache grimaced. *Shit! She's sliced herself up again!*

Along with the streams of perspiration, blood was also oozing from Malicia's body, seeping from the lines, angles and curves of the many pentagrams and devil-crosses she'd cut into her skin. She'd mutilated her breasts and belly and arms and legs—every part of herself. The emerging blood hung on the edges of the cuts, giving them visual definition, then slowly dripped down, finding fresh pathways in her creased skin. New blood immediately took its place within the magic symbols, so that Apache was staring at an obscene work of art, one wrought with razors in aged human flesh.

"Do you like it?" Malicia asked, smirking at him.

Apache gulped. *Like it? Is she nuts?* Just looking at her, with the blood escaping her everywhere like this, made him want to void his bowels. It made him want to leap up and run screaming to the nearest window and fling himself out of it, down into the welcoming yard below.

But that would be impossible. The living room no longer had any windows: the darkness had now completely taken over its walls. A quick glance over at the entrance from the stairwell revealed that it too had vanished into the encroaching gloom. So too, he realized, had the ceiling and—looking down—most of the floor also.

The heat in Malicia's living room was overpowering now. Apache's shirt was already soaked, and the sweat was making fast inroads through his jacket and pants as well.

The old woman was still staring at him. Standing there, knife in hand, immobile; watching his face until he looked directly at her again. He didn't want to look at her bloody body, but had no choice. He feared that if he took his attention off her for too long she would try to slit his throat.

"What's going on?" he gasped. "What the hell are you doing?"

The glint in her eyes hovered close to actual madness. Her facial expression spoke of her juggling agony with the most intense ecstasy. "You haven't yet answered me, Apache. Do you like what you're seeing?"

"You're crazy, old woman."

Smiling, she stepped into the middle of her pentagram. As she did so, the lines of the infernal star flared up with a brilliant purple glow. "Crazy? You'd love to think that, wouldn't you, so you can lock me away again? But you don't really believe it, do you? You know me a whole lot better than that."

"What do you want? Why are you doing this? Why are you killing everyone?"

"Everyone? Don't exaggerate, Apache. It's just four dead so far. But there are going to be many more corpses. Many, many more. You can count on that." She grinned, waving the knife at him as if it was a magic wand. "And besides, it wasn't me. I didn't actually kill any of them, did I?"

Apache was gripped by a fierce urge to pull out his gun and just shoot her, to blow her brains out and send fragments of her stupid skull spinning away through the surrounding darkness. But he didn't. He suspected that that wasn't how it worked.

Her next words confirmed as much to him:

"Don't bother with killing me," she said. "It won't solve a thing. My death won't halt what I've set in motion. Peter will go on butchering people no matter what happens to me."

"Please stop him," he pleaded. "You shouldn't still want revenge after all this time."

"Shouldn't I?" Her pale aged eyes took on a look of rage. "Shouldn't I? What else do you think I did in the asylum for fifteen years? What else, except plot my revenge? What else did I have to do in that horrible place except think about getting even?"

"But . . . but . . ." He didn't want to admit that she had a point. "You should be remorseful, old woman. You killed a whole lot of people back then. A lot of innocent people who'd never done you any harm. People you didn't even know."

"Not enough of them. I . . . no, Peter . . . is about to kill a whole lot more this time." She cackled softly to herself. "There's no way the town authorities will succeed in sweeping this mess under the rug like they did with what happened in the courthouse back then."

"So . . . you're not just going after the Bylers and their relatives?"

"Nope. It's mostly random. Peter just kills whoever catches his fancy. To his dead mind, he's still young, so that's why he's butchering young people. He should start on the old folks soon enough."

"I'm just coming from the Coopers' home. Peter killed the husband, but not the wife Sylvia, who was Max's daughter. Why?"

Malicia shrugged. "I dunno. Maybe he thought she was cute."

"She ain't off the hook yet though. He told her he'd come back to get her."

"Maybe he wants to . . . you know, get intimate with her. You know how teenage boys are always horny. Maybe he wants to make an undead baby or something like that with Sylvia. The fact that she's Max's kid will only add to the juicy pleasure of it—like kicking his tormentors in the balls."

Apache had the sense that there was more to it than that, that this crazy old witch was playing with him. But he was here in her domain and had to play by her rules.

He chanced a glance around. *Yeah, 'domain' is the right world. What the fuck is this shit?*

Now there was no suggestion that they were still inside a living room, or even inside a house for that matter. The actual walls had all vanished, to be replaced by walls of darkness that throbbed as if alive. All the light now came from the pentagram on the floor, which extruded a creepy purple fluorescent glow. This glow extended from obscured floor to smoky ceiling as if trapped inside a light bulb.

Worst of all, to Apache's mind, were the faint openings he could see in the surrounding darkness. There were seven or eight of these, spaced evenly around the vanished room. Each of these breaches in the night-wall was about seven feet high and shaped like a gray archway.

One of these openings was directly behind him. It gave him the creepy sensation of being watched, as though it and the others were the residences of living creatures. Even more disturbing, above each gray arch was set a plaque of some kind on which red letters glowed. For the briefest of seconds he was able to make out the words over an archway to his right: AGONY. Along with discerning this, Apache realized that he could hear screaming. Loud agonized cries of terror, as of people being tormented.

Now too, the detective understood why everywhere was so hot: the heat was pouring out from the openings. He visualized infernal, unquenchable fires burning behind those gray spaces.

She's opened gateways into Hell, Apache realized. *And I stupidly came here to meet her.*

He stared at the dripping old woman standing naked amidst the hellish purple light, with the still-spreading pool of her blood around her feet. She was looking away from him. She'd dropped her knife. Now, holding the pink-leathered book open before her, she was mumbling to herself; words that made no sense to him.

Okay, I've seen enough, he decided. Yes, it was foolhardy, but he had to stop her. *I recall what came through the walls the last time I heard her mumbling like this. And this time she's preparing for a real bloodbath!*

Faced with the supernatural like this, Apache Johnson didn't feel particularly brave. But . . . but . . . now, squinting, he could make out shapes inside the gray portals, and those shapes weren't even marginally human.

After a miserable glance at his mangled right hand—*I'd better just use the left one this time and hope her teeth have gotten blunter with age*—he started to get up.

And found that he couldn't. It felt as though he'd been glued to his chair.

A single glance down revealed to him why this was: seven hands from the darkness were holding him in place in his armchair. Each hand was as pale as death and was rotting. Coming from nothingness, each curled around the side of the chair to clutch its respective part of Apache's body—his forearms, his thighs and his neck. Most daunting of all, each zombie-like extremity was at least thrice the size of his own. Two of the largest of these giant hands had locked fingers across his chest, fastening his torso in place.

No, Apache wasn't getting up. There was no question about that: he could barely move.

Sure looks like I ain't about going anywhere, Apache glumly accepted.

"Hey, what's with all this bondage?" he growled at Malicia. "You turn kinky in the asylum or what?"

"Just some insurance," she replied him over her shoulder. "I don't want to have to eat the rest of your hand."

"Okay, so what do you really want with me anyway? Why the hell did you invite me over? It don't look like you want to kill me, so what *do* you want?"

She didn't immediately reply him. She put her obscene book aside, knelt down in the pentagram, and rested her forehead on the hot black stone that had now replaced the green rug. Her voice rose to a banshee's wail. At the same time, the tube of purple light encasing her tripled its brightness.

The increased intensity of the light permitted Apache to see clearly what the surrounding portals contained. He gasped, blinked, gaped, and again just managed not to fill his pants with feces.

The creatures he was seeing in there defied description. He could see eyes and mouths and tentacles and arms and legs and claws and feelers and wings and whatnot, but their arrangements on their owner's bodies made no sense to his mind; no sense whatsoever. Sometimes the limbs and eyes and mouths (and everything else) even seemed to occur *inside* one another or as bridges between themselves.

He was relieved when the purple light dimmed again and he was once more left with an audience of shadows. No one, either living or dead, should have to view those abominations that lurked behind the hellish darkness.

Malicia got up and turned around to face him. As though the Abyss had left a fresh mark on her, additional blood now seeped from a pentagram etched in the middle of her forehead. The blood traveled down around her eyes, between her nose and cheeks, and around her mouth to hang as crimson drops on her chin. Farther down her body, more blood welled from the inverted crosses cut around her nipples.

Apache was very perplexed: *How can she be bleeding so much and yet still be alive?* It was an equally baffling question to another: *How the hell did she turn her living room into this nightmare I'm currently trapped in?*

Yes, it was magic. He knew that. He'd experienced it before and hated it. And now, second time around, he hated it even more.

By this point Apache Johnson was beyond fear. It wasn't courage he felt, so much as numb. Numb because, well, 'What the fuck!?' was the only description he had for his current straits: restrained in an armchair by giant decomposing hands, surrounded by archways filled with impossible monsters, bathed in so much heat that it felt like he was sweating to death, and being stared at by an old woman who'd sliced herself open so badly that all the blood her withered form had contained now seemed to be on the ground around her, but who yet was still alive; and not just alive, but who increasingly seemed to throb with a vitality she'd not possessed on letting him into her house. Back then she'd seemed feeble and impotent. Now she appeared as energetic as a racehorse.

Apache had walked into a place that was so far from the ordinary that ordinary reactions no longer counted. All he could do now was go with the flow and hope this river of unceasing insanity didn't drown him.

"Tell me, old woman," he said in a voice that equally lacked courage and fear. "What do you want from me? Why'd you ask me over? Is it to sacrifice me to these Hell creatures of yours?"

She shook her head. "No, I'm not going to kill you, detective."

"So what, then? If you ain't ready to talk yet, just let me leave. I'll come visit you again when you're in the mood to chat."

She laughed. She appreciated his wit even though he was her prisoner. "No, we'll finish this now."

"Stop playing waiting games then. We're both old people, we ain't got that much time left to waste." He took a chance: "And for God Almighty's holy sake, tell these damn hands holding me to let go of me. They're squeezing me so hard that I'm gonna crap my pants and their damn stink's making me wanna throw up."

Her eyes narrowed. "If I release you, do you swear not to make a nuisance of yourself?"

He nodded. "Yeah, yeah, sure. It ain't like I can escape from here anyway. All these doorways lead to Hell, right?"

"Different parts of it. Alright, I'll instruct the hands to release you. But if you try anything . . ."

"Trust me, I won't. You've made your point—you're the queen of the damned. Hey, I'm so far outclassed here, I might as well be back in kindergarten."

With a cold smile, she snapped her fingers six times. The huge hands let go of Apache and melted back into the darkness.

She waited for a second until he'd adjusted himself in the armchair and seemed comfortable again. "Alright, now on to why I summoned you here."

"I'm listening."

"I want you to understand."

She left him sufficient time for her words to sink in and confuse him. They did confuse him. He pondered them. *Understand? She wants me to understand?*

"Understand what, Malicia?"

"I want you to understand *why* I'm doing this."

"What's there to understand about that? You're bitter, that's all. Hell, if *my* only kid got murdered the way Peter was, I'd be madder than hell too."

"That's *not* what I want you to understand."

He raised an eyebrow. "What then? Come on, make this easy on me. If you keep up this Twenty Questions shit, I'll need a shrink by the time you let me out of *here*." To emphasize his words, he gestured around at the darkness, which throbbed back at him as though it or the entities it concealed found his remarks humorous. "Hey, I think I *already* need a shrink and a padded cell. Lady, kill me if you want, just don't kill me with suspense."

She found that very funny and burst out laughing. Then she abruptly sobered again. Her eyes turned icy and her lips thinned to an almost imperceptible line between her chin and her nose. She was still bleeding: each time she moved a part of her body, the symbols etched there opened up and more blood spilled from them.

She grimaced, which caused the spurting of crimson jets from crooked symbols in each cheek. "Okay, no more games. I'll just come right out and tell you—"

"Thank you."

"—Because if I had you guess the answer, you never would in a thousand years, and I don't have the time to wait for your old mind to get there."

"Thanks. I appreciate your concern for my mental wellbeing. I'm now one step farther away from the psychiatrist's couch."

She stepped closer to him. "See, Apache, when at first I got to the asylum, I was repentant for what I'd done. My anger cooled and all I could think about were the corpses, particularly Judge Snelson, 'cos I knew his wife Judy. I'd sit down in my room and see all those innocent people torn open and ripped to shreds and eaten by the cot'ns, and I'd weep with remorse. Yes, I'd made my point, but at a horrible cost. To make my point to Bart and Cissy that Peter hadn't killed their daughter, I'd become as much of a monster as they were." Her voice softened. "I *hated* that. Just as I hadn't wanted Peter to be remembered as a murderer, so too I didn't want to be remembered as one either. So I spent my days wishing I hadn't gone as far as I did. I wished I'd summoned something more manageable; or maybe just used voodoo dolls to additionally kill Bart and Cissy and those other two murdering youths as well. Cot'ns are almost impossible to control; they don't think like we do; they've got on-off commands and that's about it. You set them free and they start feasting on people." She shrugged. "But it was already too late for tears then, wasn't it?"

Apache nodded. "No point crying over shed blood." He still didn't see where this was leading.

"But still, mixed in with my sorrow, I felt a little pride. Even if I'd be considered a vengeful bitch, Peter's name had been cleared. I was certain the story would spread and I'd be, if not exactly famous, at least vindicated."

"Yeah, okay," Apache agreed. At this point, he could almost sympathize with her. "Hey," he asked, "is it alright if I take off my jacket? I don't know about you, but this room of yours make a great case for explaining the concept of air conditioning to the Devil."

This time she didn't even crack a smile. "Yeah, take it off. But remember, no tricks."

"Don't you worry 'bout that. Trust me, lady: I wouldn't try tricking you even if we were both twenty again and I hadn't had sex in six months."

While Malicia Howard pondered whether his statement was a compliment on the greatness of her paranormal abilities or a putdown stating her lack of sexual desirability, Apache slipped his suit jacket off. It was soaking through and through with perspiration. The sweat had plastered his shirt to his torso and his pants to his legs. Beneath the latter, his briefs felt like a wet animal squirming around his crotch. He quickly loosened his tie also, till it looked like a black noose draped round his neck. The heat was unbearable, water beading on his temples and running down into his eyes almost faster than he could blink or wipe it away. He hoped Malicia would be done talking before he got seriously dehydrated. In this Hell environment she'd conjured up, that was certain to prove fatal.

He draped the jacket over his knee. "Alright, go on."

She resumed her explanation: "So, like I said, at first I was so remorseful over what I'd done that I tried committing suicide. Each night I'd chant spells to bring the cot'ns back to eat me. But they didn't come. There was no *blood*, see? And they only come when there's blood on offer. The first thing the doctors did when I got to the asylum was to patch me up. So by the time my remorse had replaced my rage, I was half healed, and . . . in a straitjacket. Meaning, no chance to hurt myself again. So the spells didn't work. And then—just when I'd worked out that I could simply bite off the end of my tongue and have all the blood I needed—they gagged me too, so I couldn't even pray to the darkness and plead with it to kill me."

Apache nodded. He knew this part of the story, how two interns had heard her casting spells around midnight. Of course, they'd not known that she'd been trying to kill herself in there or they might have left her alone to do it.

And saved us all this damn bother now.

"But then . . ." Malicia continued, "but then I began hearing about the cover-up. How to the public, I'd been painted as a psycho terrorist—there wasn't a single mention anywhere of magic or of the cot'ns. Hearing that was a crushing blow to me. Apparently, everything I'd done had been for nothing. Peter wouldn't be vindicated after all."

"C'mon," Apache protested, "They *had* to cover up what happened. You know no one would've believed it."

She shook her head firmly. "Yes, they would have believed it. I never used to believe in magic either. Harry always told me it worked, but I never believed him, not even when it killed him. But Tammy's death made me a believer."

"Hey, you're forgetting that the cot'ns didn't wait around to do interviews."

"Your fault." She gave him an evil smile. "Was your hand much use for masturbating after that?"

He managed a replying smile. "Nah, for six months I couldn't even make a fist or hold a pen. Thank heavens I was married; if I'd been single I've no idea how I'd have coped. But, don't sidetrack me: you're saying you're angry with everyone now just because they covered up the deaths. That's crazy."

"Not crazy. I'll never forgive nor forget you all trying to erase my work." A sudden surge of rage overcame Malicia. She leaned forward over him, bending till her bleeding face was almost touching his, her nostrils flaring, spit flecking her lips. "You went too far when you did that," she spat at him. "The entire town went too far!"

Apache saw no point in immediately replying—she was too annoyed to see reason. He sat in his armchair and sweated. He stared at her, this old woman clothed in a 'ripped robe' of blood, and waited. His throat felt as parched as if he was walking through a desert.

Maybe, right before I die of dehydration, I'll be able to convince her to reverse the spell that's brought her son back to murderous life.

She looked angry enough to bite him. He tensed, preparing to duck out of reach if she suddenly launched her teeth at his nose. But then she straightened up again and abruptly changed the topic:

"I may be angry and vengeful, detective, but I'm not entirely evil. There is a key to unlocking this mystery. It is possible to reverse the spell and send Peter back into the darkness again."

Apache stiffened on hearing this. Was she about to relent? Considering how angry she still was, it was too much to hope for. But he hoped anyway.

"How do we stop Peter?" he asked.

She scowled back. "Hell no, I'm not going to tell you that. You surely don't expect me to tell you that. I'm not going to make it easy for you. I deserve some more fun at the town's expense. You and your young partner must work it out for yourselves. The answer to your problem is a riddle I'm giving you to solve. And the sooner you solve it, the sooner the killings will end." She burst into loud mirthless laughter. "In a sense, I've just put the responsibility for any further deaths on your head, Apache Johnson: people will keep dying until you stop them dying."

Apache once again wished he could just shoot her and be done with it. "I'm not responsible for your actions," he said.

"I'm making you responsible."

"I'm not getting involved in this."

"You're already involved in this. You were there at the bitter beginning and you'll be there at the sweet end too." She laughed some more. "It's my horrible gift to you."

Then, her face solemn again, she gestured around the darkness. "But forget that. Now we've other things to discuss and attend to."

"What are you talking about?"

Before replying, she strode back into her pentagram and picked up her knife. Then she asked: "Do you know, detective, what hurt me the most about that cover-up the town did?"

He shook his head. He had a bad feeling about that knife in her hand. She was just three yards away from him and if she lunged at him, the blade could be at his throat or stuck in his belly before he could draw his gun.

However, she made no move towards him. She merely beat her left palm with the flat of the knife. "No, you wouldn't know, would you? I'll tell you—it was that nasty rumor that the Board of Selectmen spread about me having hid a shotgun in my vagina. You've no idea how much I suffered because of that."

"It was just a joke. No one really took it seriously."

"No one!?" Her gaze dulled with painful memory. "Do you really believe that nonsense you're saying!? You think no one believed I had a huge pussy? I lived in a madhouse, detective. In a *lunatic asylum.* *Everyone* in there took it seriously! Even the doctors started looking at me all funny after that. I had to endure fifteen years of being called 'Big-Pussy Malice.' Once, two crazy men actually inserted their hands inside my body, just to be certain if the rumors were true or not. They tore me up so badly that I needed to have stitches."

Apache kept quiet; too bothered to interrupt her. While she spoke, he focused his eyes beyond her, on the archway immediately to her right. He stared at the dark entity coiling and uncoiling in there. It looked like one of the dreaded cot'ns. But then again, it didn't. For one thing, it had more than one set of yellow eyes. For another, he thought he saw several heads in there, distorted heads that were of different shapes and sizes.

Malicia went on: "That smear on my vagina made my life an utter misery. I credit it with making me the woman I am today. But see, it also made me think. Yes, I *wondered.* And do you know *what* I wondered most about? . . . Hey, pay attention to me—you're not gonna want to miss this!"

Apache realized his distraction. He returned his attention to Malicia. Now she was walking in a circle inside her pentagram. Without looking down, she was tracing exactly the inner border of its red loop. She was still bleeding. Her blood was extending the red ring around the five-pointed star. Her right elbow poked through the tube of projected purple light. Reflected light from her knife bounced off the overhead blackness.

"What I wondered," she said once she'd gotten his full attention again, "was, if I *was* going to store a shotgun somewhere in my body, where would I put it?"

She's crazy, he thought.

"I'm not crazy," she said. "It's a valid question for a terrorist sorceress. I took my time and worked out exactly where to stash a shotgun inside of myself. Look—I'll show you!"

And before Apache could utter a word of protest, Malicia Howard had stabbed herself in the belly. She stuck the knife in to the left of her navel. She stabbed deep, her eyes widening with pain. Then she pulled the blade right, widening the gash.

Then, grimacing, she flung the bloody knife towards Apache.

He'd ducked out of its way before realizing she'd not aimed the knife at him, but into the darkness over his head.

When he looked back towards Malicia, he saw that she'd now stuck her right hand into the hole she'd cut in her belly and was feeling around inside herself. She was clearly in pain: she winced as she searched inside herself, and blood had begun dribbling out through her red-lipsticked lips.

"Hey! Stop it! What the hell are you doing?" Despite his desire to see her dead, he started getting up to go restrain her.

Seeing him rising from the armchair, her pale eyes flared up.

"No, don't interfere!" she yelled at him in anguish. "Just watch me! Don't you dare come near or I'll have the hands restrain you again."

Apache didn't want those undead hands touching him again. He sank meekly back down into the armchair and watched her.

Malicia had now found what she'd been looking for inside her body and was pulling it out of herself. Apache gaped as she pulled a Remington Wingmaster pump-action shotgun out of her belly. The shotgun was covered with blood.

How could she fit that inside there? How? There's no way that shotgun could have fit inside her body.

She laughed weakly at his confusion. "See? See how I'd do it? No, there isn't enough space in my vagina to hide a shotgun."

She was weak now, staggering. It seemed as if slicing herself open had finished her. The blood was streaming from the belly cut she had made.

How much blood does this damn woman have inside of her, for chrissakes?

Malicia cocked the shotgun. Then she pointed it at Apache. It was the first time in his life that he'd ever seen blood pouring from the barrel of a gun. And it now looked set to be the last time too.

"Alright, detective!" she barked at him. "The fun's over. Prepare to become food for the darknesses."

Oops, she suckered me. I'm monster food! Sweat-drenched monster food.

He desperately began thinking of how he could reach his own gun before she blew his head off. He tried to stall her, to distract her:

"Hey, hey—but you said you weren't going to kill me."

To his relief and surprise, she immediately lowered the weapon. "No, I'm not. I'm just fooling with you. . . . But do you understand now? Understand that a lady's vagina is no place to store a shotgun!? Do you get that, Apache?"

He nodded.

"Answer me in words: Do you get it?"

"Yeah, yeah, I do!"

"Apologize. Go on, do it!"

"Do you want me to get on my knees before I kiss your ass?"

She was wobbling on her feet now, but still managed to raise the shotgun and point it at him again. "If you dare smart-mouth me one more time, Apache Johnson, I'll make you kiss my vagina till I climax. Just apologize on behalf of the Raynham public for insulting it!!"

"I apologize on behalf of the people of Raynham for insulting your vagina."

"Once more. Put some heart in it."

"I apologize on behalf of the people of Raynham and of the government of the bay state of Massachusetts for insulting Malicia Howard's vagina."

"One final time. Do it like your erection depends on it." She wagged the shotgun at his crotch. "You never know, it just might."

Apache stood up. *Best to humor her*, he decided. He took a deep breath and proclaimed:

"I, law enforcement detective James 'Apache' Johnson, on behalf of the guilty people of Raynham, those of the New England state of Massachusetts, and of the general public and government of the United States of America, including our glorious leader, President Donald Trump, hereby do repent and apologize to Mildred Alicia Howard for slandering and maligning her tight and well-behaved pussy, lying instead that it was a slack bag in which miscellaneous weapons of mass destruction can be stored and used to attack North Korea and other enemies of our great nation and—"

He stopped speaking because she'd burst out laughing. She laughed and laughed and laughed. Painfully, but from her belly and with tears rolling down her cheeks. She bled all over as she laughed, but that didn't stop her. And while laughing she was waving to him to sit down again.

He did. He waited till she stopped laughing. She did finally. Either she'd laughed herself out or her pain had gotten the better of her mirth.

"Ah, that was good!" she exclaimed weakly, with blood bubbling over her lips. " 'Tight and well-behaved pussy?' 'Donald Trump?' You almost made those fifteen years of incarceration seem worth it. Have you ever considered a career in politics, Apache? You'd be wonderful as one of those sleazy, baby-kissing liars."

Now that the apology was over, he began hoping she'd die. The blood was streaming out of the fresh hole she'd cut in her belly. *Why won't you die, old woman?* he questioned in his mind. *Why won't you just die? Then I can get to work on solving this riddle you've handed me!*

She smiled at him then and there was something in her smile that chilled him afresh. Her lips projected a darkness which stripped away all his blithe acceptance of his situation and in its place restored to him all his initial horrors at her filling her living room with black barriers to his departure and gray portals that led to a Satanic otherwhere squirming with monsters.

"What is it *now?*" he gasped. Above her painted lips, her crimson-rimmed eyes had taken on a look of intense sorrow, but sorrow that was mixed with a hellish sense of purpose. Apache again doubted that he'd leave here alive.

"I'm just fooling with you, detective," Malicia said. "I actually like you very much."

"Huh?"

She nodded. "You're a good person, Apache. I really just called you over to witness my death. The darknesses—those creatures you can see in the portals around us—have asked me to make the Final Sacrifice, and I'm doing it now."

"Final Sacrifice? What's that?"

She waved the question away and spoke into the air as if he wasn't there: "My death will make Peter stronger! He'll be able to kill, kill, kill!"

"But you can't do—"

He shut up. She'd already reversed the direction of her shotgun. She placed the weapon's muzzle in her mouth and pulled the trigger.

Her head exploded. The top of her head blew away in a spray of blood and fragments of brain and bone, leaving nothing existing above the level of her nose. Still clutching the shotgun, her body collapsed into the middle of the pentagram.

Apache gaped at Malicia's corpse. Around him the darkness quivered with pleasure. He could see its black walls throbbing like an excited penis.

Even though she was dead, just a mess of bloody flesh, Malicia's voice floated around him:

"I am satisfied, detective. My Final Sacrifice has given Peter—oh, so you all call him Mr. Ugly now—more power than ever. But, no, I'm not unfair, Apache. You can still stop him—if you can figure out the riddle of his resurrection, the key to his existence. But remember— the countdown is on. How many people die from now on is entirely up to you."

"Well, if that's the case, then I'd better get to work," he replied her, angered at the evil burden she'd given him.

He made to get up, but once more found himself restrained.

He sighed. Not again. The decaying zombie hands had returned and again held him pinned down in his armchair.

"Hey, what's this about?" he shrieked at Malicia's corpse, worried that she'd changed her mind. "Let me go. You're dead! Why're you still keeping me here!?"

"Not yet," her disembodied voice replied him, echoing around the walls of darkness like the sound of invisible rain. "Sit still and watch some more. See what you shouldn't see. Observe and remember what you needn't know; and recount it to others if you dare, if you imagine they'll believe you!"

He had no idea what she meant, but a moment later he understood perfectly:

The creatures in the surrounding gray portals were stepping out of them. And they were horrible beyond belief. Apache had imagined he'd gotten a proper impression of their shapes while they'd crouched in wait in their holes. Oh, but he'd been dead wrong. The reality of their obscene presences was something from the deepest level of nightmare.

They were shadows that had gained flesh and flesh that had eroded away to shadows. 'Darknesses' Malicia had called them. And that's what they were: dark fantastical apparitions that didn't/couldn't exist until one looked at them.

They had no pure shapes, no mentally graspable forms.

Like packs of wolves, the darknesses stalked forward from their arched lairs. Their target was Malicia's dead body. These impossible creatures of night opened equally impossible maws and bared long ebony teeth. In numbers they fell on the old woman's bloody corpse . . .

. . . And ate it.

Apache fought to keep from gagging as he watched the darknesses tear Malicia Howard into little messy shreds and wolf her down. They ate her wholesale—skin, flesh, bones, shit and all—slitting her open with the ease of scissors cutting tissue paper and biting through her bones as if they were cookies. Others, with night-black tongues as long as tails, licked up the blood in and around the pentagram. The blood they spilled while consuming her first coated their deformed and twitching snouts then vanished into them, absorbed into their abominable substance.

And then, all of a sudden, it was over. Malicia Howard was finished with. All that remained of her within the pentagram were a few red smears like seals on the certificate of her passing. And then those smears too were licked up.

Their feeding complete, the darknesses retreated the way they'd come. Like black snot being snorted back up into sinister nostrils, or piles of soot being vacuumed up, they reversed direction into their portals.

The night creatures regained their homes. They faded from sight. Each gray portal became empty black wall again.

Apache was left alone in his chair, gripped by those dead giant hands. And suddenly he realized that the surrounding darkness was no longer stationary. It had begun moving inward towards him, pressing into the space illuminated by the pentagram's purple glow.

Alarmed by its steady advance, he began struggling against the hands.

They still held him firm though. The rotting fist clasping his neck was so tight around it that he feared he was being strangled.

"Let me go!" he yelled as, like a flood of black water, the encroaching wall of night swept over the pentagram, extinguishing its purple glow. Even now though, Apache could still see in the darkness: the hands imprisoning him glowed a pale corpse-flesh white. All that their light showed him, however, was the wall of night bearing down on him, like he was falling through the entrance to a black hole.

"Let me go, Malicia!" he yelled again. "For God's holy sake, I'm beggin' ya—LET ME GO!"

But all he heard in response as the wall of night came ever closer was Malicia's mocking laughter. Laughter so loud that Apache wished he had no ears to hear it with.

He fought against the hands. His struggles were as pointless as an ant trying to shift an elephant. He remained trapped in their world of midnight with their spectral glow and the unnerving noise of the witch's jeering.

The dead woman was still laughing when the darkness closed in on him. It wrapped itself around him like it was his skin. It compressed him so he couldn't see or breathe or feel anything. It filled and stopped his ears so he couldn't hear Malicia anymore.

Everything around Apache Johnson became a black blankness. Total eigengrau.

He had no idea that he'd even blacked out.

CHAPTER 32

Apache

Slowly, feeling as if he'd been stampeded over by a herd of buffalo, Apache came back to his senses.

The first thing he was aware of was that he was lying on his side. At some point during his blackout, he'd toppled from the armchair to the floor.

The second thing (and for which he was immensely grateful), was that Malicia Howard's living room looked normal again. He could see its walls and furniture and its ceiling.

The darkness had returned to wherever Malicia had summoned it from. All that remained was the red pentagram on the green rug.

The temperature of his world was normal again too.

He ached badly, his ribs still feeling the crush of those giant undead fingers. He took a few deep breaths, but immediately quit in pain.

So long as I ain't got to run anywhere in a haste, I'll be okay.

He sat up, but didn't get up from the floor just yet. He couldn't. Even that little motion had made him nauseous. Propped against the armchair he'd been sitting in, he took stock of things:

She blew her head off and then the monsters came out and ate her! No, the madness went even further back than that: *She sliced her belly open and pulled a shotgun out of it. That's impossible!*

This 'impossibility' argument was merely flogging a dead horse though, and Apache Johnson, never one given to self-deceit, easily recognized it as such: *But everything that's happened IS impossible. Magic is impossible; demons are impossible. Resurrecting a fifteen-year-dead corpse is impossible. And yet it's all happening!*

Thinking about it merely brought back his feelings of nausea, so he closed his eyes and tried to make his mind blank. This almost worked, but he found the self-inflicted darkness unsettling: it reminded him of that other darkness that Malicia had summoned in here, and of the shadowy, formless things that had stalked out of it and eaten her.

He opened his eyes again. He'd just remembered what she'd said:

A key. She said there's a key to reverse things . . . no, not reverse—even if I could, I don't want to bring the dead back to life if they're all going to be psychotic zombies like her son—she said we can stop Peter's rampage.

His hopeful expression faded. *But if we don't . . . everything's just gonna get worse.*

Already feeling the heavy weight on his conscience that Malicia Howard had bequeathed him, Apache forced himself to his feet. This instantly made him nauseous again, so he sat down in his previous armchair. He wasn't so nauseous though that he didn't first peek behind it to ensure no giant decaying hands lay waiting to seize him again.

This time the feeling of needing to vomit persisted. At first Apache toughed it out. He concentrated on the room. He marveled at how impeccable it seemed. The five wax splotches that had surrounded the red star-in-circle on the green rug were gone too. As were both the witch's knife and the creepy book she'd been casting her spells from. Her trails of bloody footprints had all vanished as if they'd been mopped up.

He had no doubt that Malicia was gone too. *I didn't just witness an illusionist's display here. No, this was the real deal. She's gone for good. But . . . she's set it up so no one will ever know what really happened to her. No one but me. Is that why she wanted me over here? As a witness to her death? Or just as company? I've heard it said that no one wants to die all alone.*

The feeling of nausea grew too strong to ignore. Apache got to his feet and staggered through the house. When the puke seemed to want out of him at all costs, he clamped a hand over his mouth to keep himself from messing up the floor.

He found a bathroom, pulled up the toilet seat, and threw up.

He figured all his breakfast came up there and then. But then he remembered that he hadn't had any breakfast yet. So what he was throwing up had to be yesterday's leftovers. But afterwards, when he straightened up again, he felt relieved. His mind felt clear and his body felt clean.

He wiped the toilet rim clean of puke, flushed it, and then rinsed out his mouth at the sink. Then, still not trusting his breath, he squirted some of Malicia's Colgate on a finger and finger-brushed his teeth. A little more water, a wide tooth-examination grimace in the bathroom mirror, some random adjustment of his pony-tailed hair, and he figured he was all right. At any rate, he wasn't about dying just yet—even his bruised ribs felt better.

He was very thirsty though, so he cupped his left hand under the spout (water tended to just run out of the gap in the right one) and drank and drank, till his belly was threatening to burst on him.

Wow, I've never been this thirsty before in my life. But then, I've never sweated this much before in my life either.

It was only now that his mind went to Sully. He wondered how Sully was getting on over at the Cooper's trailer.

Almost on cue, he heard his phone ringing out in the living room. He realized he wasn't wearing his jacket and remembered why that was.

Feeling much better now, he hurried out into the living room to answer the phone.

His suit jacket lay on the floor beside the armchair. He picked it up, got the phone out of its inner pocket and caught the call on maybe its last ring.

It was Sully.

"Where've you been, old man?" Sully immediately asked, relief evident in his voice.

"Kid, I'm over at Malicia's place. You know that."

"You're *still* there? I've been trying to get hold of you for five hours now. Your phone kept ringing but . . ."

"What? Did you say *five* hours?" He glanced at the circular clock on the living room wall and was shocked. *The kid ain't kidding. I arrived here just before noon and now it's early evening.*

"Yes, *five*," Sully replied. "I had to accompany Chief Kravitz to a meeting with the Feds and . . ."

While Sully talked, Apache tried to make up the time difference. *Five hours? I was out cold for that long?*

Even with the clock confirming the time, he'd still have liked to dispute it, except that an additional piece of irrefutable evidence was staring him in the face. This was the fact that the last time he'd been conscious, his clothes had been dripping wet with sweat, and now they were all dry again.

He returned his attention to the phone. He'd missed a bit of the conversation, but now Sully was asking, "So, how'd it go? No, since you're still over there, how's it going?"

Apache sighed. "Oh, she's admitted responsibility for the deaths, and . . ." He ran out of words, was suddenly uncertain how to go on. "Look, I'll tell you all about it tonight."

"You sound like something bad has happened. Are you sure you're alright over there? You want me to come over alone or bring backup?"

"Nah, nah. Don't come over. Don't send backup either. As for what's happened, let's just say old Mrs. Howard has left town for a while."

"What? She absconded? The dirty old witch!"

"No, no, I don't mean it like that."

"What *do* you mean then, old man?"

"Sully, this ain't something I can discuss over the phone. I'm gonna need a lot of time to explain it, and then you're gonna want to ask me a whole lot of questions, which I'll likely need a whole lot more time to explain. How 'bout if we meet up at the Liquid Solace bar again tonight?"

"Sorry, old man, can't do it tonight."

"Why not? Sully, this is frigging serious. Life-or-death serious."

"This is even more serious, old man. Tilly's parents are in town from Worchester and we're having dinner together."

"Cancel it. Do it tomorrow night."

"I can't. The reason they're in town is because they want to meet me. You might be hearing street noises in the background? That's 'cos I'm calling from my car. At the moment I'm parked outside the dry cleaners, about to collect my best suit."

"I thought you didn't know if you were serious about the girl or not."

"She's serious about me. And it looks like her love is contagious."

"Alright, tomorrow then."

"Yeah, cool. You're certain you're alright tho'? That you don't need me to come over there right now? It won't take me but a few minutes to collect my suit and then I can drive right over."

"Oh, I'm dead sure. There's absolutely no use you'll be at the moment. Even I . . . I'm no use at the moment myself. Look, see you tomorrow morning then. I can hear someone ringing the doorbell downstairs. I gotta go. Bye—"

"Hey, old man, wait!"

"Yeah?" While speaking, Apache had made his way over to the front window and parted the drapes. There was now a white sedan parked downstairs in the driveway. And the visitor was still buzzing to be let in.

"Sully, hold on a sec." Phone held to his ear, he turned from the window, quickly crossed the living room, and began descending the stairs. "Yeah, kid, you were about saying?"

"I'm just confused about something, old man: If you're saying Malicia isn't home at the moment, how come you're still in her house? You are *inside*, aren't you?"

"Oh, she left me the keys. Along with a whole lot of crappy baggage that you don't really wanna hear about, but which I'm gonna make sure to fill you in on tomorrow morning anyway."

He was downstairs now, crossing through the bookstore with long strides.

The buzzer was pressed again.

"Hey, Aunt Malicia!" came a female voice when the buzzer noise stopped. "Aunt Malicia, are you home? It's Betsy. I gotta see you!"

"I'm coming!" he growled at the door.

"What?" Sully asked. "Who's coming?"

"Neither you nor me, son. I'm just replying the lady outside. Hey, Sully, I really gotta hang up now. Have a great dinner with your future in-laws."

"*Prospective* in-laws. I ain't certain yet."

"If you were rich, that'd be the 'prospecting' in-laws, meaning their daughter's a gold-digger."

"Well, I'm glad then that I ain't rich, old man. The only prospecting happening here is when I mine Tilly's lady hole for orgasms. Okay, see you tomorrow."

Sully hung up. Apache stuck the phone in his pocket and unlocked the front door.

***

Apache immediately recognized the young woman standing outside. She'd been at Chelsea Byler's funeral. Tall and brunette, pretty and a little bit plump, neatly dressed. She seemed slightly nervous.

Her eyes widened on seeing him.

"Hello, Detective Johnson," she said, recognizing him too. "I'm Betsy Driscoll—Malicia Howard's niece. I'm supposed to see her this evening." She glanced past him. "Isn't she home?"

Her name at once struck him as familiar. He'd heard it before, and quite recently too; but his mind refused to make the connection.

He pulled the door wide open. "Come on in, please."

She stepped past him. Her eyes now displayed a slight confusion, confusion no doubt created by his presence in her aunt's home.

"Aunt Malicia . . . is she alright?" Betsy asked. "I mean, I hope nothing's happened to her."

"Follow me upstairs," he said by way of reply.

She looked indecisive. "If she ain't home, I can come back."

He almost laughed. "Come on." He turned then gestured after him with a hand. "Come on up. We need to talk."

He ascended the stairs, peering back once to ensure she was following him. She was, her face now extremely perplexed. It struck Apache that there was an ironic parallel between his current actions and those of Malicia Howard when he'd arrived here five hours ago. Then, she'd led him upstairs like a lamb to the slaughter. And now, like he'd inherited more from her dying than just resolving her morbid riddle, here he was, leading a member of her family up the same stairs in similar fashion.

Once upstairs, he sat down in his preferred armchair.

He watched while Betsy stepped past him and peered into the short hallway that linked the living room to the bedrooms.

"Aunt Malicia?" she called nervously. "Aunt Malicia?" She stamped her blue shoes in place as if she wanted to enter the hallway to go look for her aunt but was scared to. Her hands repeatedly clutched and released her blue handbag.

She seems really antsy, Apache thought.

"Come and sit down," he told her. "It's your aunt that we need to talk about."

She turned sharply to look at him. "What's happened to her?" Her lips began trembling. "Is she de-de-dead?"

"Just sit down, please."

While waiting for her to do so, Apache questioned his motives for what he was about telling this young woman. *But . . . someone has to know what really happened to her,* he decided. *Whether they choose to believe it or not, now that's their business.*

She sat on the coach opposite him, her expression that of a startled deer or a rabbit ready to bolt.

Apache smiled at the young woman. "Do you believe in magic, Betsy? I hope you do, 'cos she was your aunt, and I think it's important that someone from her family knows what actually happened to her."

She nodded, then glanced down at the pentagram on the floor as if noticing it for the first time. She stared at it for a few seconds, then looked back up at him again. She was clearly alarmed to hear him confirm that something *had* happened to her aunt. Apache figured that was only natural.

She must really have loved the old woman.

He gave her a very bowdlerized version of events. Seeing as he was the only witness, he could say what he liked.

He said the police had been consulting with Malicia Howard on the recent serial killer case, as certain strange details about it had stumped them and she had a reputation as a psychic. He and she had been having coffee together . . . when suddenly, a monster had appeared out of thin air—right over the center of the pentagram there—and gobbled her up—swallowed her in a single massive gulp. The creature had been huge and black and horribly indescribable and . . . and then it had vanished. He was still confused himself, but of course, there would be a comprehensive police investigation into her aunt's mysterious disappearance.

He made the tale as convincing as he could, layering each adjusted truth with pathos, but was still rather startled by Betsy's reaction to the news of her aunt's vanishing.

Betsy Driscoll burst into tears. Throughout the duration of Apache's tale, she'd been turning paler and paler and paler. Now the tears just exploded from her eyes and flooded down her cheeks.

"NOOOO!" she screamed. "NOOOO, this can't be happening!"

Despite knowing how evil Malicia Howard had been, Apache was touched. Really touched.

Wow, she really loved that old woman, he thought.

But then Betsy fainted outright and Apache found himself saddled with the responsibility of both having to revive her and afterwards seeing that she got home okay.

Taking her car keys from her, he first drove Betsy home, then, after finding her some sleeping pills in her medicine chest and ensuring that she took them, he made the fifteen minute walk back over to the Mr.

and Mrs. Book Emporium to retrieve his squad car. After the boiling heat he'd earlier experienced in Malicia's house, the cool evening air on his face was a wonderful pickup. He had nothing else to do today anyway.

After this, Apache didn't bother with reporting in at the station. Despite the regular strange happenings in the town, the Raynham PD didn't have a Paranormal Occurrences section. He drove over to the nearest diner, bought himself a takeout dinner and a six-pack of Diet-Pepsi and headed home.

It was only after eating his dinner that he realized he'd forgotten to give the distraught Betsy Driscoll the keys to her aunt's house.

He got the ring of keys out of his pants' pocket and stared at them. A plan began forming in his mind. But first he needed to talk to Sully.

Too much is happening way too fast and I've gotta wrap my head around it all before it drives me nuts. Hopefully no one'll die on us tonight. At the moment I'm too worn out, too mentally frazzled to even investigate the source of my own farts.

He turned on the TV, sat back in an easy chair, and did his best to forget the second most crazy day of his life.

CHAPTER 33

Danny

"Pull over, man," Ricky said. "I gotta pee."

Danny was driving his red Toyota Corolla. Ricky was riding shotgun. Danny's sister Sylvia was asleep in the backseat.

"Stop this damn ride, man," Ricky repeated with pained emphasis in his voice. "I really gotta pee!"

It was 3 a.m. on Friday morning. Ricky, Danny, and Sylvia were returning from Providence, Rhode Island, where Danny had just given a drag performance as Deirdre Fabulous at The Dark Lady gay bar.

Ricky Crampton was one of the two young men whom Detectives Apache and Sully had met with Danny at the Liquid Solace Bar. Though not gay himself, he tended to hang out with Danny a lot. The pair were great friends. In a marked contrast to the slight and blonde Danny, Ricky was tall, dark and muscular.

Sylvia had come along to the Dark Lady performance because she was 'celebrating' her escape from her murdered husband Larry. This was her first outing in six months; Larry had never let her go anywhere. She'd left Sandy with her mother. And then, not used to drinking a lot, she'd gotten quite hammered at the nightclub; hence her now being fast asleep in the back of the car.

There'd been a fourth person in the car, Ricky's brother Martin, but they'd driven up I-95 and dropped him off in Attleboro, hence their now arriving back in town via the 495 interstate, instead of via the shorter Route 44, which ran straight up from East Providence to Taunton.

It had been a great show. For Danny, being onstage as Deirdre Fabulous was the only time that he really felt alive. Once up on a stage, all the restrictions he felt elsewhere fell off his shoulders like a shed bathrobe and all he felt was free, free to express his true self.

Tonight's performance had been one of his best in ages. Singing and dancing before the audience, basking in their love and approval and their thunderous applause, he'd felt like making love to all of them in a transcending orgy.

Afterwards, everyone had commented on how great his singing had been and also on how pretty he looked. One fan had even wanted to suck him off in his dressing room; but Ricky and Sylvia had come in before the young man could get started. Still, aborted fan-fellatio or not, Danny had felt fabulous. He'd enjoyed the compliments so much that he'd not taken off his makeup, which he normally did before driving home. Silver wig, fake breasts and all, he'd leapt into the car.

They'd hit the road home, with a pumped-up Danny singing and driving like he owned the highway.

***

"Stop here, man," Ricky said. "I mean it. Park right here and right now."

Danny slowed the Toyota. They'd just turned off the Blue Star Memorial Highway (or I-495) and were about linking up with Broadway.

"Just wait till we get to my place, man," Danny pleaded. "It's only a few more minutes away."

Ricky shook his head tipsily. "Stop this goddamn automobile right now except you want me to piss in it."

For a moment, scared of their encountering the serial killer who'd murdered both his cousin and his brother-in-law, Danny considered ignoring Ricky's request and continuing on home. A pissed-up car was preferable to being sliced to ribbons.

Then he remembered that both Chelsea and Larry had been killed *at home*.

Apparently, in this case being outdoors was the safer alternative.

After a glance back at his sister Sylvia, who was safe and secure in her alcoholic dreamland, Danny pulled over to the roadside.

Ricky instantly leapt out and staggered off to in front of the hood, where he got his member out and sighing with relief, began easing himself.

Danny got out too to stretch his legs. He shut the car door and leaned against it.

At first Danny stared across the road. He'd parked right opposite the back route to Rudy's Truck Stop. The inlet was a short funnel-shaped dirt track bordered by grass lawns. At its farther end he could see the truck stop building and several parked 18-wheelers.

He looked up. The moon was a bright lamp. A cool predawn breeze caressed him beneath the brilliant lunar glow, ruffling the hem of his dress. Looking at his stage clothes—gold lamé dress, wide red belt, gold high heels and red fishnet pantyhose—brought back the delightful buzz of the performance again. He smiled, coiling the ends of his long silver wig in his fingers, then peeked over the top of the car at Ricky.

"Hey, dude, aren't you finished yet? We gotta get a move on. I got a job to go to in the morning."

Ricky wasn't done yet, the noise of his urine hitting the grass was distinct in the early morning silence. "Almost, man. I thought you said Mr. Fergusson said you could have the day off."

"Next time don't drink so many damn beers. And no, he didn't give me the whole day; just the morning half of it. I still gotta be in by one p.m. And if I don't get some sleep soon . . . Man, we really shouldn't have taken the Attleboro route. I shoulda just brought Marty back with us and let you drive him home in the morning."

"Too late. And you know my bro appreciates it."

Danny nodded. This of course, was the trouble with out-of-town moonlighting as a performer. Most times he only drove down to Rhode Island on the weekends, but tonight's performance had been a special one: a gay friend's wedding; and Danny had been asked to come sing *I Will Survive*, a request he'd felt unable to turn down.

Danny peered in at his sleeping older sister.

He was glad she'd come along and had some fun. Sure, it wasn't socially acceptable for a new widow to start partying two days after her husband's death, but Larry Cooper hadn't been the sort of fellow anyone mourned. Danny doubted even his daughter Sandy would miss him.

So, he'd dragged his sister out to his show. She'd needed a whole lot of makeup to hide her bruises, but somehow they'd managed.

Though pleased to be freed from her abusive marriage, Sylvia had also been close to freaking out. Danny didn't blame her in the least. He'd almost pooped his pants on hearing exactly *how* Larry had died— and her description of the maniac who'd broken into their trailer and cut Larry's head off. No face, swollen and rotten? Danny didn't buy those details of the killer; he didn't buy them at all. Sylvia's description of the murderer had too much of a dream quality to it to be accepted as fact. And she also claimed that the rotting man had afterwards just up and vanished. 'Poof!'—he'd turned into smoke.

No, Danny was certain that hadn't happened. The way he viewed it, Sylvia had hallucinated the extra stuff. She'd said Larry had been choking her and that she'd been losing consciousness when it happened. And when you were short of breath and dying, you were guaranteed to see weird things.

But still, Larry's death was similar to how Chelsea had been killed. So, the same maniac might have killed them both.

***

Suddenly, Danny began hearing gurgling noises. Thinking Ricky was throwing up, he looked up again.

Shit!

Terror completely jellified Danny.

Oh my God! Sylvia wasn't hallucinating.

Danny Foster wouldn't ever win any prizes for courage. This wasn't either a 'gay men are sissies' stereotype or a slur on gay character. Danny *was* a sissy, and not the kind of 'macho man sissy' who enlisted in the USMC or USAF and only wore their wives' pantyhose and lipstick when they were home on leave. Indeed not— Danny wasn't the sort of hard gay man who fucked up the nation's enemies even harder than he fucked his boyfriend's ass.

No, Danny's lack of testicular backbone was as legendary and as spectacularly limp as a non-erect penis.

Courage was for guys like Ricky: guys with muscles everywhere, even in places where one shouldn't have muscles.

But at the moment, Ricky's huge muscles were proving of no use to him at all. Ricky was in huge trouble. Over by the hood of the car, the rotting man—and yes, this definitely was the same one that Sylvia had seen: faceless and wearing a dirty blue suit and a black hat—was murdering Ricky.

The dead man had one hand over Ricky's mouth and was slashing at him with the other one, ripping him open in similar fashion to how a cat or dog might savage a pillow it had taken an intense dislike to.

Ricky's eyes were bulging as if he was screaming loudly behind the swollen and festering hand clamped over his mouth, but no sound escaped the gag of rotting corpse-flesh.

Danny thought he'd faint as he watched Ricky's guts spill out of his belly. And the faceless man kept slashing away at the freed intestines, so that short loops of them plopped onto the roadside grass. There was so much blood all over Ricky's front and thighs that he seemed to have burst open.

"Help! Somebody help!" Danny whimpered.

Then, terrified, he turned and ran off. He headed across the road towards the truck stop, where he was certain he'd find help.

This was a really bad place to be ambushed at: they were right at the start of the town, where residential houses were few and far between. In fact, the truck stop was the only building in sight. Danny had parked beside some woods, and everywhere else looked deserted. Most residences and shops were situated farther down Broadway.

At first, Danny ran in his high heels. But after twisting his ankle and almost going sprawling, he stopped to slip them off.

While unbuckling each golden clasp, he stared back across the road at the car. It was crazy, the man was still butchering Ricky. He had Ricky draped face-up over the hood of the Toyota and was raising and lowering his right arm in a fast blur in which Danny could make out dislodged drops of blood and flying chunks of human flesh.

Then Danny remembered that his older sister was asleep in the rear of that same car.

Oh my God. No!

It didn't matter how courageous or not Danny Foster was, he wasn't about leaving Sylvia to be sliced up. For one thing, if he did so he'd never be able to look his niece Sandy in the eye again. For another, his mother would never let him forget how he'd abandoned his sister to her death.

Quickly, before he'd had sufficient time to reconsider the wisdom of what he was doing, Danny ran back towards the car.

He crossed the road as stealthily as he could, ready to turn and dart away again if the killer headed towards him. But the crazy dead-and-blue-suited butcher seemed preoccupied with his task of rendering Ricky Crampton into his component parts, and that with a savagery that smacked of intense hatred.

Danny reached the car. Sylvia was draped across the backseat, with her head against the rear off-side door and her feet over on the driver's side. Danny ran around the rear of the car and opened the off-side door.

His sister's head instantly fell out into his crotch. She was still out cold, blonde hair splayed out over his waist and thighs, eyes shut, brain a million light years away on Planet Booze.

"Sylvia, wake up! Wake up, please!"

The rotting man was still butchering Ricky on the hood of the car. Danny took one look that way and puked all over Sylvia. The man was slicing at Ricky's face, digging out his eyeballs with a glittering straight razor. The entire front and top of the red Toyota Corolla was covered with blood.

Danny considered jumping into the car and trying to drive off. But Sylvia was more out of than inside the vehicle now, and bent awkwardly like she was, it was going to take both time and effort to put her back in the backseat again. Time they certainly didn't have; and as far as effort went, he wasn't certain he had the strength to complete the task. And besides, to start the vehicle up, he'd have to backtrack around the car's trunk again, which would mean moving close to the murdering man. And to add to that problem, the Toyota's windshield was so splattered with blood and meat now that he'd surely be unable to see a thing once back behind the steering wheel. The gore was also certain to jam the wipers once he switched them on.

So instead, he resumed trying to rouse Sylvia. Some of his vomit had gotten into her nose and she was sputtering awake.

"Sylvia, wake up!"

"Huh? Danny, what?"

"We gotta get out of here!"

She didn't get it, just kept goggling at him with dopey eyes. Staring down at her face now, he had a moonlit impression of a serene white oval plain with black wells for eyes and mouth. She was awake, but it was a drunk's rousing. She stared at him as if she was sleepwalking, without any true recognition. Like maybe she needed to have a quick piss and then pass out again.

Beside them, Danny heard the unnerving scraping of sharp steel on bone, then the sickening noise of flesh tearing. He heard the horrible wet splat of something falling on the car roof. A misadvised glance showed him that a pile of severed lungs now littered the car roof. Another ill-advised look revealed even more innards splattered all over the windshield.

Sights from Hell. Danny whimpered in fright. He felt his testicles shrivel up into his belly. His belly contracted as if to empty itself.

But I need to save Sylvia!

With a fierce tug, he pulled his sister completely out of the vehicle. She landed on the roadside grass, rolled over onto her belly and lay motionless.

"I feel so high," she groaned. "Feel like I'm swimmin' the high seas."

"Sylvia!" Danny bent over to haul her to her feet. He concentrated on what he was doing, not daring to turn around, because he knew that if he took one more look at what was being done to Ricky's corpse, he'd flee screaming and leave Sylvia all alone.

He got her halfway to her feet, but then she slipped from his grasp and thudded back down to the grass. Her eyes widened in surprise at the impact, then shut peacefully again.

"Sylvia, please!" He hooked his hands under her shoulders again. "Get up, get up! We need to run away from here!"

But right then, he felt a burning sensation down his right side.

"Yeeoow!" He looked down at himself. He was bleeding. His gold lamé dress was slashed open at the hip and he was bleeding from a long and deep cut there.

He turned fully around.

Oh no!

The man in the blue suit had finished carving up Ricky. Now he was standing over Danny and Sylvia. His blue clothes and black hat were covered with Ricky's blood and also flecked with little shreds of Ricky's skin and innards. He held his bloody razor poised overhead, ready to strike again.

Danny really got a good look at his face now. *Oh my God! Can anyone or anything actually be this ugly? He looks . . . he looks . . . !*

"Die!" the man hissed at him.

Then Danny spotted Sylvia's cellphone on the grass by her head, twinkling like a fallen star in the moonlight. His mind raced with desperate hope: *Maybe if I threaten to call the police, he'll leave us alone!*

He bent to pick up the cellphone, but the killer stomped on it and smashed it and at the same time slashed him across the cheek.

Danny felt the blade bite through his flesh and strike his cheekbone. He also felt a splattering of some stinky black fluid on his neck, dislodged from the man's body when he'd swung his hand. It felt like there were living things crawling in the goop.

"Die!" the rotting man in the blue suit croaked like a dying toad. "Die!"

Down on the roadside grass, Sylvia had begun snoring.

Danny took one more look at the mess on the hood of his car that had recently been a close friend of his, took another look down at his sleeping sister, and then stared his death in the face. That was how he viewed the monstrosity in the blue suit—his death.

Realizing that he could do absolutely nothing to save Sylvia now, he turned and fled.

His dress hampered his running, so he bent and pulled it up to his waist. Gripping its golden folds in both hands, he sped off.

He looked back and saw that the man was following him, coming fast after him.

Oh, but I'm not letting him catch me!

He ran into the bordering woods.

He looked back again. Almost like magic, the decaying man was now standing on the edge of the woods. Danny had no idea how he'd arrived there so fast, but he wasn't hanging around to find out. He took off through the trees.

Danny felt relieved in one sense: If the man in blue was chasing *him*, then he couldn't at the same time harm Sylvia.

Maybe, if Sylvia came around before the killer stopped pursuing him, she'd have enough presence of mind to call the police.

***

Danny's dress snagged on tree projections. Once, a branch hooked inside the slashed part at his hip and ripped a large hole around his buttock. He ran on. It had been one of his favorite performance dresses, but it was replaceable. His life wasn't.

He ran, kicking stones and dropped branches, bruising and cutting his bare feet on sharp twigs and jagged rocks, panting and feeling like his lungs would explode, but paying little attention to his discomfort. His need for safety was preeminent in his mind.

He crossed a dirt turnoff and then a tarred road, but made sure to remain under the trees until he was well away from his car. From his point of entry, the woods extended for two hundred yards along Broadway.

Finally he saw streetlights ahead of him and ran out onto the Broadway sidewalk.

Blood streaming down both his right hip and his face, he kept going, looking for an occupied house to seek help. When he remembered it, he wiped the rotting man's spillage of black corpse jelly off his neck, along with its accompanying mess of writhing larvae.

He peered back, but didn't see his blue-suited pursuer. Relieved, he moved forward, stepping fast but cautiously down Broadway. He figured his best bet at this time of night would be to get to Carver Street. The Sunflower Motel was just around the corner there. Once he reached the motel, he'd have no difficulty rousing someone and finding a phone to use.

Then, almost at the Carver Street intersection, he came to an abrupt standstill.

The blue-suited man was now in front of him.

Danny had not the slightest idea how this was possible, how the killer could have overtaken him. But there he was, in front of him and walking closer, with his huge razor flashing in the streetlights.

Danny did the only thing he could think off: he turned around and headed back the way he'd come.

Five or six steps later, he froze again.

Once again, the killer was in front of him. This time Danny had merely blinked to clear his eyes of sweat and, 'Presto!' the man was suddenly there facing him.

Danny stood there, sweating, panting and trembling in the early morning chill. With the amount of adrenalin coursing through his veins, he had little difficulty ignoring the hurt from his wounds.

The rotting man started towards him, walking with a slow, deliberate tread. About twenty yards separated them both, and that distance was shortening by the footstep.

Danny turned around and walked quickly towards Carver Street again. The result was the same. The dead man in blue was instantly in front of him again.

Cringing, Danny stood where he was and tried to figure out what to do. His surroundings weren't the most promising. Right behind him was a white building, locked at this time of night. Opposite him was the VERC Gulf filling station, similarly deserted at this hour. Left and right of these, Broadway extended as far as the eye could see.

He considered dashing around the building behind him. It might be possible to reach the Sunflower Motel that way. But what guarantee did he have that this monster wouldn't be waiting for him there too?

Shivering, Danny tried to figure out an escape. He wanted to scream, but the noise wouldn't come. The screams weren't locked in his throat either. He'd simply run himself out of breath. His silver wig began itching from the buildup of sweat on his scalp. He ignored the wig. It didn't occur to him to simply pull it off and fling it away; that was how focused he was.

All this while, he'd not taken his eyes off his pursuer. He figured that would be a suicidal thing to do. He still recalled vividly what this impossible man in blue had done to Ricky—the bloody body parts strewn all over his car.

He waited, wondering how he could save himself, hoping for a vehicle to drive past and carry him off.

No vehicle came. Illuminated by moon and streetlights, they—predator and prey—stood watching each other on the deserted street.

The killer stalked toward Danny.

Then, almost as if he'd walked into an invisible wall, the man stopped. He was ten yards away from Danny when this happened.

Next, Danny watched him vanish. Danny stared at the highway ahead in confusion, trying to figure out the riddle of the man's sudden disappearance.

Then a squishy noise alerted him to spin around. Behind him, about thirty yards off, the corpse man had reappeared and was shuffling towards him again.

But again he hit that invisible barrier and could advance no closer. Once more he vanished, this time to instantly reappear across the road in front of the VERC Gulf gas station.

Relentless in his deadly pursuit of his objective, gore and black goop dripping from his body, he stepped into the road and started towards Danny again.

Danny, his heart in his mouth, watched the killer come. The grotesque horror that was the man's face horrified him to the core of his being, with its shapeless aspect, its myriad rips and tears from which bone jutted, and the long and fat earthworms wriggling under the brim of his bloodstained black hat—brown hair and worms so enlaced that it was impossible to say which was which. And his body, which was just as bad as his face and which continuously leaked black secretions.

Danny couldn't understand how something this abominable and disgusting could possibly be alive. But no, this 'man' approaching him with such murderous intent evident in every motion of his woefully corrupted frame wasn't actually alive, was he?

But if he's as dead as he seems, he also seems intent on killing me as well; murdering me and dragging my soul down into whatever nauseating pit it was that he crawled out from.

But not yet. Once again the walking corpse hit something invisible in his path and bounced back.

Blood still welling from his face and hip, Danny stood watching the man. The predawn breeze tickled his buttocks through his torn dress; he only had on a G-string beneath it. He could sense the monstrous creature's anger toward him. The wind brought the man's stench of death across the street to him.

Danny was confused. *What's stopping him from reaching me?*

The blue-clad man remained standing opposite him. When after thirty seconds he still hadn't moved, Danny figured that he was unable to get any nearer to him than he already was. With some relief, he now turned to look at the building behind him.

It was a church. A white sign he'd been heedlessly pacing back and forth beside read: CALVARY CHAPEL.

The white building's windows were dark, but the security lights were on.

I'm standing on holy ground! Danny realized, with a quick glance back at his frustrated pursuer. *He's evil. He can't approach a church! So long as I remain here, he can't reach me!*

Danny considered the irony of his situation: he'd never liked either church or Christians with their self-righteous, preachy ways. But now here he was, dressed in the same drag apparel that the church loudly disapproved of, and yet being protected by the same stuff he didn't believe in. (Danny had once thought of proclaiming himself an atheist. But he'd been scared that God might then retaliate by giving him AIDS or leukemia or diabetes. So he'd ditched the idea. He'd instead figured that if he couldn't safely deny God's existence, he'd do the next best thing: keep as far away from Him as possible. Yes, and also ensure he never wore a cross or crucifix while getting fucked in the ass; God-hate might be great, but it was dumb to tempt fate.)

But belief or not, it's keeping me alive.

Once more keeping his eyes on the dead thing across the road, Danny backed up towards the church steps and sat down on them. The stone pillar he leaned on felt wonderfully solid against his back.

I'm safe! he rejoiced. *I'm safe! All I gotta do is wait here till daybreak!*

But then he remembered his sister, who was still back by his car. Asleep, drunk and defenseless.

He made a face at the monster watching him. *Well, so long as this creep stays here with me, Sylvia is safe where she is. And it'll soon be morning; people will start going about their business.*

But then, as if reading his thoughts, the man in blue winked out of sight again. Danny hoped he hadn't gone back to the car.

He gazed up at the sky. "Please, please, please, God. Protect Sylvia, don't let that evil thing hurt her!"

God's ears seemed shut though. The sky over Danny both looked and felt heavy. Each cloud seemed made of lead. The moonlit fluffy expanses glowed ominously, as though they were all waiting for Danny to leave the sanctuary of the church so they could fall on him and crush him dead. He had the scary impression that tonight, one way or the other, the Almighty was out to settle some of His accounts with him.

The thing was, Danny didn't dare leave the church and run back to where he'd parked his car. He just knew that the moment he stepped outside of the church's protecting influence, the monster would reappear and slice him to shreds.

In fact, he was so certain of this that he didn't even attempt to disprove his theory by putting it to the test.

He was trapped here. And—

Oh no! My phone's in my purse in the car!

—He couldn't call for help either.

Danny did the only thing he could do. There at the front entrance of the Calvary Chapel, he began shouting for help, hoping someone would hear him and call the police to come investigate the noise he was making.

The few people close enough to hear him didn't. So no one called the police.

After a while, when Danny became too exhausted to shout, he broke down weeping and hoped that Sylvia would be alright.

CHAPTER 34

Sylvia

Back at the car, Sylvia Cooper finally roused enough to look around. This happened because a bug crawled up her nose and she had to sneeze it out. The irritating ticklish feeling it left inside her head woke her up.

She rolled over onto her back. *Hey, how'd I get down on the grass with—ugh, what's that horrid smell—puke all over me?*

She tried to figure that out. She remembered Danny shaking her, then Danny dropping her. And then he hadn't seemed to be around anymore.

Where is Danny anyway? It's like I'm all alone here.

She was still pondering this when a shadow fell over her and a swollen and wet wormy hand wrapped itself around her neck and hauled her up to her feet.

Sylvia stared at the man's mashed-up head. Recognition hit her like being stabbed in the memory center of her brain with an ice pick. *Oh, no!*

She opened her mouth to scream, but the gleaming blade split her face in two, tearing it wide open from ear to ear, flashing between her spread jaws and severing her cheek muscles so that her mouth gaped uselessly and quickly turned into a lake of blood amidst which her tongue flapped like a beached pink whale or a living island.

The next razor slash took off the entire left side of her face, her flesh and skin detaching and falling off her head as messily and efficiently as if her attacker was wielding an axe.

She stood jerking in the man's putrescent grasp, bleeding from her hideous wounds, inhaling her attacker's awful stench, her terrified mind unable to find the slightest thread of logic in what was happening to her. Larry had deserved to die: he'd been an asshole. But she, she'd been good!

In a spray of gore and eyelashes, the razor scooped out her right eyeball.

WHY IS THIS HAPPENING TO ME!?

Next the pain shifted to her body. It penetrated her at random, high and low, entering her chest, her belly and her arms and legs. The agony curved in a flaming unbroken line across her torso, after which, unable to peer down at herself because of the hand holding her upright, she nonetheless felt a wet portion of her belly detach and fall out of her. She pushed at her killer and her hands sank into his rotting flesh and stuck in there. She hurt and bled and hurt and bled.

WHY THE HELL IS THIS HAPPENING TO ME!?

Tormented by an increasing and unceasing menu of agonies, Sylvia was aware of being peeled like an onion, of being sliced up like a tomato, and of being opened up like a giant pepper and having her insides scooped out and spread over the grass like red dressing on the Devil's salad.

And then she was flung away, scattered everywhere in a thousand little dead pieces.

CHAPTER 35

Reverend Hathaway

The Reverend Peter Hathaway, pastor of the Calvary Chapel church on upper Broadway, had had a sleepless night.

Reverend Hathaway, an honest and devout preacher, had woken up at 2 a.m. this Friday morning with a burden on him to pray. At first he'd shrugged the feeling off, but it had grown steadily more intense and pressing, until at 3 o'clock, he'd grudgingly gotten out of bed and, not wishing to disturb his wife, had gone into his living room to pray.

He'd prayed for an hour, then, feeling some release, had fallen asleep in the armchair he'd been sitting in.

But then, at 4:30 a.m., Peter Hathaway had suddenly jerked awake again. This time he'd not felt the urge to pray, but instead, the urge to hurry down to the church. Something was wrong there. Something had been wrong all night.

So he hurriedly got dressed, hopped into his car and drove over to the Calvary Chapel building. (At the moment, because the parsonage was being renovated, he and his wife were living in quarters on the other side of town.)

He arrived there at about 5 a.m. and found a wounded drag queen asleep on the building's front steps.

His initial impressions of the painted young man were not favorable. The sight of the boy's clothing—long silver wig and fake eyelashes and dripping mascara and long fake fingernails, torn gold lamé dress and ripped fishnet stockings—brought a foul taste to his mouth. While not exactly hating homosexuals, Peter Hathaway was wary of them. To his mind, they represented the most intense form of contamination by the world. And it was every good Christian's duty to avoid such pollution.

In fact, initially he didn't want to touch the wounded man, but he decided he had no choice in the matter. Situations like this were what the biblical parable of the Good Samarian referred too. And besides, if the Holy Spirit had roused him from his slumber for the purpose of saving this man's wayward soul, he would try to do so.

Reverend Hathaway roused the slumbering young man, who instantly burst into tears, but who, to the preacher's surprise, didn't immediately seek the Lord's forgiveness for his obvious miscellaneous homosexual offences, but instead tearfully began explaining about a rotting and faceless dead man who had killed his friend over by Rudy's Truck Stop earlier in the night, and who had afterwards pursued him here to the doorway of the church, where he (the dead man) had been unable to approach any further and attack him. He also said he was worried about his older sister, whom he'd left behind because she'd been too drunk to flee.

Hearing this, Reverend Hathaway at first suspected a gay prank designed to ridicule and humiliate the church. Rotting monsters that appeared and disappeared at will? It was just the sort of thing the homosexual community would think up to make the Lord's flock look foolish.

But then, he decided that the man in drag—young Danny Foster, he'd finally introduced himself—was too badly injured to be making this story up. If nothing else, it required checking on.

And with a young woman supposedly in danger too, Christian charity *demanded* that he take some action to help.

So he drove Danny over to the access road behind Rudy's Truck Stop . . . where they found the bodies.

It wasn't so much the two deaths themselves that so shocked the good preacher (who, of course, was used to conducting funerals), but rather the almost cartoon-like violence and brutality evident in their creation: all over and around Danny Foster's car were scraps of flesh that had come from the bodies. The corpses themselves had both been dismembered and their parts flung far and wide across the roadside grass. Reverend Hathaway thought he could even make out a fleshless human head up amidst the higher branches of one of the nearby trees. He however couldn't tell if it was the friend's or the sister's head.

The young drag queen instantly fainted on the spot. Reverend Hathaway, though made of sterner stuff than the effeminate young man, first vomited up the entirety of his previous night's dinner on the grass, then managed to dial 911.

CHAPTER 36

Apache & Sully

It was later that same Friday. Apache and Sully were having lunch at Mel's Diner on upper Broadway.

"I'd never have imagined things could degenerate so much in just twelve hours," Sully said. "We went to sleep and woke up to discover that the wheels have come off our damn wagon."

Apache nodded and bit into his burger. The burger tasted like wood in his mouth. This wasn't because it was badly prepared, but because he was so troubled by all the latest horrible developments in the Mr. Ugly case that his taste buds were in revolt.

Eating, however, was a good excuse for them to sit and clear their minds. Now was the time to do some serious brainstorming.

"Everything's so far out of our hands at the moment, we might just as well have thrown this case up into outer space." Sully's plate of food was untouched. He was so pissed off, he hadn't even sipped his coffee.

Apache concentrated on his burger. His right palm was itching, but he made a conscious effort not to scratch it. Sully was stating the obvious. He agreed with Sully, but it was better to eat.

"You're not saying anything," Sully accused him.

"Eat, kid. The brain works better on a full stomach."

Sully glared at him, then speared up a forkful of fries. His cheek muscles bunched up angrily as he chewed.

It was another wet Raynham day. Through the glass they watched the drizzle without interest. The morose weather formed a calming if actually inconsequential background to their thoughts. The cars out in the road were a man-made amphibian species, mutant metal turtles.

"What I hate the most," Sully said finally, pushing his empty plate aside, "is the damn FBI presence everywhere. Makes us look incompetent."

Apache shrugged. "Forget 'em—we got way bigger fish to fry than the FBI. But first, lest I later forget, how did dinner with the prospective in-laws go last night?"

"Fine, fine. They're nice folks. We had a Korean dinner, then came back to Tilly's and watched some old TV movies." He smiled. "I got along real well with her dad. Her mom doesn't seem to approve of me though."

"The old girl's just being cautious. She needs to be sure she'll be able to bend you to her whims afterwards. No mother-in-law wants a son-in-law she can't wrap around her little finger. Remember, Tilly's divorced. Who's to say that that wasn't her mother's doing 'cos her ex wasn't pliant enough?"

"So you say, old man."

"Trust me, kid. I've been married, you haven't. If your mother-in-law loves you on sight, you most likely have 'Wimp' tattooed in glowing letters on your forehead."

Sully sipped his coffee and grinned. He was now calming a bit; which had been Apache's main intent in steering the conversation down this homey avenue. The kid had a great brain; getting him to use it was the problem. Particularly now, when he was angry at the State Police and Feds swamping the town.

But there wasn't anything else for it. Those two killings last night had been too much to keep out of the news. The Raynham PD might have still kept a lid on things, but Michael Hathaway, eldest son of the preacher who'd found the bodies, worked with Raynham Channel TV.

Always proactive where disaster coverage was concerned, the Raynham Channel news crew had arrived at the murder scene just moments after Apache and Sully had. And with the way the two victims' remains had been violently spread over such a wide area, there had simply been no chance of preventing the reporters from getting good shots of everything. Indeed, it was the RC-TV camerawoman who—after zooming in tightly with her lens—had pointed out that the head hanging up in "that nearby maple tree" was a woman's—its remaining ear had an earring.

It had taken Apache and Sully a short while to piece things together. Clearly Mr. Ugly had fulfilled his promise of returning to kill

Sylvia Cooper. Or was it Danny he'd actually been after last night, with Sylvia just unfortunately happening along for the ride? Either way, it wasn't an easy question to answer with bits of Sylvia scattered everywhere like red confetti.

Danny Foster was currently in hospital. At last check, he'd recovered consciousness from the faint he'd had after viewing his sister's remains. Once he'd woken up though, he'd begun gibbering nonsense, so the doctors had sedated him heavily.

Reverend Hathaway had given his statement to Apache and Sully, and then gone to see a doctor for a prescription of tranquilizers. On news camera, he'd declared himself "Shaken to the very core of his Christian being," and then invited the viewers to come to the Raynham Calvary Chapel church for the salvation that these horrible times dictated their souls needed.

Apache and Sully had both given "No Comment" statements to the reporters, but the damage was already done. The murders were on the Breakfast News and after that the State Police and FBI had arrived like sharks come to eat the corpses. The brutality of the crimes and the public involvement meant there was no way they could be swept under the carpet anymore.

But Sully was more concerned with how they—the Raynham PD—would now be perceived, most likely as a stable of bumbling bumpkins incapable of recognizing a serial killer's handiwork. Hence his anger.

At the moment, he and Apache were as good as off the case. The FBI were wolves seeking prey and didn't have time for socializing with the local bloodhounds.

Apache understood Sully's anger. But then, Sully didn't know what *he* did.

Apache thought a bit. It just went on, the Summer Madness. It was here again, hot and crazy as ever. While at the most recent murder site, Apache had overheard two paramedics discussing how they'd responded to a weird death call two nights ago, right here in town, in which a guy's head had gotten twisted around twice on his neck while his girlfriend was in the bathroom. He'd asked them for the details, but neither name of those involved rang any bells with him, and seeing as the dead man hadn't been slashed to shreds, nor had his lady friend reported either seeing a stinking corpse on the premises or smelling something rotten, he'd let it go. Someone else could work out how the poor guy had died. His death clearly wasn't related to Mr. Ugly, and Sully and himself were preoccupied with that at the moment.

"I tried to talk to the Chief earlier," Sully said. "I couldn't even get into her office—it was full of men in black suits and Ray-bans."

"Forget Tina," Apache retorted. "For the next few days, she won't even have time to pee. She may need to install a urinal in her office and tape a colostomy bag to her ass."

Sully was going to reply to that, but Apache quieted him with a raised hand.

"Just listen to me," he said. "There's a truckload of stuff I need to fill you in on." He nodded. "First of all, we both know that involving the Feds in this case is as useless as bringing a knife to a gunfight." Sully was drinking his coffee, so Apache went on: "*We* know the actual problem here; *they* don't. So let the state guys and the FBI chase their serial killer. It'll give us sufficient time to fix things."

Sully nodded. "So what happened with Malicia Howard yesterday?"

Apache filled him in on Malicia's suicide and what had occurred both before and after it. Sully listened in silence, his stare widening. Occasionally he'd gulp, but he said nothing.

"Hey, put your cup down," Apache said.

"Huh?"

"Put your damn coffee down. Your hand's shaking so much that you're gonna spill it all over me in a moment."

Nodding nervously, Sully put the cup down on the tabletop.

Apache finished his tale. Sully gaped at him. "That really happened? That stuff really happened?"

Apache nodded. "You bet your future mother-in-law it did. Kid, when she pulled that shotgun out of her belly . . . let's just say I must have grade-A butthole muscles to prevent me from crapping my pants then." He leaned forward across the table. "Now listen. The important thing here is: Malicia Howard is dead, but no one knows about it yet, just us two. I was gonna tell Tina, but . . . you yourself just said she's completely inaccessible at the moment."

Sully scratched the side of his nose. "It isn't just us, old man. You told Malicia's niece that she was dead."

Apache scowled. "Yeah, maybe I shouldn't have; not immediately anyway. But the young lady surprised me there at the house, and I couldn't think up a better excuse for being there." His eyes suddenly widened. "Oh yeah, now I remember! I knew I'd heard her name just recently."

"Remember what?"

"Something that the paramedics were saying while we were over at Rudy's picking up the pieces of Danny's sister, about a Mrs. Driscoll whose boyfriend died in some weird way two nights ago. His head got twisted right around. Twice."

"Ugh. You think it's related to our case?"

"No way of telling. Besides, I ain't certain it's the same Driscoll anyway. Look, kid, let's not get sidetracked; the boyfriend wasn't attacked by a razor-wielding maniac corpse anyway."

"Yeah, alright. Go on."

Apache ran his right thumb over his lower lip. "So, yes, Betsy knows too, but . . . well, she was so distraught when I gave her the news, that after driving her home, I found her some sleeping pills in her bathroom cabinet and made sure she took 'em. I dunno how long they'll keep her out of the picture for, but . . ." He looked the younger man square in the eyes. "Anyhow, kid, my point is that, last night, I forgot to return Malicia's house keys to Betsy." He dipped inside his suit and produced them. "And so I daresay it's time we had a look around the old girl's supposedly empty house."

"You think we'll find Mr. Ugly hiding in there?"

Apache shook his head. "Not really. No, I doubt the solution to this mess could be that simple. And even if we did find Peter Howard, bullets are unlikely to harm him."

"He's already lost one finger, old man; meaning he *can* be hurt."

Apache mused on Sully's words. "You're making good sense, son, but I'd rather we didn't tangle with the dead boy. Too much could go wrong for us."

"So what then?"

"We root around and look for the 'key to the mess' that Malicia told me about. She said there was one, and if we found it we could stop Peter. Thing is, she didn't even hint at what it was. And I've been racking my brains since sunup and can't think of any kind of connection either."

"It's a fetish of some sort," Sully said.

"A what?"

Now it was Sully's turn to lean forward over their lunch table. "A fetish. Juju or whatever they call it. Voodoo stuff. You're Native American, man; you should know 'bout things like that."

Apache grimaced. "Son, stop believing all those movies you watch. That's just stereotyping—us Indians are all civilized now. Most of us don't know squat 'bout nothing anymore. We've all exchanged the Happy Hunting Ground for the Christian Heaven." Then he frowned and his brow creased up while he thought on Sully's suggested solution to the riddle. "Hmmm. Yeah, Malicia *did* use voodoo dolls to kill the two Byler brothers, but"—he shook his head—"this is a different kind of situation—"

"Wait," Sully interrupted, his dark eyes seeming to grow even darker with the intensity of his emotions. "Just hold on, old man. Last night on TV—"

Aw shit! Apache thought, *not make-believe crime fighting again!* "C'mon, kid, not *CSI* again."

"No, not *CSI*. Just listen. Let me finish."

"Okay, I'm listenin'. Go ahead and finish."

"Now, remember I said that last night we watched some movies? The second one was called *Cannibal Voodoo Massacre*. Really cheesy, mostly boobs and blood and we all had a great laugh."

"I'm delighted to hear it," Apache said dryly. "Your future marital happiness rests assured."

"Yeah, well," Sully went on, "what I'm getting at is this: in this *Cannibal Voodoo Massacre* film, this medicine man guy was angry 'cos a gang of hoodlums had raped and killed his wife and daughter—so he sicced some crazy hybrid human-dog monster on the rapists. And he controlled it using something like a voodoo doll. No, no, he wasn't sticking pins in it, but he'd talk to the doll and tell it who he wanted it to kill next and apparently it could talk back to him too." He gave Apache an enquiring glance. "You get my point here? The 'key' Malicia Howard told you about may be something like that, a voodoo doll. If we destroy the doll, we destroy Mr. Ugly." He shrugged. "It's at least worth checking out."

Apache nodded and pushed back his chair. "Let's get over there, son."

Sully looked up at him. "You agree with me?"

"Yeah, I do. She had two voodoo dolls with her in court that day. Makes perfect sense that she'll have others at home. I hope you're right about this. But even if you aren't, you've given us a very clear idea of what we're searching for—weird-looking relics, amulets and ceremonial goblets. Anything that can be tied to a monster."

He looked out at the rain, at the cars streaming past on the highway, then back in at his partner. "Get up, get up. We'd better hurry over there."

Sully rose to his feet and they started for the diner door. "What's the sudden rush, old man?"

"We wanna get over there first before Betsy tells her dad that Malicia's dead, if she hasn't already. I just remembered that Ray Howard really, *really* likes his sister-in-law. If he hears anything's wrong with her, first thing he'll do is call us, the police—"

Sully smirked. "Who are currently way too busy trying to figure out what his sister-in-law has been up to, to investigate his distress call concerning her reputed termination of existence. Except for us, of course. Everyone else is busy kissing the FBI's ass and looking for the killer elsewhere."

Apache frowned. "Yeah. Which means Ray'll most likely head over there to check for himself. And we gotta remember that he's the one who renovated the place. He's sure to have a spare key."

"That might work in our favor. He'll know of any special hiding places."

"I don't want any witnesses while we're snooping around. Too much could go wrong. Old guy like that can easily get killed."

"Yeah, I guess so," Sully agreed.

Outside, the rain had increased in intensity. And, seeing as it had been just a drizzle when they'd arrived at Mel's Diner, neither detective had bothered bringing inside an umbrella. And with all the parking spaces near the walkway taken, they'd parked out by the sidewalk.

Sully went first, running across the parking lot to their squad car. Apache waited till Sully had gotten the doors opened and was seated inside the car before hurrying over to scramble into the front passenger seat. He'd managed not to get too soaked. Sully, however, was quite wet.

"How about Betsy?" Sully asked as he steered the car out of the parking lot.

"What about her?"

Sully turned onto the highway. "Do you think Betsy will come over to the house? I'm just speculating: what if she wakes up early and . . . ?"

Apache ruminated on that while adjusting his ponytail. "No . . . no. If she wants to visit the bookstore, she'll first have to call me for the keys." He settled back and smiled coolly. "Buys us some time."

CHAPTER 37

Betsy

Detectives James 'Apache' Johnson and Frank Sullivan need not have bothered about either Betsy Driscoll or her father disrupting their intended investigation.

Today, Betsy had woken up at noon. The sleeping pills Apache had found for her weren't actually hers. They were Sammy's, and the dosage was one pill at bedtime—Apache had given her two.

The pills had knocked her out completely. She'd not even dreamt. She'd just shut her eyes one minute and opened them the next to bright sunshine penetrating the drapes.

She'd sat up in bed, peering groggily around, trying to reconnect her mind to its disrupted flow.

Then the memories had returned. *Aunt Malicia is dead? How? How!?*

Her tears came, first a trickle, then a torrent. This just got worse and worse. And this happening right when she'd decided to resolve her marital issues amicably, to give her aunt's doll back to her and ask her to bring Sammy home instead.

She sat cross-legged in bed, looking disheveled and feeling perplexed.

This is crazy, just crazy. Chuck died two nights ago, and now Aunt Malicia too?

Her aunt's abrupt passing was bad enough. But even worse (and eclipsing it) were the two problems she was now left with: Firstly, what to do about Sammy, and secondly, what to do about the voodoo doll.

The doll was still in the blue purse she'd taken to the Mr. & Mrs. Book Emporium yesterday afternoon when she'd met Detective Johnson there. On arriving home, she'd dumped the purse in an armchair in the living room and forgotten it.

She could sense the doll out there. Here in her bedroom, its evil aura was muted, but still, she perceived an unsettled atmosphere surrounding it. She sifted through the mental impressions the dark feeling gave her till she arrived at the right one:

The damn doll is frustrated again, 'cos I took all the pins out before putting it in the handbag.

She'd had no choice though. The purse was an expensive one and she hadn't wanted the pins ripping up its lining. Besides, since she'd been about forgiving Sammy anyway, she'd seen no point in continuing to torment him. She'd just wanted him back.

She forced the doll's quest for a victim from her mind. *And now? How the hell do I get Sammy to return to me now that Aunt Malicia is dead? Hey . . . how do I know that Detective Johnson was telling me the truth? But, why would he lie to me? He's an honest cop. And knowing auntie, how he described her dying is exactly how it would have happened to her.*

She thought of calling her father and informing him. Then she thought better of it.

He'll just blame me again—accuse me of having something to do with her disappearance. The old man absolutely LOVES Aunt Malicia. I'll just wait for him to discover for himself that she's vanished. Okay, maybe it isn't the responsible thing to do, but I don't care!

She honestly didn't care. She didn't even know how she felt at the moment. Distraught, yes, but for seemingly the wrong reasons.

Aunt Malicia, you can't die on me, you evil witch! YOU CAN'T! What the hell am I supposed to do now, huh?

A good amount of her worry concerned the voodoo doll itself. Now, from the looks of things, she'd inherited it for good. And from what she'd been told, it needed someone to hurt, or else . . .

No, it can't hurt me instead. Aunt Malicia assured me of that. It can't . . . God, I'm hungry. I'm so hungry I could eat the damn doll.

Yes, Betsy *was* hungry. She'd not had a meal since yesterday's lunch, which was now twenty-three hours ago.

She got out of bed, slipped her feet into her slippers, and made the short trek from the bedroom to the kitchen.

She switched on the percolator. While it made her coffee, she popped four slices of bread into the toaster. She got some sliced ham, sliced chicken breasts, and some tomatoes and lettuce and mayonnaise out of the fridge and made herself a couple of sandwiches.

She poured her coffee, then ate there in the kitchen. As her belly filled with food and the coffee energized her brain, she pondered her dilemma.

Clearly, the voodoo doll was her main problem now. *What do I do with it? Keep it or throw it away?*

Neither option was particularly palatable to Betsy. The first, because even though keeping the doll meant she'd retain her power over Sammy's body and could hurt him at will (which, seeing as she couldn't get him back now, she was very willing to do), she really didn't want the doll here in the house with her; she was tired of being frightened of it. The second option of throwing it away would have been preferable, but that would mean both that she'd lose her power to hurt Sammy (she had to remember that he was still planning to divorce her!) and also that she'd have no idea what she'd be setting in motion.

What if I throw it out somewhere and some kid picks it up as a plaything?

Betsy vividly remembered what had happened to the last person who'd 'played' with the doll. *Oh no—I don't want any more deaths on my conscience. And especially not some kid's. So no, I'm not throwing it away. But where can I keep it then? I need somewhere that's safe, where no one will tamper with it till I can find a spell to neutralize it. Aunt Malicia is certain to have such a spell somewhere in one of her magic books, maybe even in that horrid skin-covered Necromantica one. I just need to find it.*

Then the solution struck her: *That's it! That's it! I'll just leave the doll over at Aunt Malicia's place. Then I can go there whenever I like and study her magic books. Better still, I'll bring them here and . . . but I don't have her house keys. Oops, they're still with Detective Johnson!*

She finished her breakfast on a cautious high. She'd realized that given time, she might even discover the right spell to bring Sammy back home. There was no hurry, she'd get the keys back from Detective Johnson either this evening or tomorrow.

I'll have to call at the police station though; I don't have his phone number. Daddy may have his number, but . . . ugh! But then, Detective Johnson may just bring the bookstore keys here to me and save me the bother of calling around.

She got up. Leaving the lunch things on the table, she made her way back into the living room. Now she felt better. She had focus. She had a plan.

Now that she could reasonably see a light on her horizon, Betsy began feeling sad about her aunt's death. She picked up her purse from the armchair, sat in the armchair, and leaned back, purse in her lap.

She could sense the doll in her purse. Its bad desires reached her in hot psychic flashes she was powerless to ignore. But, to her relief, its anger seemed muted now, as though it expected she would soon call it into use again.

Well, you're gonna wait a long time, doll!

Her thoughts returned to her dead aunt.

Oh, but I really liked Aunt Malicia! It's just horribly sad she died the way the detective said. Oh, and this means that I'm still unemployed. No aunt means no bookstore job! I'll have to go work for dad again, and he's gonna keep rubbing it in about how I'm responsible for Chuck's death. Oh heck—I don't think I can cope with reminders of that. I don't—

Her phone rang. She fished around in her purse for it, flinching when her fingers touched the doll's queasy warm form.

She got her phone out and checked who was calling.

It was Sammy, calling via WhatsApp. For the first time in months, he was calling her. It was a video call too. That surprised her; she'd thought Sammy felt too guilt-ridden to look her in the face.

But apparently he didn't.

She accepted the call. He looked the same as always—craggily handsome in a green T-shirt, and with his short sandy hair now covered by a sombrero.

He was smiling, as if he imagined that would win him points with her. It almost did: she went weak-kneed just seeing him again after so long. But then she remembered what kind of a scumbag he was, how he'd slept with Luisa Gomez and run off with her, and her emotions turned cold against him.

"Hi—" he began.

She immediately cut him off: "Oh, it's you. Long time no see." She didn't want him dictating the conversation. Not after all the heartsick times she'd called him via WhatsApp and he'd refused to even acknowledge her calls. Even her text messages had been ignored, sometimes for days on end. "I thought you were gone for good. To Hell, I mean."

His expression soured. Then he smiled again, though now the expression seemed forced. "Come on, Bets, let's not make this any harder than it has to be."

She didn't smile back. "You're the one calling me, Sammy. You're the one who left too. So, are you calling to apologize, or what?"

"No . . . Yes, I mean, look, Bets, I'm sorry about how our marriage didn't work out and everything, and maybe I shouldn't have left the way I did, but no, I don't feel sorry that I left. I'm happy now and you'll be too when you find someone who's right for you and . . ."

Listening to him justify himself, Betsy felt herself about to cry. Hot, angry tears came knocking at the windows of her soul, but she didn't let them out. Impossible as it seemed, she controlled her emotions. She wasn't about giving Sammy the pleasure of seeing how much he'd hurt her.

Instead, she smiled coldly when he'd finished. "Alright, Sammy, so yes, you're a happy jerk now. What are you calling me for?"

He moved the phone slightly and she was able to see the background of where he was. He was outside, at a restaurant it seemed. He was sitting at a wooden table and around him were other tables, several with Mexican people seated around them.

"Talk, Sammy, I'm listening. And hurry up, I gotta go pick up the pieces of my life that you left shattered. I can't spend all day on the phone if you just called me to gloat."

The video froze up for few seconds then stabilized again.

"Yeah, yeah, okay," Sammy said. "Look, I've been meaning to call you before today . . . but . . . I haven't been feeling too good this past week."

Betsy did her best to look concerned. "How d'you mean—not feeling good?"

His handsome face expressed his confusion. "Even now I can't explain it, Bets. Every damn thing you can possibly imagine was wrong with me: I got migraines like my head was gonna blow up, ulcers like I'd been drinking concentrated acid, and my feet hurt like someone was stabbing them with knives; and then suddenly, my lungs too seemed to be shutting down on me, each damn breath I took was total agony. And just yesterday, it felt like my ass was being sliced open." Now he really looked confused. "Worst of all, Bets, both of the doctors I saw said they couldn't find a damn thing wrong with me. Nothing whatsoever. It was crazy. One of them even suggested that I go see a curandero for help."

"A *what?*"

"Curandero . . . a witch doctor."

It took all of Betsy's self control not to grin. *So, Aunt Malicia wasn't kidding me about the voodoo's potency! She didn't exaggerate at all! Mexico really wasn't far enough for him to flee to!*

But there was still the worry that Sammy might have taken the doctor's advice and gone to see the witch doctor. If that was the case, she might have lost her power to hurt him.

"What did you say to that?" she asked. " 'Bout the curandero, I mean?"

"Nothing. What could I say? I found the suggestion too dumb to reply to. Mexico ain't like home at all. The people are cool, but I'm still El Gringo to them."

"Yeah, I guess," she said with evident lack of concern. "But still, Sammy, you look okay to me. Seeing you now, I can hardly believe you've been sick at all. You're outside—"

"I'm having lunch with Luisa at her sister's restaurant."

At his mention of the husband-snatching young woman, an intense rage filled Betsy. *So you're calling me with that slut nearby? You nasty son-of-a-bitch! I bet you've even got your phone on speakerphone so she can listen in.*

Before she could weigh in with a suitably scathing retort though, Sammy went on: "Trust me, Bets, I ain't lying. I was unwell as hell. Luisa thought I was a goner."

"So how come then that you're up and about now?"

He shook his head. "That's the part I really don't understand. Late yesterday afternoon, just like that, everything suddenly cleared up. That's why I'm able to phone you now."

Betsy remembered that she'd taken all the pins out of the doll yesterday afternoon before stuffing it in her purse. *Oh, so that's why he feels better today? Okay, I can easily rectify that for you, asshole!*

"So, what did you call me about?" she asked acidly. "Luisa's pussy ain't tight enough for you anymore? You want me to give her kegel lessons?"

He scowled, embarrassed and upset by the question. "No, her pussy is fine—we're *very* happy together."

"I'm *very* surprised. I expected her hole to be as loose as her morals . . . But go on, I'm listening."

"I just wanted to ask if you've mailed back the divorce papers yet. My lawyer said he sent them by USPS and that you'd signed for them."

She gaped at him. "Why, you've got a damn nerve, you son-of-a-bitch!"

"Listen, let's try and be civil about this. We're through as a couple and that's that. *I'm not* getting back together with you. I'm divorcing you. Try and accept it and move on with your own life just like I'm trying to do."

"You horrible son-of-a-bitch!"

He smiled at her. His face and voice reflected a victory. He knew he'd scored a painful thrust through her emotional armor. "So, answer me please: have you sent the papers back yet? Luisa's mom is dying of cancer and she wants to see her youngest daughter married before she goes. That's why we're having a Reno lawyer handle it. We're trying to speed things up, so that—"

"You asshole! I can't believe you'd do this. How dare you . . ." Betsy ran out of words. Rendered speechless by his callousness, she gaped at Sammy's smiling face. She couldn't believe that he'd dared call her up to request that she divorce him quickly so he could marry his mistress.

The picture froze again. Betsy felt frozen too.

"Hey, Bets!" Sammy's voice came through after a delay. "Betsy, don't you dare hang up on me now!"

The picture unfroze and she could see him again. His eyes were cold and serious now. No more forced joviality; no more fake attempts to be friends-ever-after. The way he looked at her now revealed that he didn't care a flyspeck for her anymore. He'd wanted to hurt her and knew he'd succeeded.

She blinked. A delicate, pale-brown female hand had just rested itself on Sammy's left shoulder. Next, a female figure came into view behind Sammy. The woman didn't show her face, but the long and glossy black hair flanking her chin assured Betsy that it was Luisa. Betsy winced; Sammy was really making his point of how far she'd been replaced in his affections.

Luisa remained posed like that via the magic of WhatsApp video communication; she and Sammy a low-quality portrait by some unsung renaissance painter.

Sammy was now grinning broadly. He clearly felt he had the advantage here; that he could browbeat her into submission. "You still haven't answered me, Bets. When are you gonna mail back our papers to the lawyer?"

Feeling like she had a stone for a heart, Betsy frowned at him. "Now listen to me, you male turd. And, Luisa, you little slut, I know that that's you standing there; you listen too. The divorce papers arrived yesterday and I burnt them. Did you hear me, Sammy? I burnt the damn papers."

His shocked intake of breath at her revelation came loudly through the phone. Now it was her turn to grin at his startled face.

Delighted that she'd unsettled him, she went on quickly before he could reply her: "Yes, I burnt the damn divorce papers, ass-wipe. Would you like me to upload you a picture of them in the trash?"

"How dare you do that? You . . . you . . you . . . !"

"Because I hate you, Sammy!" she screamed into the phone. "You're a turd that God forgot to flush away and I despise your damn guts. And you wanna know what I think about your marriage plans? Well, I'll tell you: as far as I care, Luisa's mom can cut out her cancer tumor and use it as a dildo! She can fuck herself to death with it. She can die and go to Hell six hundred and sixty-six times over—I'm sure she's a worthless whore like her daughter!"

At those angry words, the phone was jerked out of Sammy's hands. Betsy had a momentary glance of a fan whirling overhead on the restaurant's ceiling and then Luisa Gomez's oval face filled the phone screen.

Luisa was irate. "How dare you call my mamá a whore, you stupid gringa puta!" she screamed. "I'm gonna come back to the USA and I'm gonna wring your silly fat neck!"

Luisa's face vanished for a second. In its place, Betsy saw fingers on the screen and heard Luisa begging: "No, no, Sammy, give me back the phone. Por favor, cariño! I'm gonna tell this crazy bitch who she is. I want to tell her how her mamá was fucked to make her! How dare she call my dying mamá a puta!"

Luisa won the tug of war. Her head reappeared in the screen, her black hair now a tousled mess about her pretty face. In the background, Sammy had lost his sombrero in the struggle over the phone, and in addition, now had a bleeding nose.

Good, Betsy thought. *He doesn't look the least bit amused or triumphant now.*

"Now listen to me, bitch," Luisa snarled over WhatsApp. "If you are not woman enough to keep your man—if your chocha is dry or has rabies—that is not my fault. Your husband wanted a hot mamacita and here I was. That is your own fault. But don't you ever mention my sick mamá again, you hear, puta!? If you do, I'll scratch out your eyes. I'll cut—!"

Betsy hung up on Luisa. Then, to ensure that she and Sammy didn't call back, she switched off her cellphone.

Then she sat back in her chair and simmered.

She'd won a moral victory. It might be a little victory, not of much importance in the larger scheme of her marital breakdown, but it filled her with a nice glow of satisfaction.

I showed those two dumbasses that I'm not their patsy.

She sat there a while longer; unsure what to do now. She felt good at having put Sammy in his place, even if temporarily. She didn't wish to lose that feeling. If she did, she'd sink back into her morass of sadness over her aunt's passing.

She pondered what to do with herself today. It was raining quite heavily outside, which put paid to any shopping plans. She could turn on the TV and watch the soaps, but sooner or later, something sad was certain to happen to one of her favorite characters and their imaginary misery would trigger her actual misery and then she'd have unintentionally put herself into the exact state of mind she was desperate to avoid.

It was quite a problem. The rain threatened to make her start crying—external water calling to internal water?—so she needed to get her mind off of her troubles and on to something else, something really distracting. The sleeping pills still had her groggy, which wasn't any kind of a help to clear thinking.

I need more coffee.

Then, about to head for the kitchen again, a bright smile suddenly lit up Betsy's face. *Why the hell am I such a ditz sometimes?*

She instead reached into her purse and pulled out the voodoo doll. Torturing Sammy was the perfect antidote to her current state of mind. He was responsible and he was going to pay. Whether or not she'd get him back in the end was immaterial, what mattered now was how she'd make him feel before then. By the time she was done dealing with him, Sammy would beg to be buried alive alongside Luisa's old cancerous whore of a mother, just to end his torment.

Her mind filled with poisonous purpose, Betsy grinned at the doll. With that similarly venomous look fixed on its ugly face, it gazed expressionlessly back at her. She felt that it sensed her purpose and that it greatly approved of what she had in mind.

"Let's do it at once! Let's get started!" its little black eyes whispered to her. This time the doll's queasy and clammy feel didn't bother Betsy. Its purpose was her purpose. She was its mistress; it was her instrument and her friend.

She got up and went into her bedroom to get the pins.

But then, once she had the pins in hand, she changed her mind. She put her handful of pins back down on the nightstand.

An amusing idea had suddenly occurred to her: *Sammy says he's been short of breath recently, right? He couldn't breathe? Oh, the bastard's about suffering major asphyxiation!*

She tried taking the doll's black hat off first. It didn't detach, but she decided that didn't matter: the hat was soft and pliable, and besides, it couldn't get lost where it was about visiting. She removed the doll's blue suit though; she wasn't looking to rub herself raw down there.

Then she was ready. She lay back in bed, undid her dressing gown, spread her thighs wide, and then inch by careful inch, slipped the voodoo doll head-first into her vagina.

Once she had three-quarters of the doll inside her body, she took a deep breath then clamped her muscles down tight on it.

"Alright, Sammy, try to breathe in here!"

She relaxed her vagina, then clamped down tight again. "How's that feel, baby? Tighter that your Latina?" She relaxed and clamped down again. The wooden image felt nice and warm inside her, almost like a penis. "How's the air in there? I'm sure you can smell me really good, darling."

She sensed the doll's emotions. It was confused, unsure what to make of this weird usage she was putting it to.

Laughing, she slid it completely out of her body. "Dammit, Sammy darling, but you do look a bit wet today. Have you been swimming? Or it just the rain? Or are you just really delighted to see me?"

She didn't want Sammy dying on her. She could just imagine the scene at Luisa's sister's restaurant now, with the tall, handsome gringo going 'loco,' clutching his neck and gasping for air when there was clearly nothing wrong with him.

"Eat some more pussy, Sam!" She slipped the doll back into her sex. As deep as she could this time. The fun and games of this had begun to sexually excite her. She figured she might as well kill two birds with one stone.

She began actually masturbating with the doll. "Yeah, fuck this pussy, you runaway son-of-a-bitch! See what you're missing, Sammy? See how sweet it is? How tight and juicy? Ooh yeah, Sammy, you're so *hard* today—yeah, just like that, baby!"

Oh wow, this is so much fun, Betsy thought. *I'm certainly going to do it again. And again and again. When I ain't torturing the prick, that is.*

Occasionally she remembered to let 'Sammy' up for air.

After a while she had a great orgasm. Then she fell stone asleep.

CHAPTER 38

Sully & Apache

Apache and Sully were upstairs in Malicia's living room.

"Well, I think this is what we're after," Apache said.

"What?" Sully asked.

Apache held up a medium-sized wooden box. "It was hidden in plain view, right here in the bottom of this bookshelf." His face creased up. "What's that you're holding?"

Sully shrugged back at him. "Empty funeral urn. It was up here over the electric fireplace. Wonder why she'd keep this. Dead lady really was a weirdo."

Apache stared at the brass container. Then frowning, he pointed to the red pentagram drawn on the floor. "I don't think that urn used to be empty. I think it used to hold her son's ashes."

Sully blanched at the information and his stomach did a twist. He quickly set the urn back down on the shelf from which he'd taken it. *Stop being silly,* he told himself afterward, but he no longer doubted the warped truths of this unreal case. He'd have loved to remain skeptical, but . . . all he needed do to reassure himself that he was dealing with the supernatural here was recall the bomb-blast-like displacement of Sylvia Cooper's and Ricky Crampton's remains. No living human would do that. That kind of callous dismemberment spoke of a hatred that had transcended death.

Realizing that, the red pentagram on the green carpet now took on a horrible meaning for Sully.

Sully had dreaded coming here again.

Viewed from outside, today the building had seemed almost normal, with no wavy lines or tricks of the light happening around its upper floor and roof. Sully had been relieved to see this. But once inside the bookstore, he'd felt (and could still feel) its walls exuding an invisible menace.

Of course, he'd told himself he was merely being silly and irrational, but he knew he wasn't. There was something wrong here; they were both in danger.

On entering the house, they'd quickly checked through all its rooms to ensure that they were really all alone. And yes, the place *was* empty. But Sully didn't feel like it was. If nothing else, he felt the pressure of Malicia Howard's desire for revenge squeezing him like a giant set of pliers.

And from what Apache said the dead woman had told him, if they didn't get this thing sorted out today, there'd be some more butchered corpses tonight; and if they still hadn't fixed it by tomorrow, there'd be yet more outrageously mutilated stiffs; and so on. The deaths would continue until they found the key to stop them.

But was it *really* possible to stop them? Sully hoped the old woman hadn't lied to Apache, and that there really was a way to break free from this cycle of madness she'd set in motion.

He hoped also that what Apache had in that box he was holding was the key they sought.

"What've you got there, old man?" he asked as he crossed the room to Apache's side.

Apache flipped the box's lid open so Sully could see. "Voodoo dolls, from the looks of 'em."

Sully studied the dolls. There were three of them. Each equally ugly, each dressed in a little blue suit and a black porkpie hat. Each, to Sully's mind, almost a perfect miniature of the resurrected killer they were after. Two of the dolls had bloodstains on them.

"Say, these look awfully familiar," Apache said, scratching his chin. He'd left home too early to shave again and the stubble itched.

"You mean they look like Mr. Ugly?"

Still scratching at his chin, Apache frowned. "Yeah, except that they've all got faces, they do fit his description to a 'T.' But that's not what I meant. What I mean is, these look exactly like the two dolls we recovered from Malicia at the Taunton courthouse fifteen years ago." He nodded. "Yeah, they're exactly like the ones she killed the Byler brothers with."

"In that case there's one missing then," Sully said. He counted off on his fingers: "Two dolls in court, three here now. But, the box looks like it should hold six." He looked hard at Apache. "You don't think . . . ?"

"What? That the missing one's the one she used, but she's hid it somewhere where we'll never find it?" Apache's face squeezed up as he considered the possibility of that. Then he gestured around the living room. "Maybe she did. But for the moment, I think the smart thing for us to do is to destroy these three we've got here first. Then we'll search through the house with a toothcomb for the last one." He pointed up at the ceiling. "And we'll have a look in the loft too. It's just the sort of place to hide creepy stuff." He resumed scratching his chin. "But how to actually destroy them though, that's the question."

"Fire," Sully immediately suggested. "That's what they used in that movie. I think once you burn a voodoo doll, its power ends."

Sully recognized the look which Apache gave him as the 'Not TV again, son' one.

But then the older man nodded. "I've been thinking that too. It's worth a try anyway. Did you find the kitchen when we checked the house?"

Sully nodded. "It's right through here. Follow me."

In the kitchen they lit three of the gas range's burners and dropped the dolls on them.

Any hopes the detectives had nursed of the dolls burning normally were quickly quashed.

The blue-garbed miniatures didn't ignite as expected, nor did they give off any smoke. Each of them just shriveled away, while all the while sizzling like it was being fried.

"Alright, old man," Sully said, feeling chills swimming up and down his spine, "if I disliked this before, I utterly hate it now. They're frying like sausages. Like there's meat inside them."

"They ain't smelling though," Apache said. "Thank the good heavens for big mercies. I'd go crazy if they actually smelled like sausages . . . I'd never eat another one in my life. . . . Sully, what the . . . ?"

Under the relentless assault of the blue/violet gas flames, all three dolls had by now withered away to mere black sizzling twigs. That in itself was creepy enough, but what now held both men speechless was that all three of the shriveled dolls had suddenly begun writhing wildly, thrashing about in the flames and kicking and flailing their previously static arms and legs.

"They look like they're burning in Hell," Sully remarked in a quiet and very worried voice. "Like they're really in agony."

"This is one of those situations the police academy didn't prepare you for, huh?" Apache said.

Sully nodded. "Yeah, at the moment I wish I'd never joined the police force. No one ever told me there'd be days like this."

Thankfully, this insane happening proved to be the last stage of the doll destruction. After another ten or so seconds of the dolls' agonized writhing on their fiery beds, each stick-insect-thin remnant abruptly crumpled into a pile of white ash.

Apache turned off the burners. "I daresay that's that then." His face was strained; his expression said he'd rather be *anywhere* else than *here* now. Sully could just imagine what Apache was thinking. Personally, he'd never seen anything as creepy as those three dolls wriggling like worms in those gas flames.

They left the kitchen.

"After all that craziness just now, do we still need to look for the last doll?" Sully asked as they reentered the living room.

Apache shrugged. "I get what you mean, son. Yeah, that should have done the trick. But still, better safe than sorry. Let's search the house anyway, just to make absolutely certain there ain't one more hidden somewhere. It might take all four of 'em to keep Mr. Ugly killing."

"He's three-quarters dead at the moment then?"

"Maybe. But if so, that's still one quarter too many for my liking."

Sully nodded. "How do you suggest we go about the search?"

"We'll both start here in the living room," Apache replied. "It'll be faster now that we know exactly what we're looking for. Once we're done searching here, I'll check the bookshop and study downstairs, while you look through the other upstairs rooms. Then we'll both root through the loft."

Apache had sweat on his brow from the heat they'd just made in the kitchen. Sully was sweating too, but not as much.

At the moment, all of Sully's thoughts were focused on how to get the hell out of this damned witch's residence and never return to it. He wanted to be home with Tilly already.

Sully's previous feeling of misgiving had returned. He felt incredibly apprehensive, expecting something bad to happen to them at any moment. He was certain both that that bad thing *was* going to happen, and that it was about happening right now. And not knowing what it was that he was scared of, he was equally aware that he and Apache would both be completely defenseless when it struck.

He reached for his gun, then withdrew his hand. He felt sheepish. *What the hell am I gonna shoot? The walls? There's nothing in here but us two cops!*

Apache, meanwhile, had strode over to one of the living room windows and pulled its drapes open, letting in a gust of raindrops. "We could do with a little more sunlight in here," he said without turning around. "I hate how dim it is. I'm starting to see ghosts in the shadows."

"Yeah," Sully agreed. "It does seem darker in here since we got back from burning those . . ." Then, realizing what he'd just said, he stopped speaking and gaped at Apache's back with a horrified look on his face.

Yes, the room *was* darkening around them. Even as Sully watched it, the window Apache was standing beside first turned opaque and then became a dull black slate.

Apache spun around. With wide strides he crossed the room towards Sully. "Let's get the hell downstairs! Right now!"

But they'd left their escape too late. The door to the landing vanished before they reached it, leaving them stranded in the middle of pulsing black walls that slowly closed in on them.

"Dammit!" Apache growled. "Not again!"

"Old man," Sully said, as intense nervousness filled his soul and an equally intense and horrible purple light filled the space around him, "the pentagram on the floor has started glowing!"

CHAPTER 39

Betsy

With the doll nestled in her body as she slept, the connection was made:

Betsy Driscoll found herself dead and rotting and holding a straight razor. This puzzled her: she knew she was alive.

Even more puzzling than the huge razor clasped in her swollen fingers though, was the anger she felt. She was enraged; justifiably so, and out to spread death and terror throughout the town of Raynham.

She saw some of what she'd already done—wielding her razor in her gross, rotting hands: she saw herself slice Chelsea Byler to bits, then butcher and scalp a man she didn't know who was walking past the Stop N Go gas station on Broadway. She both saw and *felt* herself cut off Larry Cooper's head while his wife Sylvia cowered on the floor.

Then—and this filled her with a particularly nasty thrill—she was suddenly outside near the I-495 overpass. First she was pulling the guts out of another unknown man, then she was chasing Danny Foster, who was in drag and running barefoot into the woods.

But then he ran to that church!

Oh, she was irate that she couldn't get at him on those holy grounds—she wanted to kill him so much! Oh, it was so frustrating that she couldn't. She felt weak and powerless standing opposite the church, wanting to cross Broadway and slash up the cringing painted man standing opposite her, but finding herself rooted to the ground as though her feet had been nailed to the sidewalk. She sensed an ultimately powerful presence in the church, something far greater than the infernal forces driving her, something Divine that could eat up a million of her kind and still remain hungry. She knew intense fear. She backed off.

But . . . but, oh, she found a wonderful and satisfactory substitute in Sylvia Cooper. She butchered Sylvia with great delight and relish. She took out all her frustration on Sylvia. She let out all of Sylvia's blood onto the thirsty grass, then threw red chunks of the young woman everywhere.

And now she was resting, biding her time . . . because there were many other people to kill too, and she would kill them all. Oh yes, she would. None would escape her wrath and her fearsome blade. 'Mother' had commissioned her to butcher the stupid Raynham townsfolk; young and old, male and female—everyone. 'Mother' had empowered her to kill everyone in this vile little town, and kill everyone she would.

Betsy raised the straight razor in her swollen and stinky fingers. Wet flies crawled out of holes in her hands and along the bloody blade and took to the air. A wide grin opened in the side of her face and disgorged a stream of black liquid and corpse-worms.

She laughed with glee, anticipating the oncoming night's slaughter.

Then suddenly, a massive cloud of darkness fell over her and blocked out everything.

Now she felt frightened again. Not afraid of GOOD, like she'd felt while standing opposite the church, but afraid of EVIL.

And her fear didn't let up. Instead it grew and grew.

CHAPTER 40

Apache & Sully

The darkness around them was absolute now. The rear sides of the most of the furniture was lost in impenetrable shadows. The tube of purple light emitting from the pentagram gave the impression of being in transit. It looked like it began somewhere far below this living room, maybe deep in the bookshop's foundations, and ended far above it, in the clouds currently raining on the town.

Again, the darkness throbbed like it was alive. It beat like the Devil's black heart.

The detectives stared at each other, their faces as purple as everything else in the room that wasn't obscured by the darkness. Both men were sweating profusely now in the room's increased heat, with water trickling down their faces.

"It goes without saying that we've both got a bad feeling about this," Apache said. He wiped a film of sweat from his brow. "We must've done something wrong while destroying those dolls."

"You're thinking that maybe they were booby-trapped?"

"They may have been, kid. We've no way of knowing for sure now."

"Is this how the living room was last time?" Sully asked. He loosened his tie. The heat in the room was growing unbearable.

"Yeah," Apache morosely agreed. "And therein lies our current crisis: yesterday I was stuck up here until all of Malicia's song-and-dance was over. She made it clear that she wanted me to have a ringside seat at her gory funeral."

"Well, we need to figure a way out now, old man, and *fast*." Sully pointed. "Those damn archways you mentioned have begun forming again."

Apache had already noticed the forming arches, large gray pockets in the trembling wall of night. He got out his cellphone.

"Look, we'd best try to call out. If we can get the boys at the station to—shit!"

Two black tentacles had lashed out from opposite gray arches and snared Sully. The left tentacle had wrapped itself around his neck, the other around his waist. Each tentacle was a thick living rope plaited from the darkness.

Sully's eyes bulged with fear. "Help me, old man!"

"Like you even needed to ask, kid." Apache was already stepping forward and trying to get his partner free. He put his cellphone away again and bent to the task. He'd already noticed though, that the cellphone no longer had a signal.

However, there was a problem: impossibly, the tentacles holding Sully seemed to be made of gas, surfaceless tubes packed with soot. Apache couldn't get a grip on either of them. One each attempt, his fingers closed on empty air, afterwards leaving him with the impression of something greasy having been smeared over his hands. Sully was also trying unsuccessfully to grip them.

Apache stepped back from Sully. He pulled out his gun and fired into the portals. He spent six rounds in there before realizing it was useless. The creatures in the portals didn't even seem to notice that he'd shot at them. Shades of the past.

The darkness swallowed the gunshot noises as if it was a thirsty French throat and the sounds were vintage champagne.

Additional sooty tentacles flailed out from the portals and wrapped themselves around Sully. Apache was forced to leap back and just watch, pistol dangling limp and useless at his side.

"Try hitting them with a chair!" Sully gasped, his voice sounding as if it was being choked out of him by the tentacle around his neck. "Maybe if it isn't flesh and blood, it'll—!"

A thin tentacle wrapped itself around Sully's face, wedging itself inside the young detective's mouth and shutting him up. Apache watched Sully bite down on the black cord without effect, his teeth slipping both over and through the gassy appendage that nonetheless still gagged him like a liquid rope. More tentacles lashed out from the darkness and tightened themselves around Sully's legs and arms.

Apache dropped his gun and turned and dashed to get a chair. A plastic-and-steel dining-style chair stood by the bookcase where he'd found the voodoo dolls. (The bookcase itself was now wrapped up in the darkness, its volumes black shelved ghosts.) He picked up the chair, ran back over to Sully's side, selected one of the thickest restraining tentacles as his target, and raised the chair high overhead.

Let's do this!

Apache never discovered if Sully's proposed solution would have worked or not.

As he was about bringing the chair down, something gripped him around the midriff and yanked him backwards and off his feet. The chair he'd been brandishing as a weapon went spinning away over Sully's head.

The next moment Apache was seated in his familiar armchair again and being held down by the same giant and decaying white hands as on his previous visit here.

Aw no!

Apache fought against the hands from the darkness. He wrestled against them with all his might. But all he accomplished was to bruise and tire himself. The hands had a steely grip on him. Once again, he wasn't about leaving their clutches.

Apache quit his ineffectual struggle. He could do nothing but stare at Sully.

With three tentacles now wrapped around his head, and so many of them grasping his body that he looked like a neuron, Sully stared back at him, his eyes scared and desperate.

All they could do was wait.

They didn't have to wait long.

Announced by a burst of stink that made Apache gag, Mr. Ugly stepped out of the archway right next to Sully.

***

Seeing the corpse-man walk out of the darkness, Apache Johnson was filled with a deep conviction: *Whatever is keeping this son-of-a-bitch alive, it sure ain't those three dolls Sully and I burnt!*

Of course, two witnesses had given the detectives detailed descriptions of Mr. Ugly. Neither verbal portrayal, however, had prepared Apache and Sully for the up-close-and-personal reality of seeing the reborn Peter Howard as he was now.

Grotesque mangled head without any distinct features; rotting and pulpy and swollen wormy flesh; massive hands gripping a huge razor but missing one finger on the left; blue suit dyed red with successive layers of his victims' blood, black shoes and black hat; dripping putrid black corpse-fluids from a hundred tears in his body; shattered bones poking through punctured skin; and with dead flesh hanging off his bones in places and maggots crawling over his exposed innards . . . Every single detail was exactly how Mrs. Lynn Nilsson and the late Sylvia Cooper had described them.

But in some way the resurrected Peter Howard was much worse than the sum of his individual parts, or the lack of them. He was truly a revolting and dreadful creature to behold.

But no . . . this wasn't actually Peter Howard anymore, was it? Apache had known Peter Howard in person. Peter had been a nice kid. A bit shy perhaps, like most bookish teens, but whatever the case, he'd not been this evil *thing*. No, he'd definitely not been this horrible thing. Apache could make no connection between that 15-years-dead young man and the monster now standing before him. As far as he was concerned, Sully's christening this monstrosity 'Mr. Ugly' was as right as naming a newborn child 'Jenny' or 'Thomas.'

He *was* 'Mr. Ugly'; that and nothing else.

Maybe it was the sheer atrocity of the fact that something this horrible could walk the Earth again, maybe it was his being framed against this infernal night-world his mother's living room had become, or maybe it was merely the brain-curdling knowledge that the undead young man had just walked out of Hell itself, but both detectives— both hardened, tough men—were feeling the sort of intense terror that drove little children to hide under the bedcovers so that the bogeyman in the closet didn't get them.

Yes, Mr. Ugly *was* the bogeyman, and he was out of the closet now, and that not in any kind of a gay way. He walked into the purple light, his disgusting body dripping its nasty liquids to the floor. He stood there in the pentagram, facing Sully.

The tentacles had now lifted Sully up into midair. Sully gaped down at his captor with eyes wide as saucers, trying to come to terms with what he and Apache had walked into, unable to protest because his mouth was full of floating soot.

And then Mr. Ugly raised his razor and stepped towards Sully.

"Hey, Peter!" Apache shouted at him. "Don't you dare hurt that man! He's a cop, d'you hear me!"

But the razor was already coming down and slicing away a piece of Sully's face.

Apache shut his eyes at the contact between flesh and steel. When next he opened them, Sully's left cheek was completely skinless, the masseter muscle laid bare and bloody, while the detached flap of skin swung wet and red through the gaseous tentacle securing his neck. And the blade was already back up in the air and swooping down again.

"Noooo!" Apache yelled. "Stop that, you son-of-a—"

A pale scabrous hand crept out of the darkness and clamped itself over Apache's mouth. A single breath of its putrid stench put paid to any thoughts he'd entertained of biting himself free from it. It was bad enough having to breathe the hand's vomit-inducing stink, he wasn't about tasting it as well. It felt horribly wet against his shut lips. For all he knew, it might even be poisonous.

All he could do was watch.

Watch while Mr. Ugly systematically butchered his partner, Detective Frank Sullivan. Mr. Ugly cut Sully up with incredible viciousness. The restraining tentacles unwrapped to permit him access to successive areas of his victim.

He sliced open Sully's belly and disemboweled him.

Sully died as his guts spilled out of him en masse and dropped to the floor. While staring at Apache in dismay, he shuddered and went limp.

After Sully's death, Mr. Ugly kept working. First, he carved all the meat off the dead man's chest, then he reached in under his ribs and cut out his heart and both of his lungs. These he dropped onto the steaming pile of intestines. And they *were* steaming: in addition to their normal internal body temperature, the room's oven-like heat appeared to be cooking them.

Sully's liver joined them shortly, as did his other viscera.

Then the dead man stepped back from the corpse. As if they'd received a signal from him, the tentacles now released Sully's body. It fell face-down over its innards.

The black tentacles squirmed back into their gray archways.

The tentacles were now replaced by the indescribable darknesses, those creatures that Apache imagined he saw but which he knew he wasn't actually seeing, simply because things with such horrible shapes couldn't exist. A vast horde of the darknesses stalked out of the archways.

Apache had watched them feast once. He shut his eyes so as not to repeat the experience. However, the slobbering noises the darknesses made with their teeth and tail-length tongues penetrated his ears and filled his brain. The noises made him wish for a pair of rotting hands to cover his ears.

Heard but unseen by Apache, the darknesses made short work of Sully's corpse. While Mr. Ugly nodded his approval, the demon creatures consumed the hot raw flesh with voracious appetites.

When, five minutes later, they retreated back into their lairs, all that remained of Sully was his left foot in its brown shoe. After being bitten off, this had rolled under the couch. For whatever reason, the darknesses had left it there.

Apache opened his eyes again when the noises ended.

The darknesses were gone. Sully was gone.

Tears filled Apache's eyes, obscuring his vision. He blinked the tears away and fought to compose himself. There was no point crying over the kid's death. He was in as much trouble himself now.

Here he was, held down in this armchair, with his mouth covered so he couldn't talk. He was alone with Mr. Ugly.

And Mr. Ugly was already walking over towards him with his razor raised and a toothy smile splitting the right half of his mangled face.

Apache decided to hell with dietary propriety. He began fiercely biting the demonic hand clamped over his mouth, to make it let go of him so he could plead with Mr. Ugly to spare his life and that of the Raynham townsfolk.

CHAPTER 41

Betsy

Betsy jerked awake.

She was terrified. Her dream hung over her like a poisonous cloud, tainting the world she'd awoken into.

No no no! That is just impossible. NO!

But the nightmare had been incredibly vivid. It had seemed just like real life. She could still see herself butchering all those poor people; slashing and gutting them and shredding their yielding flesh while their blood soaked her dirty blue suit. She could still hear their moans, their yelps and shrieks of agony and despair.

Yes, the pathetic and disgusting horror of the slaughter still filled her.

Feeling her lunch coming back up, she leapt off the bed and hurried into the bathroom. She just got the toilet cover up before the puke erupted out of her in a hot, stinky gush.

She let it all out. Then she stood there gagging and trembling.

When she felt strong enough to walk without falling over, she rinsed out her mouth and returned to her bedroom.

She sat on her bed staring at the voodoo doll, now both stripped of its clothes and covered with her sexual fluids. A lot of her sexual cream was packed on its forehead, caught beneath the brim of its now-ruined hat.

For a moment, the memory of why she'd used the doll as a sex toy returned and Betsy wondered how Sammy was feeling right now. She smiled.

He's most likely confused as hell. He'd have been unable to breathe at all once I stuck 'him' deep inside me. Or maybe he'd have survived on the air that makes varts? Maybe that air is a pussy's oxygen tank?

The thoughts amused her for a few seconds, but then the dream's horrors—*Hey, that WAS just a dream, right?*—returned thrice magnified.

She felt as if her mind was overheating. She felt her sanity would soon snap; snap and leave her as a raving, gibbering mess. She was completely, absolutely spooked.

Everything happening to her was just so unlikely.

She sat there shivering in the afternoon heat, her skin clammy from her chilly internal atmosphere. The patter of the rain was white noise in her head. Not comforting, just static evidence that her mental channels either weren't working correctly yet or were shutting down.

Try hard as she might to forget it, the nightmare squeezed her brain in its hot fingers.

I saw myself butchering people! Chelsea, Larry . . . and Sylvia? But . . . but Sylvia is still alive! Yes, she is!

This last 'death' seemed to prove her dream wrong, at least.

The doll; the doll; the doll!

This was the knowledge and conviction she found impossible to shake: *The doll was inside my pussy at the time I saw all those horrible things, and it was feeding the images through me, as if I was it! That's the truth of this— it WASN'T me killing those people! It was the doll doing it!*

But even this understanding seemed crazy to Betsy. *But . . . but . . . it's just a wooden image. Just a toy. And also, it's only six inches high, not six-feet tall like I was in the dream. Yes, yes, the doll killed Chuck, but that was his fault. Aunt Malicia said it was. It can't actually be as evil and violent as I dreamt it was—it doesn't leave my house while I'm asleep and go around hacking people up. No, no, no, no, no! That was just a dream. Dreams are silly.*

Betsy knew this. She knew that dreams had no substance; they were merely the tired mind either rearranging previously acted out events, or an expression of the dreamer's subconscious desires and dreads.

What I just woke up from is no different. It's just another nightmare, this one clearly due to my fear of the doll. I'm only overreacting now because I already know how evil the doll is. It was just a dream. Just a dream. Nothing but a silly dream.

Or was it? *Or is this horrible thing*—she flung the voodoo doll a scared glace—*is this thing actually murdering people at random? Yes, I know it can kill—but has it begun freelancing? Has it actually gone into business for itself because I'm not giving it enough work to do?*

The doll's emanations were as bad as ever—there was no sidestepping that. It was a nasty piece of work. One that hated and that wanted blood and misery.

The unavoidable question was simply: how much nasty work had it been doing?

Betsy thought for a bit: *I know Sylvia Cooper is still alive. So why then did I dream of her death? And the death of that other man by the car?*

The doll had shown her both deaths. She had no doubts on that score: she'd even been wearing its clothes in her visions. But she needed to clarify matters.

Is the doll predicting the future? Can it do that? Or am I actually reviewing the past? There's really only one way that I'll know for sure.

With her aunt dead and vanished, Betsy couldn't call her to ask.

But there was someone she could call.

She picked up her cellphone and dialed Danny's number.

She felt scared when Danny's number kept going to voicemail. But then, she acknowledged that he might have turned the phone off because he was at work.

Fair enough. She googled 'Raynham Public Library,' clicked over to raynhampubliclibrary.org and looked for their contact numbers. After nervously scrolling up and down the page for a minute, she realized that the phone number was right at the top of the page. She checked the library hours. Today, Friday, they'd be open till 5 p.m.

She dialed. A lady at the library answered. Betsy explained who she was and why she was calling. Then she listened in increasing shock to the woman's subdued reply. She asked how the woman could be so sure.

"Oh, it's on TV," the woman replied. "It's been the headline news story all day. The town channel is giving it detailed coverage."

Betsy thanked the woman for her help, then hung up. Then she dropped her cellphone like it was a snake. While trying her best to wrap her mind around what she'd heard, she tramped out into the living room and turned on her television.

It's been on the news all day long? Yeah, I just woke up two hours ago. That's how I missed it.

She only had to wait two minutes for the story to come up on the Raynham Channel. The TV station was running continuous updates on the murders in-between their regular programming.

Betsy watched and heard and believed. Yes, she believed.

What really convinced her of the doll's involvement were the matching gory details, like when the newscaster mentioned Sylvia Cooper's severed head being recovered from up in a tree.

Yes, Betsy vividly recalled throwing Sylvia's head up into that tree, just like she remembered slicing Danny's friend Ricky Crampton open and feeling the heat of his exposed guts on her hands as she pulled them out of his struggling body. She remembered the delight she'd felt while slicing the flesh off his bones and scattering it far and wide over the grass. She also remembered the gaping fear in Sylvia's hazel eyes before she'd scooped them out of her once-pretty face.

But Betsy also knew she'd not done any of that.

NO, I DIDN'T DO THAT! I WOULDN'T DO THAT TO ANYONE! SO . . . !

The realization had taken a long time coming to Betsy, but it finally arrived:

AUNT MALICIA TRICKED ME. YES, SHE DID LINK THE VOODOO DOLL TO SAMMY. BUT . . . BUT SHE ALSO LINKED IT TO THE MONSTER THAT'S BEEN KILLING PEOPLE HERE IN RAYNHAM. . . . SHE . . . SHE . . . SHE WAS JUST USING ME TO KEEP IT SAFE FOR HER. SHIT!

She leapt up off the couch and ran into her bedroom.

The doll lay there exactly as she'd left it, its pale wooden form glazed with her sexual secretions.

Its very gaze seemed to mock her: "Yes, I killed all those people," its eyes seemed to boldly proclaim. "I killed them all and I'm going to kill many more people. And there's nothing you can do about it, because if you dare try and stop me, I'll kill you too! Yes, I'll kill you too, woman!"

Panic filled her. Its black rose blossomed in her belly and spread petals of terror through her heart and lungs. Her breathing stuttered; her heart seemed to skip beats. Her pulse rose and the blood pounded in her head. Her skin turned cold but her hands felt hot as coals. Her mouth dried up but her eyes were watering.

Her brain was filled to bursting with the threat that the doll posed to her.

Now that she'd realized the doll's true nature, Betsy Driscoll had only one thought and goal in her mind: *I need to get rid of it! I need to destroy it quickly before it harms me too!*

She could only think of one surefire way to dispose of the voodoo doll: *It's made of wood, and wood will burn!*

After picking the doll and its little blue suit up off her bed, she ran into her kitchen.

CHAPTER 42

Apache

Apache grunted as the razor sliced through his right hand for the fourth time. He would have screamed instead, but the hand clamped over his mouth prevented this.

Mr. Ugly was cutting Apache's fingers off.

Apache watched his right index finger fall off his hand, then roll over the side of the armchair to join the other eight previously severed digits scattered on the ground around him. More blood spurted. Both of the chair's arms were red with his blood, as were the two zombie hands holding his wrists in place.

Apache had at first fought to save his fingers, clenching his hands into fists. But this hadn't done him any good: Mr. Ugly had simply sliced through each finger at its base knuckle, where bending the digit made no difference at all to the outcome. After losing one finger on each hand, Apache had been in too much pain to even form a fist anymore.

"Last," the man-monster wheezed. He was leaning over Apache, his displaced mouth open in a grotesque leer at the back of which pale glistening grubs squirmed wetly in his throat. The unparalleled feeling of disgust that his mere presence evoked in Apache almost superseded the horror of what was being done to him. The dead man's misshapen head both looked and reeked like a bag of purple pus about to burst.

"Last finger!"

"No!" Apache gasped weakly as Mr. Ugly positioned the razor right at the base of his right thumb. Then came the dreaded pain as the blade went through his skin and flesh, and between his bones, and then parted flesh and skin again.

And suddenly Detective Apache Johnson had no fingers or thumbs left at all. All ten of them were scattered around his feet on the floor.

By now Apache was woozy from pain and blood loss. His mutilated hands looked like red mittens. Blood dribbled from the newer wounds, but the older ones had begun clotting over.

What the hell is it with this family of Howard psychopaths and my damn hands?

The living room was still darkness and purple blaze.

Then Mr. Ugly stepped back, which Apache was glad for. The dead man's smell was putting him to sleep, had almost acted as anesthetic during the finger amputations. Mr. Ugly stank worse than anything else Apache could ever remember smelling. Besides which, he'd also been ceaselessly dripping black ichor and white worms on Apache.

"Now . . . kill!" Mr. Ugly said. He began laughing, a series of nasty wheezing exhalations that sounded like he was dying all over again, while his eyes gaped in the left side of his head, two side-by-side holes in which maggots crawled. "Kill you!"

On those words, the hands restraining Apache all let go of him and melted away again.

Apache staggered to his feet, then spat to clear the rank taste of zombie flesh off his tongue. "Yeah, so you're gonna kill me, you sorry-ass son-of-a-bitch. But I ain't going down without a fight!"

Mr. Ugly laughed again. "Fight!" Then he came at Apache with the blade.

The razor flashed purple in the light. The fluid arc it described through the air made it look like Death's sickle.

Having no fingers left with which to grip Mr. Ugly's hands, Apache did the only thing he could: he flung up his right elbow to protect his face.

Steel met flesh. The razor cut deep into his forearm, almost reaching the bone. Apache howled and backed off.

He didn't back off too far, however. Just in time, he realized he had another problem to contend with: the arches. He didn't dare get close to any of them because of the creatures lurking inside them. If, as he figured was the case, Mr. Ugly intended on feeding him also to the darknesses after his death, the monsters might not feel like waiting till then before starting their meal. If they caught hold of him, they were unlikely to throw him back out into the fray. Also, his hair being ponytailed meant he had to be particularly careful: if the darknesses got even the slightest grip on his ponytail . . . it would have been better to loosen it and let his hair hang down by his face, but . . . dammit, no fingers!

So now he wasn't just *facing* danger, he was ringed all around by it.

The simplest way to stay safe here is to keep a piece of furniture at my back at all times. That way there's no chance I'll fall into one of the portals. Yeah, that's the best thing for me to do.

He glanced back, made sure there was a couch between him and the black wall with its gaping pockets, then returned his gaze forward.

Mr. Ugly was already coming at him again.

Apache ducked. The razor slash missed his face but sliced open his chest instead.

He gaped down at the blood spurting from his ripped suit, then stared at his fingerless hands.

"Shit!" he gasped as he staggered back and Mr. Ugly advanced on him. *If only I knew where that last voodoo doll is right now. I'd gladly sell my soul to Satan himself to locate the accursed thing!*

CHAPTER 43

Betsy

Voodoo doll clutched in one hand, bottle of charcoal lighter fluid in the other, Betsy hurried out of the back door of her house.

It was still raining, but the house had a covered rear porch, and those areas of the porch nearest the wall were dry.

Once outside, Betsy didn't waste any time. She flung the doll and its clothes down onto a dry patch of stone, doused them with the lighter fluid and then ignited them with a lighter she'd brought along from the kitchen in the pocket of her dressing gown.

She was relieved when the doll caught fire.

Her legs trembling, she leaned against the house wall and watched it burn.

She didn't dare stand close to it though, but backed off till she was a good ten feet away from the fire.

During her mad dash through the house, she'd expected the doll to do something nasty to her, something like making her fall and break her arms or legs so she'd be unable to harm it. But it hadn't.

Its inaction had surprised her. Instead of the force of its anger increasing, it had seemed to diminish. Its continuing lack of resistance to her plans still surprised her.

In fact, at the moment Betsy felt that the doll wasn't actually here with her. Well, yes, it *was* here—she'd just set it on fire—but, at the same time, in some inexplicable way, well, it *wasn't* here. Its essential evil self, the part of it she was terrified of, seemed to be missing.

It's almost like it's preoccupied at the moment, like it's somewhere else, happily pursuing its mean desires.

Whatever the reason, Betsy was relieved that such was the case. *It just makes destroying the evil thing that much easier. Now, it's like I'm burning a Barbie doll.*

Still worried though, in case the doll either remembered her or sensed its danger and returned to save itself, she watched it burn. She wanted this over with as fast as possible. She watched from her safe distance, ready to run away the moment she sensed the return of the doll's unholy mind to its body.

The little blue suit burnt up immediately. As quickly as if it was made from paper. The black smoke of its passing blew out across the porch and was swallowed up in the rain.

The doll itself was another matter. Yes, it burnt, but not like wood should burn. Betsy watched in confusion.

It looks like it's frying. It's sizzling like it's a sausage and . . . and it's shriveling and it's—NO NO NO!

She'd just remembered something. Or rather, someone: *Sammy! Oh, my God, what am I doing!? If I destroy the doll, I may be killing Sammy as well!*

Betsy's intention of destroying the doll now immediately reversed itself into an intent to save the evil thing from destruction.

She hurried over to the little burning figurine and tried to put it out with her hands. This action merely burnt her fingers. After some desperate quick thinking, she decided to smother the flames with her bathrobe instead.

So, after a quick look around to ensure no one was watching her, she undid her bathrobe and began slipping out of it.

It was right at this point, just as Betsy had slipped her left fingers out of the robe's left sleeve and was beginning to free her right arm also, that the doll began screaming.

It shrieked loudly, in an adult male voice: "I'm burning, mom! She's killing me! Help, mom! Help me!"

Betsy stopped undressing herself. Unable to believe what was now happening, she peeked down at the little figure she was burning.

Oh yes, she confirmed, it *was* the doll shrieking for help. While its tiny body flamed and sizzled and shrunk, its previously shut mouth was now open horribly wide; and this very human and very male and very loud voice was emitting from the black opening:

"Help me, mom! I'm dying, mom!"

Then its little arms and legs began kicking and punching, exactly like those of a baby throwing a tantrum.

"Help me, mom, I'm not done killing yet! I wanna kill some more people! HEEELLLP!"

Betsy fainted. She struck the stone floor hard and lay there senseless beside the doll as it continued to burn and scream for help.

The rain kicked up in intensity then, the volume and noise of the downpour completely drowning out the doll's pleas for rescue.

CHAPTER 44

Apache

They fought in the pentagram's purple light.

Apache was fighting back the only way he could: by using his mutilated hands as if they were boxing gloves.

He flung a punch at Mr. Ugly's face, aiming for the dead man's eyes. He figured if he could blind him, he had half a chance of surviving.

The pain that flared in Apache's hand as he landed the punch was the stuff of legend, but the middle-aged detective knew he was better off hurting than dead.

He didn't want to die; not with the sort of demonic spectators to their combat that lurked in the gray arches surrounding he and Mr. Ugly. He didn't want his body torn apart and eaten the way Malicia's and Sully's bodies had both been.

No, goddammit! I don't even wanna be cremated! I want a funeral and a tombstone in a cemetery where my daughter and my grandchildren can remember me!

So he hit hard. He made contact with Mr. Ugly's face with all the force he could muster and had the instant satisfaction of watching both of the dead man's eyes vanish back into his head.

Apache had hit so hard, however, that his fist had also sunk into the man's head. It was buried all the way up to the wrist. The raw edges of his knuckles seemed to be scraping bone in there. Yet more agony for Apache to suffer through.

Now, for all intents and purposes, Mr. Ugly had no eyes.

This didn't stop the dead man though. In the few seconds it took for Apache to pull his hand out of the sucking, marshy mess of the walking corpse's face, Mr. Ugly opened him up twice down his left side.

When Apache finally managed to separate himself from his attacker, his truncated right hand was covered with a black jelly in which several maggots writhed. Mr. Ugly meanwhile, had a gaping hole in the left side of his face. No eyes were in evidence in there, just bone fragments and what might have been rotted brain mush.

Disgusted, Apache wiped the black mess off on his jacket.

It's like he's just a bag of destroyed, rotten meat! Then he remembered his first glimpse of Peter Howard's corpse in the morgue after its retrieval from Gushee Pond. *Yeah, actually, the kid IS just a bag of rotting meat.*

Apache instinctively tried gripping his slashed side, but then realized he couldn't. He stared angrily down at his fingers on the floor.

Okay, so yeah, I know they can be sewed back on to my hands, but I gotta survive long enough to get to the hospital.

Then he growled in frustration. The dead man's lack of eyes wasn't slowing him down in the least. With an unerring sense of direction Mr. Ugly shambled towards Apache, razor held high. Then he slashed at Apache with absolute precision.

While ducking to the left, Apache understood why this was:

He's been seeing without eyes all this while, you dimwit! His eyes were destroyed ages ago—all your punching him did was tuck two functionless organs away out of sight.

Apache crouched and flung another punch. Now it was Mr. Ugly's turn to duck. He shifted and Apache's hand went wide. Mr. Ugly slashed again and missed. Apache threw another punch that hit. This one went right into the side of Mr. Ugly's neck and lodged itself there.

Apache endured a long cut down his left cheek before he could rip his hand free.

They stood facing each other, Apache breathing heavily, his opponent's head now leaning crazily to the right. Apache imagined he heard impatient rustling noises coming from the demons in the arches. As though they were either cheering Mr. Ugly on, or impatiently telling him to "Kill that cop quickly, dude. Stop wasting time—we're *still* hungry in here!"

Maybe they *were* cheering the dead man on, because now, Mr. Ugly suddenly came at Apache in a rush . . .

And then, just as suddenly, Mr. Ugly dropped his straight razor and began screaming.

Apache had been preparing to duck to his left, but now he just stood staring, with a river of sweat streaming down his body.

"Help me, mom!" Mr. Ugly shrieked. "Help me, mother, I'm burning! I'm dying, mom!"

And, just like he'd said he was burning, a horrible stink of roasting flesh now filled the room. Roasting *rotten* flesh.

And the dead man also started shriveling up. He shriveled fast, faster than any of the dolls they'd burnt up on the kitchen gas range.

"Help me, mother! I'm burning up!"

Apache watched and hoped and prayed desperately that whatever was happening to Mr. Ugly wasn't going to stop midway. Because if it did . . .

He had no idea what he'd do if it did.

But it didn't stop. Mr. Ugly continued shrieking and sizzling and stinking and shrinking.

"NOOOOOOOOOOOOOOOOOOOOOO!"

And that was it for Mr. Ugly. The dead man exploded in a sudden flash of purple light that was so bright it made Apache shield his eyes.

When he opened them again, all that remained of Mr. Ugly was a small pile of ash in the middle of the pentagram.

"See, I was right," Apache said to himself as the purple light from the pentagram winked out and the surrounding darkness with its arches and its indescribable monsters from Hell faded back into plain daylight. "I was right—we *did* cremate Peter Howard."

He sank back into his preferred armchair and wiped sweat off his forehead with the back of his hand.

Okay, now there is the puzzle to resolve of why the son-of-a-bitch suddenly caught fire and exploded, but I guess we'll discover that in due course. Or maybe we won't. The fuck I care.

He looked down at his hands, then at his other wounds, feeling the trickles of blood he was losing. He expected to have a long scar on his left cheek.

He grimaced. "Now, all I gotta do is work out how to make a phone call with no fingers, before I bleed to death up here."

That took some figuring out. Finally though, he managed it.

First of all, he got the phone itself out of his jacket. This required slipping the jacket off and then upending it so that the cellphone dropped out onto the floor. Then next, using the sides of both hands like clamps, he picked it up and placed it on the chair's left arm, which was more bloody and hence more sticky than the right one. Less chance of the phone slipping to the floor from there. Next, using the same 'clamp' technique, he picked up one of his index fingers from the floor. (He couldn't tell if it was the left one or the right one.)

After that, the rest was relatively easy. Laying the phone in his lap and holding the severed finger between what remained of his hands, he tapped the screen on with the finger and searched through his Contacts list for Tina Kravitz's phone number. While the phone dialed, he made certain to put it on 'speaker.' There was no way he'd be able to raise it to his ear.

The phone connected on the fourth ring.

Tina's voice came over the line: "Apache? Where the hell have you and Sully been? I've been trying both your numbers for almost an hour now; the radio in your squad car wasn't responding either. Man, these FBI guys are driving me up the wall. Look . . . where are you guys anyway? Mandy told me you were here at the station earlier, but . . . Hey, Apache, Sully *is* there with you, right?"

"I'm over at Malicia Howard's place. Upstairs in her living room."

"What the hell are you doing over *there?*"

"It's maybe the longest story I'm ever gonna tell you, Chief. Just get me out of here first."

Her voice took on a note of concern. "Are you hurt?"

"I daresay I am. Listen, Tina, I got really good news and I got really bad news."

"The really good?"

"We've solved the Mr. Ugly case. It's over."

"Wow, that's better than incredible! For real?"

"For real, Chief. There won't be any more deaths."

"Great work, man!" Then her voice sobered. "And . . . the really bad?"

"Sully's dead. Malicia Howard too, but we won't miss her."

"S-s-sully is d-d-dead? H-how the . . . !?"

"Tina, I'll satisfy your curiosity later." He looked around the living room. "Most of Sully is gone, but there's still a foot and a shoe you can identify him from."

She sounded sad now: "Just like in the courtroom back then, is it?"

"A little bit. But this is much neater. The only blood splattered everywhere is mine. Oh, and there's also a pile of ashes on the floor here that needs to be returned back into its damn urn." He sighed. "I'd sweep it up myself, but at the moment I ain't got any fingers."

There was a long silence at the other end of the line. Then Tina asked quietly: "No fingers? Apache, you ain't bleeding to death, are you?"

"Nah, at the moment I ain't bleedin' to death, but if help takes more than twenty minutes to arrive here, I just might be: I'm slashed up pretty bad and my hands both feel like Satan is barbequing them for lunch. Look, just hurry up. I ain't joking—I ain't got no fingers, huh? I need to get to the ER and have them all reattached." He laughed coldly into the phone. "And, Tina honey, I assure you, after this I'm done with police work for good. Yeah, they can start readying my pension. Being a cop is simply too dangerous and crazy nowadays. I'm going into politics like Malicia Howard advised me to."

He hung up. Then he settled back in his armchair. Despite his hurting hands and body Apache Johnson relaxed, relaxed for the first time in over a week. He could afford to relax now, now that he was certain no moldering monstrosity was going to suddenly appear from nowhere and slash him up.

After a while he tried to think up a logical, TV-cop explanation for Sully's death, something that didn't sound farfetched and fantastical. It was the least he could do.

The kid would have liked that.

EPILOGUE

Sometimes, there isn't enough left of what originally went around to come around again.

Rosa

Rosa Fernandez would remember this Friday until the day she died. As would all of her employees and her neighbors. Indeed, by evening the story of what happened to her younger sister's lover had spread all over Mexico City and planted the seeds of several new urban legends.

It had begun innocently enough. Luisa and her new man, Sammy, had come to Rosa's restaurant, the Rosa Blanca, for lunch. Sammy was youngish and handsome. A good-looking gringo. Luisa had explained to the family that Sammy was in the process of getting divorced, and that they were trying to hurry it up so they could hold their wedding before mamá died.

Then, while their meal was being prepared, Rosa had noticed Sammy and Luisa having an argument with a woman via cellphone. Rosa had shaken her head when Luisa flared up, but on hearing her angry outburst had realized that the other woman must have provoked the argument.

But then . . .

Barely five minutes later, Sammy had begun choking.

He'd gripped his throat and gasped like a fish out of water; an apt comparison, as those restaurant customers who'd left their lunches and hurried over to help had later commented that the foreigner had a strong 'fishy' odor about him, as if he worked *en una pescaderia*, deboning salmon.

Then, just as abruptly as it had begun, Sammy's choking fit had stopped again. Everything had seemed okay. Even the mysterious fishy smell had left him. He and Luisa had thanked the other lunchers for their help and concern. They'd sat back down at their table and started their meal.

And then, thirty or so minutes later, when they'd almost finished eating, Sammy had suddenly burst into flames. He'd been sipping from his guava mint agau fresca when he'd started burning.

They'd done everything possible to put Sammy out. They'd sprayed him—literally covered him—with fire extinguisher foam, poured buckets of soapy water over him, and when both of those had failed to douse the flames, tried wrapping him in wet blankets.

But nothing helped. Sammy kept burning. Bright tongues of fire squirted from his body as if he was a living gas range. His head flamed like an ancient torch. His eyes popped like chewing gum bubbles. His clothes burnt off. Then his skin burnt off. (Two of the young waitresses—both virgins—fainted from the sight of Sammy's manhood on fire.) Then Sammy's muscles and internal organs burned up too. And while burning, Sammy screamed and screamed and screamed, until his tongue turned to ash in his mouth and he couldn't scream any longer.

(Thinking witchcraft might be the problem, immediately Sammy had caught on fire, someone had run to fetch Dona Maria Negra, the old curandera who lived next door to the restaurant; but she'd not been home.)

Unable to put out the flames, everyone was forced to watch Sammy burn. And forced also to endure the disgusting stink of roasting meat that came from him. The smell filled the restaurant. Several of the watchers vomited into their plates.

In thirteen minutes it was over. All that remained of Sammy Driscoll by then was a hollow black shell of charred meat, and brittle bones that crumpled to ash on the slightest of touches.

In fact, Pedro Mayans, who also lived next door, said the remains reminded him of someone who'd been cremated.

Luisa was of course hysterical. She'd truly and honestly loved Sammy from the bottom of her heart. Luisa was upstairs now in Rosa's bedroom, trembling and chattering her teeth and crying her heart out.

Unable to leave the restaurant, Rosa was waiting for her husband Carlos to come home and take her younger sister to the clinic. In addition to her hysterics over her lover's death, Luisa had also burnt both her hands while trying to put out the fire that had consumed Sammy. But her burns were nothing too serious, nothing that salve and bandages wouldn't fix. She'd have no permanent disfigurement. In her heart was where she'd carry third-degree scars for ages.

So, no, Rosa Fernandez would never forget what had happened in her restaurant today, the day that her American brother-in-law-to-be spontaneously caught fire and burnt to death.

The End

ABOUT THE AUTHOR

Wol-vriey is Nigerian, and quite tall.

He believes there actually are things that go bump in the night.

He writes horror fiction—for adults only, please. And also some surrealist stuff.

Wol-vriey blogs at: *http://oddityfarm.wordpress.com*

WOL-VRIEY
BIZARRO AND TRANSGRESSIVE FICTION

BOSTON POSH (BUD MALONE #1)

In 2028 AD, the USA is a nation ravaged by hungry dragons and dinosaurs. In Boston, Massachusetts, private eye Bud Malone is hired to rescue a kidnapped heiress. But nothing is as it seems.

Malone works to unravel a tangled web involving Boston Chinatown, a 200-year-old woman with a 9-year-old body, white robots, a human-liver-eating psychopath, a golem, a porcelain dragon, and a snake goddess with a crush on him. There's also a woman obsessed with chicken sex. Then Malone meets Posh Lane, a gorgeous call girl who's desperate to quit her pimp.

Romantic sparks ignite between Posh and Malone, but Posh's past suddenly catches up with her in a BIG way. To save Posh, Malone agrees to run a quest for Earth's new rulers, the Forks. But, Malone has no idea that agreeing to the Fork's odd request will send him on the weirdest trip he's ever been on in his life.

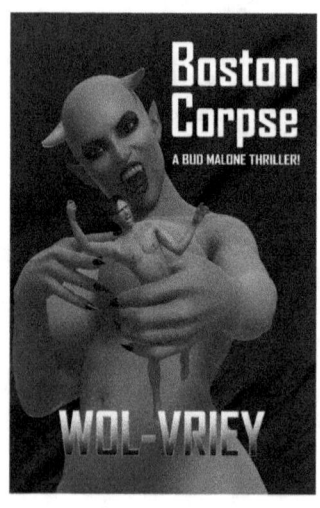

BOSTON CORPSE (BUD MALONE #2)

MAGIC CAN BE MURDER! - Drag queen Lucy Tang is back in Boston, and is hell-bent on settling her vindetta against casino owner Sookie Ling. And suddenly, Bud Malone, PI, has the case of his life to resolve.

When Boston's robot police force are baffled by a mind transfer case, they come to Malone for help. The one person who can likely help Malone out here is the witch Soledad Bathory. But Soledad seems to know a lot more than she's telling him. It's a case not made easier when Malone meets Soledad's beautiful cousin, Josephine 'Slave' Bailey. Slave has her own plans for Malone, most of which involve teaching him BDSM and making him her new Master.

Oh, and Rick Rogers owes Sookie Ling a whole lot of money, a gambling debt that's going to be literally Hell to pay!

BOSTON CORPSE - Not your average detective novel!

Burning Bulb
PUBLISHING

WOL-VRIEY
BIZARRO AND TRANSGRESSIVE FICTION

BOSTON LUST (BUD MALONE #3)

"Bless it, Father, for she has sinned."

Seven murdered gay women, all their bodies completely drained of blood. All also with large parts of their bodies dissolved away like acid has been pumped into their veins.

Bud Malone has to find the female vampire preying on Boston's lesbian population.

Then Malone meets the beautiful Trudi Carmen and the case gets even more tangled. Trudi needs Malone's help in recovering a ring that's gone missing. But how in the world is one little black ring related to either the dead women or their killer?

Resolving this case will lead Malone deep into Lucy Tang's legacy—The Abstracta. And then to the city of Genesis.

Boston Lust—Just when you thought Bean Town was safe to visit again.

HELL DANCER

Six people find themselves trapped in Detention, a nightmare realm where the demonic Schoolmaster is hell-bent on reforming them . . . until they die.

Porn superstar Venus Deluxe came to Springfield, MA to party, and next found her life hanging by a thread. One wrong answer will mean her death.

Suspended BPD detective Tanya Rockford was trying to stop one kind of violence, but found a terrifying another. With her and her companion's lives hanging in the balance, it's going to take all of her courage and resourcefulness to escape this hell she's stumbled into.

Porn stud Chad Cannon has made a career from his ten-inch penis. Here in Detention, however, it's his brains that matter. He'll soon be hoping all the pot he's smoked over the years hasn't completely messed up his memory.

The three students, Sherri, Jordan, and Mike? They were all just in the wrong place at the right time. Will anyone survive Detention? The evil Schoolmaster doesn't plan on letting that happen . . .

Burning Bulb
PUBLISHING

WOL-VRIEY
BIZARRO AND TRANSGRESSIVE FICTION

VAGINA MUNDI

Rachel Risk is a professional thief with super-strong hair that can stretch like tentacles to manipulate objects. Ashley Status has both a digitally augmented brain, and 'muscle-purses' in her arms and legs in which she stores inflatable objects—cars, guns, rocket launchers, etc.

When Raye is framed as the fall girl in a jewel robbery, the pair flee Chicago's vengeful robot gangsters and take refuge in the Hotel Bizarre, where the gorgeous 'vagina singer,' Femina, is performing for a week.

But the Hotel Bizarre is even stranger than its name suggests, and very soon Raye and Ash are involved in an deadly adventure, a struggle for survival the likes of which they'd never imagined possible—with loads of deviant sex, drugs, music, and violence at every turn. And just what is the old woman in the skin desert really doing with all those cats glued to her walls?

VAGINA MUNDI—a Bizarro Hymn in praise of WOMAN!

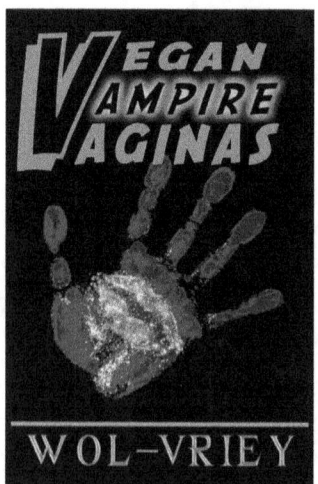

VEGAN VAMPIRE VAGINAS

The biggest bank heist in US history. And Tom Palmer can't remember pulling it off. And no, this isn't your standard case of amnesia. After a one-night-stand gone horribly wrong, Boston salesman Tom Palmer wakes up with a vagina implanted in his left hand. Then his day gets worse.

Tom is transported across space-time to a nightmare version of Boston, one where the Bizarro virus has transformed half the population into cannibals. Worst of all, Tom discovers that in this new Boston, he's the infamous gangster Pussypalm, wanted for robbing the Federal Reserve Bank of Boston a year ago. He also learns that the vagina in his hand is prophetic, i.e. it talks . . . after sex.

With 130 people left dead during his bank heist and six billion dollars missing, Tom knows he's living on borrowed time. It is in his best interests not to remember anything. Because once he does . . .

Burning Bulb
PUBLISHING

WOL-VRIEY
BIZARRO AND TRANSGRESSIVE FICTION

VEGAN ZOMBIE APOCALYPSE

In the post-apocalypse worlderness, zombies rule the earth. They're allergic to meat, and brains literally make them explode. Zombies now eat blood potatoes, parasitic tubers grown in the flesh of humancows corralled in maximum security farms. Two fugitives meet in the ancient ruins of Texas. The first is Soil 15-f, a womancow who's escaped her farm a week before she's due to be killed and her blood potato crop harvested. The second fugitive is Able Kane, former head necros food technician, now sentenced to death for heresy. But Soil is no ordinary humancow.

Unknown to herself, she's the vegan zombie agricultural revolution, and the zombies desperately want her back. And the necros equally desperately want Able Kane dead. He's fled with a forbidden discovery which will reshape the world for the worse if used. And Able is just hardheaded/misguided enough to use it.

MELANIE NEMESIS CATCHPOLE

In Springfield, Massachusetts, Melanie Catchpole is hired to fetch back a magic teddy bear worth millions of dollars from a warehouse across town. Problem is, the warehouse is down in Springfield's O-Zone—that totally weird sector of the city where Bizarro fell to Earth. The 'O' is a fairytale land, a place where dreams and nightmares literally live and breathe..

Worse still, the gingers—mutant cannibals—prowl the O. The gingers have already eaten everyone else Melanie's employers sent to get back the magic teddy bear.

Accompanied by the handsome but ruthless Doug Fisher (who she finds sexy but doesn't dare entrust her heart to), Melanie enters the O-Zone. Melanie and Doug are instantly caught up in an adventure they'd never have believed credible even if written as fiction . . . and Melanie's used to experiencing the very weird as the norm.

And now, additionally, there's a mystery to unravel: What does the dark, freezing-cold being called The Fixer want with Mary, the barkeep's daughter?

Burning Bulb
PUBLISHING

WOL-VRIEY
BIZARRO AND TRANSGRESSIVE FICTION

BIG TROUBLE IN LITTLE ASS

From Bizarro master storyteller Wol-vriey comes a truly weird western tale that will leave you awe-struck and on the edge of your seat...

In the town named Little Ass, tight-assed prostitute Rosa overhears a gunslinger's plans to assassinate rancher Edison Bennett. Once the badass Bennett learns of the plot, he ensures there'll be hell to pay for any attempt on his life!

Yes, it's going to take all of gunslinger Jude's shooting prowess, his eclectic collection of strange firearms, a trusty horse that requires an owners' manual, and the help of the lovely and invigorating Nell (who's EXTREMELY odd when the going gets weird), to survive the Bizarro hell that Edison Bennett unleashes in order to hold onto the land that he'd stolen from Madam Zizi.

BIZARRO 101 (A BASIC PRIMER)

Welcome to the strange place:

A collection of 37 flash fiction stories designed to introduce one to the Bizarro/New Weird Genre.

Weird, dreamy, nightmarish, absurd, sad, surreal, humorous . . . this collection of tales is all this and more.

***

"This primer is the very essence of any and all styles and types of Bizarro writing. Wol-vriey collects, distills, and bottles up these 37 tiny stories for your sensory enjoyment. This is an absolute must-read for anyone new to the genre, because it demonstrates the scope of what Bizarro is, and what it can be."
—Teresa Pollack, Bizarro commentator and blogger

Burning Bulb
PUBLISHING

WOL-VRIEY
BIZARRO AND TRANSGRESSIVE FICTION

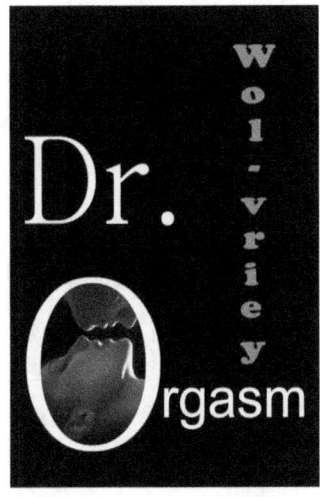

Dr. Orgasm

Courtney Taylor is young, intelligent, beautiful, and successful. She also has a boyfriend who loves her deeply. The problem is, no matter what Courtney does, she can't climax during sex.

When Florence Rigid's communist forces destroy the city of Metaphor, Courtney and her friends Teresa, Highball, Miki, and Heather are cast into the midst of a quest to find the only person able to save the land of Innuendo—Dr. Carol Orgasm, wanted by the communists for developing the O-Pill, a wonder drug that grants women sexual ecstasy on demand.

The communists will do anything to get their hands on the O-Pill and prevent its reaching the millions of Innuendo's women. But Courtney desperately wants that pill too. And so it's now a race between Courtney and the communists to find Dr. Orgasm first.

And Courtney has no choice but to win this race. She must win it: For her own orgasm . . . and for the freedom of female sexuality everywhere.

PUSSY TRANSMISSION

Pussy Transmission were the most decadent Pop Art ensemble of the 90's. Led by the beautiful painter Isis Lynch, the trio revolutionized the art world. Then suddenly, without explanation, Pussy Transmission vanished into historical obscurity. Now, twenty years later, three women come to Lynch Place. Lily and Nina are journalists desperate to interview Isis Lynch. Raven, on the other hand, wants to find her boyfriend, who's gone missing inside Isis's house. Raven's worried—she's heard that Pussy Transmission broke up because Isis began dabbling in black magic . . . with devastating results. All three women will shortly wish they'd never left home. Particularly once the rats in Lynch Place start warning them that they're going to die . . . and Raven meets Betty Butcher, the bouncy supernatural psycho who's intent on chopping her into bits. Pussy Transmission, Baby! Just because . . .

Burning Bulb
PUBLISHING

WOL-VRIEY
BIZARRO AND TRANSGRESSIVE FICTION

GIRLS ARE NOT SMILING

Welcome To The Road Trip From Hell

Pagan is demon-possessed.

Lori is suicidal.

Britt is just terminally pissed off.

Meet three young Boston women on the run from the law, each with problems that will fuse into more than the sum of their individual parts, becoming a holocaust of sex and violence and terror, a literal rain of blood and horror and gore and evil.

And if that wasn't already bad enough, Pagan's pet demon is slowly transforming her into something both unspeakable and unholy. Truly, these girls aren't smiling.

BLUE NIGHTMARES

Consummate EVIL is coming. It is relentless and unavoidable. It is Blue.

Jessica Schreiber is seeing things. Very horrible things. Since arriving in Raynham for what should have been a relaxing vacation, she's been seeing *The Big Blue*.

Jessica is smelling things too—dead and rotting things that she can't see. She is sure those dead and rotting things are dead people. Lots of dead people.

Jessica's worst nightmares will soon become her reality. Her reality will soon become a terrifying nightmare.

The tentacled residents of the House of Death have a lot that they wish to show Jessica Schreiber. They have a lot that they wish to tell her. But will she survive long enough to learn their lessons?

Burning Bulb
PUBLISHING

WOL-VRIEY
BIZARRO AND TRANSGRESSIVE FICTION

BRAINCHEW

It was supposed to be a simple jewel heist, but it went badly wrong. Chuck got shot and died.

Lance hid his friend's corpse in the Pleasant Street Cemetery. But that was a big mistake—there was something undead, something extremely hungry . . . something eXXXtremely horrible, buried in the Pleasant Street Cemetery.

And Lance had just woken it up.

They called the monster Brainchew because it ate brains. Human brains. And it preferred those brains fresh from the heads . . . of the living.

And now it was awake again, Brainchew planned on feeding big-time tonight. Oh hell yes, it did.

BRAINCHEW 2: OUT OF THEIR HEADS

After Tiff Hooper recognizes Josh Penham, the man who abducted her and kept her in his basement and abused her, she brings her three friends to Raynham for a night of well-deserved revenge on him.

Only things don't go according to plan.

It is never a good idea to leave a corpse in Raynham's Pleasant Street Cemetery. You run the very real risk of awakening what lies underground there. And that thing—Brainchew—is more horrible and more evil than anything the average mind conceives of even in its worst nightmares.

Brainchew is back! And this time the monster is extra-hungry. But there are plenty of delicious human brains about tonight, and Brainchew intends to eat them all before dawn.

Burning Bulb
PUBLISHING

WOL-VRIEY
BIZARRO AND TRANSGRESSIVE FICTION

DARIA: AN EROTIC NIGHTMARE

Even the best laid women can go wrong.

Daria Simpson is HUNGRY. She's HUNGRY for sex and bloodshed and death.

Shelly Parker just wanted to have a threesome with her boyfriend Craig and her best friend Erica. Everything was shaping up nicely for their weekend of sexual fun and games, until they stopped at the creepy Crossway Diner and met Daria.

From the moment they met Daria, EVERYTHING went wrong for them; and it went wrong in the most horrific and terrifying of ways!

Daria: Paranormal service has been resumed.

WET BONES

Greg is about learning the hard way that you don't mess with Aunt Grace.

Nine completely fleshless skeletons recovered in the Massachusetts woods. Two detectives on the trail of a horrible, hungry monster.

Broken-hearted Allie Jackson has a date with a creature from Hell.

Things are about to get well out of hand for everyone, and in horrifying, terrifying ways they don't expect.

Burning Bulb
PUBLISHING

www.ingramcontent.com/pod-product-compliance
Lightning Source LLC
Chambersburg PA
CBHW070532260626
47161CB00002B/353